FATEFUL MORNINGS

Tom Bouman's debut *Dry Bones in the Valley* won the 2015 Edgar Award for Best First Novel and a *Los Angeles Times* Book Prize. He lives with his family in upstate New York.

@Tom_Bouman

Further praise for *Fateful Mornings*:

'A terrific writer. Definitely one to keep an eye on.' Dennis Lehane

'My father always said that you can judge people by the way they keep their tools: clean and sharp or soiled and soft. Tom Bouman's tools – the words he uses to make *Fateful Mornings* – cut straight and true, in this riveting mystery about a good man caught in the ruined Eden of rural America.' Julia Keller, Pulitzer Prize-winning author of *Sorrow Road*

'Bouman's tender portrait of a widower remaking his life infuses his crime fiction with a level of intimacy that is both rare and winning.' Attica Locke, author of *Black Water Rising*

'Officer Farrell, who thinks a lot but speaks so little . . . proves to be excellent company.' *Wall Street Journal*

'You would be hard-pressed to find a finer new series than Tom Bouman's Henry Farrell novels because of the complexity of the plots or the richness of the characters, but what it really comes down to is just damn good writing.' Craig Johnson, author of the Walt Longmire novels

FATEFUL
MORNINGS

ALSO BY TOM BOUMAN

Dry Bones in the Valley

FATEFUL MORNINGS

A HENRY FARRELL NOVEL

TOM BOUMAN

FABER & FABER

First published in the UK in 2017
by Faber and Faber Ltd
Bloomsbury House, 74–77 Great Russell Street
London WC1B 3DA
This paperback edition first published in the UK in 2018

First published in the USA in 2017
by W. W. Norton & Company, Inc., 500 Fifth Avenue,
New York, NY 10110

Printed and bound by CPI Group (UK) Ltd, Croydon, CR0 4YY

The right of Tom Bouman to be identified as author of this work
has been asserted in accordance with Section 77 of the Copyright,
Designs and Patents Act 1988

A CIP record for this book
is available from the British Library

ISBN 978-0-571-32777-5

2 4 6 8 10 9 7 5 3 1

And yet the wise are of the opinion that wherever man is, the dark powers who would feed his rapacities are there too, no less than the bright beings who store their honey in the cells of his heart, and the twilight beings who flit hither and thither, and that they encompass him with a passionate and melancholy multitude.

—W. B. YEATS

FATEFUL MORNINGS

PART ONE

AS THE sun gained the eastern sky, I drove my truck through a meadow and toward Maiden's Grove Lake. On the hills, aspen trees leafed out like pale green clouds, and scattered in the grass below, violets stood up to the wet, cold spring. Everywhere you looked, summer was promised.

Who named the lake Maiden's Grove I do not know, probably the same person who named our township Wild Thyme, back two hundred years ago when northern Pennsylvania was still frontier. They arrived and there it was, a deep glacial rut fed by springs and spilling into January Creek, hooking into the Susquehanna at some point south, and then running hundreds of miles out to the Chesapeake Bay.

I came to a right turn and took the road to where a dozen cottages sat on the shore. They'd been built in the thirties, when the family that owned most of the surrounding land had sold off a few parcels to raise cash. The family, name of Swales, had evidently grown rich again down in Luzerne County. Until recently, they'd left the other three-quarters of the lake wild. The south shore cottagers were a house-proud and wealthy few who prized quiet and solitude. They stocked the lake with trout and forbade motorboats. At Cottage Seven, I pulled in next to a navy Mercedes wagon and walked to the side yard. The midmorning sun scattered white light across the lake's blue surface. You could smell the light. Rhonda Prosser, a slender middle-aged woman with the wiry limbs of a distance runner, crouched in front of a broken basement window. On my arrival she stood. She wore gray dreadlocks with silver rings and charms woven in. Her face was severe and beautiful, the face of a white woman, to be clear, dreadlocks notwithstanding. I'd seen her and her husband at monthly township meetings in the summer months. They'd made it a project to beleaguer the township supervisor—my boss, Steve Milgraham—over fracking. In particular, where was the EPA looking after us, and where was the Act 13 money going? For this they had become notable in Holebrook County despite being themselves residents of New York State, north of the border.

Rhonda peered at me over half-glasses clamped onto the very tip of her nose.

"Henry Farrell, Wild Thyme," I said.

"Yeah, I know. I was expecting state police," she said.

"Well," I said.

"So you're going to handle this? Because I called before. I left messages on your machine. People raising hell at Andy Swales's place, and you won't lift a finger."

It was true. Andy Swales was prince of the family and had, that past year, built a stone castle on a hill overlooking the northern shore, along with a small boathouse and a dock. From the Prossers' cottage, you could see a turret.

Swales leased some of his land and a trailer up there to a young couple named Kevin O'Keeffe and Penny Pellings, in exchange for their caretaking the house and grounds. Yet them two were not known for care. Child Protective Services had removed their newborn girl, Eolande, about a year ago, in a case that saw a bit of publicity. In addition to the occasional check-in relating to their efforts to get Eolande back, I'd been on a domestic call to the trailer that winter, nothing too bad, just hippies in a squabble that went too far.

Point being, with Kevin and Penny living up there, a certain local element had new access to the lake, and the cottage owners didn't like it. Starting that spring, any chance they got, they called about some scandal up to Maiden's Grove, somebody playing music too loud too late or bait-fishing their trout. I told them once you stock a public lake, the fish are the commonwealth's. But I'd called Andy Swales about the noise. He'd told me his tenants could do what they pleased, as long as they didn't get carried away, his words. Me, I also figured it was a free country and people were allowed to get drunk at the wrong lake if they wanted.

Worst of all to the cottagers on the southern shore, worse than their new neighbors to the north, Swales had signed a gas lease. At some point in the future, they all might look out across the lake to see a derrick punching poison into the earth with nothing but a thin concrete well protecting their water supply.

"Well," I said, "the state called the county, and the county called the township, and the township is me, so."

"Mmm."

"The nearest state barracks is an hour away," I said. "I may work with the county on suspects and that. Show me around?"

We went inside. The interior of the cottage was white and spare. The spaces beneath tables and chairs were empty, the countertops clean, the shelves filled with art books. Life preservers and baseball mitts hung on hooks in a shale-floored mudroom with a bench and a view to the lake. Unlike most of the homes I visited on the job, there was not a thing in this one you could call junk. In fact, the cottage was so little disarranged that I had a hard time believing it had been burgled until I came to the wall fixture that had once held a flat-screen TV, and saw the outlines where a stereo had once sat on a chest painted in blue milk wash. According to Rhonda, two vintage stringed instruments had been taken, but not the priceless barn harp, which was crumbling into something more like folk art. She showed it to me and strummed it; it did not play well. In an upstairs bedroom, the burglars had forced open a locked drawer in a nightstand and taken an HK 9mm automatic handgun. Rhonda said it was her ex-husband's, for coyotes, described it as black, hadn't touched it since the divorce. There was a touch of weariness in her voice when her ex-husband came into the story. It was the first I'd heard of the split, so I guessed it was recent. She didn't know if the gun was loaded; it may well have been. There was a nearly empty box of 124-grain full metal jacket ammunition still in the drawer. All the liquor was gone. Downstairs in the basement, any tools not bolted down had been taken. We headed back up to the ground floor.

"This is the most valuable thing in the whole place." Rhonda pointed to an oil painting in a golden frame with a picture light mounted over it. "Why turn on the light and not take the painting? Odd. I guess I shouldn't wonder." Cows in a field by a creek at sunset. She straightened it with a brush of her fingers and a flash of turquoise jewelry.

"So last night. You got a call when?"

Rhonda looked pained. "We set calls to come here, not Syracuse. He did, my ex, Evan. That's where I was last night, Syracuse. The call came to him, but the cottage is mine now, so he called me. The summers we stayed here, we rarely even locked the doors. But friends on Silver Lake had a problem. He got the system, thinking once we have it, we'll never need it. You just don't expect this."

"You're a long way out," I said.

"So we thought," said Rhonda, and then reconsidered. "No, it's more than that. You keep going along, you've got a good thing. How could you expect this? You're going along." With an index finger, she whipped tears from under her eyes. "We just have to absorb this now, I guess. There's no place to be."

"Just from my perspective, I've seen it before. It's not personal. These people, they didn't mean you harm. They don't know you. They only know what they need, and that's probably heroin. So the call came here," I continued, "the dispatcher didn't like it, she called the state police, state police called . . ."

"Evan," said Rhonda, "my ex."

"And he called you." She nodded. "I'll try to get a few prints and whatnot, but the likeliest way forward is people. People talking."

I didn't have high hopes. In the commonwealth, every house burglary was a felony, and nobody wanted to send their brother-in-law or whoever to prison over a stereo. Especially not in the government-resistant culture that had taken root in the hills of Wild Thyme. Maybe I could follow the items over the border to the small cities on New York's Southern Tier. Probably not. I took prints from the doorknobs, a few surfaces, and had a long look around. The burglars had left nothing behind. Before breaking in they'd probably taken off their boots, even. I gave my regrets and got on the road.

It took about twenty minutes to get back to the station. Rounding a bend, I rolled into the familiar valley and parked on the gravel surrounding the municipal garage. Wild Thyme Township had not always had a policeman on the payroll. I suppose it had depended on how safe people felt, and how much taxes they wanted to pay. Before my return from Wyoming—State, not County—a few years back, the post had stood vacant, and the people relied on Pennsylvania State Police and the Holebrook County Sheriff's Department. It was largely Sheriff Dally's doing that I got the job; he'd wanted to trim back his own department's ambit and felt that as long as I was up there in Wild Thyme, I could be of use.

In fashioning the police station itself, the township had cornered off a piece of the building that doubled as a garage and volunteer fire station. I unlocked the door and propped it open, then switched on a rotating fan. It never made a difference. Sometimes it felt like the air in my office had not changed since 1967 when the garage was built. Nothing in, nothing out. The desk beside mine remained vacant. My latest deputy—Krista Collins, formerly of the county sheriff's department—worked for me for about five minutes before getting herself deployed again, this time to Afghanistan. There she met a sergeant and let me know she wasn't returning to Pennsylvania probably ever. Even if I could hire somebody, there were precious few academy graduates angling for a low-paying rural post. The applications I did get were from older cops with brutality complaints and discipline problems, guys who fell out with their departments and were looking for rescue. If eleven dollars an hour was worth it, most of them had to be pretty sorry, but I kept a few applications on my desk anyway.

I considered manning one of my speed traps throughout the township, but decided against it. It was a lazy May morning after a dawn turkey hunt, and besides, as policeman of a small township, it is a fine line between making yourself useful and paining the community's ass. For that reason I tended to focus my efforts on the king cabs and tanker trucks come in from elsewhere to work the Marcellus shale play.

I called the sheriff's department and asked about any burglaries their way, any suspects. Nothing out of the ordinary in Fitzmorris or around. I filled out most of a criminal complaint, leaving space for the offenders' names, and put it in a desk drawer.

Not too long after I had done this, the township supervisor stepped in. He wore a striped polo shirt, Bermuda shorts the color of peas, and dusty work boots. As I mentioned, Stephen Milgraham was his name, the middle-aged owner/operator of a contracting business. I privately called him the Sovereign Individual, or just the Sovereign, owing to his libertarian leanings. Being a department of one, I was answerable to the Wild Thyme taxpayers by way of the Sovereign. He criticized me publicly, declined to pay for con ed, and took away my mini-fridge.

"Steve," said I, "glad to see you, please sit."

"Ah, thanks." The Sovereign scraped a chair over to my desk and sat on the edge of it. "How are things, keeping busy?"

"Always. Always something."

"I ran into Rhonda this morning."

"Sure," I said.

"You told her we've got a heroin problem."

"News travels fast," I said.

"Henry." He spat some wintergreen dip juice into a soda bottle. Steve knew roads and their upkeep, he knew the voting people of Wild Thyme, and he was well liked. It would have been convenient for me to like him too. Increasingly I had the impression that he'd be happy for me never to arrest anyone again and to move to some other county.

I said, "Come on, Stephen—"

"I have enough trouble? From Rhonda? You ask me—"

"Stephen—"

"Maybe she got hit because nobody likes her."

"Come on," I said.

"If you need more work, let me know," Stephen said, standing as if to close the matter. "But we don't want you making up—"

"I didn't make up anything—"

"—stories and then putting them in your blotter, scaring the little old ladies in the ladies' club."

"—and it isn't you who decides how much work I have," I said.

"Oh, no?"

"Okay. But please. Just read the blotter. The last few months." Heroin's arrival into the countryside had been a shameful secret at first, but you saw stories in the paper now. The truth was, within the past six months I could probably have made as many drug arrests as I had the time and inclination to make. I used to drive around what we call the Heights, a low-income community of outlaws and misfortunates perched on our highest hills, and wave to the people I saw around their homes. Sometimes I'd think, I know that guy to be a deadbeat—what's in his pockets? Now, with everything coming in, I had that thought about almost everybody, ordinary citizens too.

"I've seen the reports," said the Sovereign. "What, a few burglaries."

"A few burglaries a month where there used to be just a few all year. Possession. Overdoses, MVAs. If you think I'm catching everything . . ."

"I don't. I'm on my way to work. I'm not trying to be a prick. You've got to do your job, but you could stand some discretion. You and your reports."

As the supervisor walked out my door, I said, "Steve, it's not me that's scaring the little old ladies. You see that, right?"

It was early afternoon and I was sleeping peacefully at my desk when my phone chirped: a text message from Shelly Bray. With her two kids at school, her husband safe at work, her horses fed, and no clients at the stables, this was my signal to stop by. I had a half-hour window after every text to show up or not. Our system was simple. She never texted me for any other reason, and only ever wrote, *hey there* or *how you?* or simply, *hi*. If I could go, I would.

I turned onto Fieldsparrow Road and parked my car out of sight on the late Aubrey Dunigan's farmstead, where we'd had so much trouble the year before. I trotted through his scrubby field to the wooded ridge above. A trail led past a well pad that had been cleared but not drilled; at the moment it was just a silent expanse covered in a wisp of bluegrass. The unit in the rock far below included some of the Bray property. The lease was yet another bone of contention between Shelly and her husband. She was knee-jerk opposed to hydrofracking—a view I shared for my own reasons—but her husband saw that he couldn't keep it away. In the end, he had won.

I paused at the forest's edge to look out over the wide golden dell surrounding the Brays' horse farm. It thrummed with life, a braiding flow of light, insect buzz, and wildflower scent mixed with manure and hay. As I crept toward the house, keeping to the tree line, Shelly's two horses flicked their tails in the scant shade of a wildling apple tree, ignoring me. Wurlitzer and Pinky were their names.

At the kitchen door I removed my boots, wary of leaving imprints, and felt a rush of desire and dumb luck as Shelly padded down the stairs. She was a pretty brunette of forty or so with a huge devilish smile. That morning she wore only a clean white tank top and striped underwear. Stepping past me to the refrigerator, she removed a pitcher of ice water with lemon slices floating in it. She poured a glass and handed it to me.

"You look beat," she said. "Come on up."

Naked under a stream of cool water in the guest bathroom shower, I stood behind her and ran my hands over her abdomen, the muscle and flesh of it now as familiar as her face. My hand moved down between her legs, and my breath got short. Feeling me get hard, she bent forward with one hand on the tile, and with the other guided me inside her, unprotected. It was too good to bear. "Jesus," I said, "we can't."

Shelly gripped me to her with a hand behind my thigh. "I want you to. I want you to come."

I broke away before it was too late and stood, wild-eyed, with my back against the tile as Shelly shrugged, stepped out of the shower, and left the bathroom. I followed. In the guest bedroom, she pulled me to her and we took our time to finish what we'd started, but with protection. Afterward we lay side by side atop the bedspread, brushed by the warm breeze moving through the open windows.

"Hot," she said.

"Yeah."

"Tomorrow?"

"Okay," I said.

"What, Henry?"

"What, what?"

Shelly plucked her shirt from the floor and pulled it on over her head. Tugging her underwear up, she said, "The thrill is gone?"

"That's not the problem. That *is* the problem."

"I could leave him."

This was the second time she'd said something like this. The first time, a week ago, I'd ignored it. "Not on my account," I said. "The kids."

"Henry, I've known him years. He's not evil. But please understand: he's too broken to be fixed. Don't beat yourself up over the kids. We'd be doing them a favor."

"Just . . . not on my account."

She sighed. "Tomorrow, then?"

As I got dressed, I heard car tires. Downstairs, Shelly cursed. "Henry?"

"I'm out the window." I had memorized the house's layout for just such a moment, but never expected I'd be dumb enough to let it happen. Barefoot, and as gymnastically as is possible for a six-foot man, I folded myself through an open window and let go of the sill, dropping ten feet to the ground. From there, I slunk behind a woodpile. Around the corner of the house, Shelly and her husband Josh faced each other on the porch.

"Surprise, surprise," I heard her say.

"The AC died," he said, "you believe that? They sent us home, day off."

"I actually don't believe that."

"Maybe I just wanted to see you," Josh said.

"I'm surprised, that's all."

I heard the screen door slap shut, lay my head on the grass, and gazed into the blue sky. I thought about my boots. After five minutes, I crept to the tree line. This time the horses watched me all the way. Safe in the green dark of the woods, I stopped to look at the Bray place once more and imagined for a moment what it'd be like to live there. I felt bad skulking around in the family's house with all their pictures and things. Please don't think I didn't. But if I'm honest, it also felt good. It was something I needed. I told myself it'd be the last time, just like the time before.

I PICKED UP sneakers from home and went back to work, cut out of work at exactly four-thirty, and drove back to the tumble-down farmhouse I rented. I put on my camouflage, including green paint on my shiny sneakers and around my eyes and face where the beard didn't cover, and headed into the woods. I sat in cover by the edge of a field, trying to coax a gobbler toward a hen decoy. It was the wrong time of day, and I impressed myself by calling one in almost without meaning to. I had a feeling he was the same bird I'd heard two afternoons ago from the opposite hill, and also the huge tom that came to the edge of my yard last evening to taunt me as I ate supper on my porch, wearing only boxer shorts with a hole in the seat. I live in the country, and alone. I'd grabbed the shotgun and stalked him barefoot to the tree line, then stood and watched as he jogged straight down the road ahead of me, too distant for a shot. He'd turned, looked right at me, bobbed his head, and disappeared into the woods.

Now he played it paranoid, hunkering down in a line of maples along a creek. I scraped out another quiet invitation on my call. He didn't respond for twenty minutes. Then, far to the east of where he'd been, he made an echoing bleat and strutted into the field. His head turned blue, then red, and then deathly white as he paced in the grass, checking his flank. Saying, Where is this goddamn hen that won't move? Make me chase you, I don't think so. He was king in his world. I shot him and through a puff of gun smoke noted the spot where he should have fallen. The walk into the field stretched my legs. Standing over empty ground, I wondered at the power of this bird, half idiot, half genius, to disappear. I had shot him, I swear.

On my walk home, I followed one of my neighbor's trails into a wooded ravine, and back up to leafy woods pocketed with red pine. A clean scent moved through the forest on the breeze, so strong I could only follow. The air was sweet. I stepped off the path and into shadow. Pushing through black branches knit together, eventually I came to a small open ring with an emerald floor of moss, princess pine, and jack-in-the-pulpit. The break in the woods hid a treasure: standing three feet off the ground, in the shade of a maple, a single wild azalea bloomed pink, its flowers swaying as if exhausted with scent.

"Look at you," I said. I took a knee near the plant and

brushed aside some dead leaves on the ground. With my knife, I gathered two shoots. Fighting my way back to the path, I cradled the plants like baby birds in my cupped palm.

Back home I grabbed a serving fork from a kitchen drawer and went back outside. I considered the lay of the land and settled on a roadside tree line with a rotting split-rail fence in it. In went the wild azalea, no longer wild, nice and easy.

NEXT MORNING was clear and dry. A tom had run me around since about five a.m., and I was having eye trouble to where I couldn't see getting to work on time. I had just got home, stripped off my camo, put up the shotgun, and started the kettle for coffee, when my friend Ed Brennan called. The call changed quite a bit, then and in years to follow.

Ed is a large, loud man, but on the phone that morning his voice was a murmur, telling a story I didn't want to know the end to. I got dressed in three minutes and, with my coffee sloshing out of its cup, drove down to Fitzmorris.

The Brennans live on a small farm outside Fitzmorris, which you may know is the Holebrook County seat. Liz Brennan is the town's general practitioner, and Ed owns a high-end construction business specializing in timber frame buildings. He has a few skilled guys but he'll take his workers from anywhere, rehab placements, whatever, as long as they can work. The Brennans have two young kids, a boy and a girl. Ed and I went to high school together, oh, fifteen-twenty years ago. I'm close with their family. They've helped me through troubles. And I might as well say that if you knew Liz, you'd understand how I could love her with the purity of a dog's love, and be in no better position than a dog to express how I felt, and have no more chance of pursuing her romantically than a dog would have. She's my best friend's wife. I'm telling everything else, so I might as well admit that too. My life was much simpler when I had my own wife, but I scattered her ashes out West, and she's hard to reach.

I pulled into the yard of the white farmhouse. Ed stood in the doorway. He gave me a small wave and moved inside. On the porch, one of Ed's guys sat slumped in a chair. Duct tape held the toes of his boots shut. A baseball cap hid his face, but that didn't matter. It was Kevin O'Keeffe, the fellow who lived with his girlfriend Penny in a trailer on Andy Swales's land up to Maiden's Grove. I wasn't sure whether he was asleep or awake until I took the stairs. He shifted and tried to stand. I waved him back and pulled a chair around to face him.

"Are we doing this here?" he asked.

"Not sure what it is we're doing," I said.

"Ed didn't say?"

"Why don't you tell me?"

Kev glanced toward Ed's front door, then back at me. "You're not taking me in?"

"What is this all about, and we'll go from there." I had no place to hold Kevin in my tiny station. Not for longer than an hour or so. There was no doubt that this, if it was anything, would be kicked over to the county.

O'Keeffe lowered his voice. "I didn't kill her." He wore a T-shirt, and I looked at his arms for scratches and bruises. His sunburned skin was scraped and lined, nothing fresh, though.

"But she's gone," I said.

"Yeah. I get home two nights ago, the place is busted."

"About what time did you get in that night?"

"I don't know, two-thirty? There's some, ah . . . Jesus, oh,

God." He hid his face in his hands, which were cracked and dry, then looked up again. "But I don't notice . . . what I should have. I was drunk. I passed out. I guessed she was mad about something, me staying out late or what, and then she'd be back. No shape to go after her. Next morning, still no Penny. I called her phone, I called her sister, called her folks, no nothing. Looking around, you know, I should've seen. I went to work.

"Come night, still no Penny. Her car ain't moved. I made some more calls and went out hitting the bars. Binghamton, Endicott, down to Fitzmorris. Nobody's seen her." He raised a hand to pick at his eye. The hand trembled.

"Okay. Now, what about this, you said you shot somebody? That can't be right, right?" Ed had told me this part of the story over the phone, without details. It didn't fit. No gunshot wounds had come into Holebrook or in neighboring counties. Likely this was a bad dream or a delirium from too much or too little alcohol in the blood.

Kevin gave no reply, and then, "I shouldn't have said that. Forget that, I'm wrong, I was drunk. I didn't shoot nobody."

"Okay, so where was it that you didn't shoot anybody?"

Kevin sighed and raised his eyes to the heavens.

"Where's the gun?" I said.

He put an index finger to his temple and pretended to blow his brains out. It was not for my benefit, I don't think. Our eyes met, and I knew that something was wrong with Kevin, and with the little place where our lives met.

"Tell me where you've been, Kev. You've got to tell me right now."

"Promise me you'll go after Penny. She could be . . . we're wasting time."

"Stand up, please." I patted him down, catching body odor that was sharp like cheese, sweet like bread or beer. No weapon.

"If she's dead, I didn't kill her."

"Well," I said. O'Keeffe extended his wrists to be cuffed. I shook my head. "How'd you get here?"

"Walked."

"Where's your truck?"

He gave me a helpless look. "I don't know."

I put an arm on his shoulder and steered him to my vehicle.

On the drive to the sheriff's, I thought about my visit to their home that winter, and about their history. You show up to a domestic call expecting to see people still in the grip of the fight that got you called out, clawing, screaming. You come to somebody's defense, chances are they let you in on a punch or two. You're the person they hate more than each other. That January night when I had pulled up to the trailer off Dunleary, my blue lights dancing off the white woods, with Swales's house barely visible through the tree trunks, it was quiet. I knocked and stepped inside. The first thing O'Keeffe asked me was to turn off my lights so the landlord wouldn't know I'd been called.

When I returned, the two of them were sitting in the kitchen, Penelope at the table, Kevin on the floor with his back to the refrigerator. Penelope Pellings was lovely, with long chestnut hair and teeth that protruded slightly past her lips. A small woman, small and thin. Kev O'Keeffe had long hair pulled straight back in a ponytail and wore several ropy, beaded necklaces over a hand-knitted sweater. Neither spoke as I stomped snow off my boots and ducked inside. The only signs of struggle were Penelope's flaring nostrils, a butcher's knife in front of her on the table, and bloody paper towels wrapped around O'Keeffe's hand.

Had they been drinking? Yes, a bit. Drugs? No, they said. Back then, it didn't really matter to me what started it all; there had been an argument, a struggle, a door slammed shut and held closed against Penny. The last straw. She had taken out the sharpest knife in the block and waited.

The knife was a mirror, and what they saw in it, they barely recognized. It ended the fight, and now, with O'Keeffe's hand dripping blood on the floor, the overwhelming sense I got from both of them was shame. I asked to speak with Penelope alone, and O'Keeffe agreed.

We stepped outside and, despite the puffy jacket she had wrapped around her, she began to shiver. "We had a fight, I lost my shit." Her hands clutched each other as if preventing their own flight, the wild flight of bats. "He never hit me."

"Good."

Penny looked off into the woods. "Sometimes I can't keep on with this."

"With what?"

"What does he care? Working on these fall-down barns. Getting fucked up every night—not drunk, fucked up—waking up and doing it again. Never going to get our girl back that way. I been through the fuckin program, I been clean. But still CPS says I have to do this or that. When is our life going to be what it is? I know people have to do whatever, but I never thought I'd be living like this. Sorry. You don't need to hear it."

"You were trying to, what, get him to stop drinking?"

"Something like that. Listen, believe it or not, Henry, I didn't call for you."

"Oh, no?"

She caught my dubious tone. "Nobody tells me how it is, not him, not anybody. Nobody has a thumb that fuckin big. He drank too much to get himself to the hospital in the snow, and he won't admit he should go get the hand looked at, and if he doesn't he won't be working at all. Then we'll have real problems. I called for an ambulance." She tapped her breastbone with her palm. "He's trying to protect me, saying it isn't bad. If he isn't hurt too bad, then . . ."

Then the fight wasn't anything for me to tell CPS about. "I'll radio."

I went back to my truck and raised the emergency squad, then stepped back inside to wait. Penelope had taken a seat on Kevin's lap and was plucking at his hair. I wondered whether this show of affection might be for my benefit. At the time it seemed more genuine than not. Of course I worried about her.

I looked at them both, wondering what to say. "Please tell me I won't be back here for anything like this ever again."

"You won't," Kevin said.

"So what do you two want, where do you want to go with this?"

"Nowhere," said Kevin.

"Vacation?" said Penelope.

NEARLY HALF a year later, as Kevin O'Keeffe and I sat on a bench in the basement hallway of the Holebrook County Courthouse and waited, I tried not to feel that I had missed something important. Since our encounter that winter, Kevin had let himself go to where he was almost a street person. Teeth the color of old newspaper, voice burred by smoke, skin swollen tight on his face but dried to horn on his hands. He'd gone from an affable youngish hippie to one of those guys you see, and we all probably know at least one, riding his bicycle to the distributor for his daily thirty-pack, looking both older and younger than he should.

A patrolman led us into an empty conference room, and O'Keeffe and I sat at a chipped wooden table until Sheriff Dally knocked at the window. I left the room and joined him in the hall. Dally and the patrolman listened as I laid out the situation as quickly and fully as I could.

Dally turned to his guy. "Call the hospitals again. Check down to Dunmore and Wyoming, see if the state police have anything from last night that might fit."

When the patrolman had left, Dally said to me, "How do you want to handle this, will he talk to us both?"

I said I thought so. The question was a courtesy; Dally was going to step in. I liked him as a sheriff and a person. But he was a trifle stiff, as many descendants of the Scots Presbyterians who founded Fitzmorris tended to be, and disposed to believe he was not only right, but in the right. I'd heard him refer to his job more than once as "whack-a-mole." His world and Kevin's didn't intersect except at the point of citation, and that's maybe what the county needs out of a sheriff—distance, a lordliness. With my upbringing I didn't have the luxury of arm's-length policing. Everyone was somebody's uncle or cousin. Over the past couple years I'd been on the job in Wild Thyme, the sheriff had come to see that I could be useful talking to certain kinds of people. The indigent, the iron-spined, the woodchucks.

Dally knocked on the window and opened the door. We all said hello, and then nothing. A wary silence had settled over O'Keeffe.

"You need anything?" I asked. "Water, soda?"

"How about, you know, just a little smooth-over?" He lit a half-smoked cigarette, flattened from his pocket. "I hate to ask, you know. I understand. Shit—what time is it?" He chuckled with no happiness. "Now isn't the time, I understand that. Practically speaking, it just . . . it would help me get it together. Okay, had to ask. She's gone. You going to help me?"

"In my younger days," said the sheriff, eventually, "when I drank too much on a Friday night? I'd wake up feeling sick in my stomach, sick in my head. Soul-sick. I knew I'd done something, didn't know what. If I couldn't remember, it almost wasn't real, that thing I did." Dally paused, produced a small recording device, and placed it in the middle of the table, where it sat, drawing our eyes. "But there was a dent in the pickup that wasn't there yesterday. A rip in my shirt, a black eye, those were real. Sometimes I'd call up a buddy and say, Hey, I don't really want to know, but what happened? And it was better to know. Often things weren't so bad as they seemed. It wasn't really me. I had to remind myself of that. I'd been drinking."

O'Keeffe wasn't buying it. Dally waved a hand at the recorder. "This is what we call a noncustodial interview. You aren't under arrest, and so far as I know, you haven't done a thing wrong. You're here because you want to be and we want you to be. You're free to go anytime. Yeah?"

"Okay."

"Don't get stage fright if I record us. It's an interview. So if you say something that's useful later, we have it down."

"Useful how?"

"We don't know yet. You say your girlfriend's gone. We don't know. But if she's in trouble, details will help."

O'Keeffe sank deeper in his chair and nodded his assent.

"Say it, please, so we have it."

"Okay, I said."

There were gaps in the account he gave. Just as he had done with me, he insisted on a few things: He got home around two-thirty a.m., May 18. Penelope was gone, the place kicked apart. His search the following night had ended somewhere in Fitz-morris. Interviews don't just roll out one-and-done. They get repeated and repeated, facts change and change back, minor points get insisted on and later dropped, all in search of the one useful lie or truth. We went over it a couple more times. O'Keeffe claimed to have spent the night of the supposed dis-appearance partying with some others in a clearing on the north shore of Maiden's Grove, really just standing around drinking and, presumably, smoking weed. Locals sometimes parked on Dunleary Road and took a trail through Swales's land to do this. Sometimes they'd park up near Kevin and Penelope's place. No, nobody had parked up by their trailer that night, only on Dunleary. O'Keeffe was unsure who would be able to account for his whereabouts. Was Penelope down by the shore? Sure, but she'd left alone, back up the hill to the trailer. There were no loners, no strangers with them.

"Did she ever go swimming in the lake?" I asked. "Not nec-essarily that night."

"Yeah," Kevin said, then caught my meaning. "No, no, she

was a strong swimmer, she went all the time. All the time. Not that night, of course, lake's too cold yet. Listen. You have to get out there and find her. I'm begging you."

"In good time," I said.

"This guy you're supposed to have shot," Dally said.

"Man, come on. For the last time, I was wrong, let it go. You need to go see my place. I need you to believe me."

"Well, I would," said Dally. "Only, you said before, you shot a man last night. It's not something you'd make up or forget—"

"No, no, no. No."

"And if this guy is lying somewhere, bleeding, dying, and you have a chance to save his life, it's—"

"No."

"You'd be saving your own life," the sheriff concluded.

O'Keeffe said nothing and gazed up through the basement window. He couldn't have seen but a line of grass, sky, a couple tree branches. He settled in to the nothing.

Kevin O'Keeffe, no more than a gentle good-timer. I'd first met him one morning a few years ago, back when I was moonlighting construction for Ed. I was pulling into a site in south Susquehanna County, and there was Kevin, long-haired, pretending to make love to the rear bumper of his yellow truck. He was a young man then, actually young. Not now, whatever his age was, couldn't be twenty-five. What did he know, and what did he do, who was he? Perhaps he was just finding out.

"So, one last time. You get home," I said. "And Penelope's not there. Is that unusual?"

"Not . . . no. She went out sometimes."

"Where?"

Nothing.

"So you get home, was her car there? She has a car?"

"Yes. Yes."

"But the place was a mess," I said. "Was that unusual?"

"No, man, like I said, the doors—"

"So what on earth—"

"There was hair." His voice lifted.

"Hair," I said.

"Her hair, on the floor. I didn't find it until the next afternoon. It was bloody. Jesus."

"How much blood?"

"There was enough," he said. "At first I thought . . . it wasn't real. I'd been seeing things. Getting confused? Anyways, this shit was real."

Sheriff Dally gave the signal and we both stepped outside. "He say anything like that to you before now?"

"First I heard of any blood."

The sheriff stepped into his office to hear Patrolman Hanluain's report on area hospitals: still no gunshot wounds. He also had a brief phone conversation with the district attorney and checked in with the Marine Corps vet we used as a search-and-rescue diver. I stood guard outside the conference room door. Dally reappeared and we went back in.

Kevin sighed and said, "I'm not saying anything by this. Not a damn thing. But if you get out to my place, by the time you get there and let me know—you let me know you've seen it—I might remember something about last night."

AFTER A HALF-HOUR drive that took fourteen minutes, I was standing in front of Kevin and Penelope's trailer. Four massive oaks framed the place. The trees had begun to leaf, and the canopy blotted out most of the sun, but let coins of daylight through to shudder on the lawn. White lattice had once covered the space between the trailer's floor and the ground, but had been torn partly free; my flashlight caught nothing out of place under there, some beer cans scattered across hard-packed dirt. Two towels served as curtains to the bedroom; the other windows were covered by gappy venetian blinds. Behind several acres of woods to the right, the landowner's stone house loomed. I scraped my boot tread with a small screwdriver, pulled on some rubber gloves, and stepped inside the trailer.

The place had been scrubbed clean. Or I should say, I saw no blood spatters, no broken plates or furniture, no sign of struggle. Stacks of magazines and books strewn around, sure, dirty dishes in the sink, a thick coat of dust and dead cluster flies atop every high-up surface. But the floor was spotless. I did catch an odd, overwhelming scent of metal and smoke mixed.

The accordion door separating the living room and kitchen was in rough shape, but intact. Same with the door between the kitchen and bedroom. A bedsheet, pilled and yellowed, was stretched over three corners of their mattress. There were small piles of books on both sides of the bed. In one corner, untouched, was a crib with a mobile hanging over it, a mobile of winged fairies. The door to the bathroom was intact too, the one that was supposed to be kicked to pieces. It wasn't particularly new or old, just a cheap door. I opened and shut it. It worked fine, minus a little upward tug to get it to sit in the frame.

I lowered myself to the bedroom floor, put an eye along it.

No blood. I noticed the dried lines of a recent mopping and the smell of bleach. I sifted through some dust bunnies in the corner, but found nothing like the bloody hair Kevin described. The kitchen floor had been wiped clean too. It took me twice around the linoleum pattern before I found it: a drop of dried blood smaller than a shirt button near the refrigerator. It wasn't fresh, but it was something. Elongated, not the sun shape of a vertical drop. With my knife, I cut around it and baggied the piece of linoleum. It took a third trip around to find a small shard of china that had apparently slid to the wall and come to rest between it and the edge of the linoleum.

The sponge mop they had in the corner was dry and curling away from its metal mount. There were the usual sprays and powders under the sink.

Outside, I scuffed at the lawn between the trailer and the driveway, in which was parked a rusted compact I took to be Penny's. In the woods, I took two loops around the trailer, stepping over fallen logs and pushing aside low branches covered in buds about to burst open. Swales's land was so steep and uneven that, apparently, the Irish dairy farmers and tanners who had settled Wild Thyme never bothered to clear it for pasture, or maybe only cleared it once, long ago, and gave up. Every now and then there was a shallow rocky pit, now covered in a thick parchment of dead leaves, where long ago someone had hauled out shale for a wall or foundation. I walked to and fro from Swales's, looking for any kind of path, finding none.

After placing a seal on the door, I walked up to Swales's massive front entrance and knocked, then rang the bell. Nobody answered, so I wandered around back to the kitchen door.

I wanted to knock and talk, do a little peeping in the windows, maybe. The lights were off, the kitchen tidy and without ornament.

The path down to the lake was well trod and strewn with beer cans. I pulled on gloves and bagged every piece of trash and cigarette butt I saw. The sun rippled bright gold across the lake from the east, cutting through mist and warming me inside and out. In the small clearing, ashes drifted in a fire ring; I went through them with a stick, found broken pieces of a liquor bottle. On the way back up, I scanned the forest floor, side to side, one step per second.

I called Dally and briefed him. He handed the phone over to Kevin. "I'm here," I said.

"What do you see?"

"Nothing. Nothing unusual."

"What? No, I mean, how do I know you're there?"

"Let's see," I said, scanning the trailer's exterior. "There's like a blue-green tie-dyed towel on the second window to the right of the door."

"How could you not see?"

"Kev. I'm here, but I can't see what I can't see."

"All right. The Royal Lodges, up to Pine Street. Middle building, top floor."

ON PINE STREET, three shotgun apartment houses were stuck in the back teeth of Fitzmorris, home to some of the lowest of the community. The Royal Lodges. Not all bad people but very poor people, folks whose next step down the ladder would be a long-term motel stay, and then who knows. On the unmowed courtyard between two of the buildings, bright yellow plastic toys lay strewn, along with fast-food litter and some empties. The main hallway door was unlocked and I stepped inside to a fume of dog and dog shit. As I placed my feet on the carpeting, one after the other, I could almost see the fug rising up to meet me. Behind a wall on the first floor, two dogs bellowed.

The buildings were three stories tall and the apartment I sought was on the third floor. With each story the odor fell away and quiet settled into the building. Apartment 3A's door stood open about six inches, so I went in. What I found there was, again, nothing. Linoleum flooring, recently cleaned, peeling up in corners. No furniture, no mystery medicine behind the bathroom mirror, no hair in the drains, no bags of trash, no nothing. There was a back door that led to a balcony and an exterior staircase. A tall oak tree had laid a limb across the balcony's railing.

I knocked on the neighboring apartment's door, no answer. Nor did anybody appear to be home on the second floor. By the time I got to ground level, a man was waiting for me in the hall. He was about fifty, fat as a tomato, greasy as a pig on a spit. He had a ponytail. "I saw your truck," he said. "You're too late."

We introduced ourselves; his name was Shepcott, a precision machinist currently between jobs. "So about last night," I said.

"Last night, and every other night before that for a damn month. People stomping up and down the stairs, jigaboo music, real unfriendly kids. They usually don't play with me, they have that much sense. There was a fight last night, in the middle of the night, now, and before long up comes a white van. And they're up there throwing furniture and shit off the back stair. I come out to say what the fuck, and this kid, he couldn't have been twenty, takes his hand and pushes me right in my face. Right back into my apartment there. They're stomping up and down stairs, but damn if I can find my piece before they're gone. Everything up there, gone."

"Yeah," I said, processing. "Yeah. You get any names?"

"Nah. The one who was there most was just an ordinary kid, you know, but dressed for the ghetto. Tattoos up his arms. Nobody got any mail or nothing."

"You complain ever? Call the sheriff's, or, who's the landlord, Casey Noonan?" Noonan was a retired lawyer who owned the bulk of the rental properties in Fitzmorris.

"I tried calling Noonan. You know, what the fuck, who'd you let in here? I know everyone in this town, I don't know that guy up on three. What does he tell me? He don't even own the building anymore. Some group bought it last year. So I said, who've I been paying rent to for the past year, then? Says this company whatever, they kept him on as a property manager. He ain't been doing much managing other than taking my rent every month, cash. Other people moved out. The Covilles, nice people, they moved. Chris Parsons, he moved in with his brother's family, that ain't going too well."

"Last night," I said, shaking my head to clear the clutter.

"Yeah, there was a fight."

"What'd you see, you hear anything unusual, like a gun-shot? Any women?"

"You know, might could be," he said. "Somebody shot?"

"Just asking."

"You don't think gunshot, you think a door slamming, whatever. I mostly just hear footsteps, footsteps on the stairs all hours. Last night, could be. Could very well be. I would say so, yeah. As to women? I don't particularly notice. Whoever does go up there, they don't never stay long. But you'll know why that is."

"Why?"

"They're selling shit up there. Ain't you the cop?"

I gave Shepcott my number and walked out.

"WELP," I SAID to Dally, leaning against the wall of his office while the sheriff finished a sandwich in four bites. "Something happened."

"Hell," he said.

I told him about the two places I'd seen, both scoured, neither right.

"So O'Keeffe is lying, or he's only telling part of it. Or he doesn't even know what he knows."

"Do an alert on the girl?"

"Yeah, get me a description and we'll send it out. I'll call New York and have them do one. Release something to the news stations too," he said. "We got any kind of name for the tenant?"

I shrugged. "I'll talk to Noonan, see what we can find out about the new owners."

I set a pen and pad down in front of Kevin where he sat at the table, and told him to work on Penny's measurements and distinguishing marks. Five-one, a hundred and ten pounds, brown hair brown eyes, and a fairy tattoo on the inside right ankle. Or was it the left? He had a picture on his phone that I had him email to me.

"You saw my place," he said.

"Yup."

"Royal Lodges, too."

"Yup."

"Well? I've been sitting here."

"You got a name on the occupant down to the Lodges?"

"Uh, no, he went by Mikey, I think. You find anything?"

"How did Penny know him?"

"I don't know, town. Work." By this, I assumed Kevin meant Binghamton, New York, just north of the border. "She worked a couple bars, he did too. He moved out here, I don't know, a couple months ago. Hung out a bit here and there."

"What do you think of him?"

"Ah, he's a prick. Drives a little lime-green car, neon-pink lights that shine on the ground? Not someone who likes a small town. I guess he and Penny had that in common. Everywhere he went, someplace better to be. Plus he dressed like an idiot, like, football jerseys, big jeans." Kevin tapped his fingers. "I need a beer. Something."

I left the interview room and found Deputy Jackson at a computer, scrolling through a data table.

"Green car," I said. "Green car, pink lights, aftermarket lights around the undercarriage, you see that around town? Driver name of Mikey?"

"Seen it. Wondered. Now I know."

"Last name?"

Jackson shrugged.

Sheriff Dally came out of the office. "Henry," he said, "follow me. Ben, make sure Mr. O'Keeffe has everything he needs?"

"I'll keep an eye on him," said the deputy.

The sheriff and I took the two flights of stairs to District Attorney Ross's wood-paneled office. Ross, that retiring balding burgher of Fitzmorris, held open the door and waved us in. He was tall and bespectacled and dressed in a yellow polo shirt, probably for a late afternoon on the golf course. We sat in leather chairs and Dally filled the county lawyer in on the events of the morning. Ross listened, betraying nothing.

"Do you need anything from me?" he asked.

"I don't know," said Dally. "I was going to ask you the same thing."

"We'd never get what you've got past prelim, let alone make it out at trial. If these people are dead, we need bodies. It can be done without, but with no weapon, no witnesses, no reason to kill this girl . . . What's the history, there's something, right?"

Ross didn't handle the baby Eolande case; it had been a part-time assistant DA. "They had a baby," I said.

"Oh," said Ross, catching on. "The bottle?"

Eolande had been born small, with a struggling heart. They'd taken her away after blood work showed buprenorphine in her system. Penny had a prescription to help her kick some opioid or other, and the thinking was she'd laced Eolande's formula to get her to sleep. Child Protective Services had removed the baby and handed her over to an older single mother, also living in Wild Thyme. Penny had since cleaned up and seen her mistake, so could they give her baby back? Doctors thought that Eolande's intellect would be slow to develop and that she'd have special needs. Before she could return to her parents, there were classes to take and habits to master.

"Is it worth it to us to keep Kevin?" Dally thought aloud. "Wear him down?"

"He doesn't even know what he did," said Ross. "We don't know what happened, we're hitchhiking under the big top here. Find us some evidence."

"It'd help us more with him out in the world," I said. "He's lost his truck. That's got to mean something. Find the truck, and . . ."

"Yeah. The gun. Maybe even the girl, or something. And we'll keep an eye on him, see where he leads us."

"Right," said Ross. "Let's not take this one out of the oven too soon."

Dally turned to me. "You busy?"

I LED KEVIN out into the afternoon sun. "That's it?" he said. "That's all you need?"

"We got alerts out here and in New York."

"What happened with Mikey?"

"Jesus Christ, Kevin, you probably missed. Count your blessings. Let's go find your truck."

We did not find the truck. In my vehicle, we covered the ridge where the Brennans lived, the Royal Lodges and their surroundings, and all points in between. It was evening by the time we bumped up the driveway to Kevin's trailer. I parked on the edge of the overgrown yard.

"Listen," I said, "I don't know how you lose a whole yellow truck. There was nobody with you last night?"

"No. You know," he said, "if Penny was a kid, or like a citizen, the whole state would be out looking for her by now. But she's not a kid, she's just a girl without no money. She still needs your help. She deserves it. And you won't give it. You guys are some fucking cops, man."

"We got alerts out, Kevin."

"You can't just leave me here where it happened."

"Get some sleep. You'll feel better."

"Sleep?" Kevin gestured to the car in the driveway. "Look, where was she supposed to go without her car?" It was a good point. I walked with him to the trailer's front door, where he stood shaking his head. "Never seen the floors this clean before. Whoever did this, he took her. You find something of his, you can find her too."

"Kev," I said, not very patiently.

"You wait. Okay, you fuckin . . . you wait right there." He disappeared inside. I heard him rummaging, and then silence. "Henry! In here, you got to see this!"

I followed his voice to the bedroom, where he stood rooted.

"Henry," he said. "This ain't my door. This ain't my bathroom door, man."

I looked at the cheap composite hanging on its hinges, your typical hollow crap.

"Penny, she painted ours. She painted a scene on it, the lake, the hills, for the baby. She was a good artist, man. Come on, you got to see."

"Kevin."

"Come on."

"Kevin, you could've replaced this anytime. I don't know if it means anything." But to look in his eyes gave me an odd feeling.

"Jesus Christ." He yanked the false door open, went into

the bathroom, stood on the toilet, and popped up a tile. He reemerged holding a black glasses case, which he held out to me.

I took it and flipped the clamshell open.

"She'd never go anywhere without that. First time I found one, I took it away, broke it. The next time, she fought me. Scratched me up. Time after that, she said she'd go out and get what she needed from someone else, and I didn't like the sound of that. I didn't want her sharing."

"I have to take this," I said, staring at a spoon blackened to the color of iron, a length of tubing, and a syringe. There was a stamp-sized bag of heroin as well.

"I sure don't want it. Look, I know what it means, me showing you this." He was overcome. "We can't have everything in life. As long as Eo's cared for . . . I just want Penny back."

"Any idea where she gets it?"

Nothing.

"From Mikey?"

At this, he wiped his eyes and glared at me as if I was slow. "It used to be a friend would bring something back from over the border. Sometimes she was the one. Then the trade came here. Yeah, Mikey was one I knew of. I could get hurt for saying that out loud, you understand. I—she was trying to quit. She didn't want anyone to know. I just want her back. I'll tell you anything."

"Okay. But for now, dry out and get some sleep. Consider yourself under house arrest."

"You can't keep me here."

"No, but you go anywhere, I'll be right behind you."

"I'll stay put if you help me. You'll help me. I know you. I know you will." Kevin looked back into his empty home, and I could see the horror wash over him. He pointed to a spot between the kitchen and the bedroom. "Her hair was right there. What I saw."

"Get some rest. We'll talk tomorrow."

I parked my truck just off the driveway near the trailer, and on foot switched back and forth all over the ridge. On the southern face, the sun had punched through to the forest floor and convinced the saplings to leaf. At times the trees were so thick that I was lost in endless green.

I didn't feel I could leave Kevin alone, not yet. Reclining in my truck's bed, I got one bar on the cell phone and called the Brennans. Ed answered. I explained where I was and let him know that Kevin was home, and might or might not make it to work the next day. About Penny I said little, even when Ed asked me directly if she was all right. "Well," said Ed, "as long as you're on it, try to kick his ass out of bed in the morning. I need him working tomorrow."

"Last I knew, I wasn't his butler." I thought about how to say what I had in mind. "Maybe you don't want him around right now."

"What else is he going to do with himself?"

As evening fell I settled down with a book I'd been reading about the battle of Antietam, and then wished I could play my fiddle, which I often carried around in the warmer months for just such occasions. When I couldn't read anymore I ran through tunes in my mind. If you have played long enough, you can do that and it's just a different way to make music. For a while I let myself wander and then slipped into variations on "Ways of the World," key of A. Most old-time tunes just have two parts and you shuffle back and forth between them, AABBAABB, forever. I thought of this tune in three sections, the first being the jaunty dominant melody, the second a grumble at the base of the neck, then a wild sweep down to G that added a touch of seriousness. What are you, a woodcock on your private flight? Maybe one peeper of ten thousand in a swamp? I am one of you, and you are one of me. The music rolled down the driveway in my mind, calling Penelope Pellings home so I could go home too and live my lazy spring.

It was after ten p.m. when a Ford Mustang rolled to a stop beside my pickup. I dropped out of the bed and raised a hand for the driver to wait. I noted two silhouettes inside, and as I got closer I saw that the passenger was a woman. The driver got out of the car and I faced a bald, ruddy man in decent shape, maybe forty. Earlier that evening he had been dressed for the office, but now his tie was undone and hung from either side of his collar. His shirt was open to the second button down. He stood between me and the woman in the passenger seat, trying to shield her from my eyes. So I looked around him and saw a trim, tan woman with blond hair like she'd put her finger in a light socket. She waved.

"Andy Swales," the man said, and extended his hand. The mint he was shifting around in his mouth did not entirely hide the scent of gin.

"We've spoken on the phone," I said. "Henry Farrell."

"I don't usually get cops up my very driveway."

"I'm here about your tenant, Kevin."

"That lunatic," Swales said affectionately.

"He came to us saying Penelope Pellings is missing."

"So it's true?"

"I'd like to talk to you about two night ago. It could help us out."

Swales looked uneasy and shifted his eyes toward the car. "I've got a visitor."

"Tomorrow, then?" I said.

He handed me a business card that listed him as a partner in a law firm. "I'm not sure what help I can be, but stop by my office around four."

As the Mustang wound its way toward the big stone house, I settled back and listened to the woods creak all around me, and watched my narrow strip of sky for satellites and shooting stars. I must have trusted Kevin O'Keeffe enough that I dozed off. Then I awoke to the slap of the trailer's screen door. You know when you convince yourself that you have had a premonition in your sleep? I was on my feet and following him into the woods before I knew what I was doing. Kev was not hard to follow, swashing about in the brush, heading for the lake. As I got closer I heard him moaning. Not exactly moaning, but mumbling, repeating, "Oh," something-something, "oh." He did a header over a log and got right up like nothing was wrong. I grabbed his arm, but it took some shaking before he turned. His eyes didn't see. Then they did.

"What am I doing?" he said.

"Come on."

"She was down there."

"Come on." As I turned him toward home, I noticed a plastic bottle of rail vodka where he'd fallen, empty. It wasn't something I had seen when I went through the place before. People like him have their ways. Penny too, I guess. You had to wonder what else there was to find.

Once I got Kevin sideways on his bed and breathing slow, and I felt reasonably confident he wasn't going anywhere, I headed home. It wasn't even that late, just about midnight.

ON THE Susquehanna River between Apalachin and Owego, New York, you can kayak west to Hiawatha Island, maybe stop there to eat your lunch and hike a trail. And on this bright morning, that's just what a couple of grad students intended to do. But as they approached the first of several towheads on the way, one of the girls spotted something snagged on a branch. She drifted up alongside it, as close as she could get in the shallow water near the gravel bar. Too shocked even to cry out, she backpaddled as quickly as she could, and with her commotion scared off a carp that had been nibbling at the wound in the middle of the corpse's chest.

The Tioga County Sheriff's Department was first on the scene, bringing with them a boat to retrieve the body before the river could carry it away again. The county sent one of their coroners, but there was nothing that could be gathered or learned from the river itself. Once they'd brought the body back to the morgue and cut away what clothing remained, their sheriff began calling nearby jurisdictions.

It wasn't yet noon before I had found the Bradford County site where Ed had put Kevin O'Keeffe to work with a couple other guys. They were dismantling a barn, though not a particularly beautiful one—it was new enough to lack the grand architecture of the nineteenth century, but old enough that its roof was badly swaybacked. I picked Kevin out from among several men standing on the roof, guessing rightly that he was the one sporting the largest sun hat I'd ever seen, a straw disc the size of a trash can lid. I beckoned him down. Work ceased as Kevin joined me a little ways off from the structure, looking silly and frightened and tired. His face was smeared with tar.

"What's up, Henry?"

"I need you to come with me."

"Where?"

"Tioga County. The morgue."

He fell to his knees and let out a sob.

I heard one of the crew say, "Oh, shit, here we go."

"No," I said. "Look, man, it's not—"

"Is it her?"

"We need you to have a look, okay?"

"Is it or fuckin isn't it?"

"You need to come along."

From there we had a short drive north across the state line and the river to a dreary yellow building that housed the county's social services, coroner's office, morgue, and so on. Seated beside me, Kevin twisted his work gloves and stared out the window.

He recognized Sheriff Dally's car as we rolled in. He began to take deep, huffing breaths. As we walked slowly from the patrol truck to the county building, what remained of his composure crumbled and he squatted down right there in the lot. Glad I didn't have to keep up the half-truth anymore, I explained we were there to view not a young woman, but a dead young man.

"You motherfucker, you fuckin prick!" Kevin started back to the patrol truck.

"Kev, just get in there."

"This is your deal. You ain't done shit for me, I ain't help-ing you."

"All the same."

"Why would I look at a guy I shot? Oh, yeah, that's him. Take me to jail now. What have you done to find Penny? Any-thing? I got work."

"Then just tell me he isn't anybody you know and I'll leave you alone and start on the other thing. But you're going in, Kevin."

Tioga County employs four coroners who also serve as medical examiners. The lead was Andrea Catlin, MD, an ami-able local woman with short hair and a lift in her shoulders, as if she were in an everlasting shrug at the state of the world. It was she who had trekked out to the body, as she did in most suspi-cious deaths. Sheriff Dally was already with her, as arranged. In the doorway of her small, tidy office, she reached to shake my hand.

We four proceeded down to the morgue, where the body from the river lay on a silver table, uncovered and cut open. Kevin's breathing quickened and the color faded from his face. It was rare to see a sunburned man go that white. The kid was slight, goateed, with tattoos crawling up his arms.

"Charles Michael Heffernan," said the sheriff. "Twenty-six."

Dr. Catlin pulled on gloves and began to point things out about him. "Gunshot wound here, puncturing the left lung. That lung was full of blood, and water got into the torso through the chest wound. The body didn't have enough air to stay afloat in the river. An impact knocked it out of him. He probably tumbled along the bottom for a day or two. We took a lot of sediment out of his mouth. Some from his nose and ears. He's got fractures on his skull here, a dislocated right shoulder, broken arm in several places, broken ribs, pelvis, suggesting he entered the river from a height. A bridge, my guess."

"So he drowned," said Dally.

"I'll show you what killed him." With a forceps, Catlin picked up a long sliver of bone. "This is a piece of rib that ended up in his heart. It could be from the gunshot, or it could be on impact from the fall."

"I don't need to be here, Henry, man, let me go out to the car," Kevin said, staring at a spot on the ceiling in the exact opposite direction of the body. I caught a distinct whiff of what we in law enforcement call awareness of guilt. Dally saw it too.

"He might not have died instantly," Dr. Catlin continued. "Chances are he'd have bled out slowly, into his lung, into, I don't know, a towel maybe, there seems to have been some pressure on his chest. But there was no way this kid was going to survive it." She set down the bone needle and picked up a bullet, misshapen from its journey into the body. "Nine-millimeter, 124."

"What do you say, O'Keeffe?" Dally said. "You know this guy from somewhere?"

Kevin forced himself to look directly into the battered, soft face of the corpse; you could've spread the dead skin onto toast with a dull knife. "I couldn't tell you," he said. What he was really saying, he said only to me, and not out loud but with his eyes. This was the guy he'd shot. He had no reason to admit shooting him. And in the end, he wasn't sure he cared.

I bought Kevin lunch at a fast-food chain and we headed

back to Holebrook County, passing over the hills and creeks in silence.

"Whatever you did with the gun," I said, "I hope it's safe."

"What gun."

I dropped him off back at the Bradford County work site, where the crew stopped work to stare at us with naked curiosity.

LATER THAT AFTERNOON Dally called to relay what Tioga County, Broome County, and the Binghamton police knew about Charles Michael Heffernan. The basic measurements: five feet ten inches tall, weighing a buck seventy-five, twenty-six years old. His mother lived in Binghamton and cut hair, and his father was a bartender in Florida. He had a younger brother enrolled in SUNY Potsdam, but Charles himself had spent his college years working in various restaurant kitchens and building a criminal record of two assaults, four possessions including one with intent to distribute, and a DUI. For his efforts he'd spent, in aggregate, fourteen months in the New York prison system before winding up where they found him in the Susquehanna River.

"Any connection to O'Keeffe or Pellings?" I asked, rifling the papers on my desk for something clean to write on. "What about ties down here?"

"They're looking into it. It's possible. We'll see. Tioga County is happy with O'Keeffe as the shooter and Fitzmorris as the place. They want to send it back to us."

"How does Ross feel?"

"You know how he is," Dally said. "We've got to hand it all right to him."

"I'll tell you what, I think Kev may have done the guy. Why, and how much he meant to, I don't know. But why haul him all the way to New York? Plenty of places to sink a body closer to home."

"These are deep waters, as they say."

I brought a mug shot of Charles Michael Heffernan to the Royal Lodges to confirm with Shepcott that he was the tenant.

"Yeah, I would say so," Shepcott told me. "What'd he do?"

On my way out I ran in to Casey Noonan, the white-haired old gent who once owned the buildings. The yard was surrounded by a wrought-iron fence whose black paint had flaked onto the sidewalk. Noonan was seated in the grass beside the fence with his ankles crossed, scouring rust and priming for a repaint.

"You got ten dollars for me, I might have a spare brush in the trunk," he said. "I'd gladly give you a stretch of fence to paint."

Noonan told me that he didn't know the people who had bought him out, only that they were organized as an LLC. A lawyer from Scranton handled the deal and seemed to be a party to it as well. "Andy Swales, you know him?"

"We've met," I said.

"I think they thought this place would be overrun by now with the gas drilling. Slowed down on them, though."

I showed the retired lawyer Heffernan's photo. "You recognize this guy?"

"I don't know the people the way I once did. Rent comes cash, in envelopes. I deposit it for them, I fix a leak or two, I paint the fence. They give me a little scratch for my trouble and I get out of the house."

WHEN PEOPLE around here talk about going to "the city," they don't mean the glorified intersection that is Fitzmorris or other small towns like that. They're talking about going north over the New York border and the river to the cities dotting the Southern Tier. We have a choice of either Elmira to the west, maybe Owego if you count that as a city and I don't, or Binghamton to the east.

Binghamton, Broome County's rusting anchor, was once nicknamed Parlor City because they made so many cigars there. Not no more. After the cigars vanished, Endicott Johnson came with their shoe factory and cheap houses for immigrant labor, which drew folks to the area now known as the Triple Cities: Binghamton, Johnson City, and Endicott. The founder of the shoe factory loved carousels and set up free ones in parks all over the area. And his factory kept things humming for a while. Hand me down my peg, my peg, my peg, my awl. In the year of 1998 the last EJ plant closed for good. IBM was still around, but downsizing. Strange now to think they got their start here.

I parked in a metered spot downtown, beside one of the carousel horses that the city had bolted into the sidewalks some years back when it had proclaimed itself the Carousel Capitol of the World. With so many empty buildings and storefronts, the bright statues had always seemed about as cheerful as a roadside shrine to a car wreck. This particular chestnut mare had been tagged all over with black marker. A city living on in the echo of twentieth century bustle, now tired, with most people either wishing things could be the way they were, or never knowing they had been any different. I had little use for the place beyond the odd restaurant dinner or backyard party Ed and Liz Brennan dragged me to. It had always struck me as received wisdom that there was more to do in a place just because there were more people near each other and more things to buy. A ratty man in sweatpants and no shirt ambled up the walkway from the riverside, saw me, turned, and disappeared under the Court Street bridge. Not my problem.

Andy Swales's employer, Carmichael & Williams, LLP, was a large law firm based in Scranton. Apparently they had the idea to open up a satellite office on the border to try to rope in clients. It's possible they were counting on a bonanza of gas business once New York's moratorium lifted, but we all know how that went. Anyway, back at this time, Broome County must have looked like low-hanging fruit. Swales had volunteered to act as managing partner to this particular enterprise, and had apparently been confident enough in it to build himself a mansion in Wild Thyme.

And the firm had their pick of office space. The two partners, four associates, and six support staffers had settled into the fifth floor of a building with cast-iron trim painted sky-blue. I rode the elevator up and identified myself to the receptionist and waited. After about five minutes, Andy Swales, Esq., emerged without a trace of nervousness. He appeared to have split off midstride from a previous conversation and, without pause, gripped me by my shoulder, key-carded a glass door, and led me back to his office. After a short walk down the hall and a joke with his assistant about how she better be good because he had a cop in here, he shut the door behind us. Swales had windows that looked over on the greened dome of the Broome County Courthouse to a sparkling stretch of the Susquehanna River. Several gentle landscape paintings hung on his walls, along with two diplomas.

I apologized for bothering him at work, but he dismissed it. "They'll wonder what you're here for, and I'll let them. So," he said. "So, Kevin O'Keeffe."

"And Penny Pellings."

"What can you tell me?" he said.

"You probably know more than I do."

He shook his head, all innocence.

"Three nights ago," I said. "Any memories, impressions?"

He paused a suitable interval for recollection. "There was something, yeah. It was around twelve-thirty, I remember because it woke me and I looked at the clock right then."

"Twelve-thirty, you sure?"

"Sure," Swales said. Then he hesitated. "More like twelve-forty? I thought it was the two of them. I have to say, I heard them fighting more often than I liked. Quarreling, I should say. It's quiet, so you hear everything. This was a bit more rough, but it stopped, and I went to sleep. Only now . . ."

"Rough."

"Usually it was just raised voices. This time, I don't know, doors slamming, something maybe broke. It's hard to sort out. I was just waking up."

"Was there anything else different about this time?" I asked.

Swales thought about it. "This time I only heard her voice."

"You're sure it was her?"

"Not one hundred percent, I mean, who else could it be?"

"Did she sound angry? Frightened?"

"I don't know," Swales said, his face turning pink. "I'm trying to remember now. It can be hard to tell what's going on."

"She might have been angry or frightened."

"Yes."

"People use your land to get to the lake. Could it have been one of them?"

"Oh, yeah," Swales said with a wave of his hand. "Maybe. People take the trail down, you know that. If it ever gets to be a problem, well, it hasn't been a problem. They should be able to use the lake. Kev keeps the deadbeats away."

I doubted that Kevin did any such thing. "Yeah what is the, ah, nature of your relationship with them two? It seems, I don't know, odd that they'd be living there. With you. What I mean is, your house gives a certain impression. Yet here's this trailer."

"I do like it quiet. Maybe I should have just asked them to leave, kept the trailer nice to rent for long weekends, or, I don't know. Got rid of it altogether. It's where I lived when the house was being built. Roughing it. Kevin was working on the house, on Milgraham's crew back then—I'm sure you know him—and we'd have a few beers some evenings. A great time, when that place was getting built. Never felt so free. When construction was done, O'Keeffe offered his services as a handyman, caretaker, what have you. I'm not always there, so it's good to have someone with an eye on the place. Then they ran into trouble. What am I going to do, make it worse? Even if I wanted to, I can't put them out now. I want a better life for them, for the baby."

"Did you know Penny too, before they moved in?"

His eyes shifted away from mine and back. "A bit. I'd met her. Good kid. Serious."

"Kevin comes home when, that night?"

Swales peered at the ceiling and thought. "I remember hearing him a couple hours after Penny, and thinking, Not again, you two. Yeah, definitely around then, I remember being angry because it was the second time that night."

"And what was O'Keeffe doing at that point?"

"Crashing around in the woods, yelling for her. At that point I got out of bed and went to talk to him."

"And what'd you say?"

"I asked him if he'd been hitting the bottle. And he said Penny was gone, and I told him to go to bed, she'd be back."

"And what'd he say to that?"

"That I didn't understand." The lawyer looked pained. "I'm not sure I took him seriously. In my mind, no question she'd just taken off. And anyway," Swales continued, "pretty soon after that, Kev got quiet." He looked out the window, then turned to me. "So she's . . . something happened, then."

"We don't know. Any regular visitors?"

"The people that go down to the lake, but I don't really know any of them. No, not that I could say for sure. I wish I'd called you that night."

"Any reason you didn't?" I asked.

Swales's face burned, and he covered it with his hands, dropped them, looked away. "Why should I feel guilty? But I do. He was over the top. He drank. They argued, so why shouldn't she just disappear? I was angry too, being dragged out of bed."

"And you live alone?"

"I'm divorced. Got stuck in a rut down in Scranton, saw this as an opportunity. Professionally. A new place, but I have a connection to it."

"Anyone with you that night?"

"No."

"I hate to pry—"

"Then don't. Sorry, I don't mean to be short. I was alone that night."

I let it be. "You have a key to the trailer, right, Andy?"

"Of course I do. I think I still do."

"And you haven't been in there since . . ."

"No. No reason to."

"Does Kevin have a key to your house?"

"Yes."

"Penny?"

"Yes. She cleans once a week. It's just me in there, but I don't like scrubbing toilets. Anyway, they need the money more than I do."

"You keep guns?"

"I have a .22 pistol and a .30-06 for bears. They're locked in a closet and only I have a key. Listen, how serious is this? Any developments, you . . ."

"I will, I will. By the way, you hear anything about an altercation down at the Royal Lodges in Fitzmorris two nights ago?"

"Sir, you overestimate me."

"But you are part owner."

"Yes," he said warily.

"You know this guy?" I handed him the photo of Heffernan.

"No. I don't know much about that property, other than it isn't doing what we thought."

"And 'we' is . . ."

"'We' is a private company buying and selling real estate. You understand that the business is the business, and I'm limited in my ability to discuss it."

"Well, then," I said, "can you maybe tell me how it is you find new tenants? How'd this guy come to live there?"

"If he lived there, it's news to me," the lawyer said. "Casey Noonan must have . . . I don't know. We had an ad out in the paper for a while."

"Okay," I said, "we'll leave that. About Penny, you may be seeing more of me than usual by the lake, at least for a few days."

"You can have the run of it," he said. "Not my house, but outside, the trailer and so forth. Until we get this figured out. Tell Kev I'm thinking of him."

I left the office, got in my truck, and headed south to Pennsylvania. Over the course of several years in Wild Thyme the DA and I had intervened with two couples where, in my view, the woman was in danger of winding up dead. In one case, the boyfriend spent some time in prison, the judge issued a protective order, and the guy never came back. In the other, Ross had arranged a suspended sentence, the husband was able to keep earning for the family, bound by the knowledge that any misstep could land him in jail. Kevin and Penny had not given me the same helpless, dangerous feeling as either of those couples. Even if they had, it'd have been tough to keep an eye on them all the time, set back into the woods as far as they were. I found it hard to believe that Kevin would be hiding something so ugly. No, I didn't see it that way, but I'd been wrong before.

In an actual police department, a missing persons investigation proceeds on a couple tiers. First the patrolmen will run down family, friends, coworkers, and so on. If any of them offend the nostrils, detectives will step in. Being a department of one, I did it all. On my way back to Wild Thyme, I took a detour into Airy Township. It took me forty minutes to get to the place, a gingerbread cottage halfway down a wooded valley road. I recognized the home because the entire yard had been devoted to flowers. By this time of spring, the daffodils had given way to a crowd of white tulips and purple phlox low to the ground. I have a soft spot for anyone who works so hard on a flower garden; you can't eat what you grow, you just make yourself and everyone else happy by it. My wife was that way when she lived.

I knocked at the front door and waited, but nobody came. From the rear of the house I heard the rhythmic shush of a blade sliding into earth. I followed it and found an older woman in a floppy hat, her back to me. With a short-handled shovel she was digging into a patch of earth covered in black plastic sheeting and bordered by loose bricks. Beside her were several tomato plants ready to go in.

I called out hello. She was startled, then mildly puzzled, but pulled off a glove, shook my hand, and introduced herself as Jillian Pellings. I guessed her age at around fifty. "Reese is in town, at the gym."

"Your husband?"

"Yes," she said, warily. "Swimming laps. What's wrong? He's okay?"

"I work out of Wild Thyme. I'm here because Kevin O'Keeffe—"

"Oh, boy. Yes, he called."

"He's concerned about Penny. She . . . he's under the impression she's missing, so I'm wondering . . ."

"I haven't seen her in, oh, at least a month."

"Heard from her? Are you close?"

"We used to be. I'm her stepmother, you see, I have been since she was eight. Listen, you better come over and sit down a minute if you have questions."

Jillian led me to a broad slab of stone pushing out from the hillside and shaded by several oak trees. Around us, hosta, geranium, and a haze of lamium gave the impression of flowers sneaking from the yard to a dance in the woods. We sat on rickety teak chairs and she removed her hat and fanned herself with it.

"I've always liked your garden. Passing by."

"Oh, thank you. We get strangers stopping. Sometimes they'll get out and give themselves a tour."

"So today's no different."

She smiled. "It's fine, Officer."

"Henry. So, I'm sorry. You and Penny used to be close, and . . ."

Jillian knitted her brow. "When first I met her and her sister, they were sweet kids with a tough row to hoe. An alcoholic mother. On pills, too. Abby was her name, Abby Chase Pellings? After the divorce she went back to Abby Chase? Does that name mean anything to you?" It did, but I could not recall why, so I nodded and she continued. "As a child you need to count on your parents to be there for the little things and the big. Maybe especially the little things. The other kids at school, around here, they noticed the difference, they had to. Penny adored her mother, my god, why wouldn't she, the woman was just like a teenager. Abby hung around for a while after Reese sobered up and divorced her. There was this time—you know how kids have birthday parties at school, the parents bring something in for the class?"

I nodded.

"Well, when Penny was turning ten, Abby insisted that she'd take care of it. And she was in bad shape then, but she made these cupcakes and the kids got sick. Like, to the emergency room. Nobody ever figured out what it was, but some kind of taint was suspected, some . . . taint? Penny was heartbroken. She couldn't go back to school for weeks, she was so ashamed. To think about it now . . . Abby was on her way out by then. After that, she was more or less gone for years. So anyway, long story short, I was there for Penny and her sister, big and small. And we were close." Jillian shook her head as if angry with herself about something. "Listen, Penny had some hard things in her life, and obviously it just got harder in high school. There got to be a point where I couldn't help. It wasn't just the staying out, it wasn't just the boys. There was just a, a break in her life, and after that, she didn't think someone like me could understand."

"What about her father, would he know where she is?"

"I wish Reese had done more for her. So does he. We asked to take Eolande, but we're older now, and on a budget. Mostly CPS felt that giving Eolande to us would be the same as giving her back to Penny and Kev, that we couldn't be tough with them. That's probably right. It's more painful with Eo raised by a stranger, more of a prod to clean up and get her back. And I believe Sarah loves her and can do for her until then."

"Sarah Cavanagh, the foster mom?"

"Right," she said. "Reese wouldn't know any more than I would. Penny tended bar in Binghamton for a while, a place off Main Street called Stingy Jack's? She got fired from there."

I wrote the name down. "Any particular friends you know of? Might she be with her mother now?"

Jillian looked sharply at me. "That's not funny." My bafflement must have showed, and she softened. "I thought you knew? Abby was killed eight years ago. Found, oh, she was found under a tarp by the train tracks downtown. In Binghamton. She'd been stabbed. Maybe it was drug-related, or maybe something to do with a—a man. She'd had some arrests by then. They never found the killer."

Open murders in the region are scarce enough that as a cop I should have known. But eight years ago I was in Wyoming living a different life, one that like Abby Chase's got cut short. Or I suppose I was more like Penny, with the flow of my life dammed and redirected by the death of another. Anyways, Jillian gave me names and addresses for Penny's sister and a cousin, Bobby, from the mother's side.

I left the house and its flower garden with a slightly better idea of where Penelope Pellings might have gone, and of who she was. I put in a call to the sheriff's department and got Deputy Jackson, and filled him in on anything I considered useful. He knew of Abby Chase's murder but had not made the connection between her and Penelope Pellings, which made me feel slightly less like a chump.

I drove ahead of a cloud of dust on Owens Road to see Sarah Cavanagh. Her family owned a small patch of land next to a onetime farm that had been leased and drilled for gas. In the front yard of a yellow ranch house, two boys, maybe eight and ten, were walloping each other with homemade toy axes wrapped in duct tape. Sarah, a steely woman nearly six feet tall with a mistrustful way, emerged from the house carrying baby Eo. "Boys," she called over her shoulder. She beckoned me inside.

Eolande O'Keeffe had grown a haze of blond hair since last I'd seen her. She was still not as pudgy as I'd like, but I knew very little of babies. As Sarah Cavanagh and I talked, she held Eo in her lap, and the girl struggled to free herself. Eventually Sarah let her slip to the floor, where she dragged herself under the kitchen table like a commando.

"She's a few steps behind," said Sarah. "My boys were walking at one, before one. She's had a catheter procedure for her stenosis, they're keeping an eye on that. But she's a happy kiddo, aren't you, girl?"

"How often do you see the mother?"

"A couple hours every other weekend. They don't often miss it, even with the CPS woman hovering. Kev will bring Eo, like, a bouquet of wildflowers. An interesting stick. A CD he likes. Donuts. Have you educated yourself about your daughter's health conditions? Did you stick with the courses? No, you did not."

"And Penny?"

"She's an odd one. Standoffish, even with her own kid. I don't doubt she loves her, but. The problem ain't getting them to show up." Sarah ducked under the table to retrieve the child. "I haven't wanted to say, because at some point it's like a dog pile on them, but she's been in my house."

"Pardon?"

"This was back maybe two months? We had a thaw. I woke up because I heard something, Eolande sounded different, I mean, she's fussy, a bad sleeper, so it's unusual for her to be awake but not yelling her little head off, right, kid? I went to her room, she wasn't in her crib, and I freaked. I ran down-stairs, and there she was in the middle of the floor, like, what? Mud everywhere. As soon as it got light, I put Eolande in the car seat and charged over to their place, ready to raise hell. Kev wouldn't let me see Penny, she's sick, he said, he doesn't know what she did but she won't do it again. He begs, says it'll be the end. I say maybe it should be. But I'm a softy."

"You think they could ever care for her?"

"Not a chance," she said. "This baby girl's stuck with me, right, hon?"

I called Eolande's caseworker in Fitzmorris, Cassidy Rey-nolds, and within the bounds of confidentiality she had much the same assessment of Penny and Kevin—sweet, helpless, a little deluded about what Eolande would need. She'd had no sense of a relapsing addiction or violence in the home. What did anyone know?

I HAD AN INVITATION to join Ed and Liz and their two kids for supper. The Brennans' gentleman farm had a view south to the next ridge, where the sun bounced off a barn's metal roof, the bright spot like a leaping fish stuck in time. Liz liked to watch birds, and I found her on the porch behind a pair of bin-oculars, watching a few white-breasted nuthatches hop around on their ancient Harrison apple tree. The kids raced around the yard. I slipped inside, found a beer, and joined Liz. Flitting about high in their Douglas fir was a cedar waxwing, which she pointed out to me. I love a cedar waxwing. So perfect and aloof, on its own business.

"So," she said, giving me a glance from over top of her binoculars, "Ed says you hauled Kevin away from the site."

"I can't talk about it."

"Oh, come on." She set the binoculars down. "I'm sick not knowing."

"I don't know either. I don't think he hurt Penny. But Lizzy," I said, "he may not be who we thought he was."

"Clearly." She raised the binoculars, but the bird had flown. "We don't owe this guy. He works for Ed, that's it. A lot of people do. And he shows up on our doorstep, of all places."

"You're too nice, I always say so."

"I don't see why he has to hire these drunks and . . . ruins. Worse, even, now."

This was unusual talk from Liz, who, in the course of tending to the town's medical needs, had nursed more than one ruin back to health, including me. She treated everyone just the same and never complained in my hearing. But I could see what it would mean to her if dopey, peaceable Kevin O'Keeffe did turn out to be a killer: if him, then anyone.

"Yeah," I said, "I don't know." I picked up the binoculars and searched again for the waxwing. "One time back in Big Piney I got a call about a guy, an old cowboy turned electrician. His wife was looking for him. She told me he'd always drank, drank whiskey by the handle, you could tell that looking at him. But he'd hurt his shoulder and discovered pills. So she finally got tired of that, and, uh, she kicked him out, I think expecting that he'd clean up and beg to come back. It'd happened that way before. But this time was different. He'd been gone three weeks before his wife called me.

"Then I got word from a landowner at the edge of town who found a tent pitched in a clearing, tire tracks leading up there, an old truck, a new fire ring. Wasn't any of their neighbors. So up I go, and it's the guy's truck, the missing guy. I shake the tent, and there's a funny smell. I call out. No answer."

"Oh, God."

"So I unzip the tent—"

At that moment, Ed's truck came jouncing up the driveway. She hurried down to the yard, and I never got to finish the story.

Ed parked, opened the driver's-side door, and stepped barefoot onto the driveway. He reached into the pickup's bed and swung a case of beer onto his shoulder. He also carried a bottle in a brown paper bag. On his face was a smile of unusual transcendence and fixity. I knew he had been gunning for a contract; a local grocery store owner wanted a luxury post-and-beam outbuilding. Ed had been competing against Milgraham and at least one other crew for the contract. He left the booze on the porch steps and, without going inside, padded down to the pond, stripped to boxers, and jumped in. The kids joined him.

Treading water, Ed rubbed some of the dust off his face and said, "I am anew."

"Did you get it?" said Liz.

"Yup." Ed rolled onto his back and spouted like a whale. "Two million." He laughed. "Two million, wife! Henry, this guy, you may know him, Willard Meagher? He owns super-markets. He wants me to make him a studio up on a hilltop, to paint in; he's an abstract painter. The only thing is, he wants it done in a year."

Liz and I exchanged a glance. Ed was renowned as the best timber framer in the area, and thus one of the best in the mid-Atlantic. But he was also known to agonize and draw a thing out. Everything proper, why hurry.

After a celebratory splash of scotch and a game of croquet, we grilled pork chops from Liz's uncle's farm in northern Broome County, which we had with couscous and Swiss chard from their garden, sautéed in oil and garlic. Kevin O'Keeffe didn't come up again. Nobody wanted to frighten the kids, and Ed was eager to discuss the new project. I could almost see him spending the money in his head. After dinner, while Ed got the kids scrubbed and ready for bed, I leaned on the counter as Liz sunk her arms elbow-deep into a sinkful of dishes. I dried some of them.

When the kids were asleep, we gathered outside around the fire pit and tuned our instruments: Ed on guitar, Liz on clawhammer banjo, and me on the fiddle. It had started as a session among friends, nothing more ambitious. But with scant live music in the area other than blues-rock played by men in hats, we had tapped into a demand. Our late-night ramblings at parties had drawn some attention, as well as some gig offers. We didn't do it for the money, but the prospect of playing in public for strangers was good encouragement to learn more tunes and get better. We'd struggled over a name. I suggested the Fateful Mornings. In disaster songs, it is always on a fateful morning that you go down into the mine or set out to murder James A. Garfield. But Liz liked the Country Slippers, after the tall rubber boots most of us wore on muddy days, and that's what stuck.

We worked through some old tunes, "Soldier's Joy," "Turkey Buzzard," at Ed's insistence Iron Maiden's "Run to the Hills." Liz switched to gourd banjo for "Old Groundhog," such a strange, swooping sound, like riding a bicycle over a jump.

We played our way through the last of the beers and I packed up the fiddle. Ed's eyelids were sagging and flipping open again as the fire popped. I was too drunk to drive home but I was going to anyway. I walked across the silver lawn, my head back, stargazing. Altair, Vega, Deneb. Ed lumbered up behind me.

"Shit, man, I'm sorry. I almost forgot this." He handed me a scrap of paper.

I strained to read it:

> John Blaine. Owner, Stingy Jack's.
> Bobby Chase, cousin, Endicott
> "Dizzy." Works at Excelsior?

"From you-know-who," Ed said. "Says he's through talking to cops, can't be seen doing it. But he handed me this today, said to give it to you only."

FIRST THING next morning I put in a call to Dally's office, asking them to check New York State criminal records for the three names Kevin gave me, which would involve the sheriff calling a friend in the Binghamton PD. Then I set about patrolling my little patch of earth. Nobody seemed to want to do wrong in Wild Thyme, so I took to the road.

Penelope Pellings's sister Rianne lived in Vestal Center, New York, a tiny town on the banks of Choconut Creek, north of Wild Thyme and just south of the city of Endicott. With nothing better to do until nightfall, I decided to roll by and look for signs of Penny there, maybe ask some questions if it looked like Rianne was home. After some thought I stopped by the station, left my gun belt in the locker, and swapped the patrol truck for my personal pickup.

In Vestal Center, the homes were modest in size and brightly colored, though some were peeling paint or shedding aluminum siding. At the end of Grand Street stood an eggplant-colored two-family house, and the bottom half was where Rianne lived. A car was in the driveway, so I stopped. The young woman who came to the door paled when she saw my uniform shirt. Her hair was dyed blond, and she had none of the frailty of her sister, but her teeth were the same, the way they pushed her lips out of the way. We introduced ourselves.

"I'm here as a favor to Kevin O'Keeffe."

"Super. If you're looking for her, she's not here."

"And you don't . . ."

"No."

"Well . . . can you tell me about her and Kevin? I mean, did they fight, or—"

"What would those two have to fight about? Kevin's whole life is drinking, and Penny . . ." Rianne looked away into some memory. "She was into her own thing. I don't love Kev, but I don't think . . . If she shows up, of course I'll say something. But I doubt she'll want to see me. I can't give her what she wants."

"I'm sorry, what do you mean?"

She took breath to say more, but all that came out was, "We're in different worlds now."

"And what is Penny's world?" I asked, knowing well. "Does she have any friends?"

"I can't explain. We're in different worlds, sorry."

"So, so you knew she was using again?"

She said nothing.

"How about friends? Does she have any old friends? It could be someone from grade school, even. Anyone she might turn to, or make use of?"

Immediately, Rianne said, "Teri Filippi. She's called Teri before. They were friends in middle school. We all were." At this memory, Rianne finally crumbled and broke down crying. "I'm sorry," she said. "She lives in Port Dickinson, she works as some kind of nurse at the walk-in on the Vestal Parkway." She looked through her phone and gave me a number and an address.

"Okay, well, thank you," I said. "So this is your house, you own it? Who lives upstairs, you mind?"

"It's my uncle's. You may know him, he was a firefighter in Endicott, Ron Chase? Anyway, he's retired now. He's lived in Endicott for years. Rents this place to me."

"And you're here alone?"

"Supposed to be." She reddened. "My boyfriend stays here sometimes, but my uncle won't let him move in until we're married."

"Ah. Well, that's all, I guess."

I turned to go and she called after me. "Henry? When she turns up, let me know."

Not coincidentally, my next stop was Ron Chase's Endicott home. I hoped also to catch Ron's son Bobby, who still lived there with his father. I crossed the Susquehanna River and into a city whose downtown had emptied out. I saw a lot of it on my way to Ron's: the vacant shoe factory that had once buoyed the region, the abandoned hospital with its pedestrian bridge suspended over North Street and leading from one empty monolith to another. It wasn't mere economics that had blighted Endicott, but a toxic spill known locally as the Plume, a filthy watershed of solvents IBM poured into the earth for decades before they packed up and left.

The city still has nice areas, including north of Watson Boulevard, where Ron Chase and his son Bobby lived. I parked one house shy of the address on Oak Hill Avenue and walked up to a plain white single-family home with a big yard. Out this far, on a nice spring day, there was nothing particularly poisonous about the city, just a bustle of birds, a steady murmur of car traffic, and Ron Chase mowing his yard. A large middle-aged man in a sagging sleeveless T-shirt, Chase perched on an antique rider mower, making tighter and tighter circles over his lawn on which, far as I could tell, no weeds of any kind grew. He saw me and raised a finger, and I stood waiting while he finished the area he was on, then bumbled over to the shade of a maple and cut the engine, which expired with a shudder and cough. He dismounted, removed his ear protection, and lurched toward me, as much falling as walking on ruined legs. His niece had said he was retired. I figured him for a disability pension.

"I know who you are," he said affably, and shook my hand. We compared acquaintances. He knew a lot of old-timers on the Wild Thyme Volunteer Fire Company. There had been three fires in the township big enough that his company had responded, all of them while I was out West, at least two of them possible arson. "So anyway," he said. "Rianne called. Penny's got everyone out chasing their ass again."

"Afraid so. She hasn't been around, has she?"

"No."

"Would she come here?"

"No. We get along okay. As long as we're not asking any-thing of each other. Once we start asking, we get disappointed, and nobody likes that, so."

I heard shades of Rianne's answer in his. "How about Bobby, he here?"

"No."

"They friendly?"

"Yeah, been friendly since kids. Bobby likes the place off Main, Stingy Jack's. He got her a bartender job there even, they like pretty girls, I guess, but she got canned. Didn't stop her haunting the place. I think they might see each other there every now and then, or out in town. Not here at home, she don't come here much."

"Not even if she was in trouble?"

"Well, Penny, I'd do anything for her if it came down to it, she knows that. I think so. But it wouldn't be on her terms, it'd be on mine. And she's not one to listen to me."

"Yeah," I said. "Hey, if you see her."

"I'll send her home to the puke she lives with, or try. Or if you want to leave a number?"

"Yeah, you mind giving my card to Bobby?"

Ron lifted his glasses and peered at my homemade business card, then back at me. "I will. Listen, we've been through it before. I'd be worried, but I washed my hands and started praying a long time ago."

I drove off. Personally, I don't know how I escaped bad habits, and by that I mean serious habits. Something to do with Father and Ma, who only ever drank the occasional light beer, in company. And even then, I didn't know whether they didn't drink because they didn't drink, they couldn't afford it, or they didn't have the gene, the pull. Probably some of each. It is tempting to credit yourself as an iron man when you look around at other people and their troubles. I'd only say there's more trouble in us than we know.

I waited in my truck outside a trim little house with window-box flowers on Rochelle Road. The town of Port Dickinson lay along the Chenango River north of Binghamton, a tidy place with sweet homes and nothing particular to distinguish it. Teri Filippi had not answered my knock, so I called the walk-in on the parkway to ask after her; she told me wait where I was, as she'd be done with her shift and home in about forty-five minutes. After we'd hung up I circled the house to find a six-foot fence surrounding the backyard. I almost hoped Penny Pellings would slip out the door and try to shake me loose. But she didn't, and before long a sky-blue Volkswagen Beetle pulled into the drive, and an overweight woman with buzzed hair got out and waved me over.

Filippi's house was clean inside, the living room aglow with a large aquarium full of tropical fish, and a glass tank containing an iguana named the Overlord. The walls were lined with particle-board bookshelves full of comic books and fat paper-back novels. I saw no sign of a life partner, and Teri volunteered that she lived there alone. She offered me water or a soda, but I declined.

"I haven't seen her," said Teri. "Not since the winter. I don't think she'd show up here. Rianne probably told you we were friends. But it'd been years since my phone rang. The whole downtown thing kind of soured us . . . do you know what I'm talking about? Did Rianne tell you? No, okay. I said I wouldn't, but it seems like I should tell you now. So back in January Penny called me, she said her car's busted, Kevin won't drive her any-where, and can't or won't pay to have her car fixed. She's out of a job. She needs company, she wants to get out. I'm thinking we'll go to the bookstore, we used to do that. I'll do something nice for my friend, she's had hard times, we'll get a coffee, sit on the floor of the sci-fi section and read like we used to.

"I drove all the way out to Wild Thyme, I knocked on the door. She yells from inside that she's stuck, the front door key is behind the steps, just open the door and come in. So I did. And nobody's to be seen. And then I hear a tap-tap, and, 'Teri?' She was locked in the bedroom. I let her out. The smell was, oof, but I faked a laugh and I asked her, how do you get locked in your own bedroom? Before we could leave, she was looking through drawers, through cabinets, rooting. I ask what's it about, she turns, like she's seeing me for the first time, and smiles, and it's . . . she's herself, I think. She's beautiful. I think so. We got in the car and we left.

"I ask her how she's been, she says she's had better days, but she's on the mend. She's been reading a lot, writing a little bit. We talked about books, about who we used to be. About my life, mostly, I did most of the talking. We got to the Barnes & Noble, got settled, she's got a book she likes, some graphic novel. She wanted to buy it, but oh, no, she left her wallet in the car. Can she borrow twenty so she can buy the book, take my keys and go out to the car to get her wallet and pay me back? I say I'll buy it, my treat. No, no, she says. I'm thinking, I wasn't born yesterday. But it turns out I was, because I say just leave the damn book, take the keys, and come back with your wallet."

"Where'd they find your car?"

"Somewhere in Johnson City, two days later. Penny, they found in a shelter downtown, she'd been out and near-freezing. Kev asked me to forgive her, to let them deal with it, try to get Penny straight again, give them a chance to get Eo back. What could I say?"

"To be clear," I said, "it sounds like she was a prisoner in her home?"

Teri looked uncomfortable. "Yeah. Of sorts. Of her own making, and his. I guess she was trying to kick, and she'd want that, want to be locked up, and then . . . I let Kevin know what I thought of it. But he wouldn't hurt anybody, not on purpose. To hear him tell it, he felt he had no options left. I do believe that."

"Okay. If she turns up," I said.

"I wish I could say I meant enough to her. I don't think I do. If I see her, I'll do what's best."

BACK AT MY OFFICE I looked up the general number for Binghamton PD, called it, and was put through to the desk officer.

"This is Henry Farrell," said I, "Wild Thyme Police."

After a pause the cop answered, "Oh?"

"Yeah, we've got the missing person, Penelope Pellings? Some possible connection to Heffernan, ah, Charles Michael Heffernan?"

"Listen, it's a big department."

"Heffernan was pulled out of the river, shot. Tioga County has him. He worked there in town, lived in Johnson City, apparently. Just a courtesy," I said. "Anyways, you put out an alert on Pellings for us yesterday, she still isn't back, and I'm headed in town to talk to some people."

"Okay," said the officer, as if to ask why he was on the phone with me.

"How about 'Dizzy'? You got anybody named—"

"Like I said, buddy. I have no idea. I'd love to help."

"Okay."

"Have fun. Don't get into trouble." He added, "You want somebody to go out with you?"

"Nah, it'll be easier on my own."

I called the Holebrook Sheriff's Department and got Deputy Jackson. After I begged him long enough that he knew I wouldn't let it go, he agreed to call a friend across the border. I dithered around the office until my fax machine awoke with a start and wheezed out a photograph and a Clinton Street address for a Christian Kostis, aka "Dizzy," who was nearing the end of a parole term for third-degree assault.

Evening saw me crossing the river once again, this time in my old truck. I wore a plaid shirt and jeans. Though it was hot, I also wore a light jacket to cover the .40 in my shoulder holster. I turned left under a crumbling railroad bridge and onto Clinton Street. Many of our fathers, not the backwoods hermit who raised me, but many of them, used to do what was then called the Clinton Street Run. Back some forty years the whole length was bars, neon lights calling one to the next until you were stupefied, broke, and far from your car. Nowadays Clinton Street is a sort of concrete fairyland where parents tell their children not to end up. Most of the bars have closed, along with the shops that fed the neighborhood during the day, leaving a string of street with a few bars hanging on like granny knots. And trapped between Clinton Street and the wild hills is the First Ward, a residential cluster fighting abandonment and blight.

At Wilson Street I pulled into an empty lot bordered by Clinton to the north, and trees along the train tracks south of me at the other end. Sunbeams slanted east across the city street, catching the face of a three-story building, Kostis's address. The air was full. On the other side of Wilson, two black kids, a boy and a girl, tore along the sidewalk on scooters, never getting too far from a laundry-mat doorway where a woman sat talking on a cell phone. I took her to be the mother. A poplar branch reaching over the fence from the lot next door did nothing to disguise me, and I took out my own cell phone and pretended to be on it while I watched the apartment building. I didn't look at her so she wouldn't look at me. Eventually the kids crossed Clinton to where I was, and did some off-roading where the pavement gave way to dirt, piled in hard-packed mounds here and there.

The spidered glass door to the apartment building opened and a dark-haired, ax-faced white man with beard trotted down the steps. His hair was gathered in a bun on top of his head. He had a potbelly and carried a duffel bag. I let him bounce a good way down the street before I put the truck in gear and crawled along after him. He walked six blocks and stepped into a bar-room marked by a sign that read EXCELSIOR and had to have been from the sixties at least.

I pulled alongside the bar and went inside. Chicken wings and batter fried in dirty oil, unwashed dishrags. Odors that had worked deep into the fixtures and walls, a fuzz of grease dimming the shine on a row of glasses hanging above the bar. The sign identified it as a hotel bar, but I doubted the rooms above us were occupied, and just as well, because if they had been, the building might well have crumbled under the weight, taking with it the three smoke-cured witches bent over the bar and four slender black men in oversized clothes playing doubles pool. I took a seat at the bar and ordered a cheap beer and looked around. No Kostis. But eventually the bartender, a stern, overweight woman, made her way back to the kitchen door and propped it open while she spoke with someone inside. It took a moment, but eventually I saw Kostis's head lean into view, his hair under a white painter's cap, an apron strap over his shoulder. Knowing now I had a shift to wait through, I stood and left. There was more to see.

The front door to the building on the corner of Clinton and Wilson was unlocked. I stepped past a small pile of coupon circulars in plastic bags in the foyer and onto a colorless car-pet worn down to an acrylic hide. The place smelled unclean. I climbed two flights of stairs and stood before Kostis's apart-ment door and knocked. There was no answer, so I waited, knocked again. With each knock, the door shuddered in its frame. I took out my wallet and carded the lock in less than five seconds. The narrow apartment was set up not unlike a trailer, no room that you could get to except by moving through another room. A small television hooked up to cable in the front, windows looking out over the street. I heard a bus drive past. A mattress in the windowless bedroom and a layout of men's clothes, neatly folded on the floor. Styrofoam take-out boxes in the kitchen, and nothing of a woman's anywhere, not in the bathroom, nowhere. There was no place to hide anything and nothing hidden. I closed the apartment door behind me, made sure it was locked, and moved on.

Stingy Jack's was the lone business on a residential block in the neighborhood between Binghamton and Johnson City. On either side, rubble-strewn spaces flanked the bar, serving both as parking lots and garbage dumps. I parked my truck with the other cars at the dark end of an empty lot and walked to the door. On my left, apartment buildings talked to the night. At an intersection just two blocks away, Main Street traffic plodded along, while overhead, cars rushed nonstop on a high overpass that connected with highways and routes in every direction out of town. It gave me a lonely feeling.

I don't really enjoy a tavern atmosphere. My barroom experience was limited to the two quiet saloons Polly and I adopted back in our Big Piney, Wyoming, days. And we saw the occasional country show at the Corral. I had tried not to drink too much after she died because it led me down a path. The occasional IPA did seem to have a healthy effect on me, though. I wasn't above it.

The bar had Flower Power on tap and I get that wherever I find it. The bartender who took my money was pretty, and couldn't have been twenty-five years old. I noted her cat eyes and clean rippling arms, and tried not to ogle. The owner had

a type he liked behind the bar, I guessed, for the other bartender was also attractive and birdish in her black tank top.
Both of them called Penny Pellings to mind. I ambled over
to the jukebox. Flipping through, I used the reflection in the
machine's glass to scan the room. Aside from the few ragged
old-timers slouching at the bar, the crowd was a mix of young
people and burly men with tan lines around their eyes. It had
been some time since I had been in one room with so many
attractive young women. There was also more than the average
amount of dyed hair, ear tunnels, and secondhand clothing. I
was beginning to like the place in spite of myself. I mean, the
kids in there, trying so hard. They'd only grow up to be the
next Pats and Kellies, hanging on to a long-gone town, telling
themselves it was good enough for their kids. Why not pretend
something else until then?

I found a place to stand near the front door, and finished my
first pint too quickly with an elbow on a counter, seeming to
gaze out the front window but actually scanning the reflection.

I couldn't just stand there with nothing to drink, and soon
I was face-to-face with the bartender again, with a sweaty ten-
spot clutched in my paw, when the front door opened and
something in the atmosphere tilted. I looked over and saw two
young black men taking empty stools at the bar, oblivious to
any chill they had brought in with them. One had long braids
and weak chin; neither looked happy. The bartenders ignored
them until they couldn't, then took their drink orders.

The music on the jukebox changed abruptly, mid-song, from
upbeat pop to a shrill, thudding traditional Irish tune played
in a hard rock style. A large, sunburned man wearing a too-

large Hawaiian shirt and several copper bracelets on his wrists had moved behind the bar, and took up a post facing the two black men, his chin resting innocently on one hand, a remote in front of him. Yet another man, white, with a long ponytail and hair thinning on top, appeared at the bar, placed a drink in front of himself, didn't drink it, and took occasional glances at the black men sitting on the opposite end. And at me. As soon as the song was finished it began all over again, and the man behind the bar peered at the remote, picked it up, knocked at it once or twice, and said;

"Shit. The jukebox is broken."

It only took one more repeat before the men left without a word.

The man turned his gaze to me and said, "Them people can't stand Irish music."

"Guess not."

"John Blaine," the man said, extending a hand across the bar. I took it. "I run this place." He had a balding buzz cut, a careful goatee, and no eyebrows.

"Good for you," I said. "Been here long?"

He snorted. "Where you from?"

"Pennsylvania."

"Oh, yeah? I just got a place down Airy Township. So you know, we've been here since back in the day. Maybe your old man came in on the sly?" I shrugged, and he gave me a knowing smile. "Sure he didn't." Blaine managed a curious expression even without eyebrows. Curious and not altogether friendly. "Closed years until we reopened last spring," he said. "Used to be dancers in the back room. Old-school ladies. We re-created all the original signage, the interior . . . some of this Naugahyde we salvaged from a place out in Youngstown. Never got your name?"

"Henry. Farrell."

Blaine winked. "Now you know," he said. "Tell your friends." He turned to leave.

"Hey, man, I'm looking for someone."

"Aren't we all?"

"Penny Pellings."

Blaine returned to his former perch, but said nothing.

"From down in Holebrook," I continued. "It's been a while. Thought I'd stop in and see her."

"I had her behind the bar," he said, and shook his head. "She was a better customer than an employee. She don't work here no more."

"But you haven't seen her."

"Let me tell you a joke," he said, smiling but cold. "A cop stops a guy on the street, says, 'You look a little drunk, pal, you okay?' The guy says, 'Man, am I glad you came along, Officer. Somebody has stolen my car.' So the cop says, 'Where was it last you saw it?' Drunk holds up his hand, there's a set of keys. 'Right at the end of this key.' The cop, he looks at the drunk, looks at the key, says, 'Go down to the station house and report it.' The drunk starts heading for the station, and the cop says, 'Hey, buddy, before you go anywhere, zip up that fly.' The drunk looks down at his pants and says, 'Oh, man, they got my girl too.'

"You know what Kevin O'Keeffe is. He's a drunk, he don't see things clearly. And no, I haven't seen Penny." Blaine spun a drink token in front of me and left the bar, disappearing behind what I took to be an office door. The man with the ponytail at the other end of the bar looked at me a second too long, then returned to his glass.

I retreated into the night and slipped through a group of smokers hee-hawing by the steps. A man pissed like a garden hose behind a car. As I pulled out onto Main Street, I stopped for a red light and watched a group of teenagers pace the street, aimless and ready for war. The light changed.

After a certain hour, the desperate gather on Clinton to buy and sell sex, drugs, or both, but it didn't seem to be time for that yet. I parked a block away from the Excelsior and went back inside. A couple dozen people had descended on the bar since I'd last been there, bringing nightlife and noise with them. Only one lonely Rotarian-looking man stood out to me, seated at the trivia machine, the whirring colors of its screen dancing in his eyeglasses and across his bald pate. The jukebox insisted on seventies crap-rock and the lights were low.

I stepped to the bar and ordered a beer. When half of it was gone, I leaned in and quietly asked the bartender if Dizzy was in the kitchen.

"Was," she replied. "You just missed him, babydoll. What you want him for?"

"Nothing, just to say hello."

"You another old friend?"

"Yes."

"Well, at least you can afford a drink. Look around you, baby. You think we're hiring here? Ain't they got somebody to help you get back to the world where you're coming from?"

She meant prison. I nodded slowly, recognizing her mistake and playing off it. "It's all shoveling shit," I said.

The bartender laughed. "It's all we got here, too. What do you think Mr. Dizzy does for us? Sorry I can't help, hon."

"Well, you know where I can find him now? I came all this way."

"I don't know what he does. But he ain't gone too long yet."

I excused myself and stepped out into the night. As I walked, I passed the site of a demolished department store. Waist-high weeds had tufted up amid the rubble, and fireflies drifted from grassy island to island, their blinking a kind of grace. Several cars slowed as they passed, ordinary sedans with ordinary guys behind their wheels and alone, looking to tamp down some need. Slowing down and rolling away again.

I arrived at the door of the Georgian and entered. The barstools were mosaics of pleather and beige packing tape. A young man with spiked hair and a gold cross around his neck sloshed drinks in front of about a dozen patrons. I took a stool and ordered and had a look around. A line of low booths reached to the back wall and a red exit sign, pitchers and empty glasses and pizza trays littering them. A group of people were playing cricket on the dartboard. A stereo blasted and the bar noise was high.

It was not long before a thickly built woman with frosted hair slumped into me and excused herself. She asked my name and I gave it, and from then on I was on a tightrope between outright rudeness and trying not to encourage her. Somewhere in the middle of a long, spiraling story about her sister-in-law, I became aware of a mountainous cook in a paper hat and a stained white apron standing in the kitchen doorway, talking to a man in street clothes. But for the light spilling out of the kitchen they were in the shadowy back of the bar. The smaller man had black hair gathered into a topknot and a pencil-line beard.

"Excuse me," I told my lady companion, half standing, "I see somebody I know."

She looked confused, then hurt, then angry. She left, waving a hand behind her head in dismissal. From my vantage point at the bar, I watched as the cook disappeared into the kitchen and the other man made his rounds. He seemed to know a fair amount of people in that place, and passed right by me without a look. To keep up appearances I had a beer. The woman who'd been talking to me sent over a shot, a gesture of something, I don't know, but I couldn't leave it there. Another beer. My reality was beginning to turn fluid, my memory sinking into dark currents and surfacing again, my speech loose. Was that the same Rotarian-looking grandpa from the Excelsior now sitting across from me at the Georgian's bar? Did it matter? The woman with frosted hair was back. Before long, I stood outside in a grassless holding pen of a backyard, hemmed in by a sagging wooden fence, not quite remembering how I'd gotten there. The man in the topknot was already out there, making quick work of a cigarette.

"Greetings," he said.

"Hey, there," said I, barely nodding.

I took a closer look at Dizzy. While his samurai hairdo gave him a youthful quality, his face was lined and his voice sounded old. Peeking out from behind his Cuban shirt open at the neck was part of a tattoo of Dorothy Gale, just her head facing down as if draped on his shoulder, the pigtails, a scrap of blue gingham, her eyes closed, expression ecstatic. Two ruby-slippered feet splayed wide onto his arm below the hem of his short sleeve. I didn't want to know.

"Never seen you before. Of all the shitholes in this town you could end up in . . ."

I shrugged. "This a shithole?"

He ground out his cigarette and produced what I first thought was another, until he gripped it up between his middle and ring knuckles, sealing it to his mouth, and lit it. A one-hitter. He passed it to me. I dutifully hit it and blew a cloud of smoke, along with my good sense, into the night air. "Good," I said.

"I know," he said. "Call me Dizzy. Dizzy."

"Ah," said I. "Henry."

Dizzy looked at my scuffed work boots and worn clothes and smiled. "Country."

"I got a quarry going up to Sidney?" I said. "I cut stone, I split stone, I haul it, sell it. Make good money, all on my own, no bosses for the first time in, oh, sixteen fuckin years. I earn it all, I keep it all. Come to town, I want to spend it. My wife left, so I don't know."

"Yeah, yeah. My girl, she's got my boys? They lived over to Johnson City? The other week I get up to see them, landlord says she moved out of there. Moved to fuckin Florida, not a word to me. You believe that?"

I shook my head.

"I found a new girl. Get high, get strange. Life ain't any more simpler than that."

"I hear you."

"Oh, yeah, you do?" Dizzy moved closer.

He reached into a pocket and pulled out a cell phone. After

pressing some keys, he held the thing in front of him, and we were looking at a photograph of a topless girl on her knees and elbows, shot from the back, a thong her only defense against the world. Pimples dotted her rear. A mess of dark hair covered her face where it would've been exposed to the lens. "Here she is. She'll fuck the shit out of you," Dizzy said. "You will literally shit yourself."

The girl looked young enough that I sobered up by half. It could have been Penny, but I guessed it wasn't. Penny was a young woman, and small, but the girl in the photo looked like a teenage kid. Dizzy noticed a change in me, but read it wrong. "Yeah, her face ain't too good but the pussy is nice. Guaranteed."

"Eh," I said. "Nice. She got a name?"

Dizzy put away his phone. "Come find out."

A wicked thrill moved through me, much against my heart. I'm not the kind of man, but this is how it would be. To become something less than a man. My synapses were firing like black cat fireworks, slow and obvious. "How much?" I heard myself say.

There was silence. "Hey, now," said Dizzy.

He played it angry, but he understood that he was in the process of making a sale. And he'd turn it to his advantage, make me weak to raise the girl's price. I guessed rightly that there'd be no more discussion of her unless he brought it up again. We shot the shit for a minute longer and he went back inside.

I waited a moment and pulled the Georgian's door open, only to come face-to-face with the Rotarian. He didn't startle. By this time I figured him for a cruiser. I slipped past him and re-settled myself at the bar. Dizzy circled, avoiding me. I waited. At long last, I stood to leave. As soon as I was out in the city night, the door opened once again and there stood Dizzy.

"Country," he said. "Want to come over?"

"Where you parked?" I asked.

"Ain't far. We'll walk."

Dizzy led me in the direction of the empty lot I'd passed earlier, stopped at a tear in a chain-link fence, then ducked inside. "Shortcut," he said.

I followed, slipping down an asphalt bank and into the urban wild. We picked our way through broken brick and tall grass. Looking down, I saw empties, a child's sock, black trash bags tied shut, and several shits large enough to be from a person.

I looked about me and saw a man-sized shadow back near Clinton Street. Dizzy forged ahead. I took a few steps and looked again. The shadow moved with us. At the far end of the lot, another slope up and a chain-link fence marked where a railroad cut through the First Ward, hidden by a line of trees. Following Mr. Dizzy, I scaled the chain-link fence and dropped into the brush. We pushed through the scrub and emerged into a kind of tunnel formed by trees, with some tall grass forcing its way through the stone on the railbed. The city disappeared. Looking up and down the track, I saw the dark was shattered by thousands of fireflies, their light pulsing off the tangle of branches surrounding us. I eased the .40's safety off.

Dizzy cut west on a packed-mud path. We swept aside branches until we came to a dark residential block sandwiched between the train tracks and a supermarket parking lot far below. Two of the houses were boarded up, leaving one abutting the railroad tracks, fenced in. It was the dull green of a lily pad, and looked like you could tear the porch away with your bare hands. Two small Japanese cars were parked in a narrow driveway alongside it. We walked the other way, through a narrow side lawn and into the back, where a garage stood, one lone light burning in a second-floor apartment's window. From the garage's open door, heavy metal screamed into the night and a lank, shirtless man sat in contemplation of what looked like a Triumph Roadster from the 1980s. He raised a hand at us. We clumped up the steps of the main house and into a faded floral kitchen.

"Nice place," I said.

"This? Ain't mine. No, nothing going on in my place but picking up the mail." Dizzy opened the refrigerator, leaned in, and, finding nothing he wanted, closed it again. "I'd give you a beer if we had any, but looks like Max cleaned us out. He don't stop once he starts."

"Max?"

"He owns this place. His ma, actually. Let me go see if his ass is up right now." Dizzy disappeared into a dim living room where a television bounced off the walls.

Dizzy, Max, and whoever was in the garage. To get in and out with the girl, safe, it might be three-on-one. I made a quick set of cascading decisions. I'd spirit her away as quietly as I could, then call Binghamton PD. If that didn't pan out, I'd simply pull my badge and show my weapon and walk out into the night. If they didn't want to let us do that, I'd put myself in front of the girl.

When Dizzy returned to the kitchen, I looked at him for weapons, but his shirt was too loose. He did have in his hand a small, ornate box. He tapped it on the tabletop as we sat, saying nothing. Max, whoever he was, stayed in the other room.

"So," he said. "So quarrying pays."

"Fuckin A."

"How much does quarrying pay?"

"Got a couple hundred," I said.

"Show me."

"Where's your girl?" I said.

After a silence, he rose from the table. "Come on out back."

We crossed the backyard. The man in the garage didn't look up as we passed his door, but reached over and turned his boom box up several notches. I saw no weapons near him other than tools. We took an exterior staircase to the second story. Trees crowded in on all sides, reaching onto the small deck, blotting out the city. The door was padlocked from the outside. Dizzy unlocked it and let us in.

We stood in a narrow room. A kitchenette occupied one corner, and two couches made an L in another. There were two doors side by side, closed, a line of yellow light under one. My eye was drawn to a framed photograph of Pope John Paul II.

"Take a seat," Dizzy commanded. He tapped on one of the doors and disappeared inside.

The door opened and he reemerged. He sat on the opposite couch, pulled a small pistol from his waistband, and rubbed his eyes with a thumb and forefinger.

"Go on in," he said. "But if you don't have two hundred . . ." He glanced down at the pistol where it rested beside him on the arm of the couch. "I hear anything I don't like in there . . ." Once again, the pistol. "Get to it."

I crossed the distance to the bedroom door, turned the knob, and went inside. The girl wasn't Penny. Wasn't old enough to be, just a kid sitting in her underwear on the edge of an unmade twin bed. Clouded eyes sunk into an acne-scarred face, a nose stud that reminded me of my dead wife, an eyebrow ring that didn't. She had a hand-knit winter hat perched on the back of her head, a small rainbow in the saddest room I had ever seen.

"Nice beard," she said. You could still hear the teenager.

"Get dressed," I said. "Quick as you can." I showed her my Wild Thyme badge, which she gazed at for some time before pulling a pair of jeans out from under the bed. When she was all but dressed I asked her, "Where are your shoes?" She shrugged, and I shrugged, and I took out the .40. "Stay behind me," I said.

As I moved through the doorway, pistol hanging out of sight behind my thigh, Dizzy stood. When he saw the girl leave the room, his face grew puzzled, and he said, "Hey." He went for his pistol but knocked it to the floor. Reaching over the sofa's arm for the gun, he called out, "Bobby! Bobby!" The girl backed into her room. I leapt forward, put a knee on Dizzy, and pounded at him with the butt of the .40. He took the first few on his arm, but I landed one on his head with a thud that traveled up my wrist. He slumped into the sofa, eyes open but unseeing. Footsteps came up the staircase outside. I took a marble lamp from an end table, ripping the cord from its socket with a blue snap of electricity. As the mechanic came through the door, I laid the lamp across the back of his head. He tumbled over a low wooden coffee table and fell face-first onto the floor, the lower half of his body still on the table. Slowly, his legs followed the rest of him and thudded down. I pocketed Dizzy's automatic.

I called to the girl, but more people were coming up the stairs. I stepped on the mechanic's neck where he lay and pointed the .40 at the door.

As the door burst open, I called out, "Police!" and told the man entering to drop his weapon. It was the older bald fellow from the bars, two hands wrapped around an automatic and a badge dangling from a lanyard around his neck.

He also yelled, "Police!"

I must have yelled it back about twenty times as I raised my hands, .40 and all. The Rotarian was followed by a slender black man in baggy street clothes, and the woman from the Georgian who had seemed so interested in me, now oddly sober. After the room had settled, I kept my free hand high and slowly laid the .40 on the table, followed by Dizzy's weapon.

"My badge is in my left inside pocket," I said. "There's at least one other man—"

"We got everyone."

The black cop reached into my jacket and had a look at the Wild Thyme badge, then handed it to the older white man and holstered his gun. "I'm Detective Oates. You met Detective Larkins at the bar," he said, gesturing to the woman. "This is Lieutenant Sleight. We don't know you." I showed him that my ID matched my badge.

Larkins pushed past us and led the barefoot girl out. I realized then that at the bar, she'd probably felt my weapon through my jacket.

"So you on the job up here?" Oates asked. "Help me understand what you're doing."

"Jay," said the older cop.

"Fine, he's yours." Oates went into the girl's room.

I explained to Sleight that I had spoken to a Binghamton desk sergeant. I also told them in a general way what had led me into town.

Sleight nodded and with a faint smile said, "I know who you are."

Oates emerged, and said on his way out, "Whatever you think you're doing, it's done. Lieutenant, can you escort Officer Farrell downtown for a statement while I handle his mess?"

Sleight stepped toward me and said, "Do you mind?"

My foot was still on the back of the mechanic's neck. The lieutenant peered down into the man's slack face. "You don't know who this is?"

"Should I?"

"Bobby Chase, used to be Endicott Fire Department. Got put on leave last year for using, never went back. Bouncer now, dealer. I expect by now he's done some things he regrets. Shame. I know his dad." He gave me a meaningful look. "I've met his cousins too."

I eased off Chase, dumbstruck.

We walked to the door while a patrolman crouched by Dizzy. As we passed the garage, Sleight leaned in and switched off the music. I followed him through the narrow side yard, the sound of sobbing getting louder as we made our way out front. On the porch steps, the man I figured for Max sat with his eyes closed, his head resting against the rotting newel base. He was a big one, wearing urban clothes that increased his size. Beneath the bottoms of his too-long shorts, his fat legs were covered in bug bites. A hefty older woman sat splayed on the porch floor in a white nightgown. I guessed she was in her seventies, and she was handcuffed. It was she who was crying, and though she said no words, the sound she made had a foreign heaviness to it.

"You should see the package she kept in her pantie drawer," Sleight said. "Keep this town on the nod for a month."

We walked around the corner, got into Lieutenant Sleight's late-model SUV, and pulled away.

"Listen, about tonight," I said.

"You queered us," Sleight admitted. "We had plans to work Kostis. He's weak and it'd be his second time in. More years, more reason to talk. You showed up and it got weird. We wanted to take him away quietly, away from the house. Some rough customers there. The only chance he'd talk is if they didn't know he'd been brought in. Now the whole city knows."

"Did you know the girl was in there?"

"No. She was a surprise too."

We passed through late-night downtown easily and parked in the ground floor of a massive garage. From there, we crossed the street and up a flight of concrete stairs to a broad platform. We entered the municipal building through glass doors and a uniformed policeman waved us past the metal detector. There was a world-weary buzz moving through the Binghamton police headquarters at night, and everywhere we walked smelled like coffee and disinfectant. We ended up in a small office with a window that looked out on the Detective Division. He closed the door.

"So, you're after the Chase girl," Sleight said.

"Pellings, yeah."

"Yeah, Pellings. I've been thinking about that."

"Is that your problem? Aren't you Vice?"

"No. I loan myself out to Special Investigations every now and then because they think I look like a john. The wife would hate it if she knew. But I'm not special; I'm just an investigator. Homicide and Unsolved Crimes." Sleight shook his computer mouse back and forth and his screen came to life.

"Unsolved Crimes," I said.

"You're there for the families when they call. You keep an eye out, listen for echoes, try to make deals when you can. Open things up wider."

"Echoes," said I.

"Yeah, echoes. This thing on the East Side is just like that one North Side case that's still open. How are they connected? When we found Abby Chase, it wasn't going to be long before it was in the papers. 'Dead hooker found by railroad tracks,' nobody wants that. We had to get down to Pennsylvania to reach the ex-husband so he could tell the girls first. I remember being surprised by the house—seemed like they had a nice life, but. There's the mother, out there downtown. We get to the ex-husband's, and I had to pull him aside. It was early morning, though, the kids were there, and they knew. Right away they knew. One of them starts crying, and then we did too, me and, uh, Sergeant McKey it was back then. But the other daughter just . . . froze. Like if she didn't move, the news wouldn't get to her. Anyways. I don't remember which kid was which. I just remember the morning."

"I got to wonder, how many of these are actually unsolved, and how many are . . . like, you know who did it, you just can't get there somehow."

Sleight didn't answer.

"Can I see where she was found?"

He began to type. "Here's what you're going to say, more or less," he told me. "You were in town tonight on your own time, seeking information on a missing person, when Kostis makes contact with you. How did he . . . ?" I told him about the picture on the phone. "Nice, that's good for us too. We'll get that off the phone. Concerned for the young woman's safety, you bling blang blong, we follow you to the scene, and done."

That was more or less what happened, and I said so.

"Okay," said Sleight, "he's probably going to try to deal, but frankly, as I said, he's in no position to give up any friends without serious health concerns, so he won't offer us much. What I'm saying is, depending on what he's charged with, this may actually go to trial. Can you stick to the story?"

"Yes."

"Would your testimony give us any trouble whatsoever?"

"Look, I don't want to screw you. I'd been drinking. I also smoked a little weed."

"Yeah. If it comes up, just deny it."

"What's going to happen to the girl?"

"We'll try to connect her with some family. Treatment. What else can you tell me about tonight? Anything at all."

I thought. "Nothing."

"You're not a detective or nothing, but you had a plan. Where'd you start out?"

"Penny used to work at a place on the West Side, Stingy Jack's."

"Ah, now we're talking. Blaine's place. His, and some others'."

"'Others'?"

"You talk to anyone?"

"Blaine himself for a minute. Nothing came of it. Except—"

"That's right. Go on."

"Nothing. He told me a joke," I said.

"Okay. Picture yourself back there. Look around the room. Anybody out of place?"

The only thing I could think of was the black guys sitting at the bar, not being served, and Blaine's Irish music. I told him about it.

Sleight laughed. "Holy shit. He knew you from the moment you walked in there. Goddamn it. Now, I don't know every black kid in Binghamton, but if I did, I doubt very much if those two were from here. Somewhere in that parking lot, in the trunk of some plain little Honda Accord, was more heroin than you or I ever seen in one place."

"If you know all this . . ."

"Look, I never talked to you about it. But if Blaine was all we wanted . . ." He raised his palms. "We never talked. And you never talked to Blaine."

The lieutenant and I exchanged cards, so he'd know where to find me if and when I was needed.

"Lieutenant," I ventured. "Is, ah, who here is looking for Penny? I only ask—"

"It'd still be at the uniform level this early on. Probably. I can ask, and asking may get some doors knocked on." He turned to me. "Here's what you do. She got a cell?" I shrugged. "Get the provider to ping it. That way you know, at least, is the phone moving? Where is it? And so on. Now, I'm not suggesting you come up to Binghamton again. But if curiosity gets the better of you, stay away from Clinton Street, for poor Oates's sake, at least. We're out there every night, we'll keep an eye out for her."

We returned to Sleight's truck and he took me back up State Street, but continued north rather than west across the river. We came to an unlit area at the edge of Binghamton's railyard and parked. Sleight turned off the SUV and the blackness of the place swept in around us.

"We looked at the Canadian Northern guy that found her," Sleight said. "A utility guy. We took a long look at the ex-husband, but he could account for himself pretty well. We brought in a few sorry hustlers. Just one of those things, one of those deaths that . . . it's ugly, the way people get disposed of. We tried hard as we could to close that case."

We left the SUV and slipped down to where the railroad tracks cut a swath through the city. Fifty yards distant, two freight trains tattooed with graffiti sat as if they'd never move again. Sleight led me between the nearest track and the hill we'd just descended, to where the slope got overgrown. Again, fireflies blinked in and out of the dark. We came to a stack of rail ties nearly five feet tall, and the lieutenant pointed between it and where it was snugged up to the hill. I looked in all directions and for the life of me couldn't see any reason for this to be the place, or why anyone would have bothered to wade far enough into the tall grass to find her.

"Crows," said Sleight, noticing my puzzlement. "Carrion birds. It's not as remote as you'd think in the daytime."

I walked around the pile. My eyes fixed on something in the tall grass. Glowing in the scant light from streetlamps was a ring of white stones half planted in the ground, chunks of quartz forming a circle about three feet in diameter.

"You found it," Sleight said. "This appeared about a year after the body. Not all at once. A few rocks at a time, enough that we had a patrolman out here nights. Of course, it wasn't the killer doing it."

"Had to be Penny. Or Rianne."

"Penny. We were disappointed, but it made sense. A memorial, something like that."

"Doesn't look like she's been here lately."

Sleight named a motel on Upper Front Street, one in Vestal, and a couple truck stops. "That's where you'd be looking for a girl in the life."

"We're not looking for that," I said.

"Are you sure?"

SHERIFF DALLY wrote out a complaint and convinced DA Ross to tug on the magistrate's robe. The magistrate on duty swore out a warrant directing Penny's cell carrier to ping her phone and, if we found it, to allow us to open it and look at any recent activity. We worried that battery life would be an issue if we didn't find it soon, that it might already be dead. It turned out the phone was alive, and not thirty feet from the trailer. A PSP forensic tech out of Dunmore traveled north to help us out.

The cell was in the woods between the trailer and Dunleary Road. It didn't take too long before Deputy Jackson turned it up in the middle of a patch of fiddlehead ferns, with no signs of disturbance or human presence around it. Likely it had been flung from the driveway and had maybe glanced off a tree trunk before landing. The tech, a pudgy thirty-something man who'd given up a perfectly decent career in IT for this, took several photos of the phone where it lay, then with a gloved hand picked it up by its cleanest corner and bagged it. It was a plain flip phone, metallic gray with a smear of blood and bits of dried leaf sticking to it. We took it back to the courthouse.

Penny didn't use the phone much. In the previous month, she had only called her sister Rianne twice, and not within two weeks of the date. There were a few everyday texts to and from Kevin all throughout the month. Cousin Bobby got a call a few days before, but had not answered. There were, however, some strongly suggestive calls made and received on the night she disappeared, and after. At 12:37 a.m. she'd called Kevin, but either she'd hung up before he could answer or he'd chosen not to take the call. Then, at 2:18 a.m., Kevin called her phone, but left no message. That morning at 9:44 a.m., the same. At noon, you could hear Kevin deliver a raspy plea for her to call him back. He left a similar message at 5:54 p.m., and then in the evening messages from Penny's stepmother, father, sister, and cousin Bobby arrived, each expressing their own style of worry, each with a hint of defeat in their voices. At 10:03 that night, Kevin sobbed into the phone. "I miss you," he choked out, and the message ended. A smattering of calls came in over the next day. One that stood out because of who it was from: Andy Swales, checking in from a Pennsylvania cell number. The call would have been placed shortly after we'd met to discuss what he'd heard the night of her disappearance.

We all sat in the district attorney's office listening to tinny voices out of the phone's speaker, and we understood. She wasn't with some long-lost aunt, she wasn't shacked up somewhere in town, she had not wandered away to take stock of her life. Whatever I did now, it'd be too little, too late. Ross replayed Kevin's message several times.

"What's he sorry about?" he asked the room. He played it again.

Dally turned to me, impatient with the DA. "Henry, where are we on Kev's truck? Any sign of the weapon?"

"Been busy, Sheriff."

"Yeah," said Ross, "Tioga County called. They want us to charge O'Keeffe and wash their hands of Heffernan. I told them we're investigating on a couple fronts and to hold tight."

"Binghamton PD has been over to Heffernan's last known," said Dally. "Some shack in Johnson City with an old girlfriend and a couple kids there, not all his, I gather. She hadn't seen him in a few weeks, but that's not unusual. Said he'd called and talked to his boys, would have been five days ago. She claimed not to know Penny Pellings. Or Kevin."

Ross played Kevin's message once more. "This would be a lot easier with a body," he said.

"It's been done," said the sheriff.

"If we take O'Keeffe's calls at face value . . ." Ross said.

"Why should we?" said the sheriff. "Here's the story we tell. He killed her, carted her off in his car. Truck. Then he decided, hey, maybe I don't want to spend the rest of my life in prison, sober and apart from my daughter, what do I do? I lose the body, lose the vehicle, scrub the place down. Then woe is me. I wait a little while, I get worried. I call. I make some noise here in town, and hey, something happens I don't expect and somebody else is dead. So all the time I had to craft Penny's disappearance is gone. What do I do? I go to the police and muddy the waters best I can. O'Keeffe's no genius but you don't have to be smart to do what he did. Just motivated."

Ross nodded. "Or maybe he did her and Heffernan together, a crime of passion. Found them in town, and bang bang."

"So wait," I said, my brain grinding. "So, why does Heffernan end up in the river, but not Penny?"

"There's a lot we don't know," said Dally. "Maybe she did."

"It's loose yet," Ross said. "But the bloody phone, though. That should put the fear of god in him. I'd do a Murder One complaint for Penny and let's see where we get. No bail, and we have an extra two weeks to find something to help us with Heffernan. We'll get him for one or the other if it comes to it. I bet he'll plead." The district attorney swiveled left and right in his desk chair. "So write me the complaint for Pellings, but keep it vague. The cell is 'blood evidence found at the home.' Hit the domestic this past winter, bring in Swales's account of ongoing whatnot, and inconsistent statements from the suspect, too. I'll bring it to Magistrate Heyne, and let's try to get him locked up this afternoon."

Because I could approach Kev without provoking flight, it fell to me to execute the warrant. I drove to Ed's work site in Bradford County and parked near the workers' cars lined up in the yard, minus Kevin's truck, of course. Cock-rock guitar sailed into the air, competing with hammer blows and the creaks and snaps of ancient iron brads pried from wood. By now the roof had been entirely removed, exposing a rib cage of rafters meeting over a trio of bents. Most of the rafters would be trash, but many of the bigger bones looked worthy. After marking Kev's giant hat up near where two rafters met, I picked through the briars surrounding the structure and swung up the frame to the broad top plate where Ed stood peering at a joint. Clenched in his teeth was a smoldering pipe of tobacco and weed.

"Anything good?" I said.

"Passable. Passable," Ed said, handing me the pipe, which I declined. "You here to take Kev again? Don't be too long, now."

"About that."

"Oh." Ed searched my face for answers and I tried to give him none.

"Penny?"

"I can't say."

"Did he?"

"He'll need a lawyer. Can you call him down?"

We lowered ourselves to the dirt floor. During the couple minutes I had been on site, the crew had slackened. All except Kevin, who worked at his perch with a concentration approaching fury. First Ed called to him, then I did. He slumped in place, dangled for a moment with one hand clinging to a rafter, feet on the beam's edge, body hanging over empty space. Then he came to himself and climbed down. I took no chances with a man who was breathing what might be his last free air. I handcuffed him. As I helped him into the patrol truck, the crew stopped work entirely, offering no encouragement to anyone.

We coasted east to Fitzmorris with the windows down. As we picked up speed on 189, Kevin finally spoke, so low I almost missed it. "Where'd you find her?"

JEREMIAH HEYNE was magistrate for the district including Wild Thyme Township. He was older, with a red face, a sweep of gray hair, and a pinkie ring. Not a talkative man in private life, the few times he had communicated with me in the past, it was mainly through winks. As a judge, Heyne had the reputation of a maverick or a menace or both, depending who you asked. His sense of justice was highly individual, and he was rumored to wear a buck knife under his robe.

Fitzmorris's magistrate court was never very grand, its ceiling low, its walls covered with corporate art, and its chairs looking like they'd been filched from a church basement. Behind the bench, a picture window looked out into trees, good for bird-watching while waiting for the magistrate to get around to your case. I sat behind DA Ross, who had spread out on the prosecution-side table. He'd asked me to come, in large part, because with Heyne presiding one never knew what to expect. It was supposed to be a preliminary arraignment, the first step, where Kev would be told of the charges against him. Typically I wouldn't be called to testify until down the line, but since Kevin already had counsel present the DA worried that Heyne might try to get everything done in one fell swoop.

Across from Ross at the defendant's table sat Lee Hillendale, one of only two or three Holebrook County lawyers specializing in criminal defense. Hillendale was stocky, wore beautiful suits, and a lawyerly scent of gin followed him wherever he went. Good for Kev, I thought, but didn't know how he was going to swing the fee. I'd known the lawyer for the couple years I'd worked in the county. He'd been impossible to avoid, and though he regularly put my dick in the dirt on summary hearings, there was nothing personal between us. He and his wife were friendly with Ed and Liz, and I even liked him despite his troubling sympathy for lowlifes. The first time we went head-to-head was a defiant trespass I'd brought on behalf of a little old lady in Wild Thyme, named Lynn Lawrence, against one James Magro, who had repeatedly and, yes, defiantly hunted her land despite No TRESPASSING signs and vigorous shooings from the porch. Against some blurry pictures of a man who was probably Magro in the middle of a forest that could have been anywhere, Hillendale had shown Lynn a topo map of her land and the parcels surrounding it, and she'd sat there on the stand mute and embarrassed, unable to give the specific locations in the photos. Then the lawyer showed some exhibits where Lynn's signs were actually on someone else's parcel. It was a cheap tactic, and I said so after the hearing, after Magro had sped off acquitted and I'd bundled Lynn into her ancient Pontiac.

"I know," Hillendale had said, contrite. "But that's the system we have. I don't know why I keep taking these cases; I should just start a port-a-john business instead."

A couple months later I'd helped repossess one of Magro's trucks for nonpayment of Hillendale's fee. Glad to do it. Anyway, as far as I knew, that was the kind of case that Hillendale customarily tried in the courtrooms of Holebrook County. How he'd do on a Murder One, we'd see.

Sheriff's Deputy Jackson brought Kevin into the courtroom, cuffed, still in his work clothes. He met nobody's eye and sat with his head bowed. Magistrate Heyne swept in and we all rose without any bailiff telling us. Heyne clicked the gavel and, after peering at the complaint, commenced the proceeding.

"*Commonwealth versus Kevin O'Keeffe.* Mr. O'Keeffe, I'm Magistrate Jeremiah Heyne. You call me 'Judge.' I'm going to read these charges. Don't interrupt. Mr. O'Keeffe?" Kevin looked up. "Don't interrupt. If you have any questions, wait." Heyne continued. "You're being charged by Holebrook County Sheriff's with the criminal homicide of one Penelope Pellings of 1183B Dunleary Road, Wild Thyme Township, and obstruction of justice. Specifically murder of the first degree, that you had a violent dispute with, and did intentionally kill Miss Pellings on May eighteenth at approximately twelve-thirty a.m. Obstruction of justice, that you concealed or destroyed evidence of the crime, to wit, Miss Pellings's body. Do you understand these charges?"

Kevin was shaking his head. "No."

Heyne raised his eyes to the ceiling. "What are your questions, then?"

"So you found her?"

"Kevin," said Hillendale, gently.

"Yes, I understand. Judge."

"Dandy. Sir, I'm going to set a preliminary hearing for you on, let's see, June third at three o'clock p.m. Given the murder charge, there'll be no bail, and you are remanded to county lockup."

As Kevin returned to his cell, and Lee Hillendale walked down Main to his storefront office, flapping his suit coat open and shut in the heat, I stood on the steps of the courthouse with DA Ross and Sheriff Dally.

"Now we hope he pleas," said Dally.

"If he did it, he will," said Ross. "He'll crack if he did it. Anyways, you two, we have about two weeks until prelim. Get out there, get what you can on him."

AS I PULLED INTO the township building, the rear end of Shelly Bray's station wagon caught my eye from around the far corner, nearest my office. I parked and took a deep breath, and waited, and approached. You asked for it, dum-dum, I told myself.

Shelly waited with one leg over the other, stretched out the driver's-side door. She wore gym clothes and had her hair pulled back. When I walked up, she smiled and stood.

"I've been busy," I explained.

"Oh, yeah?" She shooed me toward the office door, which I unlocked. She carried my boots in a paper bag.

Inside, the scent of her sweat collected around us, and my breath got short.

She turned and fumbled with the doorknob. "How the . . . how the hell do you lock this thing?"

"This has to be it," I said. "This is the last time."

"Lighten up," she said.

A COUPLE DAYS earlier I had called Kevin O'Keeffe's mother to ask if she'd seen him or his pickup lately. She'd said no, she hadn't seen him in nearly a month. Since the truck still hadn't turned up, I drove to Sayre to see for myself. Yvonne O'Keeffe lived in a trailer park on the west side of town. I drove up and down the rows of single-wides, but there was no yellow truck and no place to hide one. My own truck rattled from where a heat shield bolt had rusted through over the winter. It was something I needed to fix if ever I wanted to be the least bit stealthy again, and probably a clamp or a bit of wire would do. As I passed, cats bolted from various perches in the courtyard to hide under mobile homes. Three boys in a yard several trailers to my right were contemplating bicycles that had been stood upside down on handlebars and seats—practicing the ritual of caring for their vehicles. In not so many years, their knowing nods would be directed at secondhand ATVs, then maybe an old Hyundai with aftermarket headlights, a shitheap to be proud of because it was yours. I waved and called hello to them, and they froze, then scattered. It was a school day.

As I pulled up to Yvonne's place, a young man with a buzz cut, a gold chain, and no shirt waited for me on the porch steps.

"She's not here," he called to me. "She's working over to the Pilot's. Off 17."

"That's okay," I said, stepping out of the truck and walking to him. "Who're you?"

"Brian O'Keeffe." He stood and revealed a tattoo of an anchor and DEATH BEFORE DISHONOR on his narrow chest.

"Navy?"

"USS *Theodore Roosevelt*, in the Gulf the past two years. Bosun's mate."

"Good for you."

"Yeah, well." He lowered his voice. "You here about my brother? I don't know a thing about it."

"No?"

"Except he never did that shit. You should let him out of jail. Do your job and find his girl." This was said with no real hostility, just weariness. "Or maybe you shouldn't find her, I don't know."

"It's not in him?"

"Oh, fuck, no. Man, listen, he's my older brother. So why was I toe-to-toe with kids *his age* at school? Why was it me getting popped at home for looking dad in the eye? While he was in the bunk with headphones on, going to bed hungry? He ain't a fighter. And now he's finding out what that gets him." He drained the last inch of his beer.

"You know Penny at all?"

"Little bit. Not much. They got together when I was overseas."

"Any problems there?"

"What isn't a problem with them two? Kev don't tell me. I'm saying, he doesn't tell me much."

"You spend time with them?"

"No. I stopped by the once, hey, I'm home. He was, you know, 'We're trying to get the baby back,' so on. He can't face Ma, she died of shame, so he's telling me this and that, they're turning it around, so I'll tell Ma. She—Penny—spent most of the time in the bedroom, waiting for me to leave, I guess."

"Okay." I cast my eye about the park once more. "So you grew up here, this where you and Kevin grew up?"

"Nah, this is where mom finally moved out to. Dad lived up to Waverly, but not for some time now. He's in Texas."

I gave him my phone number. "Kevin's truck came up missing."

Brian shrugged and looked blank.

"I don't know what I'd do if it was my brother," I said. "I might help him and not ask too many questions."

"I get what you're saying," Brian said. "No, if he wants to pretend the world is something else, that's his business."

"All right. Tell your mom hello."

"She don't know you." Again, the sailor said this without hostility, just a fact that he was too tired not to say.

NO TRUCK, no body, no weapon. I had been keeping myself opinion-free as to Kevin's guilt, so as not to be disappointed. But I thought about it during yet another search of the land surrounding the trailer. Men like him use their vulnerability where another man might use charm or force. You pull some-one in, you destroy them a little bit at a time, unaware even, maybe, that you're doing it, until you are revealed and they belong to you. Destroyed and killed are two different things, though. Afterward I parked my truck within sight of the trailer and Andy Swales's great stone home, where the falling sun shone magenta off a visible edge of the lake. As evening fell I listened for vibrations and continued reading my Antietam book. When the shadows began to stretch and change with the sunset, I took another turn around the property to see if anything else caught my eye, but nothing did and I went home.

MONDAY MORNING, after another slink through the woods in search of my tom, I headed to Fitzmorris to coordinate with the sheriff. He'd been deflecting his counterparts in Tioga County who were wondering where we were on Heffernan. I had little to add. Dally was also trying to push Penny's cell phone onto some kind of mythical fast track at the Bethlehem laboratory, arguing that a life was potentially still in the balance. They'd said sure, they'd see. We stood leaning on the counter in the front of the station drinking coffee and contemplating, when Deputy Jackson rushed in.

"We need a doctor." We followed him back to lockup. Kevin sat on the floor of his cell near the toilet; his face was placid, white, and sweat-drenched.

"Everything is all right," he told us, as if he believed it. "You . . . step aside from . . . the way you see, step into a new channel, and they show you the way. They're not monsters. But they're not your friends, no. No. They're not . . . they are you." He looked at me. "You were right. They are you yourself. You tell yourself how to get to the place. You have to tell yourself if you don't have help. How else can you do it?" He smiled, and then bucked backward, clocked his head against the floor, and seized.

Jackson and I held him to his bunk and I forced my wallet in between his teeth, while Dally called out an ambulance.

THAT NIGHT I sat out in the middle of the field by a fire pit I made, lacquered in bug spray and listening to the logs snap. I'd cooked a little venison steak on the camp spider, new potatoes wrapped in foil, and had a handful of the first greens of the season. I'd also smoked a small bowlful of weed. Every now and then I had to put my individuality into perspective, which is to say, I wasn't one, or didn't want to be. A self—a person—could hurt or kill another or disappear forever. If I wasn't a self, then I was everything around me, and the selves who were no longer with me were with me once again. I had brought the fiddle, but it suited me to just gaze up at the galaxy and wait for shooting stars. The stars mixed with the fireflies in the tall grass, and with the high calls of peepers in the ravine, and with the bonfire's smoke and glowing embers curling up into the air, and I belonged in the world. Having the thought brought me out of it again.

Headlights cut through the darkness, swept past my house and into the field where I sat, and my instinct was to hide. The lights cut off. A shadow stepped out of the car and stood. With some dismay I stood too. The walk through my field took a strangely long time, and then time glitched and I stood face-to-face with Lee Hillendale, Kev's defense attorney.

"Evening," he said. "I tried to raise you on the phone. I wouldn't have come, but it's time-sensitive. That, and you're the one Kevin trusts."

"What about him?"

"I've been to see him. He wants to talk, but only to you."

"How is he?"

"He got the shakes, plain and simple. The nurses said he was going on about demons. Then asking . . . asking to die, apparently." The lawyer seemed weary. "I mean, what do you do? Quitting is going to knock you sideways. Maybe kill you if you do it wrong. Not quitting just kills you slower."

"We don't always know where we are until we try to get out of it," I said.

"That's . . . yes. But how would I ever pay the mortgage without the demon rum? Anyway. He's on diazepam now, turning a corner, and he's coherent. You'll want to hear what he has to say. Ross is making a mistake. My guy didn't do it."

"I've been hearing that," I said, getting a grip on the thoughts spiraling over each other in my head.

"You haven't heard everything. Be down at the medical center before seven a.m. Room 265. The idea is you'll relieve Patrolman Hanluain. You're not coming there to talk, is the appearance. Someone else from the sheriff's office will show up about seven-thirty, and we can play it off as a mistake. Kevin's worried about being seen to cooperate."

"He should be worried in the other direction," I said.

"Henry," said the lawyer, "consider this a part of discovery. I tell you what I've got. In return, you tell me what you've got. If you've got nothing, it's in everyone's interests to know that. But I don't trust Ross to shoot straight on this. Or Dally, even. And Kevin has some interests he needs seen to."

"This is . . ." I said, shaking my head.

"Before seven o'clock, if you want to do the right thing."

"Okay."

I made it back to the bonfire. The night had been crowded out and crabbed by the lawyer, the missing girl, and whoever had taken her away. I lay back on the blanket and stared up, unseeing.

Next morning I had no time to chase the turkey. I got dressed and headed to the medical center, where Kev and Hillendale were waiting. The place had been built with money donated by gas companies, and I didn't hate that. The operators had image problems, and if they wanted to give the county a hospital or the high school a new science center, I can take that for the good. As skilled a general practitioner as Liz is, we did need something more for the county than the little Fitzmorris clinic. The hospital was built on a bare hillside. The place was wide open and I found a spot next to Hanluain's patrol car.

Room 265 was easy to find, guarded as it was by a pudgy deputy in a foul mood, leaning against the wall in a hard plastic chair. Hanluain's eyes were closed but I doubted he was asleep. "Didn't you just check him?" he said, full of wrath and without opening his eyes.

"No," I said, shrugging.

"Oh, Henry, shit," he said, rubbing his face.

"You get any sleep out here?"

"No. He's on suicide watch. Every fifteen minutes, a doctor, a nurse, a fuckin janitor, I don't know, someone checks."

"He say anything?"

"No. Not that I could tell. And I was told not to talk to him."

"Go home and sleep," I said. "You're fine."

Hanluain stood and stretched his back and walked down the hall. I opened the door and stepped inside. Lee Hillendale was asleep in a chair, head back, snuffling, book open on his chest. His head swung forward on my entry. He blinked twice and set his book aside.

They had Kevin on an IV of various dopes, and Hillendale set about waking him up before the nurses came in to drug him again or figure out what else to do with him. After some gentle shaking, Kevin's eyes raised to half-mast, then three-quarters upon seeing me. Before anything else I Mirandized him.

"You make it to town?" Kevin said.

"Yes." I told him where I'd been, and what I'd seen and done, leaving out the arrests and anything to do with the ongoing prosecutions. When I'd finished the part about following Dizzy back to the house in the First Ward, Kevin seemed fairly alert, and Hillendale's eyes were wide.

"Okay," said Kev. "Back to Stingy Jack's, though," he said, his speech slow, his voice full of false pleasure. He spoke around the edges of it.

"So . . . Penny used to tend bar there," I said.

"Yup. That was during her . . . when she was getting to be full-blown. She got fired for drinking too much, passing out, not cleaning the place."

"And you'd expect her to show up there?"

"Not exactly."

"Who is Blaine to you?" I waited for Kevin to answer. "Who is he to Penny, then?"

"Just an upstanding local businessman." He shifted in his bed. "And yet, there was that charge."

I waited.

"The story I heard is, some years back he did thirteen months for possession. Crack, I heard. He gets out, they, his friends, throw him a party. And they bring along this stripper, only Blaine doesn't know, he says, that she's just sixteen and saving up for a car to get away from whatever fucked-up place she was. Something happened to the kid, I don't know. But she ended up changing her tune."

"And nothing stuck to Blaine," I said.

"Nah. He's supposed to be a good guy. A good, good guy. He used to be a roofer, if you can believe that."

"I can." Of all tradesmen, roofers are the most villainous degenerates in America. Between roofers and quarrymen, a small-town cop can stay busy his entire career.

"Yeah, he was a roofer. And somehow he spun what savings he had into a stake in that bar. How? Hard telling, not knowing. The thing I like about that place?" Kevin continued. "It's near all the ways in and out of town. So, a drunk like me can get right on 17, west to 35, no problem. Just kind of blend in, getting in and out." Kevin had a glimmer of conspiracy in his eye. I had the notion he wasn't really talking about drunk driving. "I'd say set up checkpoints, but those are never really a surprise. Still, who's to say? You might catch a few. Drunk drivers."

"Who's Dizzy Kostis?"

"Another local entrepreneur. No, I don't know him. Not really. Know him to see him hanging around with Bobby. Penny knows these people. I want a cigarette now."

"Kostis's been inside too."

"Yeah, I guess so. Not surprised, but I don't know a thing about it."

"Kev, you got to give me more."

"Yeah, well. Sooner or later, I'll be dead over this shit."

"We're wasting time," Hillendale put in.

"Okay," said Kevin. "Here's what happened."

And this is the story that he told me. It took some work getting it all out of him. I needed the details to save his neck.

At 12:40 a.m., May 18, 2009, Kevin kicked in a basement window of Cottage Seven on Maiden's Grove Lake, slid inside, and dropped to the floor. He was followed by Sage Buckles, of Airy Township, a thirty-five-year-old former thug, new to Holebrook County that spring. Their eyes had just adjusted to the dark when a phone rang upstairs.

It continued to ring.

"Forget it," said O'Keeffe, "let's go."

"Hang on," said Buckles, clicking off his flashlight and trotting up the stairs. He picked up the phone and answered in as calm and sober a fashion as he could manage, like a home owner. "Do you know what time it is?"

The woman on the other end asked, "To whom am I speaking, please?"

"Prosser," this being the name on the cottage's mailbox.

After a brief pause, the woman said, "Mr. Prosser, this is Ann with ADT. Your house alarm has been tripped. For security purposes—"

Buckles hung up the phone. "You might come up," he called down the cellar stairs. "We tripped the alarm."

"What? Let's go," said O'Keeffe. "Come on, man."

"Look, they call the dispatcher, the dispatcher's got to send someone here. You know how long that'll take, out this far?"

"No. Do you?"

"O'Keeffe, if they're going to get us, they got us. Don't make any difference now. Get your ass up here."

In the span of three minutes, they relieved Rhonda Prosser of a thirty-two-inch flat-screen, a DVD player, and some components of a stereo whose brand, McIntosh, they'd never heard of, so it had to be worth something. It was hard to take apart, nervous as they were, and with their fingers in work gloves. O'Keeffe took every liquor bottle that was more than half full, and a loaded 9mm he found in a bedside table. By then he knew Sage Buckles well enough to want the gun. Downstairs, Buckles was about to remove an oil landscape in a gilt frame from where it hung on the wall. Neither man could have known that it was the single most valuable object in the cottage: a Hudson River School painting by an artist named Hollis Rhodes, insured for nine thousand five hundred dollars.

"What are you doing with that? How are we going to sell that?" O'Keeffe said.

"Looking for a safe."

"A safe? Come on, man, let's go."

Buckles stared O'Keeffe down, waiting a teaching moment, and walked out. But something in the painting snagged O'Keeffe. His eyes fuzzed over talking about it, and I let him tell me everything in his head. The painting showed a river meandering through a field, a couple cows, a couple trees, at dusk. He turned on the little brass lamp mounted above the frame and was stunned, rooted to the floor. The clouds above the darkened land were not merely pink, not merely gold, much more than white, and the sky behind was something more alive than the blue of day. Not since his teenage years of weed, mushrooms, and the occasional acid dose had O'Keeffe felt so strong a revelation, a sense of looking up the tube. He had seen sunsets like it in person many times, and looked away without a second thought. But this one made his heart glow even through the cheap vodka that had dulled his spirit for so long. It caught something that couldn't be sold, some end point worth pursuing. Standing there, O'Keeffe felt a long-forgotten life calling to him. His infant daughter Eo calling to him. Tomorrow morning, there'd be changes.

O'Keeffe walked away, leaving the painting's lamp on.

They stowed their haul in a plastic barrel on state game land. Then they returned to the gathering where they'd met earlier. O'Keeffe poured the remaining half of a bottle of single-malt into a red cup, joined the party, and smashed the bottle in the fire. Apparently Penny had just left, which was not a rare occurrence, as she often went her own way and it was not too long a walk up the hill. He drank the scotch in gulps, not tasting.

People filtered away. Sage Buckles's ride had disappeared, which put him in a cold fury. He insisted on a lift home from O'Keeffe, and the two men climbed into the yellow truck once more. Kevin stayed between the lines and just above the speed limit as he rounded Walker Lake, passing a couple of cottages still up and partying, tiki torches flickering on the lake's mirror surface. As they moved up and into the hills, Kevin produced a bottle of rail Irish from under his seat and the two of them handed it back and forth. Kevin dropped Buckles off at a small house in Airy and stood in the driveway for a minute. Distant thrash music pulsed from Buckles's house.

Bedeviled by mosquitoes, Kevin opened his fly and pissed under his truck, left rear, where he had replaced some of the frame with pressure-treated two-by-fours attached with bolts and clamps. Nearly everything that kept his life going was stowed back in the bed, under the truck's cap: circ saws and drills, ammunition boxes full of hand tools, nails, screws, wood oddments, empty tubs of coleslaw and tins of smoked oysters.

He slid behind the wheel and turned the key, and winced as the engine roared to life, exploding through an exhaust system patched with duct tape. His entire being vibrated, and he could almost see the noise, almost trap it in his teeth. His inspection sticker was two months out of date. Every day he drove the truck, it was a dice roll as to whether he'd get where he needed to go, or snake eyes—a cop, a fine. It wasn't good luck that kept the truck on the road those past two months, but the absence of bad. Some days it got to where he didn't even care if he woke up in the morning. But something, some sparkle in the night air, told him he could make a change, if only he could remember.

He tried to retrieve and focus on the feeling the painting had given him, the great sense of peace and belonging beyond expression. He could still see the clouds shot through with light, migrating in a different flow of life. In the moment of the painting, O'Keeffe had the odd sensation that he could have slowed down time forever. On another night he might end up by the riverside until the sun woke him, or he might go driving so far that it'd be too much trouble to ever get back. The thought gave him a quiet thrill. But he had to get back.

That night, O'Keeffe was faced with the reality that Penny needed help, and he couldn't give it to her by robbing houses or getting dragged into her messes. She'd made off with a little bag belonging to Sage Buckles, and since it had already gone up her arm, he had been willing to take payment in other forms. It had become Kevin's problem very quickly. For the first time, he decided to leave Penny. He'd call her folks and just leave, and she might get better then, without him. First she had put the shit up her nose, and it was manageable. One day he found her works and noticed the marks on her feet. The only thing more painful than watching her nod away was living with her when she was trying to kick. As he bumped up his long driveway, he hoped it was late enough that she'd be dead to the world, passed out on the couch, the floor, or the bed if he was lucky. He might remove a needle from her arm or foot and hide her gear, which she'd find again or replace.

He pulled up beside the trailer and saw that the front door was open, which usually meant she was awake. He thumped up the wooden steps and poked his head in, and found that things were not right. The accordion partition separating the living room from the kitchen was nearly torn off its hinges, and several pictures that had been hanging on the wall were lying on the floor. Proceeding into the kitchen, he found dishes smashed, silverware and pots strewn across the floor. A kitchen chair lay on its back. Kevin didn't remember if he'd called Penny's cell phone that night. It turned out he had, 2:18 a.m. He didn't remember meeting Swales in the woods. By then he was on autopilot, had been since somewhere on the drive home from Buckles's place.

He awoke the next morning with just enough time to pull on clothes and make it to the work site. On his way out he noticed that a second partition had been torn down, and the hollow door to the bedroom's half bath was kicked through and busted. It was the same door through which, over the course of a year, he'd heard the effects of her habit as clearly as if he'd been in there with her.

He'd worried, and he'd called, and he'd finished his day and gone home.

It was then, looking down, that he saw the drops of blood

leading from the bedroom, speckling the linoleum. The bloody clump of hair on the floor looked like Penny's.

And here we were.

After Kevin finished talking, I sat quietly, trying to make everything fit. For one, I hadn't ever heard of Sage Buckles.

"If you boys want to take this case further against Kevin," Hillendale said, "we can do the alibi defense, give you names of witnesses, notify them. That's what it'll take. For obvious reasons, that's complicated for my client. We've been trying to raise Buckles. Right now he's supposed to be working with Grace Services clearing well pads. Anyway, he won't return my calls or come to the door."

"Who is this guy? I mean . . . who is he?"

Kevin's eyes flicked to Lee's and back. "I first met Sage, he was spending time at the tavern here and there. He came around this spring, where from, who knows? He and Penny . . . knew each other."

"Oh?"

"The first time, I hauled her out of an upstairs room. He'd taken her there . . . he couldn't stop us in time."

"Why not?"

"He was, ah, not well. We got downstairs to the bar and out. There was another time where she'd scratched him, scratched his face and neck. Outside a bar in Fitz. People saw him after, covered in blood. You didn't hear about that?"

"No. So . . ."

"Yeah, so he wanted Penny. He tried what he could to get to her. I tried to be there to stop it, but I was in no shape myself. And I worked days, I couldn't watch all the time."

"Help me out, man," I said. "How could you throw in with him? He forced her?"

"No, he tried. He never got there. Penny owed him. She took a bag and didn't pay. That's ... straight up. He was ... it was the safest option he gave me, robbing the place. It got to where, that night ..." Kevin sighed, too drugged to summon the energy for proper regret. "I was going to give up on her. No way she was going to give CPS what they wanted, and I thought maybe I could, on my own. Go through the wringer."

"You and Ross need to incentivize Buckles," Lee said. "Give him immunity."

"Jesus, Lee—"

"This is a minor crime, this burglary. Felony two, nobody home, I'm not even sure why that is a felony. It's a life. Maybe Penny's too. At this point, you know ... you know Kevin's not the one."

"And Sage Buckles is your best bet to get this across." I thought, but did not say, that he sounded like a possible killer. Reasonable doubt in person. "I need names," I continued. "Not just Buckles, I need someone at the lake who can give me Penny's departure time. I need someone to put Kev back at the lake with Buckles after the cottage job. I need names of people at the lake with them."

"Yeah," said Hillendale, handing me a folded piece of paper. "We did our best. The call will help with timing, providing Buckles puts Kevin into the burglary. The lamp will be good for us."

"How's that?"

"Above the painting? No electric to the cottage for at least a week, probably two, and then right at that moment a light turns on. Nothing else would explain it. The utility can probably break that out."

As we spoke, Kevin had fallen back asleep, or was pretending. We moved into the hall, where Deputy Jackson had taken up the post Patrolman Hanluain had recently vacated. Jackson looked back and forth between us.

"What's up?" he said, with a note of suspicion in his tone.

"Kevin asked to see Henry," Hillendale said. "No worries."

Jackson looked at me a beat too long, turned away, spread his legs, put his hat over his face, and muttered, "Shit."

Hillendale was at my elbow all the way out to the parking lot. "See what you get from the names, from the lake people, huh? And I'll tell you flat out, so you can pass this along to Ross however you like: we want the murder charge dropped as soon as possible. Ross will want to let it go before jeopardy. Before the case gets bound over to common pleas, even. He'll lose nothing if he nol-proses and anything new comes to light, understand? He can go after Kevin again. Later. But if you go forward now, you've got a problem, and if the magistrate doesn't throw out the case on prelim—"

"It's Heyne. You know he won't, not on these facts."

"But if we go to trial on these facts, I'll win. Do you understand that?"

I raised an eyebrow but secretly agreed.

"Bottom line, I want the murder dropped even before preliminary hearing. We'll damn well plead to the burglary once the murder is dropped."

"Lee, don't get ahead of yourself."

"Be sure you're not the one falling behind." The lawyer drew himself up and tightened his tie. "I'm not asking you to help with the defense. We—Kevin and I—came to you in the spirit of cooperation so you'd get out there and find Penny. If she is to be found. That's his concern, and he knows now he can't do a thing about it himself."

"Hey, I came all the way down here," I said. "Can you do something for me? What's this about some company taking over Casey Noonan's properties? The Royal Lodges, at least. You know anything about that?"

He did not, but promised to look into it. We parted and each went about our day.

AT THE END of the list of names Lee had taken down from Kevin was scrawled "Jen Stewart." I could almost trust her. Jennie Lyn Stiobhard, sister to local ne'er-do-wells Danny and Alan, and something of a ne'er-do-well herself, had lately taken up with a respectable woman. Pamela Maddox, stout young mother of two small children, was married to a former financial advisor now in prison for soaking elderly clients. Pamela lived in Wild Thyme, in a ranch house up a driveway that switched back once through trees to a nice ten-acre plot. Tim Maddox, the husband, wasn't going to stay locked up forever, so I didn't hold out much hope for Jennie's arrangement long-term. In fact, I was a little concerned about how it was going to be when he got out.

Even so, as I pulled up to the house and found Jennie Lyn and a little girl in a princess dress blowing bubbles in the yard, I was taken aback at the irrational hope it gave me for her. She had changed her customary army/navy gear for jeans and a tank top, and her hair was pulled back and buzzed over the ears. As I got close I noted that she was barefoot; a small thing, seeing her feet, but it suggested a gentle side I'd never known. The princess was in the neighborhood of two or three, and met my arrival with silent dismay. I squatted to say hello, I do that with kids, get on their level so I'm not towering over them, and she turned her face into Jennie's leg.

"Okay, girl," said Jennie. "We'll see what's on TV, just for a sec if you don't tell your mother. Promise me don't wake up Jamie, either." She turned to me. "Her brother's having a nap. Come up to the porch."

After Jennie Lyn got the girl settled, we took canvas chairs with a view south to hilltops.

"So what do you want?" she said, friendly enough.

"Looking for Penny Pellings."

"Why would I know where she is?"

"I'm not saying that you would. But Kevin O'Keeffe? He says you might have seen her the night she went missing."

"Up to Maiden's Grove, yeah. I remember. I go up there less and less now."

"I understand."

"But I was there, yeah. I don't know, it was a strange night. Maybe I'm the one and I never noticed. I'm not above a bottle of wine these days, but I don't touch heroin. You try to talk to somebody, and you know . . ." Jennie mimicked passing out in place. "Everything was slowed way down. I'm used to it the other way. Anyhow. I could tell that Kevin wasn't happy. I mean, he's a clown, you know how he is, so it was strange seeing him that way. But something's going on with this guy there. He talks funny—"

"How?"

"I don't know, like he can't quite get the words out. Anyway, he's pissed, Kevin's squirrelly, they argue, and finally, off they go up the hill, Kevin and him."

"You got a name? What's he look like?"

"No name. Never seen him before that night. A brick house, broken nose, barbed-wire tattoos on both arms."

"Could his name have been Sage Buckles?"

"I'd remember that if I heard it."

"Heffernan, then?"

"I simply don't know."

"Anybody with him?"

"I couldn't say."

"You ever see a green car with pink lights beneath?"

"What kind of question is that?"

"Okay," I said, "what time did they leave?"

"It was after midnight. I know because I saw them go and I thought, shit, I checked the time, I got to get going myself. Back here."

"What's Penny doing?"

"Sitting. Just sitting there. She's fucked up, but that ain't news. After Kevin leaves, I look around to go and she's gone too. Seen her walking up the trail to her place."

"You sure about that timing?"

"Pretty sure." She shrugged.

"Anybody follow her?"

"No. It wasn't a big group of people there, we knew each other."

"Anybody strike you as unusual? Behaving strangely?"

"Nobody was a total stranger except for the guy I said."

"Was Andy Swales there?"

"No," she said. "But he's been known to show up drunk, sometimes with a lady. He's not a bad guy probably, I don't know. He lets us be there."

I went over the facts with her again, and it came out much the same. From inside the house the little girl began to call for Jennie, and her infant brother woke and began to squall.

"Anything on Penny Pellings you can tell me? Rumors, reputation, whatever."

Jennie Lyn thought a moment. "All the boys had high hard-ons for her, but Penny Pellings ain't no better than anybody else, whatever she'd have you think. You try talking to her, it's like talking to a tree."

I headed back to the station to do a little searching. Sage Buckles had no record in Pennsylvania, so I called my new friend Lieutenant Sleight of the Binghamton PD, who ran the name through New York's system. It turned out that nine years earlier Buckles had done sixteen months in Collins for third-degree assault. I wrote out a complaint and affidavit for the Prosser burglary so Ross could look at it, and a magistrate, probably Heyne, could sign it. Of course, I was hoping that reason would prevail, that Ross would promise immunity or something close, and Buckles would put himself into the burglary.

I tracked District Attorney Ross down as he was leaving the courthouse by the back door. He smiled wearily when he saw me.

"Sorry," I said. "We hit a snag."

As Ross ambled toward his car, I followed and told him what I had learned that morning—how the witnesses, phone calls, and timing lined up against Kevin's guilt. I had the complaint on Buckles folded in my hand. Ross, knowing very well what it was, gestured for it with some impatience, scanned it, and cursed.

"If this is true, I'm not taking the murder to trial," he said. "Got a pen?" Ross scrawled an 'Okay' and his name. "Go see Heyne."

"Assuming I get ahold of Buckles," I said, "I'd like to stop short of an arrest. What can I tell him about your feelings on the burglary?"

"What do you want me to say? He robbed a house. It's a felony."

"If he testifies—"

"Yeah, all right," Ross relented. "If he testifies and can still make restitution to Rhonda, I'll consider no jail time. For Buckles, not O'Keeffe." A breeze lifted a strand of his hair, and then laid it back across his dome like a blade of grass.

The day was disappearing on me. I called Magistrate Heyne's office already knowing that he'd be gone. I left a message and then called his home line. His wife answered, and told me to look for him at Walker Lake, where he'd gone sailing.

Walker Lake is as crowded and noisy as Maiden's Grove is lonely and sparse. People have built cottages, and cottages for their cottages, on every single spot of shore minus the state-maintained launch. There are pontoons, newly legalized by township decree. I like Walker Lake, it's cheerful. If you want to hear the ghostly call of a loon in the morning mist there are other places to go. Walker Lake is also home to a yacht club of sorts, where people pay a fee to stow small craft on racks.

The summer before, I'd gone on a regular tour of all of the bodies of water within ten miles, watching for a sailboard stolen from the club. It had never been seen again.

I walked to the end of a plywood dock kept afloat by plastic barrels, and found only one sail on the lake. My wave received no acknowledgment. I waited there for Heyne to notice me, but he kept a distance and continued to zigzag across the water to no clear end. Before long, an old-timer with a drooping mustache and a pink terry-cloth hat arrived, hoisted out a boat, and began to set it up. Then, noticing me, he nodded.

"How do you call somebody to shore?" I asked him.

The man raised a finger, disappeared into the clubhouse, and came back with an air horn. I gave the magistrate "shave and a haircut." From across the water, I heard a faint response: "Up yours."

"I need your boat," I said.

The old man, name of Fred, directed me to the front end of the little cockpit and pushed us out into the lake. The wind caught the sail and the boat leapt to life. I trailed my fingers in cold water, and as we neared the middle of the lake, I noted lake weed rising almost to the surface, suggesting a tangled forest below. The surface felt alive, and like it was playing with me when a gust shook itself to shivers on the water. Every now and then Fred obliged me to duck way down to avoid the boom as it swept to the other side on a tack. It was my first time on a sailboat and I was learning what things were called. We were gaining on the magistrate, who lurked by the far shore.

When we got within speaking distance, Heyne called out, "Look, damn it, Fred, you rat."

"Magistrate," I said, "I hate to pester you."

"Can I have one, just *one* afternoon without thinking about which dimwit killed the other?"

That was overstating his burden considerably. "Well," I said, "no, you can't."

"Damn it."

But Heyne let the mainsheet go—that's not a sail, it's the rope that controls the boom, I have learned—and the sail lost its wind. We came alongside and I gave him the complaint and affidavit. The magistrate tossed Fred a light beer from his cooler, and I crossed over to his boat and explained the developments as he read. The sail flapped above us.

"So this Buckles claims to have done the Prosser B&E with O'Keeffe? The night of the Pellings girl's disappearance?"

"The other way around, but yeah. Buckles is an alibi witness for Kevin. For the Murder One."

"Bring him in," Heyne said. I handed him a pen and he signed the complaint with a flourish. "Horrible hunting."

GRACE LANDSCAPE SERVICES was one of the local successes that came out of the Marcellus shale boom. Until just a couple years ago Alexander Grace ran an equipment business only, renting excavators and skid steers to small-time sometime contractors in the area. With a mid-sized wood chipper, a dump truck, several chain saws, and wages for three workers, Alexander had formed a side business, Grace Tree Service. They cut down and hauled away dying and unwanted trees all over Holebrook County and the surrounding area, no job too hairy, no power line too close. East of Fitzmorris, Alexander had a fenced plot where he split the wood that he brought home, which he then sold to the lazy and infirm at a premium. He also began a quarrying operation, both on his own land and as a contractor for others.

In the early days of the shale play, when landsmen were carousing the county like raccoons—*Hey, can I have this?*—Alexander saw how it could be. He sank god knows how much, probably at least a hundred grand, into a feller buncher, a heavy-duty stumper, and a skidder. Then he plied the gas companies with phone calls, emails, and letters, and took out ads in all the little local papers. Grace Landscape Services was ready to clear the way. If the operators were unwilling to use local labor, he'd feed that refusal into the anxiety that was gathering around the industry. I'd seen him in action at our township meetings, and so had the community relations people working for the gas companies. When Grace got its first contract, he invested even more capital in equipment, and in that way made one of the myths of gas development true: job creation. Any man who could use a chain saw, or who had heavy equipment certification or what, could now find a job. You had to admire it.

Sage Buckles had one of those jobs with Grace, and good for him. I guess it didn't pay quite enough, though. At my station I wrote down his license plate, make, and model—a fifteen-year-old domestic sedan, brown—and switched into my own personal truck. The Grace businesses were spread out over a valley floor. Logs were milled in huge corrugated steel sheds, and wood, as I said, was split in the yard. Trucks hauling flatbed trailers stacked with lumber or pallets of shale inched out of a gate and onto the road. Trucks returned empty. Dirty men in fluorescent T-shirts moved to and fro. I waited and watched as four-thirty approached, then stepped through the gate and scanned the parking lot for Buckles's car. It wasn't there.

I pulled open the door of the office trailer and met the cheery smile of a fortyish woman behind the counter. It turned out Sage Buckles had taken time off from work to attend to a family matter, no idea where. The personnel manager gave me a look at his file without a fight, and his ICE contact was Hope Martinek, address in a little town way across the state in Beaver County, no phone number listed. I wrote it down, along with Buckles's address in Airy Township, and left.

It took about forty minutes to drive to Airy. The southernmost part of it had been home to a little pocket of coal mining, which was unusual, as most mining had been done farther south in Lackawanna, Luzerne, and so forth. Whatever coal worth taking was gone, leaving odd right angles in the land, pools of strange color and unknown depth, and the highest hilltops with trees that clenched like arthritic hands and never grew above eight feet tall. Head down into the valleys, though, and you found woods and clusters of houses, mobile homes, none too close together, very few farms or relics of them, just little places people had carved out to be alone in.

Sage Buckles lived in a white one-story cottage with black trim in the middle of an unmowed yard, up a steep driveway off of a nowhere road called Hurrier Lane. The house was backed by a hill with forest thinning to scrub near the top. I pulled alongside the home and parked, noting the absence of any cars, the windows shut and blocked by curtains. Knocking got me nowhere. A rusty canopy behind the house was empty, with tire tracks ground into the grass. It was bordered by machinery, presumably saved for parts or for lack of another place to put it. I made out a rider mower with no seat, a child's four-wheeler missing two wheels, a shopping cart with nightshade growing up through it, and like that. Mr. Buckles had skipped town.

I called Sergeant Louis Resnik, the PSP station commander in Beaver, to ask for help in case Buckles turned up there.

"Don't know the guy," he said. "No warrants on him. What's it to do with?"

I explained to the sergeant in broad strokes what had happened. "I'm comfortable calling him a material witness at this point," I said. "We need to know where he is. How about his girl, Hope Martinek?"

"They connected, are they? Her, we know. In and out of treatment, petty larceny, solicitation, prostitution. I don't see an address in our system. Okay, I'll get word over to Beaver PD, maybe the county. Good luck to you."

THE LAB sent a report on Penny's cell, and we all gathered in Ross's office to make sense of it. The gist was that the phone had Kevin's prints all over it, which we'd be able to Branch in as evidence at the preliminary hearing. None of them printed in the blood, mind you, and of course he'd have reason to handle the phone in perfectly innocent ways. But there were only the two sets of usable prints, his and Penny's, which we'd matched off of other personal items of hers.

And something else. Bethlehem sent a disc containing data and files from the phone, everyday text messages and photographs, including some that Penny had attempted to delete but were still lurking like germs in the circuitry. There were a few photos of Eolande in and around the Cavanagh home, in Kevin's arms, in hers. Images Penny had taken of herself in the bathroom mirror were from a limited palette: sultry, sad, mysterious. I was reminded that her beauty was rare and startling for the area; once you really knew what you were looking at, it was like finding a morel or an arrowhead. She was also a devoted photo-chronicler of Maiden's Grove, near and far. I would have liked to have stopped there but the lab dug deeper, into a darker seam of Penny's life.

A watch of white gold lying on a bedside table. A naked man from the back, silhouetted in a bathroom doorway, and in the foreground, the form of a woman I took to be Penny herself, stretched out on tangled sheets, also naked. The man was not Kevin and the bedroom was not the trailer's; the furnishings were too fine, the light too soft, the bed too large and white. For good measure, Penny had taken some other images from that bedroom, including art on the walls. And then a self-portrait of just her face, her dark hair swimming around her in a large white bathtub. Next was a series that, per the Bethlehem lab, had been sent to Penny's phone by another device. In this series, Penny was featured first giving oral sex and, from there, other acts. We saw very little of the man in the photos, but from the hints we got he was younger than Kevin or the other figure pictured, and in an unfamiliar living room.

"You don't like to see that," Ross said for something to say, closing out the last of the photographs and leaning back in his chair. "And yet."

"It's a motive," said the sheriff. "She was stepping out."

I drew breath to speak and stopped myself. Ross cut his eyes sharply in my direction and said what I was thinking. "Hillendale's going to say it could easily have been one of these guys, or even yet another, with motive and opportunity. A jealous lover, whatnot. It goes both ways."

"Who are these guys?" the sheriff asked. "Could this one be Heffernan?" he said, pointing to the second series of photos. "We should send these up to Tioga County, see if they can match him up."

"Can we go back to Heffernan's girlfriend with this?" I asked. "Talk to her again?"

"Oof, you want to have that conversation, go ahead," said Dally.

"Hillendale wants a discovery conference this week, so he's going to see these," the district attorney said. "And I'd be interested to put them in front of Kevin, see what his reaction is. We haven't got Buckles. So Hillendale will ask for a continuance and get it, and we'll be running around doing his work for him. Or, I should say, you all will," meaning me and Dally and whatever troopers we could rope in.

We parted ways and I headed out. I patrolled a fair amount in spring and summer, usually on a wooded hill up a dirt road where it intersected with 37. Sometimes I'd leave the vehicle and find a stream to put my feet in and listen to the water click the rocks, and I'd snooze until the radio woke me up or I felt guilty enough to make myself useful. There was this one ravine, I don't know whose land it was, but there were no houses nearby and nobody ever told me not to go there. You cut down a steep slope and you'll find at the bottom a carpet of moss and a creek going through it. I went there and took my shoes off and was content. My cell phone chimed. It was, of course, a text from Shelly Bray, the only human being who ever texted me. Her visit to the station the other day had made me know that I should not continue with her if I valued my job and cared what people thought of me. But she had also made clear that she was not going to take my no for an answer, nor my silence. What better place for the final conversation than this neutral ground, this pretty glade? A place to say goodbye. I told her where I was.

It wasn't long before I heard her car pull up behind mine on the road overhead. I watched as Shelly swung herself down, tree trunk by tree trunk. She wore hiking boots, shorts, and a V-neck T-shirt. She smiled when she saw that I saw her, and though it was my instinct to discourage her, she looked happy and I liked her and was glad to see her. I smiled back and waved.

By the creekside, she put her hands on her hips and glanced around at the fluttering sunlight through aspen leaves, the stream, my bare feet. "Make many arrests down along the creek?"

"Creek isn't going to police itself."

Somewhere nearby a robin reasoned with itself and a wood thrush sang, *Frito Lay.* Shelly settled down beside me, nestled in, and I felt the weight of her breasts, free beneath her shirt. "I'm glad you answered." She kissed my neck and began to work at my belt with her hands.

"We've got to talk. I'm serious."

"There's time. God, you're always thinking. Can't you just."

I've got to tell you something. As Shelly tugged my gear and clothing away from me, I was saying to myself, Why not, why not, why not. I say that to myself. I'm a person, and we need things. Why not. And when she in three or four simple motions stood, pulled off her own clothing, enclosing herself within the forest, with me, without the flow of time, I kept thinking it, Why not, why not. We made use of the glade. And I remember the very moment that I learned what I had to tell. Shelly lay on her side on a flat, mossy rock, one leg over my shoulder, looking at my face and trailing a hand in the stream. I knew I didn't have long. She closed her eyes and reached a hand between her legs. The feeling was life itself where we connected and there was something blameless in it, and that felt new. And suddenly I was overcome, nearly, by a new kind of guilt, or an old guilt made new again. Shelly had been no threat to my wife, my Polly. And then she was. And that was the answer why not. She arched, and I came, and we lay side by side. I couldn't end things there.

Back at the station, I put a call in to Francis Sleight to see what, if anything, had been done on our various cross-border matters. The lieutenant wasn't in and I didn't leave a message. I received an email from Lee Hillendale, saying he'd spoken with Casey Noonan and learned little more than what Noonan had told me. An LLC fronted by Andy Swales had bought out a number of his properties, including a piece of land with a new house in Airy Township, unoccupied. A search of the registry returned only the name of the company, Ton L, LLC, and a Scranton street address. None of the members were named.

But around lunchtime I did get a visitor from upstate. A knock on the door from Penny Pellings's uncle Ron Chase, large and sagging. He shambled in and took a chair unbidden. And though he greeted me genially, there was something aggressive in him, like he owned the place. I asked him what had brought him out all this way, having a notion of what the answer would be.

"You know, I was just curious what's been happening with the Penny thing, and then I thought, why not just head out there and see some of the boys from the squad?" By this I took him to mean the Wild Thyme Volunteer Fire Company. "See how everything's getting along." No mention of his son Bobby, who I'd seen arrested in the First Ward the other night.

"Yeah. Well, we've got some active, uh, ongoing..." I flipped through some papers on my desk. "Anything new on your end?"

Chase's eyes narrowed. "You know very well."

"So you talked to Bobby?"

"Yeah, I talked to him. He was behind glass on a damn phone, surrounded by all the finest niggers in town."

"Hey. How do you want this conversation to go?"

"What do you want me to say? I'm his father. And I want to know what the—what's happening."

"Even if I knew a thing, I couldn't tell you."

"You were there."

I shrugged.

"Admit it. Bobby described you exact."

"All right. Yeah. I didn't know it was him at the time, but."

"Who was he with?"

I tried for a mix of pity and irritation, and kept my mouth shut.

"What was he doing? You see him do a thing wrong? I know they got him charged on, uh, drug conspiracy. But this prostitution thing, this underage girl . . ."

I repeated my last answer.

"Listen, I can't talk to no Binghamton cops. They're pissing in my face. But I think you understand. Bobby's not one of them. He's one of us."

"He is?"

The old man cursed me and stormed out.

CHARLES MICHAEL HEFFERNAN's girl Vicki Jelinski lived with their children in a two-family home in Johnson City, down where the houses end, across from a concrete contracting business. Mac trucks and flatbeds in corrugated metal stables, all going to rust behind a chain-link fence. To the north, Highway

17. To the south, a railroad track cut a green path through the city, same line that ran through the First Ward.

The house itself was shingled in yellow asphalt, with some pieces missing to reveal a layer of brown beneath. I looked at the doorbell, looked at the file in my hand, which contained printouts of some of the explicit images from Penelope Pellings's cell phone. The Tioga County coroner had matched one of the unidentified men in the photo to Heffernan's corpse using forearm tattoos—it was him, no doubt. But his ex didn't know anything about it, and I had been tasked with getting all I could out of her, anything useful. I had shown up during school hours, hoping to avoid any complications from kids being home. What a thing.

I rang the bell. Vicki herself answered, unsurprised. Her hair was slicked in place with some kind of gel and dyed purple and red. She had a baby on her hip.

"Come in," she said. "Nothing I say's going to be any different than what I told the other cops before." Her voice was deep and round and unhurried, and she spoke in a near-monotone. The baby stared at me, silent and unknowable.

The house smelled like fried eggs and was littered with bright plastic toys. Framed photographs of four children decorated the walls and shelves, including one professional portrait showing Heffernan neatened up and in the role of father. I saw nothing that would indicate a man's permanent presence in the home.

Vicki laid the baby on a blanket on the floor and took a seat on the sofa, and pointed me toward a leather chair that had been scratched by a cat.

"I don't know his friends, I don't know why anybody wanted to kill him, and I didn't do it. I was working," she said.

"Where is it you work?"

She named a chain restaurant on the parkway. "My ma helps with the kids," she said. "He was good giving us money, but he's not the home type."

"He has, what, two kids?"

"Yeah. She's his. Daniella," she said, gazing at the infant lolling on the floor. "And a son, Colin. My other two boys are older, like eight and ten."

"She's a sweetie. He get along with the other kids' father?"

"They don't know each other."

"Would he have any other children?"

She looked alarmed at the suggestion, but said nothing.

"But, he saw other women, and you, you two weren't exclusive, I'm saying."

"When he was around, he was with me."

I nodded, but didn't understand her answer. "So Mikey, that's what he went by, he worked in food service? That how you met?"

"He sold drugs."

I laughed.

"He's dead, so why lie? And you got to know that about him already, being a cop. I don't know who he did business with. I wouldn't tell you if I did."

I looked down at the file on my lap, then back up at her. "I just want to understand what your relationship was. You're not aware he saw other women?"

"I don't know." I heard vulnerability.

"The name Penelope Pellings mean anything? Penny?"

Vicki's eyes widened. "No," she said.

I didn't believe her. I looked at the folder in my lap again. "What would it mean to you . . . what would it mean if I told you we knew he was stepping out?"

"What would it mean?" Vicki's voice raised in pitch and volume. "He's them kids' father. He's dead. What do you want? What's it mean to you?"

"I want to know who killed him and why."

"He got killed over some whore? That what you're trying to say?"

"I don't know, hon. I think maybe."

"He was in the business he was in."

"Yes." I stood to leave, the photographs hidden in the file under my arm. "If there's anything more I should know . . ."

She showed me to the door. I looked up and down the street and saw, in a parked sedan, a man watching Vicki's house. I got in my patrol truck and idled a moment, then pulled away. The sedan followed me all the way back downtown and then passed once I pulled up to the bay doors of the police station. I didn't get a good look at the driver and he turned the corner and disappeared before I could follow.

Since I was near enough, I stopped by Carmichael & Williams. I had no appointment and didn't want one. It cost me nearly an hour waiting in the lobby until a secretary led me to Swales's office. The lawyer waved me in and I shut the door and sat, and took a moment to look him over, without hostility or judgment. He was too self-contained to break the silence. His face betrayed very little, but there was something he couldn't quite keep inside himself, some haze of rude health rising through his shirt.

I opened the file and took out the photographs that concerned him, and set them on his desk. He didn't look down.

"What am I going to see there?"

"It's nothing you don't know."

He reached out his left hand and his shirt cuff slid back to reveal a white gold watch. He took Penny's nude self-portrait and stared at it awhile. "I'm going to miss her. She's dead, isn't she?"

I said nothing.

"So you tell me, Officer. You're a lonely divorced guy and you had some pretty young girl cleaning your house. And for whatever reason, one morning she comes into your bed. And she does things for you . . ."

"For whatever reason."

"Things that wake you up. For whatever reason. She's not feeling loved at home—"

"Come on, Andy."

"No, I mean it. That and, I don't know, she has hopes for a bigger world. For herself. I don't love what that maybe says about me, but that must have been . . . somewhere on her mind."

"And what did she get?" I said. "I mean instead. What did you give her?"

"I know better than this."

"How much did you pay her, actually, to clean your house? Did you know she was an addict?"

"This conversation is over. If you need me again, you'll go through my lawyer." I stood to leave. Swales pushed a long breath through flared nostrils. "Henry. Don't pretend you don't understand this. You do. You're no better than anyone else, friend. And it doesn't make you a murderer any more than it does me." There was a knowing look in his eye, and a faint false smile that took as much out of me as it did him.

"Don't leave Holebrook County," I said. "Not till this is over."

FREMONT LAKE is near Pinedale and Big Piney, Wyoming, where I once lived and worked and was married. It was ten, eleven miles long, narrow and deep, undeveloped at the shore, other than campsites where people sought seclusion or a place to go wild. Six hundred feet deep toward the middle. I fished my share of trout out of there. We had a canoe.

We were all trained and certified rescue divers, us in the Big Piney department, and some firefighters and EMTs too. Trained and certified, but never had to use the training because there were experts around. Back home in Wild Thyme, I was going to have my chance.

Nine a.m., when the sun rose and skimmed across the surface of Maiden's Grove, I was pulling on a wet suit alongside a beefy ex-Marine named Matty Lehl. Matty was an assistant chief in the Wild Thyme Volunteer Fire Company, a grumpy cuss full of procedures. Anyone could see he lived for mornings like this. Me, I did not. Death and rot didn't bother me on land, not even the smell of it that much—it was easy enough to fool myself that I was separate from it long enough to get the work done. The landlocked dead caught up with me only after, and not to horrify, but to connect, it seemed. On the other hand, I felt no safe distance from the drowned. They come apart with no mercy and spread death everywhere, death out of proportion, coating you with it inside and out.

I set my mask atop my head and tossed borrowed fins into the county's inflatable dinghy, which Deputy Jackson manned. Matty joined us, Jackson tugged the outboard to life, and we cruised into the lake. The boat rode low in the water, weighed down with tanks and grappling hooks and all. Matty lounged at the bow.

"State police didn't want to send a team? Lake this size, a few pair of us, we'd finish in a day. This could take through tomorrow." It was clear he hoped it would.

"Yeah," I said. "Well, we didn't ask. I don't think she's down there."

"That won't make the dive go any faster. You think the boy did it, the O'Keeffe boy?"

I didn't answer. On the south shore, Rhonda Prosser stood watching through field glasses. I wondered if we'd have a TV crew joining us before we were done.

"Well, if she's down there, and she moved, she'd have moved toward the outlet to January Creek." Matty inclined his head toward the southeastern corner of the lake. "You want to start there, sweep up to the north, and back around, or what?"

"You're the boss."

"My view is, what is the middle, about seventy-five feet deep? Let's not get down that far unless we have to. If she drowned, she'd likely be toward the edge anyway."

Privately I felt that if she were anywhere below us, she'd be wrapped in a chain and sunk deep, eyes open, waiting. But we did it Matty's way, chugging over to the outlet and falling backward into the shallows. Once our splashes had calmed, I was drawn into the weird tapping silence of diving. We moved to within three feet of shore, a plain of mud and rock. Sunnies darted out of my path. January Creek's pull was gentle, and we lolled northwest against it. No matter how clean Maiden's Grove was supposed to be, our flashlight beams caught tires maybe every sixty feet. We yanked them loose, and anything else man-made we saw, billowing sediment into the water all around us. The work was slow and cold, punctuated only by fallen trees rising out of the gloom. Toward the center of the lake, starweed grew in fine green tendons, mixed with pond-weed of red and purple. Seen from the surface the underwater jungle had always brought home a feeling of not knowing what lay beneath and not wanting to find out. But I could get used to them underwater, a curtain from the shallows and a dense forest up close. When I swam too near they swayed and clung to my fins.

I moved through it and was startled when, all of a sudden, the forest disappeared; I looked behind me at a line the vegetation wouldn't cross, a wall of it stretching right and left as far as I could see; I looked below at a steep slope into black; I could not see the other side. Above me, sunlight roiled on the lake's surface far more distant than I liked.

After breaking for lunch we searched the south shore, dredging up a collection of beer bottles, tires, televisions, flip-flops, and toys, but no sign of Penny. A sunken dinghy contained no secrets.

Matty and I surfaced to change tanks, put our elbows up on the county inflatable, and floated with Deputy Jackson, turning our faces to the sun. A kayaker had joined us on the lake. Rhonda Prosser's gray, twinkling dreads gave her away, even at a great distance.

"I guess we have to go down there and see Davey," said

Matty, crestfallen. I took that to be a diver's expression I wasn't familiar with. "I don't know how much you've done at that depth—"

"Not much."

"So stay close, stay in sight of each other. It ain't pretty down there."

We circled down, the beams of our flashlights cutting through the dark, the dark closing in again just as quick. I blew out my ears. At fifty feet I began to feel some pressure and, looking up, fought an urge to surface. We got to within sight of the lake's bottom, which might as well have been another planet, so empty was it, at first. A small cylinder rose out of the mud. I picked it up and the mud coating it swirled away: salt stoneware with a faint blue pattern, a bird. A toddy jar left by an ice fisherman long ago. My light caught something distant, a reflection of metal or glass, and my heart started to pound. I gestured to Matty and moved in closer. Under a fine layer of sediment, a vehicle, too small to be a car. A snowmobile upside down. From its body type, it was older, maybe as old as the sixties or seventies. Under it, a shapeless wad of fabric was disguised by the lake's floor. I pulled at it and it flaked away into the water around me, revealing bone beneath. I swam back in a panic. Matty caught my attention and directed his beam around us. Several more dead hulks of machinery lay scattered in the mud, though nothing else that looked like a body. We surfaced. Back at the boat, I removed my mouthpiece and said:

"What was that?"

"That was Davey," said Matty Lehl. "Davey MacCabba. He's one reason you don't see too many of us at Maiden's for sport."

"Well," I said, "why is he still down there? I mean . . ."

"Good question. Been down there, oh, thirty-nine years now? And a half? Since '70 or so. Bunch of old boys went out ice fishing too early in the season, ice started to crack, they all left their machines and ran the fuck back to shore. But Davey, he—do you want to hear this?"

"I have to, now."

"So the story goes, he was going about sixty, he doesn't know the conditions, and he busts through. But it was fast enough to where all of him didn't make it under in one piece. The ice took his head clean off and it rolled a good way north. The littlest guy in the fire department tied a rope around himself and walked out there to get it. They thought they'd get the rest of him come spring, but they never did."

"But . . . why not?"

"Davey didn't have much family. And they had the head."

LEE HILLENDALE asked Magistrate Heyne for a continuance, given that the alibi witness, Sage Buckles, was still nowhere to be found; Heyne gave Kev three more weeks before prelim. No good reason not to. The continuance worked for us too, and I logged many an hour searching for the missing yellow pickup and signs of Penny. The weather got hotter, and though with every passing day Penny's chances of survival withered away to nothing, there was a certain kind of grim freedom in those days for me. Not so for Kev, who remained locked up in county.

At the sheriff's urging, I visited once to show him the pictures we found on Penny's phone. This struck me as cruel, but we had to have his reaction, so in I went to the cells to show him through the bars, so as not to have to chain him to a table.

He did reach for them, likely to destroy them, but with no real violence or hope. "It don't make any difference," he said.

He didn't have much to say after that, not any of the times I saw him. It was hard to tell whether sobriety had killed a part of him or brought something back to life, some channel of thought or sense long stifled.

Kevin's jail time was a headache for Ed Brennan, who was on the hook to the grocery store magnate regardless of labor shortages. Though Kev was a drunk, and unbelievably simple in some ways, he had been able to focus on the subtleties of carpentry and joinery to a rare degree. Ed valued his work highly. Through some tortured logic, he partly blamed me for the loss of his worker, and thus, early that June, he convinced me to moonlight after my shifts policing Wild Thyme.

So one day after closing and locking the station door, I stowed my belt in the gun safe and stripped naked. From a bag under my desk I took a pair of work shorts and a T-shirt that was still stiff with yesterday's sweat, and put them on. Then I locked the office, got in my personal truck, and headed to Fitzmorris. At Liz and Ed's farmhouse, a rooster strutted across the driveway. Little Ed, who was seven, had a rusted lawn tractor up on ramps, and lay beneath it turning a wrench, only his elbow and bare feet visible. I drove past the house to the scrubby woods behind.

Ed's workshop had escaped the bounds of one mere building. His materials were scattered over several acres of field turning to forest behind his house: a lumberyard full of ancient wooden beams, rafters, and siding, some scrap metal and scaffolding, and half a dozen large trucks that almost ran, shoulder-high in blackberry brambles. At the center of this maze stood a lofty garage with several bays cobbled onto a much older barn and surrounded by a gravel apron. A radio blasted classic rock and Ed sang along, a pipe clenched in his teeth. He stood poised over an ancient beam with a wooden mallet and a two-inch chisel. While he had a boundless, almost religious capacity for work, his rotating gang of employees did not. So here was I, wrestling beams and hogging out pockets with him until dark, once the others had gone home for the day or out to the bars. I'd asked Ed to apply my wages against my land contract for his late Aunt Medbh's house, where I lived.

"Henry," he called. He set down his hammer and chisel, sighed expansively, and said, "You know what? I like to drink beer and work on buildings."

"Yessir, I know."

"There's nothing better, I find."

"I can think of some things," I said.

"What, Saint Francis, finding a bird's nest in the forest, alone?" He looked around him, up into the leaves, and pointed with the stem of his pipe, from which he smoked a mix of tobacco and homegrown. "Hey, an indigo bunting." Bending over his work once again, he shaved a sliver of wood out of a mortise and peered at the result.

Inside the garage, I passed a roadster convertible half covered with a tarp, raccoon prints crisscrossing its dusty windshield. On a workbench I found the mallet and chisel I had been using, and returned outside to where a beam lay on mason's lifts. The timbers had been salvaged from a Bradford County barn dating back to the 1850s. Our first job was to convert them to the dimensions of the new, smaller building that, as of yet, existed only in blueprint. We had been measuring and measuring again, dadoing pockets in the sills for the rafters and floor joists to sit in, and hogging out mortises where beam would meet beam, pinned with fresh locust pegs. I studied Ed's pencil markings where they lay over the original craftsmanship; you could see roman numerals scratched into the dark surface a century and a half ago. Fitting my chisel to a line, I struck a blow and was lost in work.

The truth was I did enjoy those evenings, the sun kaleidoscoping through the trees, seeing Liz and the kids. Later, as the mosquitoes took flight and the sun was almost gone, Ed and I perched on the tailgate of my truck, drinking bottles of cold pale ale.

"I don't know anymore," said Ed.

"Yeah."

"Willard Meagher came by today." He shook his head. "I had the feeling he didn't think we were going to get this done."

"Yeah." I didn't either.

"It's like the artist who sits still for three years and then, whoosh, a perfect butterfly. You follow me? We're sitting still now. But Willard sees sloth, junk in a heap. He thinks, where's the progress?"

"Progress is overrated."

"Yeah. What're you going to do when you're done making progress?"

"Make some more, I guess."

"Exactly. And if all you ever do is make more progress, doesn't that call into question the very notion of progress itself?"

"What about hiring more hands, any luck?" I asked.

"I'm not rushing into new commitments," he said.

We had dinner and the kids got put to bed over their strong objections, and as the night got dark we—me, Liz, and Ed— made it to the fire pit to rehearse once again as the Country Slippers. We had a gig coming up in July, so we took it fairly seriously, always remembering to drink beers before they got warm.

After a long, veering drive back to my place in the hills of Wild Thyme, I bumped to a stop in my driveway, stepped out, produced my johnson, and took a long piss, gazing up at the stars. The world was blinking on and off, and I was the kind of drunk and high where I'd spend about an hour muttering to my wife Polly. While I often thought about my wife and tried to reach her with some purposefulness, this was not that; I'd long avoided this particular approach as self-deception. I may already have begun telling Poll about things, when I noticed I was not alone. With some difficulty I put the buzz to one side and focused on the set of headlights moving slowly past my driveway.

I N THE hot afternoon Ed and I rode in his flatbed up a rutted track. Several large timbers were strapped down behind us, on their way to Willard Meagher. It was a silent journey, no bullshit, no radio, no toughening up on any dank homegrown. After having seen nothing recognizable take shape either in Ed's studio or at the site, Meagher had, in the nicest possible way, demanded assurances. Waiting for us on the hilltop above Walker Lake was Willard himself. His brown hair was turning to silver and his silver goatee was turning to yellow. There was nothing showy about him save a large gold watch on a hairy wrist. He wore a short-sleeved shirt and shorts, and leather sandals.

A young woman, blond, stood beside him in a tank top and work shorts. Hands were shook, and Willard introduced the woman as Julie, his daughter. We knew each other. She was an EMT with the professional crew out of Fitzmorris. I had seen her at many an MVA and one murder scene of sorts, spoken with her some. She knew her job, and we each had the thing of, hey, we can skip the part where we talk about what a shame it is. Of course it's a shame.

After lighting a small cigar, Willard put his hands on his hips and gazed about him. Ed led him off to the site, which they framed with their hands, imagining the barn there. Julie looked as if she wanted to join them, but stayed.

"Never seen you out of uniform," she said to me.

"I don't get out much," I said.

"Second job?"

"Just a few hours on the side," I said. My contract with Wild Thyme forbade moonlighting. "A favor. Don't tell anyone you saw me, or I'll get fired."

"Ha. I hear you. Or, wait. Are you even here?"

"I never made the connection with you and Willard."

"Yeah . . . yeah. Dad's got his projects. This is one I'm taking an interest in." We watched Ed and Willard rearrange the air and sky around them.

A word about Ed Brennan's way of putting a building together. He was a master in reconstruction and restoration, carrying history forward in structure. It mattered to him where a particular post or tie came from, how it had been joined to the frame as a whole, where the building had stood, who owned it and how it had been used. Because it mattered to him, it mattered to me. If you didn't care about this, if what you wanted was a sturdy outbuilding with few concessions to history, you might build your barn square rule. This means you take your timbers, rugged individuals all, some still retaining the shape of the tree trunk on three sides, and fit them into a standard system of measurement, frame them that way, one and done. Ed worked scribe rule. Scribe rule construction embraces the unique timbers you have at your disposal. You love the pieces you have for what they are. But it means you have to lay everything out, over and over, frame it in your mind, frame it on your shop floor, then assemble the components, take them apart, and reassemble them until it's proper. And then you mark them—the old way was with roman numerals scratched near the joints—take them all apart one last time, and then comes the raising.

We had brought three timbers only: two posts and a tie beam. Ed had a dozen or so pegs hand-hewn from green locust wood and a couple mallets.

Ed said, "Henry and I are going to show you the very heart of your barn."

"Oh, good," Meagher said. "I've been curious."

We dropped the timbers gently to the ground. I took one of the posts and held it in place while Ed slid the tie beam to it, fitting the tenon into the mortise a mere inch before gripping up a mallet and pounding at the exterior face of the post. Bit by bit the tenon moved home, until you could look straight through the peg holes and see daylight. It was Ed's most favored joint, a wedged, dovetailed mortise and tenon in a diminished housing, through the post. He hammered locust pegs into the joint, and then a long wooden triangle into the mortise from the exterior side. We attached the other post to the tie beam in the same way. Ed let the cable out from the winch on the front of the truck, threw it over a high branch on the ash tree that provided the only shade in the field, looped it around the tie beam, and raised the H-bent so that it loomed over us like a piece of Stonehenge.

"There it is," said Ed. "The heart."

"This is my barn," Willard said. He stepped through the massive gateway with no little ceremony. When he was done, he said, "I'm almost tempted to sink this in concrete and call it good. What do you think, kiddo?"

Julie nodded without conviction.

"Let me explain," Ed said, pointing to the two mortise-and-tenon joints. "In a manner of speaking, this structure is the stuff of your barn, your studio. This is a dropped-tie bent. You're going to have six of these in a row, connected by plates up top. Plates, they're beams the length of the barn, long ones. And then six smaller bents on the second floor, with plates on top of them. The plates support the rafters, and the rafters support the . . . roof . . . yes?"

Willard had placed a hand over his goatee and was scrutinizing one of the joints. "What's this?" He pointed to where the end of the tenon came out the exterior side of the post. "Can this be fixed?"

"That's what you call the relish. That's the part of the tenon that extends beyond the peg holes. In this joint, you could say the relish is proud of the post."

"What does it have to be proud of?"

"Because it's a strong joint, a through housing. The tenon passes all the way through the post. It's stronger that way. The more tenon, the less apt it is to split."

"Oh," said Willard, brightening. "That's the way it should be."

"Now, in order to find material that'll work for the barn, that can be sized right and is from the correct era historically, we go all over the county. All over the area. Sometimes we're lucky, sometimes we strike out. We get it while we can, right, Henry?"

"Right."

"And we puzzle it together. Each individual member within a unified whole."

"But . . . you could just knock a barn all together and be done by now. I mean, you could just *make* it fit."

"That's one way," said Ed, his horror visible only to me. "But it's not my way."

"These days, I don't know anymore," said Willard. "I don't look for comfort, I don't look for material things. I look for real things. I don't have your expertise, Ed, but I believe that's what I see here."

We had beers and talked a bit of nonsense. When we had a moment to ourselves, Ed muttered to me, "He understands."

Before long, Willard and Julie stood to make the walk down to the lake. "Ed," said he, "I can't give you more time. That's the other thing in life I want, and I can't do without it. But I can give you a pair of hands, no additional cost."

"Oh," said Ed, all politeness. "You know your way around this kind of work?"

"Ha! Not me," he said. "Julie, though."

Julie gave a cheerful wave. A hilltop breeze scrubbed some of the day's heat away. But to Ed it offered no relief. "Sure," he said. "Sure, sure, sure. Welcome aboard."

"My schedule's all over the place," she said. "Afternoons tend to be good? I'll text you."

"The place'll be hers one day," Willard said. "She takes an interest."

"Proper," Ed pronounced it. No woman or girl had ever worked on his crew. It had simply never come up before.

As we drove away, Ed glowered.

"What?" I said, amused.

"Meagher," he said. "Meagher's daughter."

"She's just keeping busy," I said. "Everyone needs a hobby."

"She's a spy." A minute or two passed before Ed muttered, "I'd bend one into her, though."

"Shame on you."

"What? You can see she's got a nice rear end. Like a shelf. To set a drink on."

Sometimes I find it is best to be still.

"Anyway," said Ed, "she'll keep the boys coming to work on time."

ONE MORNING: a lone sunbeam on Kevin O'Keeffe's ass. I had been making the occasional drive to Airy Township to look in on the Buckles place, to no avail, the cottage had remained abandoned, but as I pulled up this time, an eggplant-colored car was parked in the driveway and a woman answered the door. She appeared fortyish, with frizzed, graying hair and the yellow skin of a longtime smoker. Before I could reach the porch, she called out to me.

"He's up to Grace Services. Getting back on the job."

"Oh? I didn't know he'd quit." I left a silence for her to fill, but something shifted and she became wary. I introduced myself. "What's your name?"

"Hope Martinek."

"I don't know you, where you from?"

"Beaver."

"May I come in?"

"He's up to Grace."

"Good, we've been looking for him."

"I know it. He's had some family issues. In Beaver. So, yeah, he ain't been here."

"Family issues?"

"Look, my worker said I was fine to come out here. The court signed off. I been clean for a month now. What do you want?"

"Tell him from me he needs to come in. Tell him no jail time if he comes in and tells us what he needs to. But if I have to use the warrant, no guarantees. The window is closing."

"I'll tell him. Whatever that means."

I raced over to Grace headquarters, but of course he'd left by then. I called over to the sheriff's department to let them know to be on the lookout.

After my shift was done, I headed over to the Brennans to put in my time with Ed. I didn't see Liz. Ed rattled away in customary high spirits until night fell on our work and I drove home, my arms coated with sawdust, a bottle of beer between my thighs. I would have preferred a quiet evening with the fiddle and a book. But Shelly Bray's wagon was in my driveway and she waited for me on the porch, looking puffy and tear-streaked.

"He knows." She burst into angry sobs. "I don't know if he's been looking at my phone, it's not like I give him the chance, I delete everything, I told *nobody*. Nobody, Henry."

"Come inside."

"He's going to take the kids."

"Come on in."

I gave her a scotch with ice—it was the only hard liquor I kept in the house—and we sat at my kitchen table. It was difficult watching her cry. I put a hand on her shoulder, bare but for the strap of a tank top, and despite myself I felt desire for her. She froze at the gesture, and I took my hand away.

"He'd been saying things, little harmless things. Then Steve

Milgraham would be over for a beer or whatever, and he'd—
Steve would . . . talk about you."

"And say what? I've heard it all."

"The smug shitheel . . . it was so small I can't even tell you.
They have their little jokes between them. Waiting for me
to crack."

"You don't know that."

"Oh, yes, I do. Because then . . ." She broke down again, and
I had to wait. "Josh has this other friend up here, some long-lost
guy from high school. I don't know how, because—anyway,
Andy Swales is his name. And he all but told me everyone
knew. And, ugh, he put his hands on me."

"Okay." I stood.

"Where are you going?"

"Out."

"Oh, no. No. That's not what I want. Henry, please."

I stopped and choked out, "What did he do?"

Shelly took a deep breath. "It wasn't like he groped me. It
was like a caress? On the small of my back? And he said something like if I ever get bored, he works from home Fridays,
come over to the lake. 'But you don't get bored, do you?' It was
clear what he meant, I can't say exactly why."

"Okay." I sat back down. The remark Andy had made to me
at his office was now clear: he knew. And probably Josh knew,
but I could not be certain of that, because what kind of man
would tell his friends that his wife was running around? Maybe
Swales had passed our cars together on the side of the road, or
seen something in Shelly she hadn't meant to betray. Maybe he
was bluffing. Whatever the case, I now felt as trapped as ever a

person can be and, despite myself, angry. At myself and at her. "I've been saying, all this time."

"I know. I just love my kids, and . . ."

"Easy."

"I don't want to choose, every time I think of their faces . . ." She trailed off in weeping, then drew herself up. "Jesus Christ, I get so mad."

We both knew that didn't say it. Anger hides pain. So does lust, love, and getting high. But only for so long.

"See you, Henry."

And I thought that she meant it. I thought we both did.

NEXT AFTERNOON, Sage Buckles walked into the Holebrook County Sheriff's Department and identified himself. The receptionist had trouble understanding him; he spoke through an obstruction inside his head that muffled and rerouted sound through his nose. I learned that it was an untreated cleft palate that you couldn't see from looking at his face, except maybe for a quality of pinchedness between crooked nose and mouth, a lack of upper lip.

Later that day in the sheriff's private office, I reflected upon the odd face before me, wondering whether the blow that had broken the nose had also cleft Buckles's palate, or whether the problem had been with him since birth. I wouldn't have wanted to go up against the man who dealt that blow; Buckles was an ox, but more: he reminded me of the time I saw a leopard sleeping at the zoo. Because of his trouble speaking and because of a strong odor of sweat, I caught on slower to the fact that he may have been drunk. Certainly he was operating in a state of permanent befuddlement I'd seen in longtime drug users before: craftiness without logic, talk veering out into the world in repetitions, contradictions, and leaps.

District Attorney Ross was in the middle of explaining for the fourth time that total immunity was off the table, and didn't Buckles want a lawyer?

"I haven't done nothing to require that type of service."

"Then why do you want immunity?"

"You tell me."

"As I may have mentioned," Sheriff Dally said, "Kevin O'Keeffe has named you in a burglary up at Maiden's Grove Lake. We could just charge you."

Buckles's nose whistled. "I don't know who Kevin O'Keeffe is, but I'll knock his head off for him."

"Oh, Jesus Christ," Ross said.

The DA got up and gestured for Dally to follow him, and the two left to discuss matters. I considered leaving the room myself, but sensed Buckles looking at me from his chair, waiting for something.

"You're the one who came to see Hope," he said.

"Yeah."

"You wouldn't have never brought me in. Not on your own." He waited for me to respond. I didn't see the use. His smile was almost tender, and it, more than his strength or his ruined face, told me I was in a room with a dangerous person. "I told them, and I'll tell you. I'm not going to prison, over what? Somebody said I did something."

"Yeah, you did something and a girl went missing. Same night, same place."

"So now I done every damn thing you can't figure out?"

"Account for your time that night. People are telling me all kinds of things. Not you, though. You haven't said shit."

"Who's telling things?"

"How'd you get to Maiden's Grove on the night of May seventeenth?"

"Who says I did?"

Ross and Dally reentered the room. "I'll tell you what," said Dally. "You plead to the burglary and tell us under oath, in detail, about that night—specific times, places, items, and so on. We can't give immunity but we can keep you out of prison. Depending on your health, the judge may require some drug and alcohol."

"Don't need it."

"We'll see. And you need to make restitution to Ms. Prosser."

Buckles opened his hands.

Ross said, "That's, you need to pay her back."

"With money? What if I return the shit?"

A head-slapping conversation ensued where DA Ross tried to get Buckles to understand his need for counsel; he would not be able to enter a plea without a lawyer present. Nobody in the room trusted Buckles to waive counsel knowingly or intelligently; without counsel, he could walk it back on appeal. "I said it all just now," Buckles maintained. Finally, Ross waved his hands in dismissal and told him that he'd have the court appoint him a lawyer to move him through the process.

"There you go," Buckles said. "Thank you, sir. I ain't made of gold."

I followed Buckles out to his car, where Hope Martinek

was waiting in the passenger seat, sweating with the windows down.

Before getting behind the wheel, Buckles faced me. "What now? Ain't we said all that needs to be said? I'll be here on the day."

"I'm just curious," I said. "May seventeenth, then it's midnight, so the eighteenth, Kevin said he had to drive you home."

"That guy talks too fuckin much."

"Yeah. So we know how you got home. How'd you get to Maiden's Grove in the first place?"

"I drove my car," he said. "A car is an invention that runs on gas that takes you here to there? And then Dopey Hopey wasn't feeling good, so she went home. Right, hon?"

Hope looked miserable; she didn't deny it.

"You didn't have a good time?" I asked her.

"I didn't know nobody," she said.

SAY YOU ARE a poor man facing a year in prison for burglary. A year in state, followed by six months of probation and outpatient alcohol monitoring. That's the arrangement we came to for Kevin O'Keeffe, all parties, including Rhonda Prosser, whom we were required to consult as the victim. She was cool with it. Hillendale was able to keep DA Ross from bringing either murder. There wasn't enough there, not yet. Between Kevin's claims of innocence to all but the burglary, the witnesses putting him elsewhere at key times, the phone calls suggesting he had no knowledge of Penny's whereabouts and believed her alive at the time he'd called, the other parties with motive and opportunity, the missing truck, no weapon—the outcome of a trial would be uncertain, and Ross knew it. By not attaching jeopardy to the murder charges, Ross could revive them at any time the evidence allowed. Whether Kevin would eventually have to answer, we'd see.

From a law enforcement perspective, it suited us to keep the sentence light. If Kevin did kill Penny, what good would it do to keep him away for a small-time house burglary? Out, he would have to face his act, and maybe lead us to her in time. It gave Ross a headache. He would be up for reelection, and I suspect he would have preferred a murder conviction or at least a showy trial. It was only fair to him that Kev should get some time in state for the break-in. The judge had fifteen years on the bench and was likely to stand uncontested until retirement age. He tended to sentence right down the middle of the guidelines. We—Dally and Hillendale, mostly—were able to convince him that the lighter sentence was not only practical, it was fair and modern.

So say that's your situation: a year in prison. Your belongings don't merely drift off in the same way yours or mine would in ordinary life. The things of a poor man are carried away by a strong wind.

The sky was gray and smudged with charcoal clouds hanging low. Up at the trailer by Maiden's Grove, I watched as folks picked over appliances and furniture while Kevin O'Keeffe's brother collected what cash he could for them—soggy bills and in some cases handfuls of quarters, destined for Kevin's lawyer, I supposed. And all the while, Rianne Pellings defended Penny's things against the scavengers, boxing them up with slow, sad attention, as if the objects were themselves pieces of her sister, as if all together they were her, or all that remained.

At the county lockup that morning, Kevin had requested that I salvage a book for him. It was actually Penny's, a kind of diary glued into another book's binding and hidden in plain sight by the bed. I had been taken aback, and then angry, that he'd kept it from us.

"There's nothing in it," he'd assured me. "Trust me, I looked. It's just art, writing, and that. It's private. It's the one thing I want."

At the trailer that afternoon, I'd waited until a moment when Rianne was in the yard, walking armfuls toward her car, and headed in. By Penny's side of the bed, there had been a stack of about a hundred books, mostly fiction, many of them long fantasy novels with wild cover art, some nineteenth century poetry books too, Wordsworth and Keats, I remember. I don't know what was to be learned from her tastes other than she was or had been a fan of escapist stories. The book pile had been disarranged by several searches of the room. I found the one I needed, a leather volume claiming to be *Bullfinch's Mythology*. A glance inside revealed blank pages darkened by handwritten verse, what looked like diary entries, and pencil sketches.

The diary remained on my passenger seat for much of the afternoon as, parked behind a closed-down miniature golf business, I lay in wait of speeding cars. Back at my desk, I placed the book in front of me and stared at it. There would be no easy way for the diary to make the journey into county lockup, let alone from there to SCI Dallas (Pennsylvania, not Texas). The question was, would I lock it away out of deference and superstition and honor, or would I read it for the sweep of Penny's life leading to the disappearance? Of course I would read it. Maybe a name or a place would stand out. But as the day dragged on, duty interfered over and over again. Folks needed help stamping out a brush fire, and I was able to show up and do what little I could before the squad sent out a truck. I also responded to a mini-B&E. A window open and only a jar of change missing. I was on the scene about three minutes before a neighbor marched her son over to return the silver and apologize.

AT HOME in my armchair with a growler of the local IPA, I opened the book I came to think of as *Pellings's Mythology*. The first pages were pencil sketches of a triangle of lake at Maiden's Grove seen from the hills. I didn't remember the exact view, and wondered whether it was done from the trailer's roof or from imagination, or a combination. There wasn't much to feel at first—the work of an untrained artist, and something fragile in the little piece of lake nested into the land. The drawings evolved. Different vantage points, different subjects. Kevin O'Keeffe's truck overgrown with grapevine. A tattooed barroom patron leaning back and puking laughter from a mouth three times too big. A man's figure from behind, a shaded-in haze for a head, folds sagging off the torso. A man's mouth and chin only, too close. But always a return to the lake. Penny began to introduce seams of color into her work, thin lines of green running through the woods, dots of crimson. On one page, she'd sewed silver thread over the surface of Maiden's Grove.

One page was left blank except for three words, center. "Tonight's the night."

Song lyrics followed, whether hers or someone else's, I couldn't say. I didn't recognize them.

About a quarter of the way into the book, a woman's figure appeared. In the first drawing, she hung over the surface of Maiden's Grove. The law of gravity would suggest she was diving in from a height, from the middle of the air. But something about the image suggested floating. She had no face. In the next, she had disappeared into the lake without a splash, leaving only one foot and ankle above water. Why did I know it was the lady's, I don't know, something about it.

When writing at length first appeared, smeared by palms and erased words, scarred by cross-outs, it was of a piece with the images and fragments that had come before. The entries spanned several pages, or trailed off after a few sentences. A lot of it repeated itself or simply wasn't clear. The words themselves weren't enough to tell the story, and neither were the pictures. But you put everything together like a dream, and there's something there. If I were to tell you, I'd tell you like this:

It begins with Anna, a young woman creeping through the woods, pursued. The moon was high and nearly full, and she couldn't risk stepping into the light. But staying in the dark of the forest too long would be dangerous. Soon she came to a lake ringed by tall, soft grass in a rising wind. Beyond, a lantern shone in the window of her father's house up in the hills. The fastest way to get home would be to swim across the lake. Of the three possibilities—a sprint around the moonlit shore, a slower creep through trees beyond, or a straight shot across the water—she didn't know which would allow her to live. She stood frozen at the water's edge. It wasn't so much fear of the creatures she couldn't see in the lake, but of the vast, unknown depth below her, or was it, in the end, above her? She had a vision of herself on the surface, a crawling shadow surrounded by moonlight. A vision from a great distance.

She pulled off her boots and flung them away, then waded in. At first the water tugged at her dress, seeming to drag her back the way she'd come. She swam as silent as she was able, listening, keeping her arms and legs below the surface. The sound of the stone hitting the water and the pain between her shoulder blades arrived both at once. She cried out and choked on a mouthful of water. Black against the moon's lilting reflection, her head was breaking the surface in a clear line. He would be able to find her again and again. She dove.

Instantly she was as free as if floating through the air. But there was something else, a current going through her, something more than the lull from her father's moonshine, but less than the nights in bed when she'd put a hand between her legs and brought herself. She now remembered the threat above water only at a distance. Part of her knew she shouldn't want the feeling, but it was too good to give up.

Another stone shot past her into the depths, trailing air. She followed it with her eyes. There was light below, or above.

The next morning, an angler found a dark-haired stranger drowned at the edge of the lake, facedown, arms floating in the water, his legs hooking him to shore. Nobody in town knew him. A newspaper item describing his person went unanswered, and though it was odd to have found a small pair of boots not far from the body, the sheriff had him buried in a potter's field and closed the matter.

Anna had not only lived that night, but awoke safe in her bed the next morning, damp bedclothes the only sign of her swim. For days, she kept silent about the drowned man and avoided the lake, until she couldn't.

One bright day Anna put on a light, too-large dress of navy blue cotton, and brought another old one to change into. She approached the lake through the green woods, avoiding the deer trails that the fishermen took to get there. From behind a mountain laurel, she watched and waited. Sure she was alone, she slipped down a bank of red pine needles and into the water, then under.

She felt no change. She surfaced, dove again, this time forcing herself to open her eyes as she had done that night. She saw nothing but mud, rocks, roots, and pondweed. Swimming out farther, Anna took a huge breath and descended as far as she dared, just to the tops of the weeds thicketing the lake floor. She stayed there until she would either have to surface or die. She tried to breathe, couldn't, and panicked. Her dress flowed around her, dragging. She thrashed close enough to shore to climb her way above the surface.

She waited several more days and into a night when her father passed out, his liquored breath filling the cabin. She eased out the door and walked down to the lake under a belt of stars. She stripped to a thin dress and stepped into the water, the mud squirming up between her toes. She felt leeches on her feet and floated to brush them off, then gave up and let the worms feed. Beside her on the surface was a bladder she'd blown up and cinched with twine.

At first, Anna was unaware that she'd gone under. But at some point, she felt the absence of air. The surface above her—or was it below?—filled her with peace, and though it had been some time since she'd taken a breath, she didn't miss it. In the deep of the lake, she became aware of currents, gentle at first, fanning out in a direction she could no longer be sure of knowing. A glow near the lake's floor. From even a short distance, it appeared as if the weeds dancing below her gave out the light, but, sinking closer, Anna found strands or locks of something very small, possibly alive, moving with some purpose, twisting in the underwater grove.

Again, she awoke safe and damp in her own bedroom, with sounds of her father stirring beyond her door in the room that worked as their kitchen, dining room, and parlor. The odor of pipe smoke and liquor would cover, she hoped, the wild rot scent of the lake.

Alone on one page, "The oceans of other worlds."

Anna did not plan to live with her father, Bernard, forever. He was a distiller tolerated by their community, and for reasons unknown to her, he wouldn't move from their homestead in the hills, not for anything. Anna was not tied to that spot. Though she was young and poor, and lacking in the education to cut a self-reliant figure in any kind of town, she could hunt, fish, farm, butcher, cook, sew, and read.

Anna was both drawn to and frightened of Maiden's Grove. She knew in her body that she could live beneath its surface, and she knew in her mind that this was impossible. If her mother had been home, Anna would have found a way to see if she wasn't alone after all. But as long as Anna had been aware of the lack of a mother, her mother had not been there. Questions about it drew only silence from her father, then suspicious glances, then threats, and one night, the beginning of a beating that Anna escaped after the first few blows. She'd walked to town, the handful of houses scattered into a valley like seed, there to seek the protection and maybe work from the tavern owner who regularly bought Bernard's spirits and always had a kind word for Anna. But he hadn't been there, and being a girl she was not encouraged to stay. A dark-haired stranger had followed her home and lost his life in the lake.

Anna could only guess from her own face what her mother had looked like: high cheekbones, pointed ears, and hair straight as a bolt of black silk. Men noticed Anna now, and they must have noticed her mother then. Bernard had once been a respectable farmer who had cleared one hundred acres for feed corn, wheat, a garden, and a small orchard. That would have been the least he'd need to bring a beautiful woman to his side, Anna supposed. Long ago now. Bernard had sold much of his equipment, including wagon, plow, bridles, horseshoes, scythes and other tools, and much else useful besides. To find the orchard, she had to sift through the saplings that had sprung up everywhere around it, overlaying what used to be producing fields and concealing the odd skeleton of a starved dairy cow.

Alone on another page, "EO."

At a farm seven miles distant, a Mr. Morris did everything her father now would not, taking great yields from his two hundred acres. His herd of belted Galloways could serve as beef or dairy, and he bred his bulls throughout the county. Morris had several sons, the oldest John about her age, and he and Anna had played at romance. She hadn't felt for him the love she'd read about in books; in her heart he was not much more than a possible future to live through. Even so, they'd met in field and forest over the past year. She recalled her wonderment, as they lay in an August field of Queen Anne's lace, at the cock springing from his unbuttoned trousers, dense like iron under its cloak of skin, and, when she took it in her hand, wonderment at the spurt that dripped down her knuckles. He'd lain in a daze and then rose again. He wanted between her legs. Not yet, she told him.

Her father drank more and stopped wanting to eat. A pencil drawing showed Anna tending Bernard's still fire at night, herself alone, with a moon cutting through the forest, small eraser marks making fireflies in a mist. One early autumn evening Bernard collapsed. His breathing turned shallow and he was unable to wake. She ran seven miles to the Morris farm.

What happened there, we can't know, as the journal is silent. We return again to Maiden's Grove, to Anna before a shining surface, otherwise surrounded by black.

"Beyond time, a new space. It was. It reached for Anna, and she reached for it."

Next, a nude image of Anna striding up the hill, the old homestead in near-ruins, a tree growing a branch through a window and up through a hole in the roof. Beside the cabin, her father's headstone and her own.

Penny's notes sketch out the rest of the story: It is sixteen years since she was last seen anywhere, and she has not aged. She is disoriented, strange, naked but not weak. Anna fends off a hunter's attack, breaks the man's neck, and buries the body. She steals clothes under cover of night, passes herself off as a long-lost cousin and nearest living relative arriving to claim the property. But it's no good. She returns to the lake.

PART TWO

PAT GEORGE took a final shot of bourbon, palmed a beer into his sleeve, as was his usual practice, and walked out into the cool September night. He had managed to take first place in the horseshoes tournament at the marina bar in Watkins Glen, New York, that evening. The win came with a two-hundred-and-fifty-dollar prize. As the twilight glow gave way to black, he bought rounds and drank, drank until closing, and now, in the near-empty lot beside the bar, he readied himself for a drive.

Pat slid behind the wheel and turned the key, and the engine of his rattletrap Japanese sports car came to life. A middle-aged car salesman and hard drinker, Pat George was not a successful man, or lucky. He himself wouldn't say so. But something, some sparkle in the air that afternoon, guided his hand, helped send those iron horseshoes home. He could still feel the winning throw leave his fingertips, see it float through the light, high above the watchful faces in the crowd. In that moment Pat had the odd sensation that he could have slowed down time forever as the horseshoe sailed on.

And he had left the bar that night with a woman's number in his pocket. A taste of water after a long dry spell, that ringer clanking down. Bam!

In the safe darkness of the hills beyond, Pat drank his beer, which was already half gone. He turned west on Sugar Hill Road through the state forest. He knew it well, which was good, because he was starting to feel just a bit spinny around the head. Faster he drove, letting the night pull him. There was nobody on Sugar Hill this late; only when he connected with 23 would he have to worry and slow down. As he roared over a rise, it was too late to avoid the sedan pulling out of a blind, nameless road, a road that went nowhere and stopped. His left front grille struck the car's hood with great force. Launched into motion beyond time, beyond control, his car bounced heavily across the road and into a hemlock, sending Pat through the windshield. The car rolled slowly back into the road. They believe Pat remained conscious for some time, tangled in branches overhanging a creek, before fading out and waking up days later in a hospital, permanently unable to breathe, eat, or move on his own. He signed his own advanced directive by blinking his eyes, and died that afternoon.

A late-night passerby, probably also drunk, called it in as a one-car MVA and disappeared, not seeing the other vehicle where the impact had spun it back against a tree in the shadows of the nameless road, or hearing Pat's ragged pleas for help over the creek. So, for all intents and purposes, Schuyler County Deputy Alex Poole was first on scene. By the time he arrived, he would have driven into a scene washed in false dawn by Pat's car, now melting into a white-hot tangle of metal, glass popping, oily flames billowing into the night. And out of the trembling shadows where the second car came to rest, a woman with purple hair lurched toward Poole, screaming through her duct-tape gag, her wrists tied behind her. The deputy didn't know her, but we all did: she was Vicki Jelinski, mother of the late Charles Michael Heffernan's kids.

From Deputy Poole's tape, Jelinksi's account, and the examination, we can reconstruct some of what happened. When the sedan bounced off of Pat's speeding car and slammed into the tree, it broke the trunk's latch. The trunk was lined in plastic sheeting, and contained nothing but Vicki, a spool of vinyl-coated steel wire, two jugs of drain cleaner, a shovel, and several cinder blocks. On impact, Jelinski briefly lost consciousness. When she came to, she realized the trunk was open a crack and she could kick free. She was afraid at first. Then she recognized the red-and-blue pulse of police lights, and knew it was then or never.

Seven minutes passed between Deputy Poole's arrival and that of the next emergency vehicle. We know the trooper reported on scene at 1:17 a.m., and at 1:20 we have the first mention of Vicki Jelinski, the sedan in the woods, and an urgent request for backup. Jelinski begged Poole to stay with her in the patrol car, to get her away and safe. He couldn't leave the scene as it was, and locked her in his vehicle's cage. Weapon drawn, scanning the trees, he approached the sedan and found no sign of the driver.

Poole stepped in front of Pat George's burning car, which hid him from Jelinski's view. Had he not done this, he might have lived. She heard a bang and assumed it was a gunshot. It wasn't: a gas-filled shock absorber in the car's front bumper had become superheated. It exploded with the power of a fifty-millimeter field gun, passing through Poole's left leg below the knee, pulverizing bones and leaving just a narrow strip of skin attaching lower limb to thigh. Jelinski heard the deputy's scream, then saw the man who had taken her crawl from the woods and move across the road. The screams stopped. Poole died quickly, his throat opened with a fishing knife.

As her abductor approached the patrol car, he gave Vicki Jelinski her first direct look at him. He was wearing a ponytail and was thin-faced, almost handsome if not for an overbite, though pain contorted his features and exposed his large upper teeth. He walked clutching his side. She curled up on the floor. With Poole's service weapon he shot out the window glass. I don't know why he didn't finish her right there and then, I guess he had planned it differently. He pointed the .44 at her and told her to get out.

This was when Mrs. Alice Campbell arrived in the ambulance, which was also carrying two volunteer EMTs. A seventy-seven-year-old great-grandmother, Campbell braked to a crawl, not quite believing what she was seeing. But when the man turned the gun on her, she floored it and ran him over.

Orange 2, a fire engine, screamed down the valley. County sheriff's cars and state troopers followed close behind, but not quickly enough. In the distraction of the fire engine's arrival, the man somehow made it to his car, which still ran, and drove away. Alice Campbell thought about following him, but instead turned her attention to the scene.

Five county sheriffs' departments, six municipalities, three townships, and New York State police cast a wide net that night, but the man found a hole and got through. No hospital for three hundred miles in any direction reported anyone like him. Several days later, they'd found the car, a 1989 Cadillac de Ville with VIN numbers removed and New Jersey plates last belonging to a 1994 Honda Accord whose registration had lapsed, abandoned near Wolcott, New York. It suggested a path in the direction of Canada. A reward of ten thousand dollars was offered for information leading to the man's capture, and still he was nowhere.

Vicki Jelinski herself had never seen the man before. He'd struck her, bagged her head from behind, and thrown her in the trunk of his car, her with her youngest still inside the house in Johnson City. The first and last she'd ever seen his face was as he was shooting out the glass of the patrol car. She had no idea why anyone would want to hurt her.

HELICOPTERS THUDDED over my head and gone as I took slow steps through a field in Wayne County, New York, one link in a search line near where the kidnapper's car had been found. There was about thirty of us—state troopers, local police, and volunteers—hunting the wounded animal among the farms and country homes south of Lake Ontario. Wayne County was well north of us and autumn had taken over there, firing the land with gold and red. Cars on a nearby road pulled over to watch our progress.

Sheriff Dally and I had taken a road trip north for the search. We viewed the scene on the state forest road, looked over the sketches of the kidnapper, talked to local and state cops. Vicki Jelinski had been spirited back to Binghamton, gathered up with her family, and relocated. New York State forensic techs had crawled over the car like monkeys picking bugs. They found very little in the way of evidence, and nothing they could use to identify the driver.

By the time Dally and I had arrived, the rush of the manhunt had slightly faded into bureaucracy and scheduled shifts of New York state troopers. We were not much use, and we knew it.

Back home in Holebrook County, we filled a spare sheriff's department office with criminal complaints, records, and court documents. Police sketches of the man had been pinned to the wall—narrow-faced, toothy, long-haired but thinning on top. I'd gotten copies to Jennie Lyn Stiobhard and Andy Swales, but they didn't know him. Swales had communicated through a Binghamton lawyer.

Kevin O'Keeffe had been shipped off from SCI Dallas to SCI Mahanoy in Frackville back in July. One afternoon in September I sat across from him in a private interview room in the prison. His face had hollowed and grown mean in just a couple months. He regarded the sketches with no hint of emotion, finally giving the slightest shake of his head no and leaving without a word.

THE DAWN AIR was cold and heavy and gave up its water to the earth. I lay camouflaged in the tall grass. When it was still dark I had parked my patrol truck up a logging road and walked the unposted triangle of swampland where three roads met at the tip of an arrowhead, including Hurrier Lane, where Sage Buckles lived. His place looked like a junk heap, yeah, but you had to know what that meant—it wasn't that he couldn't get to the dump with his broken washing machine, kitchen stove, old bicycles, lawn mowers, blue barrels, pallets, and so on. To a capable hill person, these were elements, and their usefulness would emerge with a need. I'd grown up in a backyard like his. We never had new things because there was always some fool who didn't know the value of his old things.

Since the summer, Buckles had been doing D&A outpatient treatment in Fitzmorris. Showing up to the center had kept him out of jail, or I highly doubt he'd have come within a hun-dred feet of the alley off Main Street, where the county's misfortunate young, middle-aged, and old addicts waited for their partners, waited for rides, ran down job placements, kept their kids from drifting away for one more month. The first time, I'd watched Buckles take the door of the treatment center, and after, reviewed his report. Neither good nor bad. He'd sworn up and down that he never touched the hard stuff anymore, meaning methamphetamine or heroin, I supposed. But he'd dug in his heels over the bottle, until his caseworker had threatened to send me to his house. For support, he'd listed Hope Martinek as his "live in wife." The next appointment, Hope had come with Sage, and the report got a little more rosy. He'd passed all his urinalysis in that first month, so the county hadn't seen the need for a SCRAM anklet. I'd let up, only driving by his place or Grace Services every couple weeks but not making contact.

This morning Sage Buckles was home, or at least his brown sedan was. I saw no sign of Hope's purple car. Just before eight a.m., the front door swung open and Buckles emerged. I made myself low to the ground. He stomped down the front steps with a cooler in his hand, got in his car, and drove away. I waited to see what would happen once he was gone: for twenty minutes, nothing. I stood, slipped out of the tree line, and walked to the driveway, where I wouldn't leave a trail. From there, I paced around the house, trying to get a look inside the windows darkened by blinds. So far as I could tell, he was the only one using the place.

I headed back to the woods and took another glance at the topo map I'd brought with me. An ATV trail ran along the edge of the scrub, leading north. On the far side of the hill, out of sight, was the Ton L parcel, twenty-five acres climbing the ridge north and over. John Blaine had come and gone there all summer. The southeast corner of the plot kissed the northern edge of six acres belonging to Buckles. The connection surprised me at first. I took the trail.

On the Ton L parcel was a large modern home built into a steep slope. It had four entrances: the front door on the east side of the house, which nobody seemed to use; the kitchen door to the north and out of my line of sight; the sliding double doors to the deck facing south; and the basement door of metal. I slipped through the trees and crouched in some cover to the east. Nothing stirred. I moved down the slope toward the corrugated steel garage, to within sight of the rear of the house, the kitchen door, and the aboveground pool. No cars were in the driveway, and the place looked shut up for the season. I watched it for some time, then headed for my truck and a day of writing speeding tickets.

Late afternoon I was back to my blind on the edge of Buckles's property, waiting. The brown sedan clanked up the driveway just before five-thirty. Buckles's Day-Glo-yellow shirt was covered in black smears, and he looked tired. He slumped up the stairs and into the house, but surprised me by reappearing on the porch in athletic shorts and sneakers, and setting out for a jog. I put my face in the grass and listened to his steps vanish up Hurrier Lane. It wasn't too long before he returned. Buckles had gone to fat but iron lay beneath, and each step up the drive was a sledgehammer falling. He stopped by the house, bent over with his hands on his knees, and puked a small amount. Standing, he rocketed stray vomit out of his ruined nose, wiped his mouth, and looked around him with particular care. My face was down, buried in field grass, and when at last I raised my eyes again he was picking through the junk in his yard. He paused before a blue barrel, lifted the lid, and looked inside. Something tightened in his face. He reached in and fished out a fifth of some neon-green spirit, probably schnapps. He downed a mouthful and put it back and went inside.

I trotted back to my patrol truck, removed my camo, traded my boonie hat for my cap, and drove back to Buckles's place. I had not climbed the stairs and set one foot on the porch before I heard a bellow.

"Back out! Back out! Back out!"

I put my hand to the .40 on my hip and identified myself as police.

"I don't care," said Buckles, shirtless, thudding onto the porch with a loaded crossbow pistol in his hand. A felon's handgun. "Back out."

"You know me, Sage," I said. "Put that thing down before you end up on the news."

His expression lost no ferocity, but he raised the crossbow in the opposite direction from me and without looking, pulled the trigger. The bolt took a chunk of wood out of the porch railing and winged into the yard. He set the weapon down and said, "What do you want?"

"Can I come in?"

"No."

"Sage, I'm authorized to come in on the terms of your plea."

"Fuck you, then, do it."

I put my head inside and smelled old food. "Hope around?"

"She ain't here no more. She's back in Beaver. It gets to

where you can't do what you want to do in your home without someone stepping in. I told her the woods ain't no place to get sober, but she thinks with me in my situation, with you all up my ass, it'll work. Of course it didn't work. She's back home."

"In rehab?"

"Something like that, I don't know. What do you want?"

"I'm here to show you something."

Sage took both police sketches in his hands and said, "Seen him on TV. What do I know him for?"

"I don't know. I just had a feeling."

"Yins always blame me. I don't know him, what am I supposed to know him for? How? You see where I live."

"You know Vicki Jelinski?"

"Who? I don't know anyone."

"You knew Penny Pellings," I said.

"Yeah, I knew her, but . . . so fuckin what? So did a lot of guys."

I took a moment to assess the man before me. Arms folded, chin back, eyes like a pinball machine. "You knew her. Penny."

"I'm telling you, she was out nights, and I was out. A lot of people knew her."

"And you had something she wanted."

"I could say something but I won't."

I ignored his ugly smile and said, "How come if you live out here all alone, you have enough of what she wants to draw her in?"

"I don't know what you're talking about."

"Heroin. Where'd you get it?"

"Can you hear right?"

"Maybe not. But I can smell good," I said. "And I smell something fuckin awful. What kind of ladies' night you having up in here? Is that . . . watermelon schnapps?"

He fell silent. "Hope," he said. "Dopey Hopey came out from Beaver with a bag. I was just trying to make money, get on my feet."

"And your straight job wasn't enough."

"Sure it was. I was just spinning straw to gold."

"I'm curious," I said. "How'd you come to settle in this place, anyway? What's here that isn't in Beaver?"

"Work, I don't know. I did the same thing out there, but it dried up. So I head east." Buckles seemed glad to get on a new subject. "I see this place, ain't nobody lived in it years, it's cheap, I think maybe I'll fix it up. Flip it, maybe."

"Ah. If nobody lived in it, who'd you buy it from?"

"A local guy. A lawyer."

"Andy Swales?"

"Who? No, an old guy named Noonan."

"You get along with your neighbors?"

"I'm telling you, bud, I don't know anybody. I used to clear trees and get drunk. Now I just clear trees. Is this America?"

WITH KEVIN GONE, my moonlighting job with Ed Brennan became permanent, and I followed his crew from site to site as they gathered material that they would need to build Willard's studio. Ed was in full artisan mode, exploring, spending his own money, and making fine distinctions.

One evening I worked along the side of a barn, jamming a crowbar under the fascia boards and ripping them off the ends of the roof. A century of bird, bat, and rodent shit, straw, dust, and powdered wood had gathered in the spaces between the rafters, and I'd gotten a faceful pulling my first few boards. I peered up, shoved the crow under the board, and heard a squeaking scrabble within, just as a warm, wet spray coated my face, some in my eye, some in my mouth. I spat, but it was too late: bat's blood. Part of the animal came out on the tip of the crowbar. A quick, unfair death.

I cursed. Below me and off to the side, Julie Meagher was prying nails out of siding boards, every so often stopping to retrieve the metal off of the driveway with a magnet on a stick. She had been doing this all day. Hearing me, she looked up and saw my bloody face.

"A bat," I said.

"Sick!"

I threw the bar in the dirt. "I'm going up to the creek."

"Me too." She unbuckled her tool belt, revealing a band of sweaty cloth around her midriff. We walked in the direction of the woods. "Don't get me wrong, I love pulling nails," she said, "but it's not as if I can't use a speed square and a circ saw. We're always tearing shit apart. When are we going to actually put this thing together, is what I want to know?"

"We don't always know what we're doing until we're doing it."

"I'm going to dream about barn siding."

Often I had occasion to consider what made Ed's timber-frame buildings rise to the level of art, at least as far as some people thought. In art, I'm told, there is nothing new under the sun, nothing new since man tamed fire. Except ways of seeing things. Everywhere in Holebrook County barns lasted long past their usefulness, until they became land itself. If you cleaned one up, laid its joinery and beams bare, put in windows, evicted nature, I guess you could call it what you want to. If it was art, you couldn't make it without spilling some bat's blood.

Julie removed her work boots and sat on a rock upstream from me as I cleaned my face and hands. I took a couple glances at her as she reclined, the thickness of her body, the way everything about her fit together in a kind of easy strength. She was I guess a bit younger than me but had grown up in the area, and had been a jock, a soccer player in fall and a miler in spring. I'd played high school football, so I was familiar with the edges of that—go, Hawks. But our worlds were different. We were different. She seemed to know everyone in town, young and old. An enthusiast, a joiner. Where I'd been raised by a father like an ironwood tree. He never took off his camo except on Sunday, when we'd sit in an off-brand church and hear peculiar, harsh beliefs. My family's home had been small, and in the hills, and I barely graduated high school. I hardly knew what to say to somebody like Miss Julie if we didn't have an MVA or an overdose to occupy us.

When we got back to the barn, two of the crew shook their heads in mock disapproval. Ed had arrived from some other site and was sticking his nose into everyone's work. Julie sidled up to him, hip-checked him gently, and followed him inside the structure. Them two were always joking.

That night I called Liz to ask what I ought to do, and she said come in to the clinic and she'd give me the brace of rabies shots I probably didn't need but couldn't risk skipping.

So early the next morning I was waiting for her in the clinic parking lot. She smiled kindly enough when she pulled in. We walked up the stairs and into the white-walled suite, white walls with scuffs and dings and mismatched waiting-room chairs. I told her, in some detail, what had happened.

"I don't know, though," I said. "Rabies is in the spit. So isn't this backwards? My spit, his blood."

Liz shrugged, pulled her hair into a ponytail, and unwrapped a syringe. "I'm going to stick you."

"Bats are everywhere. I have one behind one of my shutters on the porch."

She gave me the injection. "You don't have rabies, man, but if you do, it's a bad way to go. It's best to be careful." She gathered the trash and the syringe and disappeared into the next room, calling, "You are being careful, right, Henry?"

"What do you mean?" I said. But I knew.

She returned. "I just wish that if you have . . . unfinished business out there, that, that you don't screw the pooch. It's a small town. I hear stuff."

There was forgiveness in her tone, but it was clear she knew something. The truth was that I missed Shelly Bray's company, but even if I wanted to see her, there was no way I could, not anymore. I nodded. "It's over with."

"Okay, honey," she said. "You have two more shots to go. Come back in a week."

THE BARN of the moment was in Susquehanna County, north of the borough of Susquehanna and east of the river. Evenings, I joined the crew there and spent a couple hours cutting briars away from the structure and heaping rotten siding in a pile. The hills were still green, but starting to burst out in vermilion and orange. Still, summer had elbowed its way into the fall, and it stayed hot. I had just removed my shirt and doused myself with water when Ed arrived. He put his hands on his hips and examined the frame where the siding had been peeled way.

"It's a Frankenstein, a kludge," he said. "Everything sistered on everywhere. I don't know what does what. We'll see what we get. Hey, I want to show you something."

At that moment, Julie Meagher came up, her face raccooned in dust from where she'd worn safety goggles. "Can I come?"

"Sure, sure, sure," said Ed, too quickly to be cool.

We got in his truck, Julie riding the middle seat, her hip pressed against mine. Ed drove up a logging trail just to the tree line, where he parked and we got out. He took a small cooler and we walked a trail through brush and into deep woods. The day had been like the flat of a knife in the sun, but turned cool and fluid in the trees. Pale green ferns curled around boulders. We crossed where a stream had dried and left only cracked mud, and proceeded up a steep slope to where daylight broke in again. A quarry, now abandoned, had been cut into the mountainside, a clatter of gray stone sliding into a leveled clearing. Pinks grew in clusters among the stone pieces. The view east encompassed the entire Starrucca Creek valley, the creek itself where it met the Susquehanna River below, sparkling in the slanting light, and the railroad viaduct winding north in the crook of a mountain.

"The Erie Railway," Ed said. "The bridge is what, a hundred fifty, hundred sixty years old, actually. And they still use it. It's made of blue shale. We might be standing on the place where the stone came from." We each opened a beer. Ed patted at his overalls pockets, found a corncob pipe, and filled it with tobacco and weed. "Look at how it fits right in there." He framed the viaduct with his hands, and placed them in front of Julie's face. "All nice."

"All nice," she repeated, handing me the pipe without smoking.

On the walk back to the truck, a low patch of color caught my eye: a cluster of mushrooms the color of saffron with whitish undersides. "Oh, ho ho!" I said, dropping to my knees. I gathered a handful of interlocked fungus and showed it to the others. "Chicken of the woods," I said. "You wouldn't believe it. Fry them in a little batter and it's just like chicken. Or in an omlette. It's . . . magic." Without thinking, I stuck my arm out in Julie's direction, and she took them, thanking me.

Ed idled by our parked cars a moment and said, "Want to get beers?"

"I would," I said.

"I won't," said Julie. "I'm going to go home and cook these, actually. Eat 'em."

"Good luck," said Ed. "At least you've got medical training. You know, I should head home too."

That night I looked through my three guidebooks on fungi, fretting over the chicken of the woods. When they had been in my hands, I was sure of the species; I had picked and eaten them many times. But now that I had foisted them on someone else, my brain began to play with me. Had it been *Laetiporus Cincinnatus* or *Laetiporus sulphureus*? That didn't matter so much, but if it had been *huroniensis*, good night, that could poison Miss Julie with vomiting, chills, and hallucinations. It got to be ten o'clock and I got out my Fitzmorris telephone book and found "J. Meagher" listed. It took me some minutes to force myself to dial her number. My relief when she answered was beyond reason.

"Henry Farrell here," I said. "Sorry to call at home. Uh, you feel fine, right?"

"Should I not?"

"Did you eat the mushrooms?"

"Sure did. I had them in an omelet with a glass of pinot. Why? Wait, man, actually . . . I don't feel very well."

"Okay. Uh—"

"Kidding, I looked them up first. How sweet of you to check on me."

"Sure. Sure, sure."

"Sure."

"Well, uh, see you tomorrow, maybe."

"See you."

LIEUTENANT SLEIGHT and I sat in a hall on a bench beside a Broome County courtroom door. The older cop had testified earlier in the trial of Christian "Dizzy" Kostis, as had Detectives Oates and Larkins. The lieutenant was keeping me company while I waited. I had wanted to move away from that night in Binghamton's First Ward, far away from it, and I had convinced myself everyone would plead out like they always do. Only, Dizzy hadn't, so I'd come into the picture.

"Don't fuss," Sleight said.

"Yeah."

"It's just a bench trial. It's a show. It's all over but the years."

Kostis had waived a jury and pinned all his hopes on the cold, clear-eyed reasoning of one lone judge. Meaning he didn't want a jury full of citizens to get their hands on the facts. An assistant DA named Michelle Knobel had filled me in the night before by phone. Bobby Chase had testified against both Max and Dizzy for reduced charges and a lighter sentence, casting himself as a hapless visitor there at the wrong time, bludgeoned and accused of terrible crimes. The prosecution had gotten the victim to talk as well, so there wasn't much left to fight over. On the stand, on direct I'd give a bare account of my night with Dizzy leading up to the arrest. Kostis's lawyer would certainly cross me, but the DA told me not to worry, I'd done nothing wrong, everyone knew that. I'd authenticate the handgun I'd taken from Dizzy. He already had a felony conviction on his record, so simply possessing it was a misdemeanor, and he had used it in connection with a slew of Class B violent offenses, separate felonies all their own, likely to bury him in prison for at least fifteen years.

As I waited to take my turn at the crank of justice, I tried to recall that night, a haze of alcohol and weed smoke burned off by a violent end. I thought of the teenage girl and other things.

"Any word on Penny Pellings these days?" I asked.

"No. I'd ask you, but . . ."

"Yeah. Everybody's looking someplace else. For the fugitive."

"Yeah, about that—"

A sheriff's deputy leaned out the courtroom door and beckoned to me. Sleight patted my knee kindly and I stood and went in. The lieutenant followed behind and took a seat in the rear of the gallery, which was otherwise empty. Judge Mondello, a large balding gray-bearded man with a nose like an eagle's beak, watched me enter and take the stand. Assistant DA Michelle Knobel stood at the prosecution table. A tall, middle-aged lawyer sat with legs stretched out beyond the defense table, hands clasped behind his head, leaning over while Dizzy murmured something behind his hand. The prisoner met my gaze with hatred. The bailiff swore me in and I took a seat under what felt like an enormous weight of wood paneling all around.

After a couple preliminary questions—who was I, what was my job—Knobel tackled the gun, probably thinking if I was going to be impeached, what she most needed from me was testimony of the weapon in Dizzy's hand. She held up a plastic bag with the gun inside. Had I seen it? Yes. When?

"That night, I was with Christian Kostis, in a house here in town, uh." I blanked on the address, and Knobel refreshed my recollection with an arrest report. "Yes, at that address. He had it there."

Did I see Mr. Kostis here in the courtroom? Yes, right there. Dizzy breathed heavily. I could hear it from the stand.

"Mr. Kostis had the handgun," echoed Knobel. "Did he wave it around, or . . . ?"

"Mr. Kostis took me to the house—"

"Objection," said the defense lawyer.

The deputy led me out of the courtroom while the two attorneys argued some fine point in whispers before the judge. Before long I was brought back in and re-sworn. The rest of the direct proceeded more or less chronologically through the early events of that night, up until the moment of arrest. I put the pistol in Dizzy's hand and Knobel had no further questions.

The defense lawyer's name was Pirro. He looked about fifty, and the spikes in his gray hair were out of place above his sagging eyes.

"Officer Farrell, I want to be crystal clear. You do not work for, or with, the Binghamton Police Department, do you?"

"Asked and answered on direct," said Assistant DA Knobel.

"No," I said anyway.

"And vice—drugs, prostitution—is not your specific area of law enforcement, is it?" said the defense lawyer.

"Asked and answered," said Knobel.

"What I mean is," said Pirro, "you're not an expert in that particular area."

"I see a little of everything out my way."

"That's a no?" he continued. "Officer Farrell, tell the court:

What were the precise circumstances in which you first met Mr. Kostis?"

I waited a beat. "I was searching for a missing woman."

"Yes, we understand that. We got that. What I want to know is, while you were out at the bars and so on, how did you actually meet Mr. Kostis? What were you doing?"

"I was sitting at the bar at the Georgian. I saw someone of Kostis's description—"

"And where did you get that description?"

"His, his record—"

"Judge?" Pirro said.

"I understand."

I did not, but Pirro moved on. "So you saw someone you thought could be Mr. Kostis, then what?"

"I went outside, out back, and Kostis started a conversation."

"Kostis started it, are you sure?"

"Pretty sure."

"Had you been drinking?"

Knobel objected with no real conviction, and was overruled.

"Yes," I said.

"How much?"

"A few beers."

"How many is a few?"

"I don't know."

"How many bars had you been to before the Georgian?"

"Just two."

"And after you met Mr. Kostis out back, didn't you smoke any marijuana with him?"

I waited too long, thought of the girl locked in the room, and said, "No."

"Liar," Kostis said, drawing a sharp look from the judge.

Pirro changed direction. "Are you married, Officer Farrell?"

This was another question I had to think about. "My wife died a few years back."

"I'm sorry for your loss. So you're not married now?"

"Objection, relevance," said Knobel.

"Your Honor, it goes not only to Officer Farrell's perception of the encounter, but to credibility, to why he was in a prostitution and drug market not in his jurisdiction, out drinking on the town—"

"Objection!"

Judge Mondello raised a hand and sighed. "I hear you, Ms. Knobel."

"Your Honor, just because there's no jury here to prejudice shouldn't give Mr. Pirro the right to root around in Officer Farrell's private life, for information with no probative—"

"Overruled, but feel free to renew if need be. Mr. Pirro?"

The defense lawyer restated his question.

"No, I'm not married."

"And you weren't seeing anyone romantically, sexually, at the time of this incident?"

"Objection."

"Overruled, Ms. Knobel," said the judge. "Mr. Pirro, we get the thrust. Let's wrap it up."

"Your Honor, Mr. Kostis's freedom is on the line here." The judge raised his eyebrows, and Pirro raised his hands. "That's my last question, then."

I thought about it, about Shelly and her family, and I thought about the girl. "Not at the time."

"No further questions," the lawyer said. Everyone in the

courtroom seemed to settle into a dull relief, all except Kostis, who tried and failed to pin a death stare on me.

Sleight and I trotted down a set of concrete steps to the cool blue day outside.

"Kostis probably told Pirro about the grass. He had to bring it up," Sleight said. "But he wasn't going to nail you to the wall, not over a lost cause like that."

"What's with the fuckin judge?"

Sleight smiled. "Believe it or not, he was with us. So was Pirro, or at least he understood his position. We just needed your cross to be good enough to shut down an appeal before Kostis can even make one. If the judge had sustained any of our objections, there's a chance of error on the record. Mondello wants Kostis to go to prison and stay there. No chance of error, nothing to reverse, no appeal. You did fine."

"Oh, yeah?" I had committed perjury, and we both knew it. As to the weed, it was my word against Dizzy's, airtight. But I had a new concern: if somehow Kostis found out I'd lied about the thing with Shelly Bray, it could be a cat's paw to a colorable appeal. But nobody knows, I told myself. Nobody knows who would want Dizzy out of prison anyway, and Shelly won't talk.

"We got kidnapping, predatory sexual assault, compelling prostitution, the gun, the whole boat."

It was hard for me to shout hooray. I thought of the girl, and it got easier. Something puzzled me. "No drug charges?"

"Nah. Conspiracy for Max and his mother, possession with intent, but not for Chase or Kostis. We couldn't make it out. Guess where they all said the chain ended?"

"Charles Michael Heffernan."

"And why not? He's dead; let him deal with it." Sleight

swabbed the top of his head with a folded paper napkin. "And who killed him? Let's say a couple nameless black guys from downstate. It's a shame, though. They all pin it on Heffernan, naturally we go to Miss Jelinski to talk it over, and all of a sudden she's supposed to know something. The poor kid doesn't know jack, she's just the only one around to take the heat. Someone up the ladder freaked, and it's just blind dumb luck she's not dead in the woods up there.

"There's something you should know," the old cop said. "I'm not sure what it means. Late in the game, after we'd gone to trial, Kostis floated info to, I don't know, reduce his sentence, probably. Info on the guy, the fugitive up north. He didn't have what we needed and we told him to fuck along down the line, but it sounded like he could talk about a murder or two."

"Penny," I said, my heart beginning to race. "It has to be."

"Penny's nobody, begging pardon. She's just trouble, or was. These murders sounded more like hits."

A FALL MORNING parked in the shadow of a church. Then came the distant rumble I'd been waiting to hear. Faint light spread out over the road, resolved into headlights, the engines buzzed closer, and then, wham, a convoy of four tankers passed by, all unaware. I clocked them at twenty-one miles over the limit and swung out from behind the church. It didn't take me long to catch up, and the drivers pulled over, one by one. I parked at a diagonal in front of the first truck, gathered licenses and registrations, and began writing tickets.

Toward the end of the summer, SRI had hired Grace Services to clear a well pad up to Swales's land north of Maiden's

Grove Lake, fenced it off, and sent in the thermos bottles, in with water and out with waste, as the wells got fracked. In the beginning I'd welcomed the operators, if only because the process of tearing out acres of trees and leveling the land might have turned up Penny Pellings's body. It hadn't. With the well being fracked, tanker trucks hauling water and waste were passing through the township at a furious rate. On winding, bumpy dirt roads with low overhanging branches, the trucks slowed to a crawl. But out on larger routes like 189, they bombed it, potholes be damned. Over the past two years I'd been to a couple grisly accidents where passenger cars got in the way of these guys. Early on I'd had a report from a little old lady who lived on a state route, on a straightaway just beyond a curve. The truck drivers tended to shift just as they passed her house, and the engine vibrations got so bad that one of her front windows shattered. Sure, they've got to get where they're going fast. It's business, and if that's the way they wanted to play it, fine. But I was going to take a bite where I could.

As I was finishing the third of four, my radio murmured, catching the odd weak signal. Then, loud, the Wild Thyme first responders were toned out with a long high note, followed by two staccato lows. The dispatcher was, as ever, hard to decipher, but I heard, "Man down," "Maiden's Grove Lake, north shore," and "SRI well pad." I struggled out of my truck, flung all of the IDs and registrations through the frontmost truck driver's window, and pulled out.

As dawn broke I turned up the hill onto the access road cut by the gas operator, in this case SRI, Southwest Resources International.

I pulled right up to the well pad's closed gate, fully expecting the sentry to rush out and let me through. His silhouette stood out plain in the guard station. I hit the horn. Beyond me, around the bend amid a haze of the rig's artificial yellow and orange lights, blue and red blinked through the trees. I leaned on the horn. The sentry stuck his head out of the window and, with an impatient wave of his hand, beckoned me over. This was irritating but I figured I didn't yet know what was going on, so what the hell. I kept the truck running. The young man wore blue coveralls and a yellow helmet that seemed unnecessary to his particular job. On the side of his neck he had a tattoo of what looked like three wolves running, and he was unshaven. He held a finger up before I could speak, ear pressed to a two-way radio.

"Open the gate," I said. "Hang up and open the goddamn gate."

The sentry looked up at me in surprise. "Who are you?"

"Officer Henry Farrell. Wild Thyme. That's this township, did you know? What's going on here?"

"Officer. There's nothing you can do now. We're good."

"You're good? Open the gate."

"Hold on." He slid the window shut and, after a brief exchange on his radio, emerged from the guardhouse to unlock the gate and swing it open.

At the well pad, another worker waved me over to where a Fitzmorris ambulance had parked, its lights still rotating, at the end of a line of trailers. All around, generators groaned, though the rig itself was quiet. A dirty apron of railroad ties surrounded the derrick, making a level surface half the size of a football field. A loose line of men stood at some remove.

"Hey," I said, approaching the man in the ambulance driver's seat. Damon was his name, I recalled; he'd grown a mustache for a touch of authority. "What is this, what happened?"

"One of the Grace Services guys. Someone found him in the reserve pit and dragged him out before I got here." He pointed to a murky pond extending from the edge of the rig, a place on the far side where it met the woods. "Don't know if maybe he fell or what."

"Julie here?"

"Yessir." Damon gestured toward the rig.

She was deep in conversation with an older man in blue coveralls, a man like a great big bag of beer. I walked over and joined them. Julie introduced me to the other fellow, who turned out to be the safety officer, Ahern. He carried a clipboard.

"What's the story?" I asked.

Ahern looked uncomfortable. "You understand, this was a Grace guy, not ours. Tate, he pulled the poor son of a bitch out." He nodded toward a young roughneck talking with an older man, off to the side.

"What was Grace up here for?"

"Routine inspection." Ahern waved a hand in the direction of the woods. This set off bells. I made a note to go out and look as soon as I had time. "It was busy; I don't know that anybody saw anything. Once our tool pusher's done with Tate, you can talk to him." Ahern ambled off.

Julie raised an eyebrow at me. "I heard something else."

She led me back to the ambulance, steered me around a puddle of foul liquid and used food, and opened the rear door. Taking up the entire compartment with a blanket around his shoulders, an oxygen mask on, and a bandage wrapped around his head, was Sage Buckles.

He raised his eyes to me. "I got nothing to say," he said, muffled through the plastic mask.

I closed the ambulance door and turned to Julie.

"He was attacked," she said. "He almost died. Arguably, he did die for a minute. He got clocked on the head, and if you look, you can see the beginnings of bruising around his neck. A few of the workers out there saw it and chased the guy into the woods. Another one gave the victim CPR, got him breathing again." She pointed to the man identified as Tate.

"Okay. Don't let Buckles go anywhere."

I approached the group of roughnecks. Tate was a pleasant, long-haired kid who seemed slightly wildered by the morning's events. Shaking my hand, he introduced himself as Potato. I took him for a worm, a low man working his way up. "Just a few questions," I said.

Early in the morning Tate had been on the platform, uncoupling drill segments as they were pulled out of the well. From there, the thirty-foot pipes were swung up and slid onto a steel rack. One of them had failed to catch on the rack and took a bounce onto the ground behind, where a reserve pond from an earlier well stood between the rig and the woods. Tate had gone around to mark the pipe's location, and there saw a man kneeling by the water's edge. This was strange in itself, but when Tate saw an extra pair of legs splayed out behind, he ran toward the pond, calling for help. When the kneeling figure stood, he revealed a man lying facedown beneath him, head and shoulders below the pond's surface. The man ran and disappeared into the woods. A few roughnecks gave chase but turned up nothing.

"I pulled the dude out," said Tate, "gave him CPR, mouth-to-mouth, and he starts to cough up."

"You see his face? The other guy."

"Nah."

"Could he have been one of you?"

"No, sir. He wasn't dressed for it. He was skinny, had on some busted camo and boots, that's about all I saw. He was quick enough, but something was up with him. Not exactly a limp. Like his body was twisted?"

I took the names of every other man who claimed to have seen something, and returned to the ambulance. Buckles had forced his way out and was moving toward his car and the gate, sweeping Damon and Julie out of his way with tree-branch arms. He was shirtless and his hair gleamed like a puddle in asphalt.

"Oh, no, you don't," I told him. "We need to talk."

Buckles was barely able to speak. "I need to get home," he croaked.

"That's exactly where you can't go." He smelled like diesel. I gave him the name of a nearby motel and told him to park in the back. "When you get out of the hospital, the township'll put you up for a couple days." Buckles started to move again. I put a hand on his chest. "You're going to tell me what happened, and why."

"I'm the victim here." He stepped back into the unit.

I couldn't hold him or arrest him, and he knew it. The best I could hope was that he'd see the use of laying low for a while. The ambulance disappeared beyond the edge of the pad.

I radioed down to Fitzmorris—the hilltop helped—and the

dispatcher promised to send someone. Tate directed me to the exact spot where the assailant had disappeared into the woods. Beyond the saplings there was a steep slope that formed one bank of the reserve pond. I slid down it, noting the commotion on the ground and in the brush where the workers had gone in.

I listened with the other animals, folded in shade. Daylight and the grind of industry from above faded as I moved. It wasn't many steps before I found an oozing patch of earth the size of a picnic blanket. Whatever was bubbling up there was orange, and I'd never seen its like. I stood looking at the place too long, then continued on, picking up the scar in the soil, again, bright orange, grass washed flat and coated further down the hill.

For decades the stream that flowed south out of Maiden's Grove had pooled in a hillside flat that had been arranged by beavers into their kind of place. It was smaller than your usual swamp, but it had made up for that in location. Since it was not near any roads, the township never felt the need to drain it, and I had always been fond of these particular beavers. The place had changed. The water was ringed with an orange sludge, an orange ring speckled with dead insects. And in the pond's outlet, several beavers were balled together and dead. I took pictures of the pond and followed the stream back up the slope.

Voices approached from the well pad above. Ahern and a younger roughneck lowered themselves into the woods. Ahern carried a metal pipe with him.

"This what a safety officer does?" I said.

"We didn't know it was you," he said. Ahern stood on the blighted place as if to hide it. He introduced me to his companion by the nickname Chickenwing.

"What's that?" I said, pointing to the ground at Ahern's feet. He shrugged.

"You been having any problems up at the site, anything I ought to know about?"

"Other than the Grace boy? No."

"I haven't been clear on what he was doing up here, anyway. The pad was all cleared and done, you've been working these wells awhile now."

"Ask them that. It's nothing we did. Tell you what else," Ahern said, pointing at his feet, "we're not alone up here. Chicken can show you. Be good for the policeman, boy. Show him the place."

The worker beckoned me back into the woods. I stood still a moment, pointed to the ground below Ahern, and told him, "I'll be back again."

I followed the worker as he pushed through saplings around the pad. We came to a gap in the trees and a shale scree, which we crossed, sending rocks clacking into the valley below us. Where the mountain rose just above the well pad, Chicken-wing, whose real name was Lonny, stopped at a stone fire ring. Surrounding that ring was another ring, but different: white stone spheres half buried in the earth.

"You go on back," I told him. "I'll stay up here awhile."

"Ahern told me bring you out to the gate."

"I'm not doing that."

It had turned into an itchy, sunny day and the air was stubborn. I moved around the fire ring and found views to the well pad, the lake below, even part of the roof of Swales's house. There was nothing left in the pit but cinders. Closing my eyes, I listened beyond and below the thrumming and clanking of the rig. A person approached through the brush. I lowered myself down and watched as Patrolman Hanluain worked his way into the clearing, sweaty and aggrieved.

"What the hell?" he said as I stood. "What the hell anymore?"

We two searched the hill, checked the closed-up cottages for signs of disturbance, then tipped our hats to Rhonda Prosser, out on a deck chair reading, and asked if she'd seen any strange customers that morning. Nothing turned up. Back at the station I called our wildlife officer Shaun Loughlin to tell him about the dead animals. He said he'd check it out and notify the DCNR and the EPA, see if they'd do their job. I also left Andy Swales a message, as it was his land. I couldn't very well not. Buckles had not done as I asked; the motel desk clerk in Fitzmorris hadn't seen him. I passed by his house several times that day and into the night. What a unique chance, I thought, to reverse-engineer some fracking waste, but no. How much he'd swallowed or inhaled, or what effect it would have on him, I couldn't tell. We'd never know if he stayed gone. More immediate than that was getting to why he'd been attacked. I left another message with Sergeant Resnik out in Beaver and kept my eyes on the country roads.

THE JUKEBOX cut off in the middle of a southern rock jam, and crowd noise swept in to take its place. Ed handed a flask around. We Country Slippers filed out to our corner as the room fell silent. A group of Shure SM58 microphones, duct tape on the mics, duct tape on the stands, stood between us and an audience of about forty or so well-wishers. As we took our places, Ed's microphone slowly drooped to the floor in its stand like a monk touching his head to the ground, with an amplified thud. He raised it. It fell again. He looked over at me with naked terror in his eyes. A kind soul emerged from the crowd and wrapped yet more tape around the stand. To the left of us, a mechanical hiss: someone had turned on a smoke machine. A spurt of white vapor turned psychedelic in the flashing lights of the juke. Fogged in, I started us on "Shove That Pig's Foot Further in the Fire," a favorite of the band with a triumphant part B, a tune we eventually merged with "Fire in the Log," also known as "Who Shit in Grandpa's Hat."

The High-Thyme Tavern was an institution of long standing, ill repute, and several personalities, depending on season and time of night. In winter, you might find a gang of snowmobilers giving off fumes of fuel and sweat, bibs undone and hanging at their waists. Or you might see one old-timer measuring out a night in cigarettes, old jokes, and jukebox dollars. Summer drew all kinds, including well-to-do folk, known reprobates, and everything in between. Naturally Ed Brennan might be found there any time of year, and earlier that September evening I'd found him and Liz socked away at the far end of a screened porch, tuning and plunking. I caught a drift of marijuana smoke. Ed craned his neck around me in an exaggerated gesture, then palmed me the pipe, which I crouched down to hit. The day had been hot, but autumn nights came down colder, and as the sun set, we began to see the foolishness of trying to tune outdoors only have our strings go wild again once we brought our instruments into the bar.

Two sets at the High-Thyme Tavern, for money. I wasn't worried, as I ranked pretty high among fiddlers in Holebrook County. Ed, though, had the mee-mees and twice walked stiff-legged to the men's room to empty his bowels. Over the summer we'd added a drummer of sorts, a hippie of Ed's acquaintance named Ralph Lilly who was near sixty and wore thinning white hair in a ponytail. I'd been skeptical at first when he'd hauled congas, a cabasa, various sticks, shakers, tambourines, and djembes of different sizes to the Brennans' backyard for a "jam." It wasn't long before he settled on a kind of wooden box on which he sat and slapped out a punctuating rhythm that reminded me of Jim Keltner's drumming on early Ry Cooder records. When I stopped noticing he was even doing it, I knew it was working. Anyways, this guy didn't drink, only indulged in weed and other things I didn't ask about, and he showed up just before eight. By 8:25 we were on the dance floor, sweating into the suits we'd all agreed to wear except Liz, who looked fresh in a dress of Day-Glo paisley.

We were several tunes in before I came back from the unstruck chord and looked around. I stood far left so my bow didn't poke anybody in the eye. Liz was to my immediate right playing an open-backed banjo, clawhammer style; we stood close enough to touch shoulders. Guitar and box provided texture and bottom but it was fiddle and banjo that needed to interlock to make the tunes danceable. And we did that: not only Julie and her people were out there, but rednecks, hippies, and retirees. Their whoops and off-time claps became part of the music. I clogged a bit and did a couple fiddle tricks.

A few more dance tunes, and we took time for a ballad, "Gathering Flowers," which Liz sang sweetly and without a hint of costume jewelry. Out in the wildwood gathering flowers, you know. I stepped back because it was just the vocal for the first verse. I looked around. Julie Meagher was easy to pick out, I'd seen her about three or four people back, her blond hair tucked behind her ears, a lodestar out there. We'd made plans to meet at the bar that night and get a beer afterward. But someone else was pulling my gaze in. I cast my eye about and there was Jennie Lyn Stiobhard with Pam Maddox in a rare public appearance. Having caught my eye, she winked, then gestured for me to meet her outside. I missed a few bars of the tune.

During the break between sets I checked in with Julie, who was most complimentary of the band. Outside, I took note of Ed, pissing into the tree line out back, hands on hips, gazing at the stars above. I waited by the horseshoe pits until Ed had gone back inside, and there was Jennie, stepping out from the shadows of the rear lot.

"I didn't know you could play like that," she said. "My great-uncle Colum could play that way. I remember him visiting. He could barely even see. I'd pay to hear you guys play, man, that's something."

"Kind of you, Jennie."

"Yeah. Yeah, man."

"What's on your mind?"

"Some little squirrel been making his nests," she said, naming three remote locations in the township.

"And?"

"We'd talk to him if we could catch him, but we only see what's left behind. He moves around—he's good at that. Anyways, brother Alan thought you'd want to know in case it's to do with the girl. He thinks it may be."

"I appreciate it."

I sensed someone, and Julie walked up, smiling.

"Evening, sweetheart," Jennie told her. To me: "We'll be out tonight. Out along Sprains Road." I nodded. Jennie Lyn ambled in the direction of the parking lot.

Julie's eyes showed curiosity, but she restrained herself from asking questions. We found Adirondack chairs and talked nonsense in the dark for a few minutes.

Some folks headed home after the first set. Those who remained got drunk. My mind was elsewhere; I made an approximation of fiddle music. After "Rose in the Mountain" ended, I set the fiddle in its case and ignored the smattering of calls for one more song.

With pain in my heart, I found Julie Meagher at the bar, ordering two IPAs. She handed one to me, and I looked down at it.

"You earned it," she said. "What?"

"I've got to go."

"Huh?"

"It's work."

"Oh, really," she said, giving my old-fashioned suit an up-and-down look. It was a chocolate-brown three-piece with yellow stripes. I had bought it for five dollars at the Christian consignment store in Fitzmorris and hung it on my line for two weeks.

"Really," I said. "I've got business out there. It can't wait, or . . ."

"Can I come?"

Ed appeared between us and took my untouched pint. "Horrible hunting."

In a drawer at my station I kept an unofficial plat map on which I had scribbled landowners, rough estimates of pooled tracts, the locations of well pads, and wells sunk and fracked. Sprains Road was a piece of rubble that ran for 1.3 miles off Route 37 between a quarried-out hillside and a bend of January Creek on the eastern edge of the county, and then rejoined the paved road. There was nothing on it yet except a quarry owned by a partnership, the quarry now idle.

Cassiopeia was out among the stars of the Milky Way, and moths and bats rode invisible currents in the air above me. I drove through the township without meeting a single car, and left my pickup on a dirt shoulder of Route 37 with an old T-shirt hanging out the window, looking like one of many abandoned trucks across the county.

Brother Alan was the Stiobhard to worry about; I'd shot him once, but it wasn't serious, and he had nothing particular against me these days. In fact he probably trusted me as much as he could anyone who wasn't family, though he was not one to seek out the company of police. Alan had been running wild since we were teenagers, getting by however he could, some-

times with honest work, sometimes poaching, theft, sometimes making and selling drugs even after the cartels moved
in with their supply of mass-produced crank and now heroin,
automatic rifles, and loose teams of local animals to handle the
business. They'd get busted and somebody new would come in.
It put me in mind of a fast-food franchise. But Alan would not
be pulled into anyone's system. And if I had to predict, he was
not going to die of old age, either. He'd stand toe-to-toe with
someone bigger and lose, or he'd let down his guard and one
night a jealous man would put a bullet in him.

Sprains Road led to the creek valley. The quarry was ahead,
behind a chained and padlocked gate. Quietly I walked the
road in the dark, stopping to listen, hearing nobody out there
with me. Softly, almost in my ear, a whistle through teeth. A
hand found my shoulder, pulling me into the brush, and down
to the earth behind a fallen tree. I turned my head to find
Danny Stiobhard, whom I thought of as the loud brother of the
three Stiobhard kids, and, behind him, the shadows of Jennie
Lyn and Alan.

Our group split, with Jennie and Alan moving silently past
the entrance. Danny and I crept up the road and waited. There
in the trees was an ancient two-door Oldsmobile, white and
rusted, with New York plates. Beyond it, a faint orange flicker
coming from the quarry, and the scent of a campfire. We moved
into the woods along the edge of the hollow and up.

We took a position beneath a patch of wild sumac. I'd
thought only kids used the quarry anymore. Spray paint covered the rock faces: 2008. 2009. Elsewhere: WE HAVE ALL BEEN
HERE FOREVER. Stone, cut but not worth enough to haul out
and sell, lay stacked and piled below us, some of it racked on

end. There was trash, too. And deep into the quarry, hard up against a cliff wall and shielded from the road by a bunker of stone and brush, a man sat beside a small fire. Through my field glasses I saw a shotgun and two blades set out on a cloth. A piece of mystery meat lay there, bloody. Tucked into the cover and facing the quarry gate was a rifle; I almost missed it. The man wore an army jacket with the collar up, his back to our position. One leg was tucked under him, and another was stretched out on the stone floor.

Danny got so close to me I could feel the bristles on his face as he whispered in my ear. "You're the cop. Go talk to him." He braced a deer rifle to his shoulder and put the scope to his eye.

He was right; if the stranger turned out to be someone, I'd want to go down and identify myself first thing. Arguably, his weapons gave me what lawyers would call an exigent circumstance, yet there wasn't any law against being out in the woods with protection against coyotes, and there had been nothing to show the man was dangerous. I waited, watching; he hadn't tipped that he knew we were there, and yet a hitch in his movements told me he was on alert. Silently as possible over fallen leaves I lowered myself to where the quarry leveled out. I stood hidden by the last line of brush, east ninety degrees out of the range of his rifle. The man was just below my sight line, about forty feet west.

I took a deep breath and called, "Henry Farrell, Wild Thyme Police."

There was no answer at first. Then, "You have a gun on me?"

"Should I?"

The fire went out with a hiss and a smell of wet smoke. I heard movement and dove into the lee of a rock pile. He would go for his car. Maybe not first, but that's where he'd want to end up. I scrambled across the stone plain to the smoke where he'd been: no knives, no shotgun. I pulled his rifle out and unloaded it, then stopped to listen. He'd lured me to his own exposed position, and I needed to get back to the woods.

Up the hill, a shotgun thudded. I ran through the tree line into darkness, slid down, and listened. Silence, another shot. In the echo, I ran in the direction of the car, stopped. Heavy footfalls tumbled down the hill toward me. I pointed my .40 into the darkness and startled as bodies collided half seen. Two men grappled on the forest floor; a shotgun fired once more and buckshot scattered into the trees around me. I dropped, looked up, and saw Danny Stiobhard grinding the stranger's head into the earth. Then a flash and a scream as a knife punched into Danny's side. Danny rolled away and the man crawled from under him. My finger was on the trigger and I had his galloping, broken body in my sights, but I lost him in the shadows and pulled up against an ash tree.

Below me, a car door opened and shut. I sprinted toward it; no sound followed. Hard to see into the car, but as I came to a stop I counted one head in the driver's seat. I walked up slowly behind my .40 and hollered for the man to drop any weapons he had out the window. A gleam of metal, a hand clutching it, an arm: Jennie Lyn Stiobhard was in the back seat with a pistol to the back of the man's skull. The two of them were talking low, and as I moved around the car I caught the words.

"If you move again, I'll kill you," she said.

"Do it, then," said the man. "You ready?"

He swept behind him with an arm and Jennie shied and cursed. Twisting himself around, the man slashed at Jennie with a knife, catching her jacket and maybe flesh. There was nowhere for her to go, no door out. For a long split second I readied myself to shoot, and once more was saved from having to—Alan charged out of the woods, broke the driver's-side window with a rifle butt, and clubbed the man to sleep. I ripped open the door, pulled the stranger out, and handcuffed him while Alan wrapped a cord around his ankles. I told Jennie where I'd left brother Danny, but she didn't have to go far; he was walking slowly down the access road, hand to his side, pale and fuming.

He called out, "Did we earn our ten grand?"

AS THE AMBULANCE shot toward Fitzmorris, the stranger opened his eyes.

Out cold, stripped to a ragged pair of underpants, and handcuffed to a gurney, he had appeared almost helpless. He'd buzzed his hair and grown a patchy beard. The lump on his head, planted by Alan Stiobhard and his rifle, was the size of half a baseball and growing. His mouth hung slack, giving us a view of too-large teeth going yellow. Nowhere in his possessions had we found a toothbrush, anyway. No wallet either, no papers in the car, nothing with a name on it. From his ribs to his right knee was a wash of purple, green, and yellow bruise, like a kid's fingerpainting. On his hip was a sharp line of red cutting through the bruise. Julie Meagher had told us it was a sign of a fracture. If he was who we thought, this was where the grandmother had hit him with the Town of Orange ambulance.

It was to Julie that the stranger turned. His eyes contained no plea or sign of physical pain. It was an empty stare, compressing the space in the unit even further, shutting me and Lieutenant Sleight out, filling the air between himself and her with the promise of death. Sleight snapped his fingers in front of the man's eyes, then, when that produced no change, turned the stranger's head with a slap. "Right here, son." The man looked up at Sleight, tested his restraints once, then rolled his head back in the direction of Julie Meagher.

"Tell me all about it, honey," Julie told him, cold. "Tell mama."

I read him his rights.

After I'd left the tavern, Miss Julie had gone home. But the radio squawked, and Wild Thyme's rescue squad couldn't put their team together, so the Fitzmorris gang had gotten toned out. Julie had taken the call, putting her unit in the center of a whirl of red and blue lights bouncing off the quarry's cliffs and into the woods beyond. Sheriff Dally had come, and as news of the encounter traveled among the departments in the area, so had officers from PSP, New York State Police, and a couple Binghamton detectives, including Lieutenant Sleight. With so many of us in one place, even in a forgotten hole like the quarry, the news media wouldn't be far away. So the most pressing question was where to take the show next.

There was no question that if the stranger was who we thought, a New York State shop would take him. But he needed medical care immediately, and Dally was in the process of convincing a Troop C BCI detective that the hospital to the south, in Fitzmorris, would be quicker, quieter, and more secure. Lieutenant Sleight was arguing for Binghamton, making the point that, again, assuming the stranger was who we thought, his crimes originated in the Triple Cities. The NYS investigator was trying to get someone to tell him just how far the arrestee could travel in his condition, as Schuyler County had the best claim out of anyone by reason of Deputy Poole's murder, so why not get him close as we can?

Me, I was content to use Dally as a shield; he had the air of authority, not I. With the arrival of police, the Stiobhards had dissolved into the night air like a dream, leaving me to explain. I had given my account to Dally, written it down, told it once more to Sleight, who had pulled me aside, and told myself the story a dozen times or more; in the telling, it had taken an eye-blink, but what exactly had happened in the woods out of my sight, the Stiobhards had not yet said. I had kept their names out of it thus far and weathered stern looks from my fellow officers. It was easiest, then, to stand next to Julie Meagher and look busy.

"It's my damn county," Dally had announced back at the quarry. "Settle down. We don't know the shape he's in. We need X-rays and an MRI. We need to tell the techs where they can get his samples. And he'll have to go before a Holebrook County judge down here anyway as a fugitive of justice, if that's who he is. It's my county and I'm calling it. He's coming with us until he's cleared to travel." The sheriff slapped the ambulance twice. "Henry, you ride down with him. Take . . ." he said, searching for a familiar face he could spare.

"I'll go," said Sleight.

The BCI detective looked sour, and said, "You clean him up and then he's ours. I don't want to find out you've been talking to him."

And we didn't talk to him, not really. PSP patrol cars ran silently front and back, their lights bringing the trees up close around us, at least from what I could see out the back windows. A hospital administrator met us at the ER doors, and conferred briefly with Sleight and a PSP corporal before leading us past sad and bewildered old faces in the waiting area to a secure room at the end of a quiet hall on the second floor. Two nurses, a DNA tech, and a doctor went inside.

Cops began to gather now by the nurses' station, bringing cold air in on their jackets and bad coffee on their breath. "Dirty motherfucker," said one, to nobody and everybody.

I pulled Sleight aside. "I know he's headed up north. I want him back," I said. "I want him for Penny Pellings. At least to talk to him."

"One dead junkie over the state line won't get you much," Sleight said. "We'll send you what we can, samples, information. You can work from that."

"It's not just her," I said. "A guy just tried to kill O'Keeffe's alibi witness, Sage Buckles. This guy shows up same area, same time. And I don't know for sure, but I think Buckles went on the run."

"Somebody's been trying to kill Buckles all his life. Find out who he pissed off lately, and there you go. It's not necessarily this guy. But noted," he said, not unkindly. "Now, you get with your friends up in the hills, impress upon them the need to talk to us about tonight. Us, you, somebody. I assume they won't be too hard to find. The reward's waiting."

Come four a.m. I decided that there was nothing left for the Wild Thyme Township Police Department of one to do or hear at the hospital, and hitched a ride with a New York State trooper back to the scene at the quarry. From there, I walked to where I left my truck on 37 and drove home.

A compact car was parked in my driveway, and a person was behind the wheel, face buried in the collar of a too-big coat. I tapped the window with my knuckle and the driver started, put her hands over her face, and cursed. Seeing it was me, Jennie Lyn relaxed, opened her door, stood, and stretched.

"Where you got him?" she asked.

"Fitz. They'll move him before too long," I said. "Out of this county, anyway."

"Good."

"So next step, we'll need to get you three together for a statement—"

"I don't think so. They're on the road."

"What? Why?"

"They don't want to be on the news," she said, as if to an idiot. "Neither do I."

"But you want the money. If you want the money, you have to show up for it."

"More than that, we want your assurances," she said. "I ask for my brothers, not myself, you understand."

At my kitchen table Jennie Lyn pulled a black-and-white map of Holebrook County, the kind you get free at the gas station. On it were circled three areas I knew to be Stiobhard hunting grounds, junkyards turned shops, trailers running off generators, whatever served as their infrastructure. We were looking at a map of black market auto parts, small-time marijuana farming, maybe a lab or two. Of particular note was a swamp fanning out from a valley bordering the Heights. Rumor had it that a lowly dealer from out of town had been killed and buried near it long ago. Forgotten now, almost. "Nothing goes on at any of these places we don't know," she said. "This guy up to the quarry is nothing to do with us. He killed that cop, I get that. But remember who found him, and who told you."

"Fair enough," I said.

"Damn right," said Jennie. "Now, how do we get our ten thousand smackers?"

EARLY THAT week I had a summary proceeding at the courthouse, late afternoon before Magistrate Heyne. Some poor dumb juggins had driven his truck halfway over a guardrail, got it stuck, and then fled the scene. He blamed it on prescription medication, but I had witness statements from a tavern in Great Bend that put him on a barstool just prior. After the hearing, I paid a visit to the sheriff's department to learn what I could about the stranger.

"He's already gone," Dally said, sounding partway relieved. "New York State and Binghamton PD took over. Welcome to him. I've never known a guy to stay dead silent as long as he did. His prints weren't in the system, so we didn't even have a name. Still don't. We called him 'You There.' They matched his blood to the scene up in Schuyler County, and he had a closed-circuit hearing with a court-appointed lawyer and a judge down here yesterday morning. Judge read him the charges—assault in the first degree, kidnapping in the first degree, endangering the welfare of a child, driving an unregistered vehicle without insurance, fraud, first-degree felony murder. Did he understand the charges? 'Yes.' That's it, and he was shackled to a gurney and shoved in an ambulance."

"We still have blood evidence from the Pellings scene," I said, recalling the droplet I'd pulled from the trailer's kitchen linoleum. "It's untested. I didn't think we'd need it because of the phone, but—"

"Send it in. That's the best we can do."

I thought about the stranger's silent leer during the ambulance ride. "So even if we had a chance to dig into him in an interview room . . ."

"No way he's talking."

I DIDN'T SEE Julie Meagher again until one early morning the following Friday, when I got a call to Maiden's Grove. I wouldn't waste a chance to haunt the place, and I got there in a hurry. A line of bystanders stood on the shore, and Fitzmorris EMS had wedged an ambulance onto a cottage lawn. There was Julie, looking sleepy. She waved to me from the bumper. I wondered why they'd been toned out too. Shaun Loughlin's Game Commission truck was parked in a nearby driveway and I pulled along beside. Out in the middle of the lake, a group of kayaks, canoes, and rowboats moved through curls of morning mist. A breeze lifted some of the gray cover, and I saw moving across the lake's surface a stag's head with a huge basket of antlers. Even from shore I could see the animal's tongue hanging red from the side of his mouth, and his neck straining forward and back with the motion of his body beneath the surface. Then it was gone in the fog.

Rhonda Prosser approached me, a coil of dreadlocks teetering atop her head. "He's been out there at least since five this morning, poor guy," she said. "At first he was just wading. By the eastern shore? But then something spooked him and he won't come back. They're out there now trying to, I don't know what they're doing. I don't think it's helping."

"I saw Shaun's truck," I said. "He out there too, or?"

"He's getting patched up," Rhonda said, nodding in the direction of the ambulance.

"Oh."

"Yeah, the ambulance isn't for the deer."

Shaun sat shirtless on the unit's rear bumper, staring at his right forearm, which was wrapped in bloody gauze. He was a military veteran, like me, but still in his twenties. He'd been to Iraq.

"Hey, pal," said I. "Looking mighty green."

"I had a hand on him, and he tagged me."

"That's what you get."

"That and some stitches. He's all yours now."

"What am I supposed to do about it?" I said.

"I don't know," Shaun said. "I'd of shot him by now if there weren't so many kids watching. And Rhonda." He dangled his head between his thighs, and sweat dripped off his nose. "I'd have made him into chili. Wait." He puked between his shoes, then glared at the wound on his arm. "What the hell."

"Let's just let the poor bastard sink or swim."

"That's been tried," he said. "He just keeps in circles like he's in a giant shitter. And the people have spoken: no drowning in their lake."

"It's a lake, it's full of dead things."

"They're beyond reason at this point. They're involved. It's a dog down a well; you've got to get it out."

Father raised me with the belief that game wardens existed only to make money off of honest, self-reliant men, and as such their authority was illegitimate. To wit, he quoted Psalms, "Shall the throne of iniquity have fellowship with thee, which frameth mischief by a law?" No, was Father's belief. It helped him put meat on our table. I liked Shaun. Father would, too.

In the dinghy Shaun had borrowed from a cottager, there was a length of rope tied in a noose. I quickly retied it as a taut-line hitch and shoved off. Four heavy pulls on the oars, and I was adrifting toward the buck. I came in at an angle to the animal, his eye wide and white around a rolling black hole. I shipped the oars and took up the rope. As soon as I got within range, the buck stilled, shuddered, tossed his antlers once around, and sank. Where he had disappeared, I looked through a mass of air bubbles into the dark.

Back ashore, the onlookers headed back to their cottages with an air of defeat. I don't think anyone ever found that stag.

As I was getting in my truck, Julie beckoned me over. "Come here a minute," she said, and steered me around the side of the ambulance, out of view. "About last week."

"I can't say much," I told her. "They moved him already."

"So it was him."

"I couldn't say."

"It was him. I looked online."

"It was him, yeah."

"I still keep my lights on all night." She gazed across the lake, then turned to me. "Fuck him anyway. Want to pick apples tomorrow?" She said it plain enough. But there was a challenge in her eyes, a riddle of some kind.

"Sure, sure," I said. I couldn't really say no without a good reason.

"You can come over to my place around nine," she said. "Can you bake? Never mind, I can."

That night I took down my sky-blue *Joy of Cooking* and read what there was to read on the subject of pies.

Next morning I arrived at the address Julie gave me: a white carriage house with black shutters in the town of Fitzmorris, at the foot of where the wooded hills rose out of the river valley. A wind chime clunked, hanging from her porch, and in the side yard there were three raised beds, two of which had been turned over for the fall, while the third ran riot with pumpkins and winter squash. A line of dwarf peach trees marked the edge of her yard, each leaning at forty-five-degree angles and propped up by pitchforks. Julie answered the door in jeans, a sweater, and hiking boots. She carried canvas sacks.

"Morning," said I. "Ready?"

"Yessir," she said. "I thought Anderson's." This was the main u-pick-it orchard in the area.

"We could," I said.

"What, what's wrong with Anderson's?"

"Why pay money when I know a place that's free and nobody'll be there?"

The noise of my truck's engine made talking nearly impossible as we crossed Holebrook County and headed toward the Heights. I stopped at the edge of a dirt track that bisected the main road; it had been fenced over and branches crowded the intersection. The road we stood on had only ever been a little detour from one paved route to another, and the lone place on it, a dairy farm, had been abandoned for years. I knew a path through the woods that would take us there.

Leaves rattled overhead and fell in glowing sheets around us. Once we hit the acre of grapevine claiming second-growth trees, I knew we were close. Julie swung on one. Before us, the shape of the house waited, the ground floor shot through with multiflora rose, still green but no longer in bloom; beside what was once a barn, the remains of a silo was supported by an oak tree growing through its middle and up to the sky. What was left of the farmhouse was surrounded by several acres of brown scrub, with a layer of green above it: an orchard living on, becoming wild.

"I went here when I was little," I said. "You paid fifty cents to an old lady who dipped snuff, and she gave you a brown paper bag. Nobody was working the farm even back then."

Julie pulled a yellow apple off a tree next to her. "I couldn't even tell you what to call this," she said.

"Me neither. Too old, some of these varieties. The names get lost. I saw that you grow peaches."

"The trees came with the house. I do what I can."

"Before they clear-cut most of the hills for pasture, you could walk through the woods and find wild peach trees everywhere," I said. "They used to be called Indian peaches because the whites thought the Indians had planted them, before we moved them down the line. But actually it was Spaniards who brought them to Florida. They migrated north. When we were kids, Mag—my sister—and I used to want to find one. Never did."

"Not yet, anyway," Julie said.

It felt great out in the sun and cold air, and the orchard was full of fruit like pirate treasure. At one point I boosted her up into a tree so she could shake down a branch of deep red apples. I felt her thigh flexing against my chest and a sensation of flight as she stepped off my clasped hands and into the tree. Where the apples dropped, deer sign was everywhere. This place would draw them all winter, and I made a note to return and hunt next month.

Back at Miss Julie's we pried our boots off, she got the oven heating, and made us strong coffee from a ceramic dripper. Her kitchen was light-drenched and centered around a chopping-block island. Public radio murmured from a device. I rinsed and sliced apples, while Julie heaped flour on the clean countertop and first drizzled water into it, then scooped out a mysterious substance from a jar from the freezer. Bacon fat, it turned out. It being a carriage house, there wasn't much room in the kitchen, and so we slipped around each other as the place warmed from the oven and ourselves. At one point Julie disappeared and returned without her sweater, just a tank top on her and a film of sweat on her shoulders. At one point as we moved about I found myself looking down right into her face, which showed amusement and mischief. She brushed by with a hand on my arm. Another man would have done something brave and found himself in a new life. But we kept talking, and the conversation turned to the places where our shops met.

"I worked down in Asheville, North Carolina," Julie said. "It's about the size of Binghamton. We had homeless, addicts. Some violent, mostly not. Some kids came to us with gunshots, lacerations, bloody, calling for their mommy. I don't know, it's not right to say, but there's something sweet about a hood who thinks he's going to die. It takes him out of himself, shows you who he really is. So you'll save his life, I guess. Now, the guy we picked up last weekend, he wasn't dying, but . . ."

"Yeah," I said.

"There was nothing in him beyond what he showed us. Not that I could see."

"I don't guess he cared one way or another about dying."

"If he ever talks, I wonder what he'll say," she said.

We fell silent. "How'd you like Asheville?" I said. I imagined barbecue, coffee shops, and guitars in open tunings.

"Asheville's a long story," she said evasively. "You ever been to a place before?"

"I have," I said. "A long story."

For lunch we ate good cheese and fig bread she'd baked in her Dutch oven, and apples. I left her in the afternoon, reluctantly, with a lattice-crust pie in my hands.

I KNEW I was in trouble when I arrived at the work site after my shift, saw Miss Julie's car there with the crew's jalopies, but no Miss Julie and no Ed. I asked a fellow prying siding off the barn where was everyone, and he told me they'd hopped in Ed's truck to see about another frame in Bradford County. Well, I thought, never mind he's married, of course it's him she likes. It's all over before it even began. I contemplated the already eaten pie, the dish waiting to be returned on my passenger seat. Before it got dark, before they returned, I made myself drive home.

ONE DAY without any warning, the stranger's face appeared on the local news: the mug shot beside artists' renditions from the Schuyler County incident. The anchor tiptoed around the facts of his capture, leaving me, Holebrook County, and anyone else out of the picture. Authorities were baffled, said the reporter, and cut to a brief interview with a New York State investigator in plain clothes asking folks for any information about the man. Him and his 1989 Cadillac de Ville with New Jersey plates, his white Olds. The pictures disappeared from the TV screen just as they started to mean something else to me. I looked the report up on the Internet and stared at the images awhile. Then I picked up the phone to Lieutenant Sleight.

"So," I said.

"Yeah. That's the grand total of what we know. Except we have a lead on a first name. I can't give it out yet."

"He started talking?"

"No. No, someone else did."

"Who?"

"You know who, Mr. Dizzy up there in Mid-State Correctional."

"He getting out early for it?"

"He's not getting dog-dick for a first name and 'maybe I've seen him around.' A definite ID, known associates, something more, maybe. But that—"

"Could get him killed," I said.

"And he knows that. So it's up to him," Sleight said. "I think what's-his-name will plead to the Jelinski thing and to the deputy in Schuyler County and try to disappear. It's what he seems to want to do already."

"Got anything else for me?" I said.

"DNA profile, prints, tests from his clothes, report on trace evidence from his car, that's about all I got. He's left no presence online, no credit cards, nothing. Nobody in town seems to know him, so."

"If I were to try to get up to see him . . ."

"He's a stone. You'd be wasting a day."

Since the news report, I'd had a feeling that I'd seen the stranger somewhere before. It could have been that I was placing him where my brain wanted him to be, supplying meaning where there was none. But I didn't think so. The man we'd arrested had short hair, but when I superimposed the stringy ponytail of the artist's rendition from Miss Jelinski's description, I was almost sure. I said, "What if I know the guy?"

"Henry, nobody does."

"I mean, I've seen him."

Sleight expelled a long breath. "Tell me, then."

"At Stingy Jack's, sitting at the bar that night. He looked at me wrong."

"This is about more than Penny. Give it some time. At this point, she'll keep."

A folder thick as a magazine arrived in the mail from Binghamton's Detective Division. The comparison between blood taken from the Schuyler County road and the stranger postarrest was a match, a smoking gun. DNA profiles matching Vicki Jelinski and him were found in the Cadillac, as well as two more unidentified samples from the trunk. His clothes were just a lot of noise, but his coat and pants contained surprises. The techs had noted several foul-smelling stains, and the coat sleeves and trouser knees were particularly saturated with heavy metals, barium, calcium, and silicates.

Closing time, I tucked photos and sketches under my arm and took a cruise over to Airy Township to see if Mr. Buckles had returned. The leaves were still unraked in his yard, but a rented dumpster stood next to his swaybacked cottage.

The curtilage had been partly cleared and as I pulled up, Sage was heaving a roll of rusted wire fencing into the bin. As I approached he said, "How can I miss you if you never leave?"

"Last we talked, I told you to stay put," I said.

"What do I got to stay put for? I had business in Beaver." He seized a plastic tub and threw it into the dumpster. Where it had been, insects fled the bare dirt for new cover. "Won't be here long," he said. "That should make you happy, finally drive a workingman out of town. Drive a strong man out. Keep the weak ones. Makes your job easy, don't it?"

"What can I say? Good luck to you. Where you headed?"

"Selling the place. Getting it ready, anyway. I can take a hint. Since I been here, I been accused, beat, harassed, my old lady moved away, shit."

"How is Hope these days?"

"How should I know?"

"Know where I can reach her?" If Buckles didn't know the stranger, maybe Hope did.

Sage pried a sheet of tin off of a great lump in the yard, and seemed delighted to find half a face cord of firewood underneath. "What?"

"Hope, where is she?"

He shrugged. "You here to see her, or me?"

Sage peered once more at three images of the stranger, this time with photos accompanying the sketches, and handed them back to me. "I told you before, I'm supposed to know him? I know a million guys like him."

"Not like this one," I said. I listened to the silence Sage was putting out. "This one tried to kill you."

"I got hit from behind. I didn't see."

"You didn't have to see, did you? You know. You have a job, you have a house, you managed to tiptoe your way past jail time. But you're clearing out. What kind of trouble are you in? Let me help."

He turned away from me and unearthed a sodden computer chair missing its wheels. "I'm good. Never seen that guy before except on the news. I don't know what happened to me up at the pad, I don't know what people say happened. People talk a lot of shit and don't know."

"You ever spend any time at Stingy Jack's?"

"Who's that?" said Buckles, facing away. I left him to his work.

In among the stunted trees and the leaves still clutching to them, I looked from the ridgetop to John Blaine's vacant country house. I left, returned that evening, and waited until after midnight. Nobody showed. The next day I did the same. The third morning, I gave that up, looked in the Internet white pages, and found a J Blaine living on Binghamton's West Side near Main Street.

AT 7:37 A.M., the city was alive but not yet overrun with car traffic. Kids with backpacks nearly big as themselves tripped along the sidewalks to their schools. I never could walk to my school, which was miles away from the house I grew up in. I waited for a bus at the end of my dirt road by a hutch the township had built for us. When it rained or got cold, there were fights over who got to stand in it, but I knew better than to scrap over a thing I never wanted. I was happy outside in all weather, miserable in school, whether school was merely a roof in the cold, a bus, or a concrete holding pen run by teachers as mean as their students. Sitting in my truck at the end of the residential block there in town, it came back to me and my heart hurt for those kids, knowing it'd be years before they'd get out.

I waited on the far side of a triangular park with coffee and donuts and a pocket scope. From my position, I could look straight to a little blue house on the corner of Schubert Street and Mendelssohn. There was a fat SUV in the driveway, and a copper-colored sport wagon parked out front. The wagon was new as of that morning. Every twenty minutes I drove away and parked somewhere else with a view. In the light of morning there wasn't much I could do to hide; the neighbors would see me and wonder.

Yet that was how I had spent four days that week. In the early evenings after my shifts I drove back to Binghamton to follow Blaine the couple miles to Stingy Jack's. Late into the nights I switched up my positions, watching cars as they moved in and out of the bar's dirt lot.

Around nine that morning, a young woman trotted down Blaine's driveway in tight jeans and a short jacket. They looked like clothes she might have worn out at night, not what she'd put on for a quiet Binghamton morning. The night before, I'd given up waiting for Blaine to leave the bar after two-thirty a.m., and hadn't seen her go home with him; possibly she was a bartender. Stopping at the SUV, she opened a backseat door and pulled out a small duffel bag, took it with her to the car out front. I started my engine. Two blocks, two turns, and her sport wagon found Main Street, with me following a few cars behind. At Front Street she turned left to head north, and I followed, until a car swung in front of me and slowed to a crawl. I tried to pass him, but he straddled the yellow lines, blocking me. In the distance, the copper wagon drove under a trestle and onward to one of a couple highways. A black muscle car with tinted windows pulled out from behind, sped up the block, and slowed again under the bridge.

The car in front of me stopped dead. A dark-skinned hand emerged from the driver's-side window and pointed down a side street. I followed the driver there and parked. The hand beckoned to me. I left my truck and walked slowly to meet the owner of the hand: Detective Oates of Binghamton Special Investigations.

"No," he said. "No, no, no."

KEVIN O'KEEFFE called my station three times that week, and I managed not to be there to answer any of them. I later recognized the Mahanoy number on my caller ID. After the final call he left me a message: three seconds of silence, then, "Who's that on the news?"

JUST EAST of the Heights there is a roadside car dealership and junkyard climbing up a hill. A man named Cy Stokes owned and operated it. As far as I knew, he'd never sold a running automobile to anyone off of his lot; his business was scrap and parts. He'd called me once about tweakers up to his or his brother's junkyard, yanking the best parts out of his best cars. I'd told him there was no way to help; I could never verify what trailer hitch or exhaust sytem had or had not been in his possession at one time, even if I'd found the guys. If he'd caught them red-handed, had a photograph or something with the stuff visible, maybe.

I returned from a spin around the township one morning to find Cy Stokes waiting for me at the station, a little kobold of a man dried out by work and cigarette smoke. He followed me inside and stood twisting his hat in his hands while I hung up my coat.

"Sit," I told him. "What's on your mind?"

"Well, I seen the news," he said. "Seen a fellow on there and it looked like I knew him from somewhere. And then I heard about the car, and I . . ."

"Go on," I said.

"Well," said Stokes, looking itchy. "Well. This was back in May or June? Months ago, anyhow. Long-haired man comes to my lot, early morning, he's got a hat on but I can see he's got the long hair under, and he's got a truck that ain't running good, but it does run, inspection's overdue, registration's about to expire, and he wants something else, a car. Something less noisy, he says."

"A truck, you say."

"Yessir, he had a Nissan pickup. So I take him around, show him—the truck ain't worth a quarter, I'll tell you what—but I show him. Says he likes an old car, a stick, he likes a Cadillac I got on the lot. I tell him straight, you buy that car off this lot today? You better put a case of steering fluid in the trunk, because the rack-and-pinion is shot. Been meaning to replace it. He don't care, he'll get it fixed. He wants to take the car. But the funny thing is, he don't want me to sell the truck, he wants me to store it up on the hill there, in case he ever wants it back. Says he'll pay a grand for me to just keep it, but if he comes back and it's gone or anybody's been taking parts, he ain't going to be happy."

"A yellow Nissan?"

Stokes fell silent.

"You got paperwork on this?" I said. "Titles? A name, even?"

"The man needed a car right then. I didn't have the title right then. He didn't have his title. I know it ain't right, but at the time . . . we're talking about two vehicles that ain't worth a quarter. I'm telling you now because it is right: I sold this man a Cadillac de Ville car, and damned if he didn't turn around and put a girl in the trunk of it. I seen him face-to-face. And yeah, the truck he give me was yellow as a buttercup."

TWO FORENSIC DETECTIVES from the Binghamton Police Department's Identification Services, a woman named Mason and a man named Riva, picked their way around Kevin O'Keeffe's pickup where it stood in the shade of a red maple tree. Brambles had grown up around it, knee-high, and the truck looked natural among the other wrecks waiting for the crusher in the Stokeses' yard. It was a cold, gray morning and several of us had hiked up the hill from the garage. Lieutenant Sleight wore a tracksuit and ate plain donuts one by one from a small box. Sheriff Dally and DA Ross were there, as well as a New York BCI detective named Portiss. At a distance Cy Stokes watched, accompanied by his brother Ollie, fat and soft as a wad of Kleenex, with white in his beard.

Sleight turned to the Stokes brothers. "You say you didn't let anyone else near this thing?"

"I mean," said the little man, "I called Henry about people snitching parts a while back. But far as I can tell, they didn't take nothing out of the truck." Stokes shot a look at his brother. It was in a blink, but I saw it. Sleight did too.

ID Services began their work with powder, brush, and tape. Mason crouched by the opening with an elaborate dust-buster to gather particles. From what I could see craning my neck, the truck's cab had been swept clean. The interior panel would eventually be removed once they lifted any prints, and the steel innards of the vehicle scoured for contraband and trace evidence. I peered into the bed and saw that it, too, had been cleared of Kevin's things.

Not until we reached the underside of the bench did the detectives perk up. The vinyl upholstery had been torn away from the seat, from the looks of it with a razor. Much of the foam had been gouged away, exposing some of the metal bones. Some of the floor rubber had been peeled back and stripped.

Mason crouched with a flashlight, then waved a hand behind her, signaling for quiet. We watched as she dropped alcohol on a contact strip and pressed it to a spot on the floor beneath the seat. Then she opened a chemical applicator and tested the solution in the tube against the paper. It turned the bright blue of a gas flame.

"We need to take all of this," she told Sleight. "We should haul this whole vehicle back to the hangar. Anything around it we find."

The lieutenant raised his eyebrows.

"Blood," she said.

Out front of the garage, Cy and Ollie were passing between automobile husks, opening hoods and rubbing their chins. Sleight called Cy over.

"We've got to take the truck," he said.

"I thought so," said Cy.

"Nothing in and out of this yard until we say so," said Sleight. "You're closed."

Cy removed his hat and swatted his leg with it. "I got Northern Scrap expecting ten tons this week. I can't do business that way."

"That's right, no business," Sleight said. "We have questions."

"What you see is what it is."

"Yeah, a sale with no papers. A sale and you don't even know the party's name. When did the VIN come off the Cadillac? Did you do it?"

"No."

Sleight took off his glasses, rubbed his forehead, replaced his glasses. "Jesus Christ," he said in a rare loss of temper. "People have been killed. You didn't think?"

"That's why I went to Henry," Cy said. He looked ready to cry.

"This truck is stolen; you knew it, you received it, you hid it. Theft and obstructing justice. Then you got conveying a Cadillac without title. And the VIN coming off the Caddy, the VIN thing is federal."

Ollie Stokes had not spoken a word since we arrived. He stepped forward, and in a shaking voice said, "Sirs, this ain't the first one."

"Ollie—"

"Well, it ain't, Cy."

Cy held up his hands, weary. "We'll tell you what we know. You want to charge this and that, I can't stop you. But I came to Henry on my own. We never knew what we'd got into. Have you tried to make a buck out here?"

The first such "trade-in" between the stranger and Cy Stokes took place a year prior, and concerned a Japanese sedan with over a hundred thousand miles and light rust on the doors' edges. The man had brought it in early morning and exchanged it for another mid-sized. Cy didn't say this, but we guessed that the transaction had to have been unbalanced in the Stokeses' favor, and in cash. The car Cy had bought was clean enough to put on the lot, but the stranger did not want it sold, he wanted it destroyed, so when he passed by the Stokeses' used car lot and found the sedan out for sale, he paid a visit to the brothers and made that clear. They'd crushed the car the next day and sold it to Northern Scrap. There had been two more, both sedans, both exchanged for the same money, the same arrangement. Why the fellow had wanted the truck saved, Cy could not say.

"Them cars were clean," Ollie maintained. "Whatever he used them for, them cars were clean when we got them."

"Smelled like Clorox," said Cy. "Except the truck."

Sheriff Dally took Sleight and the Stokes boys to his department to wring every detail out of them. They were shown photographs of both the stranger and Kevin O'Keeffe into the bargain. Cy pointed to the stranger, but could not say for certain.

Lee Hillendale, the sheriff, and I drove south to visit Kevin O'Keeffe in Mahanoy. His face had further sharpened and turned to stone. I guess Kevin had general instructions from Lee to say nothing to the police, and he did not, raising an eyebrow and leaning back in his chair, asking a question we still couldn't answer. Had he ever done any business with the Stokes brothers? No, he didn't know them. Once again, did he know the man pictured here? No, only from the news. Who was he?

Binghamton ID Services hauled the truck north. In Holebrook County, we were content to send it all up north to the investigation in New York and trust that it'd come back down to us. But the look on DA Ross's face when he saw the match between Penny Pellings and the blood found in O'Keeffe's truck said what was on his mind. Kev was still in play for Penny's murder, and always had been.

SEVEN O'CLOCK Friday evening, I parked under a crisscross of bare oak limbs with orange streetlights shining down through them, near the Civil War memorial on the square in Fitzmorris, PA. I had a dinner engagement, and with forty-five minutes to go, I was at a loose end. Around the corner from the courthouse was a tavern called the Low Road. I took the four concrete steps down from the sidewalk and ducked into the door. The bar was beneath what was once a four-story hotel, now empty. Staring in the bar's mirror, I noted that though I had attempted to comb my hair and beard, I still looked like a dead Civil War general. At the jukebox I punched a few Alan Jackson tunes and returned to the bar. After forty minutes ticked by, I stood, ate a breath mint, and went out to meet my doom.

Night had settled over Fitzmorris. Around the corner stood a building that used to be a feed and hardware store. The interior was well lit and conversation spilled out the windows. I stood at the door for a moment, and then I went in. Of course, everyone was at pains to say it wasn't a date; who goes on those anymore. Yet it was something. A distinct pairing-off.

The new restaurant, called Dry Goods and Sundry, was full of unfamiliar people—natural gas management, folks from over the border in New York. I slipped through to where Ed, Liz, and Julie Meagher sat. Julie smiled. I smiled back and reminded myself not to start talking unless I had something to say. Sitting at a table was not like baking a pie. Though—again—I had no particular reason for it, my mouth was dry and my heart thudded.

With a glass of syrupy Finger Lakes wine in hand, I unclenched my mind and drank enough to where I could talk without stammering. Ed, Liz, and Julie handled most of the conversation. I hardly tasted my brick chicken and braised greens. The restaurant was new, and the idea of it was farm and field to table, meaning as much local, game, and wild food as they could get, they'd serve to the public. Julie had ordered the venison ragout, but I had decided against it, reasoning in my mind that I didn't deserve it, having gone out with the bow only twice in October and come back empty-handed. Rifle season started the end of the month, and I was already scouting. I found myself asking Miss Julie did she hunt at all.

"I can shoot," she said cautiously. "We hunted duck, quail, shot clay pigeons. Soda cans with a .22. But with something as big and soulful as a deer . . . I've never tried. I'm not sure I'd want to."

"There are a dozen ways to go worse than a quick bullet," I assured her. "Starvation, chronic wasting, coyotes . . ." Julie looked down at her dinner in dismay. "And it's an ancient part of life," I continued, veering away from biology. "The hunt is the oldest thing there is. It brings us close to the soul of the animal, like you say. You wouldn't have to shoot a thing to see that." Not even Polly had gone hunting with me. I'd kept her at bay, probably, saving for myself the wild, cold dawns in communion with my fellow beasts. The soul of the animal is the soul of the whole world. The life of the world. Most humans had a hard time seeing that. So I surprised myself when I said to Julie, "If you ever do want to go out in the field, let me know."

When our table had been cleared, and the check split and paid, Ed suggested a bonfire at their place, as they had to relieve their babysitter.

In the flickering firelight on the Brennans' lawn, Julie stayed close to my side, not touching me, but within range. We kept an easy silence, lulled by the fire. She yawned, then backpedaled out of the fire's range to view the stars. I fought the impulse to follow.

A couple days later we were digging through the splinters of a collapsed barn outside Owego, New York. There were a few good timbers and many more rotten ones half buried in animal dung. The days had shortened, and I could sense Ed's anxiety build as the year ticked forward.

That weekend I'd driven up to see Ed in his shop, and waited for him to finish a phone call, seeing disappointment on his face. He'd hung up, turned to me, and said, "We're in trouble." He grabbed a scratch awl off of the workbench and stalked back outside. Then, almost gently, he'd plunged the awl three inches into a section of timber from the big Bradford County barn. Then another, and another. "Rot. They're all gone," he said.

"You'll find something else," I said.

"No time. Everywhere I look, rot!" He stomped back into his workshop, shoulders hunched, and picked up the phone. There was a negative to Ed's vision, of his faith in work and works to improve the world: total Armageddon. If he couldn't find the timbers to get Willard's studio done by the deadline, he stood to lose not only the five percent bonus for timely completion, but also his break-even number, his future contracts, his reputation. Nobody understood his work or why it had to take so long, everybody just used the amateurs because nobody understood landscape, he had been born in the wrong century, all would be ruined. Or it'd be fine, I tried to tell him.

Anyway, we were scrambling now to fill out the frame with new material. Ed had asked me not to reveal the trouble to Julie, so of course I hadn't mentioned it. She worked gamely with us through the bracing nightfall, digging deeper into the pile until we couldn't see what was under our feet.

Some of us stopped at an Owego bar called the John Barley-corn for supper and beers. I only went because. One by one, the guys made exits to cross the state line into Pennsylvania; Ed was among the last to leave, gazing longingly in Miss Julie's direction, but I outlasted him. Only she and I were left of the crew, elbow-to-elbow at the bar. As we sucked down our final pints, she reached into her pocket and slid something across to me. Lifting her hand, she revealed a rectangle of yellow plastic: a hunting license.

THE THING about hunting deer is, there's no sense in going unless you are going to beat the sun. It's the dawn that plugs you right into the Oversoul, into the earth's systems, to where you can understand what's around you. We could've done a night stand, but I wanted to show Julie the morning, where you almost don't need a rifle. Almost.

But she lived more than thirty minutes away from me, in Fitzmorris. She told me straight she wasn't going to get up that early, not on her own, but could she stay over at my place the night before? That way we wouldn't lose any time with her getting up and driving all the way to me. We made plans for her to stay over Friday night and go into the field Saturday morning, and we parted ways from the John Barleycorn in all enthusiasm. In the sober light of the next couple days, neither of us backed out.

Friday: After a supper of homemade ravioli made by Julie with a pumpkin from her patch, we sat on my couch with glasses of wine. The space between her knee and my leg was competing with the TV, which was tuned to a singing contest that Miss Julie could not miss: she'd seen too much to turn back now. The music said almost nothing to me, so to the extent I had any skin in the game, it was because of the stories. Between songs, one contestant cried for a lost brother, one had struggled through an inner city childhood, sustained by faith in Jesus. One had lost over sixty pounds. Again, Jesus. I don't watch very much television because it gives me the feeling of life slipping by unseen. If I'd had the place to myself, I'd have run scales on the fiddle, maybe tried some tunes, maybe thought my thoughts, maybe read, maybe watched one of my movies over again. I felt a heavy silence. If I was somebody else I'd have had more to say.

I got up to go to the john, and when I came back she was standing, peering at a framed photograph of my wife Polly and me in camping gear, a huge western vista behind us. You could see the wind in her hair, Polly's. This was the problem with my living room—Polly's bodhran perched behind a lamp in the corner, the photographs, the hat she'd knitted me hung in a place of honor on the back of a chair.

Polly Coyne had been my constant companion, at least

in my mind, for many years. Most of my adult life. From the moment I'd met her in the Wind River Range, through my first return to Pennsylvania and a dreary year of training academy in Allentown, through a sloggy time of tree service with my uncle in Bradford County after finding no police jobs anywhere I wanted to live. A boyfriend of Polly's and a girlfriend of mine in the way, letters and late-night phone calls, my own reluctance to leave the Pennsylvania hills—I'd hardly been anywhere else. A confusing time where we lost touch. I worked and saved what I could. Always, the thrill of meeting her that one summer stayed with me. And it was that same feeling that had faded to where I almost couldn't get back to it now. It would almost—almost—be easier if I could forget.

Aunt Medbh's guest room came furnished with a cot-sized bed from the Great Depression, a cheap pine dresser from the eighties, and a closet full of rolls of crumbling fabric where the door didn't close all the way. I had wrung my hands over the sleeping arrangement, and decided that it'd come off weird, not gallant, to offer my own bedroom and full-sized, twenty-first century bed. So that morning I'd dusted, swept bunnies out from under the guest bed, vacuumed, washed the sheets and quilts, kept the windows open, boiled apples and cinnamon sticks on the stove and then left the pot in the room all day, repurposed a milking stool and a lamp from the living room as a bedside table, and hung a cross-stitch done by my mother in a Currier and Ives style decades ago.

At bedtime, Julie and I stood in the doorway. "Cute," she said.

The upstairs bathroom was at the end of the hall, not far from my room, and I could hear more than I'd expected as she brushed her teeth and washed her face. I lay on top of my covers, fully clothed with my boots on. She tapped on my doorframe and stepped in, wearing sweats and a tank top that had rolled a little bit up over part of her hip. She looked around at my room and its newly clean floor, the bare walls, the blue hospital blankets that I'd favored since boyhood.

"All right, we're doing this. Four-thirty wake-up. But I never go to bed this early."

"No?" It was nearly ten-thirty. "What do you do all night?"

"I talk to my plants. So this is how you sleep, in your clothes, like Dracula?"

"Ha ha, no." I slept naked, like everybody.

"Good night, then. I like this old house. It's very you. But I'm leaving my door open and can we have the hall light on? I don't want Aunt Medbh sneaking up on me."

I suppose we both lay awake for a while, yet four-thirty seemed to arrive about five minutes after she went to her room.

We stepped outside in darkness, Julie clutching my .243 by the stock and shivering white breath. I had my .270. The trail through the field was silent, but in the woods we crunched brittle leaves on our way to my go-to spot, a crag at the base of a ridge that faced a clearing to the east. Black trees marked where a creek went through the field. The air was perfectly still, and we each sat against a tree trunk and waited for the sun.

Sunrise will push air west. The faintest breeze came just before the first gray light added depth to the landscape. Julie reached out and clasped my wrist. I looked, she cocked her head south of us. We waited; millimeter by millimeter I turned my head to see what was coming. Climbing the ridge behind us was a line of deer, six or eight yearlings led by two does. Julie had heard them and I had not. They walked without fear, dumb and incurious, until they crossed our downwind, snuffed, and bolted. In their commotion I turned my head back around, just as the sun gained the opposite ridge and caught the frost in the grass, pooling golden light in the clearing and reaching into the woods. I snuck a look at Miss Julie: she saw it too.

The temptation is to move. If nothing comes our way, we're hardwired to think we can stalk game to where it is. No. But with nobody driving, Julie and I were relying on luck just sitting there. I kept us in the same spot as long as I felt she could stand it, but she was shivering, so up we got, shook the cold out, and began our slow way back. I took her the long way, on a four-wheeler trail that passed by a grove of red pine. We took a seat on a bank of moss behind some rattling beech scrub and peered into the dark. Julie sat on my left. The slow, stately pace of a lone buck coming toward us. The world crowded in to my vision from all sides, telling me now, now, now, here it comes. The cold air hovered in front of my face, thick. The buck was to Julie's side, it would cross the trail any moment; she raised her rifle and the animal streaked into the woods and gone. It took effort to listen to my own good sense and head back to the house for Miss Julie's sake.

Back in the kitchen, I put on the kettle, and my hands buzzed. My blood was up and I tried to contain myself.

"Holy shit, man," Julie said, tearing off her jacket. "That was . . ." She shook her head, searching for words. "The real thing." She folded herself into me to get warm, and the next thing I knew we were pawing at each other like bears, right there in the kitchen.

MID-DECEMBER, AND we were socked in under two feet of snow that had come down over less than a day and night. After a melt and another freeze, icicles grew all the way down from my porch roof in a sheet. In the morning, Julie and I were at my place, and neither one of us planned to go anywhere until we were toned out. We both would be. Our uniforms waited upstairs. Until then, we would enjoy a blizzard like normal people. I'd made coffee and we had some ham and eggs going in the kitchen. Our sleepovers had become something of a cold war, in that each one's home was about half an hour from the others' work—mine in Wild Thyme, hers in Fitzmorris. Clothes and necessities had traveled back and forth across Holebrook County to lodge either in her white Victorian cottage in Fitzmorris or my creaky hilltop farmhouse.

I left Miss Julie reading a book at the kitchen table and went out barefoot to the porch to collect firewood. The snow on my skin was a jolt that cut through the beery fog of the night before. I stoked the stove, then put on my country slippers, hat, and coat, dug a path to our cars, pulled the rider/mower out of the shed, and plowed what I could of the driveway. When I came back I caught Julie snooping in the living room again. Winter had made Polly's life, the nothing that remained of it here in the farmhouse, an intimate companion. A too-sweet, too-heavy breath hanging in the air, a half-heard pleasantry said in the next room, waiting for an answer.

Julie smiled and said, "You two look very happy."

"Yup."

"She has a kind face."

"She was," I said.

"I like that." She placed a hand on my arm. "You must miss her."

"Come on." I tried to smile, too late, and it didn't work.

"I just wish you would talk about it," she said.

"Please. I don't need to."

"It's not for you," she said. "I'm trying to get a look at the competition."

That brought me up short. "Dead people don't put up much of a fight," I said.

She sat on the couch and said, "That's what you think."

Julie's point was—and I heard about it at length—that if I included Polly in my life openly, then Julie could share it, this unreachable part of my self when I was happiest and maybe the most myself that I ever was.

"I'm still an outsider," she said. "I can only guess. I want to know."

You want to put Polly in her place, I thought to myself and didn't say. I saw the sense but I did not want to share. I wasn't ready, and I hated being asked. Then and there I decided to box up and stash the things. If only she knew what it took to reopen the box in the first place—everything in that room, Polly's parents had shipped to me in one package once they'd found where I was. It had been kind of them, but I didn't want to look.

Eventually I made myself, and it hurt. And now Polly was going back in that exact same box, up in the attic. I'd have to talk to her about it. She was mine, always would be.

Julie watched as, without a word, I collected and boxed everything of my wife's that was still downstairs. I was angry all out of proportion, but I couldn't stop.

"Henry," she said, and decided to leave it alone.

My radio toned one high, two low. A gas station's alarm had been tripped. The place was almost to Airy Township. I got dressed while Julie lay on the couch in her pajamas and slippers, her face hidden in a book. She was gone when I returned in the afternoon, and her stuff was too.

THE SNOW hung on a few days, and then it snowed some more. I figured I might as well just stay in the station during working hours, as nobody was going anywhere by car anyway unless the township building was clear. Big John Kozlowski was plowing overtime for the people, and even the Sovereign Individual took a shift behind the wheel. Fitzmorris was in better shape than Wild Thyme, but Julie felt she should stay there until the blizzard passed; many old-timers got trigger-happy for an ambulance when they felt trapped. All except one: I'd had to travel to the edge of the county to check on an aging pedophile yellowed by bile duct cancer who had missed his Megan's Law check-in. You could understand it, given the conditions. People had been civil and full of the can-do spirit, apart from the gas station burglary a couple days back. Junk food and soda only. Whoever it was had smashed the glass doors easy enough, but couldn't get into the register, much less the safe. A two-car MVA where one car had flipped and the driver ran, leaving his buddy in the passenger seat. I'd followed the driver's tracks and found him shivering on the roadside. Both passenger and driver of the flipped car tested positive for heroin. That to deal with, and the usual trespassing calls on snowmobilers.

The fourth day of blizzard had come down over us like a gray-and-white coma. The daylight didn't change at all from one hour to the next. It could have been night, or morning, or the ashes of a long-dead fire in some dimension beyond space and time. How long until I could eat my sandwich? My cell phone beeped with a text, and I stared at the name there, and my heart did a clumsy little dance because it thought nobody was looking. I got in the truck.

Shelly Bray had almost made it down the driveway from her horse farm to Route 189, almost but not quite, and she stood there on the packed snow beside a ten-foot moving truck whose right front tire had buried itself in a three-foot berm of snow, while the rest of it sat diagonal across the entire width of the driveway like an old dog. On Shelly's head was a pointy cable-knit hat, jaunty and out of place for the occasion. She hugged me and said thank god I was there.

"It had to be today?" I said.

"Court order," she said. "I can't drag it out any more. I wouldn't want to. He was going to sell my shit online."

"You don't have anyone to help?"

"I have you," she said.

I knew what would happen. I did it anyway. We got to work getting the truck unstuck. At one point, her husband Josh appeared some forty feet up on the driveway, a slight figure in sunglasses and a hat, his coat weighed down with what I was pretty sure was a handgun. As Shelly and I shoved at the front grille, I muttered to her, "Should I be here?"

"It doesn't matter now."

"Should I talk to him?" I said.

"And say what? Trust me. It doesn't matter."

Maybe not to her. Josh reached into his coat pocket. My hand crept toward my belt. Josh produced a little silver camera, took several photographs of us, turned his back, and left.

With a couple sheets of cardboard and some main force, we got the truck pointed toward Binghamton, where Shelly had taken an apartment near downtown. She asked me to follow her and I did. All the way in, I steeled myself against what was coming. All the way back and forth from the truck, through the falling snow, through the lobby of a massive Front Street building intended as low-cost housing for the elderly, into the elevator, and down a long hallway with door after door leading to tiny apartments just like hers where the old folks watched, and into number 11F.

When the last box was stacked in her new home I said, "Well."

Shelly cut me off. "You need to hear this."

We faced each other across a small patch of empty floor near a picture window. Below, if I could've seen through the snow, the Chenango River was crashing into the Susquehanna under a jagged field of ice. Snow that once clung to me had melted and I could hear it tock-tock onto the floor.

"Take off your hat, at least," she said.

I did. My glasses were fogged and I unzipped my jacket to

find a piece of shirt to wipe them. "This isn't how I pictured you," I said, meaning the apartment.

"It's a quick fix. The kids like it because it's high up. Like a big city. I won't be around longer than a few months. Maybe you shouldn't be either."

"I'm good where I am," I said.

"Henry. The divorce didn't go well. You can see that. I'd usually get something to live on. In a no-fault, that's just the way it always goes. I'm the kids' mother. But I get them every other weekend while that sociopath raises them. I get no money. Why am I here in this funeral home and not him, do you think?"

The old worry came back. "He knows."

"It's worse." She looked away. "The house was rigged with cameras. If I'd fought for custody, for anything, things would've gotten personal. Real quick. For both of us, you and me both. He made sure I knew that."

"It's a bluff," I said, knowing it wasn't.

"I've seen video. I came down to his den, in the basement there? And he was watching us, ugh." She squeezed her eyes shut. "What tipped him off, I don't know."

I felt sick. "Where does he keep the tapes?"

"You can't smash and grab, not with him. They're digital, on his computer anyway, uploaded to a server somewhere too. There's no way to make them disappear. So that's him, that's who he is. I tried to tell you." She swept away an angry tear. "I swear, I almost called you, I was going to kill him then and there."

I sat there facing the idea of being on somebody's video, having that hang over me and my life going forward. If I'm honest I wanted to kill him too. "What do you want to do?"

"There's nothing to do. He's got us. We could bring it out into the open. We could say we don't care."

"I'm with somebody now." As I said it, I knew it wasn't entirely true.

"Just like always," she said. "Is she what you want, then?" Shelly stood, brushed past me, bent down, and put her mouth on my neck, her hands to my belt.

"I can't do it, Shel. I'm fond of you as can be. I can't." I left guilty and lonely from my secrets.

The drive to the West Side was hairy and out of my way, but so few people were out that I could cruise ten miles an hour right down the middle of the streets. Nobody had shoveled the sidewalk in front of John Blaine's little blue house on Schubert Street, the driveway was empty, and the lights were off.

THERE WAS an ice storm, and a thaw, and a freeze down to minus two, and so on until one night, up on that wooded ridge overlooking Maiden's Grove, Kevin and Penny's trailer caught fire. By the time I arrived, there was a line of engines down the driveway to the road. I could smell the plastic fusing together and escaping as gas, along with the cheap wood, almost like a campfire smell fighting with the plastic. I walked up the hill, passing squad trucks and idle firefighters from neighboring companies, narrow, wide, old, teenage, ready for action with not much to do. The closer I got to the house, the more I heard, around me everywhere, a great hissing separate and apart from the rumble of the fire. Whirls of flame rose out of the trailer's windows and merged into one as the roof lifted and disappeared into air. The hissing, I understood, was from trees overhanging the mobile home losing their water to the heat.

With no chance of saving anything, the Wild Thyme crew still had hoses on the trailer and the surrounding scrub. The fire would be knocked down before long.

I got on the phone to Sheriff Dally, who said he'd heard about it but wouldn't bother to see the show now that I was there. He offered to call PSP Forensic Services and ask them to send a fire investigator as soon as they could. I told him I'd get ahold of Binghamton and see if they'd oblige. Sleight would have to be told about this, anyway. There was no doubt in my mind the place had been torched intentionally. The ultimate scrub-down. Whoever had done it probably should have done so months ago.

The Wild Thyme assistant fire chief, Matty Lehl, stood back from the fire beside a red super-duty pickup with chrome decals on the doors. He wore no SCBA and neither did any of his guys; they just turned away from the fumes. Seeing me, he excused himself and sidled up.

"A fire like this is over soon as it begins," he said, shaking his head. "At least we know nobody's home."

"What are we looking at?"

"Oh, I don't know, some little rat-bastard chewing through a wire, my guess."

"Has the owner shown at all? Swales?"

"Oh, yeah. He was so helpful we had to send him out for sandwiches. He shouldn't be too much longer."

"When he gets back, I'm going to search his house, just quick. Keep an eye on him if he's outside?"

"All right." Matty spit black juice on the ground.

"Any way you could avoid pulling the site totally apart, so much the better. We got an investigator coming. Should have."

"All right. We'll just do what we're doing, leave the rest to you. Hope you don't find anything you don't want to."

"And keep it to yourself, please, Matt."

"Who am I going to tell?"

Just the whole county, I thought. As we stood there, a pair of headlights threaded the needle between the trucks lining the driveway and the trees on the other side. I figured it would be Swales returning, but I was wrong. Out of an elderly Dodge Ram eased a large man who gripped the truck's bed a good while before hobbling to where Lehl and I stood. Ron Chase.

"Ronny, hi," said Lehl. The two men shook hands.

"Buddy of mine in Endicott let me know, structure fire up on Dunleary, I thought, I don't know. Just, I'd see her place one more time."

"I hear you."

The old man turned to the trailer as the front exterior wall, what was left, toppled forward into the yard. "And that's that," he said. He turned to me. "What are you going to do about it?"

I shrugged.

"Too bad my boy's still locked up, you could blame this on him too," he said, quiet, and shambled off to find somebody else to talk to.

"He ain't been the same," said Lehl.

"Excuse me, Matt," I said, and stepped into the woods.

Leaves covered earth and rock in a stiff layer almost like plastic. It was disturbed here and there around the trailer's curtilage, but deer tracks only, nothing as purposeful as a human's. The driveway in front would be totally useless from the firefighters. By the time I'd circled around again, Swales had returned. His back was to me; he was glad-handing some of the firemen as they clustered around his muscle car. He turned and saw me and cursed.

"Yeah, it's me," I said. "You got a minute? You can leave the car where it is."

In his garage, Swales and I stood in the space where his car usually went. I took note of the state of his clothes: jeans wet to the shins and splattered with soot and mud from the driveway. Ski gloves that he pulled off and tossed aside, dirty. He opened his work coat and released a smell of sweat. Black smoke residue had collected at his nostrils. I opened my mouth; he raised a hand.

"What do you want?"

"When did you first see the fire? It was you who called?"

"Yeah, me. Ten-thirty, I smelled it, looked out, turned on my outside water, and started filling buckets. There's a spigot."

"Was the fire on the left or right, let's say, east or west side? The middle, front, back?"

"On the west side. The east side, toward my house, there's a fuel tank. I was keeping my distance. Turns out it was empty. It never blew."

"And it was a small fire at first? I mean, small enough that the buckets made sense."

"Yeah, just climbing up the side of the trailer. I was pulling as much water as I could with a wagon on the ATV, going back, filling up, going back. I knew there was no saving it before the company even got here."

"Any visitors today, tonight?"

"No."

"Trailer insured?"

"I let it go. Nobody stays there, obviously."

"I'm going to take a look at the garage. House too."

"If you must." He left.

I took off my coat and shoes and rolled up my pant legs.

There was fresh mud and plant matter in the tires and on the undercarriage of Swales's four-wheeler. Nearby stood a small plastic gas can, half full, dusty, no spills in the cement around it. I opened the inside door between the garage and the house and stepped into a small carpeted hallway leading to the kitchen. A bottle of expensive gin stood on the counter, along with a lowball glass, half a lime in it. I opened his garbage can; the remains of a salad, ranch dressing, gristle from a steak, paper towels, no chemical smell. Under the kitchen sink: what you'd expect. I stood, told myself just a quick sweep and if it needed to happen again, it would. Upstairs, the rooms were dark. I left them that way. The place was carpeted and everywhere I looked there were lines from a vacuum. The home was clean, impersonal, with nothing of life, nothing to embarrass. A white canvas. A man who sets a fire and then calls the fire department about it would have been careful. He might not even use fuel at all. Something told me Swales hadn't torched the trailer, at least not personally. I headed upstairs.

We have no streetwalkers here in Wild Thyme. We have no trafficked girls locked away; it's a small town. We have a woman or two you may know yourself or have seen at the supermarket going about her life. She could be raising kids without a partner, she could be out of work and it's her own fault, or not, but she needs more than she can get the honest way. Maybe just for a time. Maybe it gets worse, as it did for Penny, one piece at a time scattered here in this bedroom and beyond. I crossed the bedroom and opened a set of glass doors leading to a private balcony. The night washed in with its smoke and flicker as I opened the doors and stepped out. Below me, the ridge sloped to where a solitary set of cottage lights marked a triangle of lake, naked beyond the trees. It was not a view you could see from the ground, but I recognized it.

I put in a call to Sleight, who answered on the third ring. I told him about the fire.

"I'll be goddamned," he said. There was silence on his end of the phone. Then, "Let me call in to the shop. What do you need?"

"Investigators."

"I'll send Mason and Riva down. They do good work, especially if there's OT in it. They won't talk either."

I returned to the garage, pulled on my boots and coat, and stepped outside again. The line of emergency vehicles was starting to break up and disappear into the hills. Soon I was all that was left. Swales had long since gone to bed, and I shivered in my truck, waiting for ID Services. At some point I did fall asleep but did not dream that I can recall.

The trailer, what was left, reignited once in the early morning. It only took Matty Lehl, one squad truck, and one hose to put it out for good. It was six a.m. before Mason and Riva arrived with their van. I told them nothing of Swales's account of the fire, where it had started and so on, to see if he'd be consistent. They talked to him separately in the house. I asked Mason if any alarm bells had rung: not particularly. She asked me what kind of smoke had I seen and smelled. Black, chemical, I said. Though the sky was clear, the detectives pulled on heavy-duty rain suits and galoshes before they strung a perimeter and grid over the charred remains of the trailer.

By the afternoon they had few answers. The fire had started on the west side of the structure, just as Swales had said. They'd found no burn trails, at least none visible to the naked eye, to indicate the presence of an accelerant. They had sealed samples from the charred remains, as well as the ground surrounding it, in metal canisters for hydrocarbon testing. There were, to their knowledge, no bones of any kind. They'd let me know if it looked like arson.

I watched as the two detectives gathered the grid they'd strung over the dead fire, now a black hungry patch on the hillside. Three of the massive oak trees that had once framed the trailer would survive. The fourth and most westerly of the oaks had been directly in the path of the blaze pulling itself skyward; the trunk of the tree and several of its lowest branches had been charred black and still glowed red in the wind.

LIEUTENANT SLEIGHT had paid weekly visits to the stranger's cell in Schuyler County. Road salt from the highway coated his car, then the rain and sleet would wash it off, then the next week it'd collect again. The old cop sat across from the stranger, and the stranger sat shackled to an interview table, silent. Sometimes Sleight laid out a new fact they'd learned, or a theory, or sometimes it'd be stories from Deputy Poole's short life. The stranger never asked for a lawyer, never even spoke, not once through his arraignment or his preliminary hearing. The Schuyler County judge had granted the DA several continuances so that the loose task force of state police, Binghamton cops, and local law enforcement could figure out who the hell they were talking to.

We had him cold for Poole's murder; that wasn't in question. Vicki Jelinski's abduction raised questions. Kevin O'Keeffe's truck raised questions. What was the connection to Charles Michael Heffernan? Was he, as an informant had told Sleight personally, responsible for at least two murders in Binghamton—a black man up from Brooklyn, as well as a local crack addict who had been sexually assaulted and had her throat slit three years ago? Was he Coleman Tod, a Lackawana County, Pennsylvania, native who had been raised by his grandpa until Grandpa died, after which Coleman had taken everything of value from the house, including Grandpa's Roadtrek 190, and wandered over the hills and gone? A PSP detective had found a strong resemblance to early photographs from when Coleman Tod had gone missing, but the boy had been gone so long that if anybody had been interested in declaring him dead, he would have been.

"You think keeping your mouth shut's going to save you? You think they won't hang whatever they can on you?" said Sleight. "But you could talk. You could give us something."

Nothing was given.

"I'm going to play a game," Sleight said. "I'm going to assume that you are Coleman Tod, born in Clarks Summit, 1978. I see you have a mother in First Hospital in Wilkes-Barre. We could test her, see if there's a match. I see here a mother, a brother and his wife, and they have two daughters. Would they recognize you if I asked them?" Sleight fell into silence.

"I don't know," the stranger said. "Let me think about it."

YOU GO along and things happen and you don't know why. If you stop and think, you get pushed out of your own life. And when that happens, do you put up a tent in the yard, or do you go back in the house? There's a song about it. What I mean is that your life can get to feel like a current all around you, floating you along, but if you go back and look at the way things happened, there's fate, and then there's you. That's why I have to remind myself how Polly and I began. Not that chance meeting in the mountains in Wyoming, but what came after. Now that she's gone, the story I tell myself about her is like a flag, colorful against the sky, commanding devotion. The pattern shifts in the wind, but never changes very much, and it's been there so long I take it for granted. And all the while, the earth-bound struggle of our life together fades until it's almost gone from memory.

Certainly, if I allow myself, I remember the autumn trip to Jackson before Polly and I were anything. I had saved and gone hungry to pay for a drive across the country, gas tank by gas tank. The first night she took me to the ski hill and we rode a gondola to a fancy restaurant that specialized in wild game. Seams of aspen trees glowed gold in deep green pine trees, everywhere. I had pheasant medallions on a kind of green paste that looked like oil paint and tasted like the sun, never had the like before or since. It became clear that I had no plans out there that were independent of her, and the dinner had hit my wallet so hard I almost cried. Polly stayed quiet as she drove me back to my lodgings, and I had to remind myself even then that she hadn't asked me to come, hadn't asked me anything, and owed me nothing. The motel sat in the perpetual shadow of a steep valley outside of town. We got there and idled in the parking lot for a bit, then she came in with me, claiming she was curious to see my room. I believe I was the only guest at that time.

"Oh, brother," she said, her eyes flitting from the stained ceiling to the single bony armchair to the mattress swaybacked by decades of humanity. More than anything, the creek running behind the motel gave off a dampness that slicked the fabrics and the wallpaper, fogged the mirrors and glass surfaces, and mixed with the lack of light to choke the very happiness out of the air. "You can come sleep on my floor."

She didn't know what the journey had meant to me, or what she meant to me then, and that's probably a good thing. We tiptoed around each other for years without honesty getting in the way. Whenever I liked someone it was always, whoa, nelly. Slow down. Lately I don't know anymore.

AT FITZMORRIS'S tiny art supply store and coffee shop on Main, old hippies in funny sweaters sipped wine and sat and tapped their knees or ignored us. The Country Slippers rode again. The gig had come to us through a friend of Ralph Lilly's, a local poet throwing herself a book party; she'd read a number of poems, some of which made me blush, and we did our thing after.

We finished a set and a potbellied old man with a long yellow beard cornered me, smiling. It took me a moment to recognize John Allen, my fiddle teacher from when I was a kid. Back then, I'd thought him old, biking slowly up the hill in the summer months. But now, in the store's backyard some twenty-five years down the line, he was a true old-timer.

Last I'd seen him was the mid-1980s at a bluegrass festival in Bainbridge, New York. Somehow they'd gotten Del McCoury and the Dixie Pals to headline at the little fairground, and Father and Ma took us. I was eleven or twelve. Back then, hillbilly and bluegrass music was controlled by societies of men in fire halls and garages, and presented for the enjoyment of old folks in lawn chairs. Newgrass had arrived with competing flavors of jamminess and precision, but at that time it had not yet elbowed out the gospel and country blues of true bluegrass, which itself had elbowed out something before. That older thing is what I play to this day.

As I wandered the field, I saw John Allen standing with friends, and had that odd feeling of betrayal when you catch teachers escaping the lives you had imagined for them. Onstage, a fiddler was getting some on a tune that had gone foreign, that had to be in Hypolydian mode, a strange ancient feeling of becoming that went well with the kicked-up dust of the field attaching itself to my teeth. Thinking back, it couldn't have been Del's band. But I remember feeling awe at this new sound, and meeting eyes with John, and him calling over to me, "Listen to that loose-armed idiot!" I considered his authority absolute, and that was his harshest criticism of a fiddler. He was a purist.

So as I faced John Allen once more, I expected a rebuke for the band, for our peregrinations and abominations.

What he said was, "That gal can play the banjo."

"You said it."

"Ten years ago, I'd have stolen her for myself."

"Stay away, old man, she's ours. Do you have your fiddle, you want to play a tune with us? Let me bring you on."

"You got a time machine?" John held up his hands, curled and frozen. Unable to handle the fiddle any longer, he offered his services going forward as a dobro player, and he knew a bass player way over in Honesdale, and what about reviving the Holebrook County Old Time Society, and and and. "I hear you guys and I think you could be . . . I don't know. I don't know how to put it," said he.

"Better?"

John Allen gave me a guilty smile. Over his shoulder, I caught a glance from eyes I knew and excused myself from John, only to face Miss Julie Meagher.

"Who's that guy?" she said. "You sound like summertime."

"You look like summertime," I blurted.

"Aw."

"Listen, I'm sorry I haven't called."

"No, me too," she said. "Just . . . the winter, and you and your boxes," she said.

I got dragged back for a second set. Julie was gone by the time we were done. John Allen was still there, but I snuck out the back door.

YEAH, the winter was bad. One sunny day in May, I lay in the yard with my cheek pressed to the grass. In the distance, hills poofed out in light green for another spring, and up close, right in front of my face, violets bloomed purple and white, shivering on green stalks. It was then I caught the scent.

I had no shoes on, and the muddy water oozing out of the earth began to numb my feet. In I went, into the woods, into the stand of pine where I'd once found that wild azalea and brought it home. For longer than I should have, I sat and contemplated that wildest of wildflowers. The seat of my pants got soaked. I dug up a shoot, found a pot to plant it in, and drove to Fitzmorris. I caught Julie on her way out the door; she was in her uniform and headed to work. I explained what the plant was.

She put her nose to it and said, "Goodness."

"Not many like that."

"Ain't that the truth," she said.

"Well, goodbye."

"Meet me at the Low Road after my shift? Nine-thirty," she said.

And at the Low Road we got drunk. We both needed to. Much was said about our pasts. It turns out Julie was more like me than I ever knew, a kind of refugee from another life. She'd been a sometime drug user from age fourteen on. Weed was easy to get and much beloved of the jam band culture up north, where she went to college. She'd bought from a late-night takeout counter. There was also code for cocaine, pills, ecstasy, heroin (which she never touched), certain words you had to say while ordering certain items, and there'd be something for you in your greasy bag.

Come med school down in Chapel Hill, the dealers were on the delivery model. Her boyfriend was from a wealthy Jewish family in Philadelphia, secular and left-leaning, and he'd come to school already deep in cocaine.

After they got expelled and he later stepped in front of a commuter train and died, she ended up a certified EMT in Asheville, where she knew a friend of a friend from college. Though it was lonely, she didn't go out unless she was working, and cut drugs out of her life. She leaned on her family for human contact, followed her parents on vacations, marked off her calendar until holidays. Then came the end of a long shift marred by a stupid accident. A young man on a bachelor party weekend had wandered out behind a barbecue place and fallen into the river. That was it, he just fell. It was enough. He drowned but didn't go far, got snagged on a tree branch right there while his friends inside had not a clue. Everything he ever thought he was, gone, no getting it back. She'd had flashes of her own dead boyfriend, knocked into someone's backyard and out of existence by the train up north. Her shift partner had found her hiding in the trees, sobbing. He palmed her a hydro pill, telling her it'd feel just like Saturday night. She knew that. She took it, and many more in the months that followed before she was caught, suspended from work, and brought home by Willard.

"It felt safe here in Holebrook," she said. "Simple. You understand, I've been to college in Vermont, a year in France, bareboating in the Caribbean. I've been to Vietnam, Ireland. My dad worked but my mother's people started out well off. I was eight before I understood that not everybody's grandparents have a huge old house on the hill with a swimming pool and a home theater. My mother, I think she feels a little lost out here, she put pressure on me to belong to the other world. But I grew up in Fitzmorris. I tried for so long to find out, to feel right anywhere. In the end I had to decide on one place and one person to be. That's what I mean: simple."

"I never had a choice," I said. "I only had the one place to go." I told her about Polly; our chance meeting, our courtship, our marriage. How she got sick and how it was too late for her to get well. How bad I felt that I hadn't seen it, and how much I wanted to go back in time and give her more life, even if it was without me. I'd been heartbroken, near-dead; no way I could live out there alone without her. I had taken my shot at life, and had returned to Wild Thyme to become the nothing I already was. Julie did me the favor of listening without trying to say the right thing.

"What do you most miss about her?"

"Possibility," I said, after some thought. "Adventure. Bending the world to my will. The older I get, the more I see fate in the corner of my eye, lurking. When Poll was healthy, in her prime, she went toe-to-toe against fate, her and me. She was my moonlit mountains way out West, and I was her something, I guess. It was early love, before you see that it takes work. You'd follow that early love anywhere."

"I know what you mean," she said.

"It's still early for you," I said.

"Don't pull that shit, man," she said. "If you don't like me, if you don't see it, just say so. It's easier in the end. Or if you do . . ."

"Of course I see it," I said. Once spoken, the words showed me what we would become. And even through a painkiller drip of booze, it made me so sorrowful for my wife, so guilty. I knew I'd have to talk to her, but for the first time in memory I thought: What if I just leave it until tomorrow.

Miss Julie Meagher, alive and there in the bar with me, said, "Good enough." We locked faces like drunk people do, like learning to swim, while the bartender gazed mournfully at the muted TV. "One thing," she said, pulling away. "What's Liz to you?"

"Liz Brennan?" I said stupidly. "She's a friend. My best, her and Ed."

"Right." She stared at me, and I willed myself not to look away. "You don't," she said, "mess around with married women, do you?"

"Where'd you get that?"

"Do you?"

"No. Especially not . . . Liz. No." If there was ever a time to come clean about Shelly, it would've been then, but there was something about her that I wanted to keep for myself. The lie had gotten easy. I'd need it to be true now.

"Okay, okay." Julie looked into my eyes. "There is one thing you need to promise me before I set foot in that house again. And I don't want you to get the wrong idea: it's for your own good."

WE RENTED a dumpster, got cardboard boxes from the supermarket, and opened all the windows at Aunt Medbh's. Out went the sofa bed that had wasted away to a skin of cloth over metal bones. And it went in pieces, as the thing had come with the house and I had no idea how it had gotten inside in the first place. Tucked in its folds were mouse droppings that I hid from Julie. Out went the brown hook rug of the living room floor. As it flew out the window and through the sunlight, it unfurled one last time to show the portrait of a dog I never knew, then whumped into the dumpster, gone.

All that May, between our jobs and my evenings working with Ed's crew, Julie and I scrubbed the house's interior,
scraped the trim outside with an eye toward painting it laven-
der, and generally made the place shine.

Julie favored direct sunlight and plain things, and slowly I
bought cheap and used furniture at her direction. I didn't actually care except that I wanted it to feel like a home. And it did,
when our days were done and we couldn't possibly do more,
when the night drifted in and we sat reading or talking nonsense, moths tapping against our windows, me with a sweating IPA and she with her glass of rosé wine. One time we had
Ralph Lilly over to burn sage in the corners and chant.

DAYS, I went on patrol. The thunderstorms and cool rain of late spring gave way to the low drone of a heat wave. It broke records. As the ditches dried up, frogs braved the roads to look for new homes. Cars flattened them and they baked into paper, too empty for crows to pick at. The heat drew cottagers to the lakes and bars, but also turned the lake water warm as a bath. I patrolled with my truck's windows down, stayed away from the station, and let everybody try to cool off according to their own lights.

Over the past year I'd had visits from Penny's family, as well as the odd telephone call from Kevin. Once I'd gotten word from a state police lieutenant assigned to Troop P, saying he'd been calling his office too. The calls eventually stopped.

I took a quick turn up the driveway to the empty patch where the trailer once stood, still thrumming with vibrations, then back down to the station to stow my gun belt and change for a couple hours' work with Ed's crew. As the birds settled down and the mosquitoes took flight, he and I sat smoking weed together on the purlin plate of a half-dismantled barn.

"Did I tell you I heard from Kev? O'Keeffe," Ed told me.

"Lucky you."

"He made mistakes. You can let a man fall, or not." It sounded like an argument he'd made before, probably to Liz.

"He wrote me letters, called. Usually I wasn't there for the phone, even if I was home. Anyway, he's getting out."

On paper, O'Keeffe had pled only to the burglary. Not that that would matter: in peoples' minds, what he was convicted for paled in comparison with what he wasn't. "And you're giving him a reason to come back."

"He didn't kill his girl, you know." Ed passed the pipe to me. "I don't believe it, whatever they say. We don't know if she's even dead. She could be just . . . gone."

"She's more than gone. She's got to be." I shook my head. "And I might add that simply not killing your girlfriend is a low standard to meet. Possibly the lowest."

"He asked for my trust."

"Does he know I'm working for you, too?"

"Well, since you're not a hard-on, you two'll get along fine." Ed puffed his pipe in contemplation. "You can let a man fall, or not."

SOME NIGHTS I feel I am not paid enough to sleep with my scanner on, and don't. Many local people know my landline and will just call. I was asleep when, around twelve-thirty a.m., my telephone rang. I thumped downstairs to answer it. The woman on the other end had to yell over a crowd; it was Connie Conley, who often tended bar at the High-Thyme Tavern.

"Henry," she yelled. "I need you. Can you come?"

I rubbed my eyes. "What's the problem?"

"We've got a fight about to go off."

"Can't you just buy a round? Kick them out, I don't know."

"They been kicked out. It's to where they could get hurt."

"Who is it?"

"Kevin O'Keeffe, himself."

"Already?"

"You should know, dipshit!"

"On my way." I pulled on a wrinkled uniform and kissed Julie on the top of the head. Deciding I didn't have time to get a vest and service weapon from the station, I thumbed four shells into my own shotgun and drove into the night.

It being a weekend, the High-Thyme's dirt lot was full. I heard the fight before I saw it. Around the corner, a man staggered in the open. It was O'Keeffe, almost unrecognizable. His bare torso was now clenched as tree roots, nothing extra save a circle of loose flesh on his waistline, some tattoos and scars. A stream of blood flowed from his scalp down his face and into a long brown beard. He held a hand over his forehead and one eye.

A man charged out of the darkness, made a swipe at O'Keeffe's knee with a metal bar, and missed. O'Keeffe caught a blow on his shoulder, seized the other man's wrist, and pounded him into the dirt, knocked out. It took just an instant, neat and quiet. A woman in the crowd screamed. O'Keeffe yanked his attacker up by one limp arm, at the same time keeping a foot on his neck. The next instant he'd be broken.

I fired my shotgun into a horseshoe pit, sending a cloud of sand into the night air. The report startled O'Keeffe into stillness. He didn't turn at first. Likely he thought I was another one come to finish him off. When he did look, what he saw didn't calm him down.

"O'Keeffe," said I, "drop him down. Let him go."

He looked away and nodded his head. He tensed his shoulders and pulled on the arm, and the woman in the crowd cried out again. Out of the corner of my eye I saw her struggle; someone was holding her.

"O'Keeffe," I said, and racked a shell.

He dropped the man's arm, kicked him lightly in the head, walked to a nearby pickup, dropped the tailgate, and sat. "Jesus," I heard someone say. "Jesus Christ."

A rail-thin middle-aged woman with long platinum hair escaped the crowd. She stumbled forward and knelt at the man's side. In the darkness, the stars-and-bars on her black T-shirt glowed. She wore a pink baseball cap.

"Where is she, motherfucker?" she called around me to O'Keeffe. "You hear me? What'd you do with her?" This she repeated several times. She took a step back and looked up me. "Oh, look, it's the cops to save the day. Where were you when she needed you?" She burst into choking sobs. Rianne Pellings, Penelope's sister.

"Go back inside," I said.

She pointed to the man. "He's my cousin. Until somebody comes to care for him, I'm not going nowhere."

I looked down at the cue-bald, gym-built man on the ground, and saw it was indeed Bobby Chase. He began to stir. She brushed his hair with her hand, and rose now and then to curse in O'Keeffe's direction. In response, Kevin began to mumble in a weary voice. He sounded sad, and I knew how he felt. Nothing ever gets done with a fight. If a fight leaves you through fighting, it simply goes somewhere else. And it'll probably come back too.

I walked to where Chase lay. Rianne knelt, peering into his

face and telling him to wake up. I squatted down and placed a hand on her shoulder. I was close enough to catch the scent of shampoo and sweat.

"He going to live?"

"He's breathing."

I stood and scanned the crowd and saw angry faces. Recognizing a member of the VFC, I gestured to him to call for an ambulance. He trotted to the bar.

"Rianne, things are going to get . . . I'm taking O'Keeffe away." I moved my head in Kevin's direction. "He'll answer for anything he ought to. If you all want to press charges, if there are charges to press, we'll talk."

She turned away. "Just take him while you can."

I stood. "And tell him when he can listen," I said, meaning Chase. "I don't know anything and that works both ways. Tell him don't go nowhere or I'll call Binghamton."

"I don't tell him what to do. Neither do you."

At some remove sat Kevin O'Keeffe, still muttering.

"Let's see that eye," I said, approaching slowly.

He looked me up and down, then dropped his hand. The blood on his face came from a lump on his head, bisected by an open seam, as well as a tear in the flesh above his left eye, which had swollen shut. "How's it look?" he asked.

"How'd it happen?"

"A rock."

"Been there. Give me the alphabet backwards."

He did, slower than I liked, correcting himself twice. I heard the ambulance's wail in the distance.

"Okay, get in the truck, we're leaving."

"I'm getting in your truck?"

"That's right."

"I don't think so."

"No?"

"I'm fine."

"Kev. I could let someone else handle this."

He looked down at the blood on his hand, some of it his, some not, and up at me, pushed himself off of his perch, and stood. He walked over to a rusted compact car—Penny's—and locked it.

We hopped in my truck and drove away. As we moved through the darkness, I considered what to do with the ex-con. "There's a first-aid kit under your seat," I told him. "Patch up your eye, at least."

He rummaged underneath him, found the white plastic box, yanked the rearview in his direction, and began to tape gauze over his eye.

"What happened?" I asked him.

"Huh?"

"How'd it start?"

"Are you asking as a friend?"

"Talk, and maybe I won't call your PO."

"Well, I didn't start it." He tore off a piece of medical tape with his teeth. "Not any of it. I'm sitting there at the bar, next I know I'm called outside. I can take a punch or two. Nothing like prison for that. But them two weren't going to let it go."

"So?"

"So what am I supposed to do, let him kill me? It ain't time yet. I fought back. You saw."

"I saw something. So he just started swinging. You didn't say anything, they didn't want anything."

"Rianne . . . I took her car back, Penny's car. It was over to her place, but she can't have it. It's in my name, man. I can show you the title. I still have a key. You got my truck, so I have to live out of that car. I mean, my ma's place in Sayre's where I live, but. Somebody at the tavern must've called somebody, and next thing you know."

"Been drinking?"

"Don't anymore." Bandaged, he turned the rearview mirror back to me, and I saw headlights floating in the distance behind us.

"Jesus Christ," I said. It occurred to me I wasn't in my patrol truck.

The lights lurched forward, and a truck swung alongside me. I stepped on the gas and pulled ahead. We made a right at Walker Lake. When I went around bends and the cars were out of sight, I floored it for a few seconds here and there, creating distance where I could.

"Soon as we pull up to the station, you get out and head to the door," I said. "Don't look, don't talk. Just get inside."

We bounced over a gravel yard and pulled up sidelong to my station, next to the garages. The truck roared up behind, then parked at the edge of the empty fairgrounds across the road. I backed around the hood of my vehicle, shotgun hanging by my leg, unlocked the door, and we were inside. I left the light off. Then I opened my locker, pulled out my belt, and buckled it on. The weight of the .40 was a comfort. I caught O'Keeffe staring at it.

I led him behind my desk and told him to stay down. Outside, the shadow of a man passed in front of the headlights, which were pointed at my station. Then the lights went dark, the engine silent. I got on the phone to the county dispatcher and requested a second pair of hands. He told me there weren't any state police in the area but he'd try to find someone. I sat where I could see out the window. Kevin craned his neck.

"Settle down," I said. "We might be here awhile."

O'Keeffe tried to make himself comfortable on the cement floor. I listened for voices across the road, and sat for a while and thought. With my eye pressed to a scope, I peered out the window. One man, as far as I could tell.

I called the county, and the dispatcher placed me on hold for about five minutes while he tried to raise Sheriff Dally. When he came back on the line, he was abject.

"Henry, sheriff says he's sorry, he can't send any of his people. He says to sit tight, call PSP, and don't bring him anybody new down to the lockup tonight."

"They're full? What the hell happened, a riot?"

"I'm telling you what he told me. You want me to call PSP?"

"So they can get here even slower than the county?"

At long last I secured the gun locker, told O'Keeffe to stay where he was, and stepped to the door.

"I'll go with you," he said. "Give me a gun. It don't have to be loaded."

"Just stay where you are."

Beyond the yellow floodlights of the township building, a ridge swept up to a horizon crowned by stars. Down in the real world, as I stepped outside with the shotgun over my shoulder, the man across the road raised his hand.

"Evening!"

"You," I said. "Step across the road."

The figure moved slowly—very slowly. I recognized the

man's ruined gait; it was Ron Chase, Bobby's father. "Woah, Officer," he said. "You got the wrong idea." He had his hands in the pockets of his windbreaker. "I just want a word with your pal." He peered over my shoulder to the station's closed door.

I cleared my throat. "Go home." I raised my voice. "Any harm to O'Keeffe, you look at him wrong, anything, you're getting a visit from me. I'll make you pay and it'll hurt. If you test me now, I'll cuff you right here and bring you in."

Chase stepped closer and lowered his voice to a murmur. "You sure about that?"

I let the shotgun fall off my shoulder and into my hands. "On the ground with your hands behind your head."

Ron smiled. "No."

From around the bend, I heard a car approaching, and saw the trees light up blue. Wild Thyme 5, our ambulance, came to a halt in the middle of the road. John Kozlowski, township mechanic and a stalwart rescue squad member, stepped out of the driver's-side door and walked up to us. He was a hulking, shambling, drinking man, and everyone I knew liked him. He met my eyes and showed me he understood there was something wrong.

"Why, Ron," he said. "You here about Bobby already? You're in luck, we got him right back there in the unit. Kelly McCann is back with him, he's awake, but he had his bell rung for him. Go see him and tell him what year it is."

Ron grimaced, looked away down the road, turned, and walked to the ambulance.

When he was out of sight, Kozlowski leaned in and spoke low. "We found this in his sock." He handed me a small bag of white powder. "He should probably spend a night in the hospital. What do you want us to do with him?"

"These guys," I said. "Shit. I still have O'Keeffe in the station. What's your view on giving young Bobby a pass this time?"

Kozlowski shrugged. "You tell me. I just hauls 'em."

In the end, Kozlowski, McCann, and I got Ron to agree to take his son to a hospital of their choosing over the border. I told Ron to have Bobby come see me as soon as he was able about the way he'd carried on. The old man nodded his head and didn't speak a word. By the time I unlocked the station door, Kevin O'Keeffe was gone. I trotted out to the wooded hill behind the township building, drove to the tavern only to find Penny's car gone too, recognized my situation for what it was, and headed home.

JULIE AND I walked through waist-high daisies on the hill behind Walker Lake. Ed had begun dropping materials off at the site of Willard Meagher's studio, and the mason was pouring a concrete foundation and basement, which would be disguised on the exterior by a layer of blue shale pulled from the surrounding woods. It was our job that day to find the stone.

"When we were kids, we mapped this whole hill out," Julie said, pushing aside a branch and stepping onto an ATV trail. "We'd be looking for treasure, fairies, rocks with holes in them. We each had kingdoms. Creeks, foundations, boulders—they all got names. One time we were panning for gold in a stream, and we pulled out all these shards of pottery, like dozens. White with blue flowers. But our big thing was finding tree stands in the woods. Nobody used them in summertime. First Georgia and me, and then Georgia was chasing boys around the lake, and then Dee followed me everywhere. We never had a TV in the cottage, so at night we read a lot, or looked at stars." She stopped to catch her breath. "They were good summers. I'd stay in the cottage year-round if they'd let me. Here," she said, stepping off the trail, through a patch of ferns, and onto a mossy patch. Beyond, the land we stood on fell away and revealed itself as a stone outcropping. In the dell below us, great slabs of rock rose out of the ground. "We called this place the Pitfalls."

We sifted through layers of dead leaves. Several troughs at

right angles showed the area had been quarried in the past, probably for the Loinsigh farm just north of the lake, since subdivided and built over. The shale that remained would do for the mason. As the shadows stretched away into twilight, we exposed what we could.

Julie yelped; I startled, and followed her gaze to the lip of the quarry. There stood Alan Stiobhard above us, a statue in full camo and thick eyeglasses. A braid in his beard suggested the presence of a woman in his life. As far as I could tell, he was unarmed; if he'd wanted to hurt either of us, he already would've. He doffed his hat to Julie.

"Henry," he said, "been wanting to catch up."

Later that night Alan drove up to Aunt Medbh's, bringing his customary gift of a gutted perch on a line. We sat on my porch where a couple punk sticks burned, and pink hairy moths with yellow spots circled an oil lamp.

"If it's about the reward," I said, "I've done all I can for now."

"It is about the money, in a way. Here it's been some months. He's been on the news, then off it again. He is who you were looking for? Who killed that cop up north?"

"Between us, yes."

"And the ten thousand was to come from New York State?"

"Yes."

"There's got to be a reason the matter isn't closed," Alan said. "I hear they're going to haul him back to Holebrook County before they're done."

"Where'd you hear that?"

Alan declined to answer. "If he's coming back here, we'd rather have your help than the money. Help it not get out of hand."

"Alan, you know me. I'm lazy. I never want anything to get out of hand."

He smiled. "Try to find out what you can," he said. "Maybe give us some notice, if it's no trouble. You got the map to work from if it comes to it."

A FEW DAYS LATER Sheriff Dally knocked on my station door and let himself in. Under his arm was an accordion case file. He sat, and I asked him what brought him around.

"I had a meeting across the border. Binghamton, Elmira, Schuyler County, New York State."

"Ah."

"You got a choice," the sheriff said. "We could use you. You know the area, you can work quietly."

"However I can help," I said.

"All right, then," Dally said, placing the file on my desk. "Put this in your locker when you're done looking through it. And don't talk to anybody. He's coming."

THE PRISONER wore a white T-shirt and a pair of gray sweats. Shackled hand and foot and flanked by sheriff's deputies, he shuffled out of the Holebrook County Courthouse's back door. Sleight and I waited in the belly of a Black Maria with New York plates, an unmarked van belonging to Binghamton. A vehicle like that will typically have no windows in back for obvious reasons, but for what we were doing, the prisoner needed to see around him, so the van had windows, but tinted. The guards handed Coleman Tod up, set him on a bench in front of me, ran his chain through a ring in the floor, reattached it, and slammed the door shut. Tod twisted his neck to look behind him, and a faint smile lit his face when he saw me. He turned his gaze to the window.

It was my first time in his presence since the night of his capture. I'd seen photographs and videos of his interviews with Sleight and others, read transcripts and reports. Whatever was in the file. The details of his supposed killings remained murky, contained by a computer screen, limited to talk or a list of evidence found with a body. I was glad of that. What I found out was that even with all he had done to escape the everyday world, he could not escape himself. In captivity, his wants and needs had boiled down to a new pair of sneakers he wasn't going to get, a cigarette, more time in the yard, a pack of Ho Hos from the vending machine.

Detective Larkins from Binghamton Special Investigations was in the driver's seat. In front of us, Sheriff Dally idled in the county's unmarked radio car, ready to lead us on a tour of the county, one dirt road at a time. ID Services would follow behind in a black SUV. In the past few days, we had pored over maps and made some guesses as to where Tod had been. Based on hints and recollections from his interviews, he was drawn to abandoned structures, man-made hollows, power line cuts: places where his tracks could blend into others'. But he had been careful not to give us enough. Larkins flashed her headlights, and Dally pulled out with the easy slowness of a veteran lawman. We hit the road and I watched the pleasure on Tod's face as we moved through the open fields.

Two days previous I'd met with the Sheriff, DA Ross, and Lieutenant Sleight to discuss the new VIP guest in the Holebrook County lockup.

"It's not just victims we're looking for," Sleight had said. "He stashed money, tools, and weapons as he went along, so he could disappear if he needed to. Knives, a thousand or so in twenties, MREs. Anytime we can find something to confirm what he tells us, it's something we can use. It'll buy us more time in the field."

"You find any guns out there?" I asked.

"Not yet," said Sleight. "But we haven't ruled it out, just like we haven't ruled out traps, bombs, and the like. He's never mentioned an accomplice, but he'd have no reason to. Bodies, weapons, materials, trace evidence of anyone other than Tod or his victims. That's what we're out there for. But we've got to take every precaution.

"He's more than what he seems, but less than what he wants

us to believe," Sleight continued. "He doesn't want to go up to Dannemora, but he doesn't want to work with us, either. Just when we were about to send him up and wash our hands, he led us to a body in the basement of a half-burned house south of Elmira. A woman's. We think he may have done a rape-murder in Binghamton too, a prostitute. He won't admit to that one. He's been protective of his family. That's the one thing that got him to talk, to cooperate to the extent he has. I threaten to go to his mother—she's in a psych ward. His brother. He doesn't want that."

"You ask him about Penny?" I said.

"Yeah," he said, "but sideways. At a slant. You can't say the wrong thing to this guy," Sleight told me. "And anything could be the wrong thing. Best not to draw his attention. You're here because you know the county. But I know him. Listen, don't talk. We don't need you giving him any kind of a cat's paw. If he addresses you, keep it civil. A wrong word from you or anyone and this whole deal is trashed."

We fetched up by a swamp that fed into January Creek near the New York border. There was a natural shoulder and a trail worn down to the inlet, littered with beer cans and overhung with trees. The water was black and alive with bullfrogs. Though it was only noon, mosquitoes rose in clouds and worked us.

"Here we are," said Sleight. "What can you tell us? Where do we start?"

"All good things in all good time," said Tod. He leaned his body back to take in the blue sky where a hole in the forest let its light in. "You should look around. I can't be sure anymore."

"Well, if you're not sure—"

"Look around. You're the professionals." He inched his way to my side, put his back to a tree trunk, slid down it, sat, and closed his eyes. The sun crawled west.

The ID guys found nothing but a child's sneaker; it was enough. At the end of the day, Tod returned to his cell at the far end of the Holebrook County lockup and I drove home. Walking to the door, I heard Julie plunking on a ukulele in the backyard. I thought of her out there, sunny and free. I stepped inside and undressed and washed my face, and searched my eyes for secrets.

The next few days, Tod put his feet up in Fitzmorris while ID Services took their tweezers and baggies to the swamp. I stood sentry on and off. We were in a quiet pocket of the township, and the team worked unnoticed, far as I could tell. Nobody came down the trail. Still, I walked the land searching for signs, finding none.

AFTER THE NIGHT at the High-Thyme Tavern, Kevin O'Keeffe sank out of view. I called his mother, who said he was in and out of her place, and that his parole officer was also calling, and threatened an ankle bracelet if he didn't check in within the next two days. Thinking I could keep him on the map, I decided to pull out the file I'd made for him, where I had collected names, addresses, last known addresses, arrest records, and so on for many of the folks who had come into the burglary or Penny's disappearance. It was not where I'd left it. Then I looked where Penny's file was: no. I had a half memory of taking them home, but couldn't be sure.

One early evening, after a day of standing sentry near the

swamp, I showed up at Ed's shop. Ed was in the cab of his skid steer, tumbling twenty-foot beams from his forks onto risers. You could hardly hear them thunk down over the roar and rattle of the vehicle's engine. These timbers had been buried in the depths of Ed's yard for a few years; weeds had sprouted from some of them.

Off to the side, a gas-powered pressure washer idled. Who was there but Kevin O'Keeffe, standing beside the machine, cradling the spray gun in his arms. The nozzle leaked a rainbow mist into the air. His jeans were soaked to the thigh. I pointed at him and called, "Don't go anywhere until we talk." He stared at me without hostility or life before turning to his task. The bruise on his face had flattened and turned yellow. With a blade of pressurized water, he stripped a green scrim of fungus off of the nearest timber, turning the surface silver-black again.

Ed left the machine and stalked inside, and I found him sitting at what passed for his desk, peering into a handwritten ledger, which he snapped shut when I arrived. "I think I saved our asses," he said, "but we're going to have to blur over some of the history. There's another barn out in Susquehanna, built much later, the twenties, a real heap, but it could be they recycled some older material to make it. If we can pull enough out of there, we just might make the date," he said. "Whatever's going on with you and the Meagher girl, can I count on you to just not volunteer anything too damning? Nothing she doesn't notice herself?"

"You know me."

"So it's for real, you two," he said.

I shrugged.

"You son of a bitch," he said with a brave smile. "You keep it close to the vest. I had hoped against hope that you'd rise to the occasion."

"Sure," I said. "Sure, sure."

Out by the lumber pile, I found Kevin facing the woods, his eyes closed.

"What are you up to out here?" I asked.

"Listening."

"Good place for it?"

"It was."

Kevin in daylight, after his stretch in Mahanoy: distilled, burned away to stone, to iron. Even without the wound surrounding his eye, his face would've been different.

"You talk to your PO, you good?"

"Yeah."

"He ask you about the shiner?"

"Yeah. He don't need to know it all."

"Be careful," I said. "You could end up back where you were."

"Then I'll just come back here again."

"Kev," I said, searching for words. "Your place is gone. Start over."

"Nothing's gone," he said, "and nothing's here. Nothing but clear light." He opened his eyes and gazed into my face until I looked away, then started toward his car, backed into the trees by the side of the shop. His car, I should say Penny's, now rusted to a fare-thee-well.

SET BACK from a quiet road behind a weeping willow and a grove of larches, there is a boarded-up trailer that once belonged to a man named Leslie Skaggs. Why it's abandoned is, ten years back Les won a hundred thousand dollars in the lottery. The very next day he quit work as an excavator and landscaper. From there he proceeded to spend it all on food and drink, losing his legs to diabetes and his life to a heart attack. Skaggs put no further money into the place, reasoning, I guess, that he'd worked since boyhood and didn't want to miss his chance to sit around. A distant relative auctioned off what was worth selling and left the trailer, several derelict vehicles and heavy machines, and a rusted shed. Now that relative, who had been unable to unload the land at the price he'd wanted, stood to collect gas royalties from afar if they drilled. Good old Les. You can't take it with you, and you can leave it any way you want.

The midmorning sun caught a black van as it turned onto the dirt driveway. A black Suburban followed. Sheriff Dally and I stood behind the trailer in our own trucks, watching the motorcade push aside briars and tree limbs as it crawled up the track.

"You think this is going to be anything?" I asked Dally.

The sheriff spat. "Going to be a waste."

Sleight descended from his truck. With Deputy Hanluain's assistance, the prisoner hopped out of the van. He was dressed in plain clothes and manacled. He rotated his head, cracking vertebrae, took a deep breath, and looked around. Confronted by Hanluain's stony face, he scowled.

"You want to," he said, shaking the cord connecting his wrists and ankles. "Stop breathing on me."

From the Suburban, Detectives Mason and Riva emerged, skeptical and bored.

Tod turned a full revolution in place. I watched him. We took in the same air, the same swim of time. He stretched his body as far as his restraints allowed. Thought and memory passed across his face, and I had the feeling that the greenery around us was allowing him to blossom. He revolved once more, contemplating the hills. I stepped back and quickly picked a couple strawberries from the grass at my feet. This was a mistake.

"Hey," Tod called. "I'll take some."

I peered down at the crushed little berries in my hand, then up at him. "No."

The killer shrugged and sat down on the grass.

"What," said Hanluain.

Sleight hustled over and took a knee by the prisoner, all concern.

"It doesn't seem like that much to ask," Tod said to me.

"What do you mean?" I said, my voice shaking. "It's everything." I threw the berries to the ground and walked away. Behind me, the killer laughed angrily and said something I didn't catch.

Sleight was already sweating through his dress shirt. I moved off and tried not to listen as he soothed Tod, stitching up the delicate mood I'd torn into. Before long, the lieutenant made his way to my side. Meeting my eye, he gave me an almost imperceptible wink. With a big hand on my shoulder, he spoke so only I could hear.

"I need to look like I'm ripping you one. Nod your head."

I nodded.

"In medieval times we'd have wound this guy's guts around a spit. I used to think about that. I wanted him to suffer. Now I'm too tired. I'd just put a bullet in his head and leave him where he falls. He doesn't deserve the effort. Get me?"

I nodded.

"I understand how you feel. I feel it. For the job, I put it away. Of course, you can't do what I'm doing. I wouldn't want that. I just need you to understand that he's not worth the effort."

Once more, I nodded.

"There's a way to tell him no and not give a fuck. That's where you need to be. Be smarter than him." Raising his voice and turning abruptly, he said, "Fucking strawberries."

I followed the lieutenant to the edge of the small group gathering in the overgrown yard, and tried to be invisible. It was no good. Tod called out.

"Officer?" Silence fell. "Officer? You." I looked up. He pointed to an eastern hillside of scrub and saplings leading to a wall of green forest beyond. "That way," he said, and smiled.

In a procession slowed by Tod's chains, we moved up the hill and into the woods. I'd never known what was back there; like everyone else I probably thought it was a junk heap, known only to marauding boys. Skaggs's land extended farther back than I'd imagined, over a wooded hill sprinkled with tires and beer cans, beside a ravine that was dry and rocky. The creek had washed away earth around a huge maple's roots, leaving a tangle of archways and tunnels. After a gentle turn north and a rise, a column of sunlight reached the trail, marking the entrance to a clearing. In a field full of saplings and purple-topped bergamot stalks, a barn stood two stories high.

Tod waited at the edge of the meadow, as alone as any man can be who has an armed cop on either side of him. "I don't know," he said. Sleight waved us off and moved to the prisoner's side. You had to strain to make out their words.

"What don't you know, Coleman?"

"I just don't know, man. I don't know."

"Coleman—"

Tod's voice raised in pitch and speed. "Because you've been telling me my interests are being looked after here. And all along I've been trying to, to do what you've asked—"

"No, you haven't."

"Yes, I have, I've tried, without any, any material demonstration that what I've asked for, you're going to give me. So . . ."

"Coleman."

Tod looked at his feet.

"Coleman, what have I always said? There are no guarantees. We can't give you everything you want. There are things we can do, and we have done them."

"No—"

"Whether you want to say it or not, we have done them. We handled the family in Elmira. We haven't slipped since."

"Yeah, but that one time—"

"What are we doing?"

"That one time—"

"What have we been doing since we met, Coleman? Talking. With our words, with our ideas about the way the world is. Getting to know each other. Building trust. We needed to build that trust, we all did. But now we're here. And it's time for more than talk." Sleight gripped the prisoner's shoulder with a heavy hand and kneaded it. "Not another package, not another dead end. We need a forward step."

Tod shook his head and stared at his feet. "I don't need to be here. I could go to prison. Just quietly."

Sleight cocked his head to look straight into the killer's eyes. "No, you couldn't," he said. "Not quietly." A look of horror passed over Tod's face. Sleight continued. "You know what I see here? I see a man who wants credit for owning up to what he did, a man with some sense of honor. I also see a man who won't own up. What do you always say about morality, that it's a convenient fiction? That it's useful in inverse proportion to your position in life? If that's really, really how you feel, what do you care what we find here? But just for the sake of argument, what if that isn't how you feel? Then hear this: you know and I know there's families that need relief. You can give it to them."

"I don't know."

We all stood there, looking elsewhere, pretending not to listen.

"We could dig this entire place up," Sleight said. "If you don't help us here, we probably will. But you need to help. Here's why: The conversation we're having? It has moved beyond words. The next statement you need to make is an action. You know what that action is."

Tod exhaled. All around us, green. He shuffled forward.

As we moved through the field, bobolinks lifted into the air, their bouncing songs taking on more urgency, luring us away from their young. I was touched by their bravery. Polygamous, bobolinks, did you know? The vegetation had an itch to it, too much pollen, too many things hooking on to you, causing some in our party too wipe watery eyes and sneeze.

I put the barn's age at about one hundred and sixty, modified English style. Seams of sunlight escaped the decayed siding. Otherwise, it was in plumb and sturdy. I had the insane, fleeting thought that Ed should take it, and then recollected myself. The prisoner stood before the frame of a massive door at ground level. Tilting my head back to look at the gable, I felt a pulse from within: the structure gave the impression of a memorial, like a headstone washed away by centuries of rain or a lesser pyramid half buried in sand. Sweeping aside some tall grass with his leg, Riva seized the rusted handle and pulled. The door jerked along the track, obstructed by stones and weeds on the ground, until he'd made a four-foot opening. At the opposite end, the southern end, another such sliding door had fallen off its track, framing a bright square of green beyond.

"Yeah," said Tod. "I remember this." He turned to Sleight. "Tell them to let me be for a minute. Please."

Sleight gave a nod and the two ID Services detectives stepped back. Tod slid his feet forward into the barn, making parallel tracks on the dirt floor. His presence dislodged about twenty barn swallows from their tight, muddy nests, and they swirled about him in a cloud, squeaking. He moved on.

With hand signals, Dally sent Hanluain trotting around the outside corner of the barn to post up at the far door. Probably unnecessary, but we had no reason to take chances. In a stage whisper, Mason said to Sleight, "Francis, that's far enough!" The lieutenant held out a silencing hand.

Tod called over his shoulder. "It doesn't matter. This is the place."

Quiet, Mason said, "It does matter."

Tod turned and shuffled into the dark depths of the farthest bay, and there dropped to his knees.

"Okay," said Sleight. Duffels thumped to the ground, and the detectives pulled white jumpsuits out of them.

As the team broke out their tools and taped off the area, Sleight helped Tod to his feet and led him outside. "Thank you, Coleman," he said. "Thank you, son."

The body we found buried in the barn floor was a man's. The skeletal structure was clear to the field experts. Wrapped in a blue tarp, flesh melted away with lye, the bones were all that was left. There was blood in the soil. A lot. Sprays, distant from where his body became earth. I hate telling you about this, it makes me sick.

ONE MIDMORNING on Saturday, as Ed Brennan and his crew stripped shingles from a barn roof outside Susquehanna, a purple thunderhead rolled over the western hills and lay about itself with lightning and dime-sized hail. Kevin O'Keeffe was there, working. In haste to get off the roof, one of the fatter gentlemen forgot to walk on the rafters, and put a leg through the decking. It took some pulling to get him free, and afterward the crew ran for their cars or roughed it in the barn itself. The storm blew over and disappeared, and so did Kevin.

Days passed. Then I got a call late night about a prowler. As I had turned my radio off in an effort to help Julie sleep a little better, the dispatcher had had to use my landline. So much for sleep. The address was Swales's, so I called him to make absolutely sure I couldn't just go back to bed.

"It's O'Keeffe down in the woods," the lawyer said. "I told him to leave."

"Did he threaten you?"

"Not with words. Look, if someone doesn't get him the fuck out of here I'm pressing charges." Swales hung up.

Julie watched as I got dressed, then headed downstairs to put on the kettle. I kissed her and got on my way.

There were no vehicles to explain Kevin's arrival to the

ridge above the lake. The ground where the trailer had once stood was bare and streaked with black. The dead spot gave way to open space and a slope of hay washed in silver starlight, and deep forest beyond. O'Keeffe wasn't trying to cover his trail, and I followed a swath through the tall grass, clicked off the Maglite, held aside a branch, and was in there with him, in the dark.

A smell of the woods in summer, strong in old places, of decay giving way to new life. Damp, green, and secret. There's a species of lichen called British Redcoat, ever see it out in the wild? The brightest red caps atop the palest aqua-blue stalks. It—they, the lichen and its partner, a photobiotic algae—can live in extremely tough places, much more so than these woods. It takes them years to grow a millimeter. In this forest, they had grown several inches tall on melting tree trunks, glowing plain as the moon. A deer snuffed alarm and bounded away unseen. Thinking I heard something man-sized and furtive to my right, I called out in that direction. No answer. Stones clicked as I crossed a streambed.

I came to a flat expanse where the forest floor was covered with a wisp of grass, shin-high and swooning back to the earth. Broken light glanced off something bright in the green. I got closer and found what appeared to be a circle of apple-sized white stones, non-native, smooth and crystalline. Several steps brought me to the edge of the ring, probably six feet in diameter. Some stones were partially covered in leaves and dead grass, some in bird shit. And sitting cross-legged in the middle of the ring was Kevin O'Keeffe.

"I don't mean to intrude," I said.

"What do you mean, then?"

"We got a call."

"Swales?"

"Right," I said. "So you'll move it along now."

"I'm in the middle of something."

"And what is that?"

"Take a seat, I'll tell you."

"I'm not . . . it's time to go. Or he'll press charges, he says."

"You lost your wife," Kevin said. "Is she gone completely, or can you still feel her with you sometimes?"

I squatted. "You know the answer, or you wouldn't have asked. Not that she's your business."

"So my business is yours, but yours isn't mine," he said.

"Glad we're clear on that."

"Are we?"

"Okay, buddy," I said, standing and gesturing for him to get up.

"It's not time yet." Whatever small light reached Kevin's eyes made a kind of film over them, a gleam. I couldn't get through it. "Penny made this place. I know it. But I can't feel her out here."

"I'll drag you," I said, "time or not. Or we can have dignity. We can get up together and walk out like gentlemen."

"I guess it's all the same. You might tell Andy this place isn't his any more than it's mine. What a fool he is." Kevin inhaled sharply and stood. "Where does he think I've been spending my nights?"

THURSDAY, JULIE and I had an invitation to join Ed and Liz and their kids for supper. After cleaning off with peppermint soap in the pond, we sat down to spicy basil tofu and noodles with sugar snaps from their garden. Liz and Julie carried much of the table talk, while the kids rattled on at me and each other. Out under the stars with our instruments, we ran through the Country Slippers songs without really sinking into the music. Something was keeping us apart. Now and then I'd catch Julie, under her breath, add a wavering harmony vocal to Liz's voice.

I hadn't told Miss Julie about Coleman Tod's presence in the county. I couldn't. The investigation was ongoing and sensitive as they get, I just couldn't say even if I'd wanted to. But I wondered if the secret had added drag somewhere. I could already get lost in a spiral of worry, almost to the boiling point, about my history with Shelly Bray and what could happen when it got exposed. Julie had to know I went somewhere when I thought about things like that, but she rarely asked me.

Once Ed had begun his drooping journey toward a drunken six hours in the sack, Julie and I drove to her place and went to bed too, leaving plenty unsaid.

Had I been able to tell her everything, I'd have said that the DNA profile of the corpse buried in the barn matched Marcus

Quade, the black man from Myrtle Avenue in Brooklyn who'd gone to Binghamton and never returned home. This discovery confirmed Dizzy's information, unfortunately: Coleman Tod operated within Binghamton's hometown trafficking structure as a killer, and the Brooklyn man was an early victim. We had Quade's record: possession, sales, contributing to the delinquency of a minor, assault. But when we asked Tod who Quade had been and how his death had come about, Tod simply said, "He was the first. The admission ticket."

Sleight took Tod to mean that there had been more than one source feeding the Triple Cities. Whoever Tod worked for had made a deal with one of the suppliers, and thus not the other. This Quade had either been a rival or an upstart with a package, time on his hands, and the wrong idea about Binghamton. Whoever he had been in life, in death he kept Coleman Tod out of prison and in our company that much longer. And since the day of the body's discovery, Tod had taken a special interest in me.

Under the hemlocks by the shore of Maiden's Grove Lake a few days later, Tod announced, "I need someone new to talk to. I'm going to talk to my friend . . ."

"Officer Farrell," I said.

"Farrell." He gestured for me to sit. I glanced at Sleight but he was no help. I sat. Sleight hovered nearby. "You can go," the prisoner told him. "Old man. You should go." Sleight moved off, and the prisoner and I sat without speaking some time. "You from here, from this county?"

"Yes."

"Do you know this place?"

"Yes."

"Not as well as you thought." Tod tilted his narrow face to the sky. "I'm not from here. I bet you're wondering how I found it. Any of my places. Simple: I see a road that's closed and I take it. I see a trail, and I wonder, and I take it." He leaned over to me. "I see a girl—or whoever—and I take her. Farrell, I did what I did and it's done. These hills aren't yours anymore."

I heard Mason call out.

"What?" said Riva.

"Let's tape the place off."

Tod looked me straight in the eyes. "I wonder what she found. I bet it's nothing," he said. We watched the cops gather and converge on a single point. "While we're waiting, let me tell you about a girl I took one time. The girl in Elmira."

I stood and moved away.

"You are going to sit and listen, or whatever I lost in these hills will stay lost."

FOR ALL I KNEW, I was spending my days with Penny Pellings's killer. But I worked when I could on the building, with O'Keeffe on and off, and he appeared to be none the wiser. Because he had no particular place to be, he often worked as long as Ed would let him, which overlapped with my own hours. One evening it got down to just me and Kevin left, tearing the skin off the barn in Susquehanna. Toward the end of a long day like that, you get punchy, body and mind. It's when you're likeliest to hurt yourself or someone else. We were tethered together, each on the end of a long rope, taking turns descending one side of the gambrel roof or the other, prying decayed decking away from the rafters and leaving empty space below us. Once we were done, we were supposed to burn the burn pile, which had grown to a mighty height, and make sure that it went out. A little diesel was all it took and the scrappy and rotten wood lit, sending sparks way high. Night was growing around us.

"I did some reading down in Mahanoy," Kevin told me. "About the afterlife. Different ideas about the afterlife," he said. He squatted and poked at the fire.

"Oh, yeah?" I could sense he was not done.

"You ever hear of the Empyrean Fields?" he asked me.

"Nope, where are they?"

"Oh, come on, man. The sky!"

"Sure."

"The fire in the sky. The pure light, man. Clear light. Empyrean Fields, it's where we all want to go. That's just one name for heaven. How do we get there, that's the question. In the Empyrean Fields it smells like smoke, you know why?"

"It's a fairy tale," I said, feeling surly. "We told stories because we needed to, and now we don't. Who cares if it smells like smoke. This is our world. Our world smells like smoke."

"Our world?" Kevin shook his head. "Well, you're wrong."

"What?"

"You're wrong," he said. "Look up. A power of love is telling you how to be, and you ain't listening. You're betting on yourself."

"Fuckin A."

"I don't even believe you right now. You know it comes from us. The story comes from us, the only one that matters."

"Yeah," I said. That was my point.

"Sacrifice is the story. Sacrifice is how we save ourselves.

I don't see you as different from me. I save you, I save myself. It's, isn't that the way to the Empyrean Fields? They smell like smoke because the ancient ones burned offerings to get there. Sacrifices. You don't want to listen."

"No, I don't."

"You don't have any sacrifices to make."

"I've sacrificed plenty, Jailhouse Jesus. I'm here listening to you right now."

"You don't know everything."

"HOW DO YOU THINK animals feel about dying?" Coleman Tod asked me. "You're the hunter. You ought to know. Do they understand it?"

"They understand survival."

We had switched up our schedule and moved our search to nights after a neighbor out hiking had stopped to ask Deputy Jackson a passel of questions. It was now past midnight in the woods near another corner of Maiden's Grove Lake.

"The funny thing about people is, they just can't believe it." Moonlight pooled on the lake's surface. "I once knew a girl who talked too much, and she had to go. She fought like hell not to. She couldn't believe it. And then she could. She kept asking to make one call first. To write one note, take care of one thing. Of course, she couldn't take care of anything. But knowing she had to go, what was so important to get done? She'd given her kid up to another family. She wanted this kid to never know she existed. She wanted to tell her boyfriend, whatever, the family, to keep her secret from the kid. That was interesting.

Mostly they just can't believe it. This one did. And that's what she wanted. Imagine."

"So what happened?"

"She disappeared," he said, with a laugh. "She had to go, and she went. That's how the story ends. Who gives a shit about the baby?"

"Why'd she have to go?"

"Another time."

"Coleman? You don't have to go through this alone." I waited, then spoke again. "Do you remember me? We were at the bar in town. I was there talking to John Blaine, looking for a girl named Penny. I remember you there. Do you know me?"

He stayed silent. We slapped at mosquitoes and I held my tongue. Penny Pellings had never felt so close; if I could have, I would have tore his horde open to pull her free.

ONE TWILIGHT evening at Ed's shop, he and I were chiseling pockets into timbers as classical music played on the radio. One of the garage doors was open, admitting many moths and the night itself, hushing through the trees outside and beckoning to me. A tap at the door, and Kevin O'Keeffe appeared. Neither Ed nor I had realized he was still at the Brennans' place.

Kevin beckoned me outside. "I need a favor," he said.

My call to Child Protective Services the next morning was partly successful. At Kevin's parole hearing, a judge had limited his privileges to visit his daughter Eolande to one a week with a court-approved supervisor present. Eo's caseworker Cassidy Reynolds had never liked him, Kevin told me, and he couldn't connect with Eo while she was there hovering. Could I talk to Ms. Reynolds and get him some breathing room with his kid? The bargain I struck with the caseworker was that I could come with Kevin on a visit, never let him or Eo out of my sight, and Cassidy would spend the time with Sarah Cavanagh, the guardian, in the house.

I found Kevin late afternoon at the work site, and waited while he rinsed and sponged himself from a jug of water and put on a clean shirt. He carried with him a small package wrapped in a bandanna and tied with ribbon. I had on my most official uniform shirt—the one that stayed ironed—clean pants, no gun belt, hair combed, fresh. Kevin's case might have been hopeless, and the gestures he had planned empty to all concerned but him. Still, I wanted to reflect well.

He was silent on the drive to Sarah Cavanagh's place, gathered around the cloth-wrapped parcel in his lap, which he held in two hands. I asked what it was.

"A diamond," he said.

"Oh, yeah?"

"A bubble."

"Forget I asked."

"What do you think you are?" Kevin asked. "What do you think *you* are?"

"A long-suffering—"

"I've heard of an indestructible drop in your heart. It's from a book I read. This drop, diamond, whatever, is made from your mother and father, one red drop from the father, the other white. That indestructible thing is you. There's a diamond inside of you. I'm serious, Henry. You're the one who asked."

"Forget it. Save it for your daughter."

As we came to a stop in the driveway, he took a deep breath and smiled at me, his brow lifted, and his eyes terrified and sad. Cassidy Reynolds met us on the front steps in slacks and a little blazer, a dab of officialdom in a country place. She and Kevin exchanged pleasantries, and she reminded him not to expect too much, and not to try too much too soon. Eolande would set her own terms.

Inside, Kevin's daughter wore a pink dress with a cartoon character on it, and was lolling on a couch in front of a television turned low.

"It calms her down," Sarah Cavanagh said.

I don't know about kids. I'm not sure I could have said what was supposed to be wrong with Eolande, except maybe a lack of curiosity and eye contact that I thought all toddlers kind of had. She was at least two years old by now, the blond hair she'd gotten from her daddy pulled into spouts.

"Eo," said Sarah, loudly and with deliberation. "Kevin's back. He's going to visit us for a little bit today."

The child turned to Sarah, gave Kevin a skeptical up-and-down beyond her years, and returned to her show. Kevin sat beside her on the couch, still cradling the present he'd brought. I accepted a cup of coffee and sat at the kitchen table in a chair with a view to the living room. This is it, I thought, and I hoped he saw it: you spend a lazy hour with someone you love, and it doesn't have to be more. Before long Kevin requested to take Eo for a walk outside, and the women agreed, as long as I went too, and Sarah sat on the porch steps to put Eolande at ease.

Armed with bubble stuff and a wand, Eo waddled around the yard, marveling at bubbles and then popping them. I'd yet to hear her speak a word.

Kevin sidled up to me. "You ever wonder what they know?"

I shrugged.

"They're so close to it; what do they remember? Could they tell you? Could you understand if they did? I don't know."

"What are they so close to, pal?"

"The in-between. Wherever they were, whatever, before they were here."

"My niece used to talk about the mommy she had before my sister." I shrugged again. "Nobody knows what she meant. Kids don't understand things any more than us."

Kevin thought about that. "In the end . . . she's never going to understand me, alive or dead. And that's good. But she contains me."

For me, sensing Sarah's unease, Cassidy Reynolds's disapproval, and Eo's indifference to Kevin's attentions, the visit dragged on. When Cassidy stepped out to the front steps, it was a signal to wrap things up. Kevin knelt before his little munchkin, whose nose had started to drip, and placed the gift in her hands. Sarah stood up, and Cassidy took a few steps in their direction. I held up a hand. The little girl had no idea what she was holding, but she understood it was a present of some kind, and pulled at the cloth. Kevin helped her unwrap it: a round white stone, glittering.

"You're not going to remember this," Kevin said to himself. "Eo, baby, you have a mommy and a daddy. Hold this in the light: it's not your mommy, but it's the best way I can explain her. She . . . if you ever wonder about me . . . your mommy got lost, and I'm helping her get where she needs to be. If you can just remember that. I helped her."

On the drive back to work, he cried without shame. In his sorrow I heard a faint harmonic of joy.

WHEN KEVIN failed to show up to work the following day, I wondered. His mother hadn't seen him in a week. He stayed missing the day after, and I went out looking for his car in the usual places, and called Lieutenant Sleight with the make and model. The third day I got another call about a prowler by Swales's place and thought, Kevin. This one came right to my station in the afternoon. I drove the patrol truck up and parked beside a small Japanese car with New York plates. At the edge of the black empty space where Kevin and Penny's trailer once stood, I found not Kevin O'Keeffe but Bobby Chase. Tall, muscled, and shaven-headed, he held his hands clasped over his crotch and barely registered my arrival. I couldn't see his eyes for the black sunglasses he had on.

Chase was the first to speak. "So he called you."

"He's going to complain if you don't leave."

"I better get out of here, then," he said. "I ain't going back." He swept a finger and thumb under his eyes and replaced his sunglasses. "I mean," he said, gesturing in front of him, helpless at the ruination.

"I know."

"She was my girl," he said. "You find her," he said. "If O'Keeffe didn't do this, then you explain it."

"What makes you think he did?"

"That's the way it always is. You think because he smiles in your face he won't? He will. He has. Anybody can."

"You a hundred percent on that?"

"I don't know what to think anymore," he said. "Did you know he kept her locked up? O'Keeffe did. In the bedroom. My cousin, locked up like a dog."

"Like that girl up in the First Ward."

Chase tensed, and violence was in the air. For a moment I thought he'd come for me, but he wrapped his head in his hands. "I can't go back, I can't go back. About the night at the tavern, please don't. Rianne got me going, Dad got me going, I was drunk. He had her car. I want to start over. I just wish she was here."

It wasn't until the fifth day, the night rather, that something of Kevin O'Keeffe resurfaced. Miss Julie and I had returned to my place from burgers and beers at the High-Thyme, tipsy and leaning on each other as we walked from the truck to the front door. There was a message blinking on my answering machine. I pressed play.

"Yeah, Henry? Frank Sleight. Just calling to let you know O'Keeffe's car was found on a back lot off Clinton Street here. It'd been there for I guess a couple days, and the lot owner called to have it towed. It's been impounded. You want to give me a call, I can show you the place."

In town, I met not Lieutentant Sleight but Detective Oates in plain clothes, in a parking lot beside the DMV office. Fifty yards back and one lot over was where Kevin had left Penny's car nosed into the trees. In any direction, a man walking could find bars, hotels, highs including strong drink, crack, heroin, and bridges to jump off. Downtown, a man could board a coach bus to take him anywhere.

*   *   *

I HATED being so busy. Ed called and called; I told him I needed to take time off the building, and he cursed me. The township was not to be denied. In the late afternoon I heard a car stop in the parking lot with a familiar wince of brakes; Shelly Bray had come to visit once more. My office door was locked, and she twisted the knob and shook the door in its frame before thumping on it with her fists and feet. I hurried from behind my desk and let her in.

"Jesus," I said. "Quit it. You can't stay, you know that."

Shelly wasn't listening. "I feel sick," she said. "You have any water?"

I freed a plastic bottle from under my desk and handed it over; it was warm, but she drank some anyway, then focused and turned to me.

"You have to go out there," she said. "Wurlitzer's dead."

"I'm so sorry," I said. "Wasn't he pretty old?"

"He's lying out there. Josh won't let me up. You have to go, Henry."

"I can't."

"You have to. Henry, he killed my horse. My kids are home."

Shelly followed my patrol truck in her car, but at my insistence she did not turn up the driveway, and I left her parked on the shoulder. As my tires crackled up the dirt driveway and the Bray house came into view, Joshua emerged with a nod of his head and folded arms. In a gesture of peace, I was without my gun belt, but kept a .22 mousegun in my pants pocket. Though I didn't know Josh beyond a couple conversations a couple years ago, I had seen the guns in his basement. It being a Saturday, he was dressed for leisure. I couldn't tell if he had something on him. I got out of the truck.

Into the silence between us I said, "Shelly came to see me at the station. She was upset. One of the horses died?"

Josh blinked impatiently. "Yes?"

"Well . . . can she see him?"

"No."

Dismayed, I pressed on. "How did he die?"

"I shot him."

"Okay, I need to see the horse."

"If you must," he said.

Behind the house, a golden field bordered the woods. Turkey vultures wheeled in the sky above. As I watched, one tumbled down to join others around a dark form in the grass. Joshua and I approached the place. Wurlitzer was a bay whose shine had been dulled by shagginess and patches of gray. I'd ridden him once, and though horses were not my favorite, he'd been a real sport. I hated to see him lying there in so much blood. Once the birds moved on, leaving only a cloud of green flies, I could see that the horse had been shot four times, high-caliber, three to the abdomen and one to the head. In the distance, Wurlitzer's girlfriend Pinky, a rose-gray, raced along the fence by the tree line, keeping as far as she could get from the house and barn.

"What happened here?"

"He broke his leg this morning, and he went wild." Josh shrugged. "He was scared, pacing, hurting himself. I had to do something."

A blade of bone emerged through the skin of Wurlitzer's foreleg. "How'd he break it?"

"No idea. I just heard him carrying on, and I could see it was serious."

"Shelly's upset."

"Yeah. Yeah. If she doesn't like how I care for the animals, she can find a way to take them on herself. You have some land up by you, don't you?"

"Did the kids see?"

"I don't know. They probably did see something, yeah. I told them to stay in the front room. Of course that only made them curious."

I looked at Joshua for a long moment. He looked back at me, waiting for something I wasn't going to give him. He'd seen much more of me than I had of him, and as his eyes flicked up and down my person, I wondered what was in his head. His calm was perfect.

Back at the road, I swung the truck behind Shelly's car and joined her in the passenger seat.

"You can't go up there," I said. I explained about the broken leg.

"You're kidding me," she said. "You bought that?"

"I don't know if I did, but you still can't go up."

"What are you going to do?"

"I gave him the names of a couple excavators. He's got to have it buried, he knows that. I'm sorry, Shel."

She landed a punch to my neck and was winding up for another when I took her wrists. "Get out," she said. "Get out. What are you going to do? Who's going to take care of them? My god. Get out."

*   *   *

AT THE CLOSE of a god-awful day Sheriff Dally came to assign me an overnight babysitting detail in the county lockup, just Coleman Tod and me.

"It's not my shift," I told him.

"He asked for you," the sheriff told me. "Sorry about it."

We sat for a minute at my desk with our heads bent over a map of the county. It was clear we were running out of places to search. There was a spot off of 37, and then on the edge of my township, a vast swamp of berms and channels leading nowhere, and emerald bogs cut off from the main body by the slow buildup of silt. Your one step could be on grass, your next step thigh-deep in rusty mire that was and wasn't water. Known Stiobhard territory. They'd been clear with me, and I owed them a word about where we were going.

Before heading to the county lockup, I drove the dirt road up to the Heights to visit the Stiobhard homestead, where Michael and Bobbie Stiobhard lived, parents of Jennie Lyn, Danny, and Alan. Last I knew, Jennie was still living with Pam Maddox in Wild Thyme, Danny was probably in a long-term motel somewhere, and Alan was likely out in the woods. But none of them got too far away from their folks for too long. In the front yard was a rabbit hutch with two checkered giants nestled in whorls of hay within. A vegetable patch took up the side yard. Bobbie emerged from between two rows of corn, raising a meaty arm in my direction.

"They're out and about," she told me. "Been over a week since they've visited. They never tell me where they go. The boys don't, anyway."

"How you been?"

"We're managing. Less weeding without the rain. Less of

everything, but still we do all right. What do you hear from your folks?"

"They don't use the phone much," I said. "Neither do I. Mag tells me they're doing fine, though."

"Tell them hello. Not many of our people left out here," she said. "I know Michael would send his best to your father."

"If you can get word to Danny or Alan, or Jennie, whoever," I said. "I know they're often scouting game out to the swamp. We'll need to get in there on county business, next week or two. So to avoid a misunderstanding . . ."

"I'll let them know," she told me.

The county courthouse basement had one row of six cells for men and an annex for women, and this had served as the lockup for decades. It had never been intended as a permanent deal: sleep one off, think about it, wait for your hearing if you can't afford bail. This was distinct from the multitudes taking plea deals and getting short sentences in the new century; those folks ended up in the county jail proper, south and east of town. People not bad enough for state prison, but not good enough or rich enough to be free, wound up in the newer facility.

They had given Coleman Tod a temporary cell in the court-house basement, at the far end where nobody ever went any-more. Sheriff Dally's people took extra shifts to keep watch on him, and I'd seen them bleary-eyed and cranky from having stayed up to do so. Deputy Jackson met me in the fluorescent hallway and repeated what Dally had told me earlier: "You won't have any reason to open his cell door. If you think you do, call me first, then the ambulance, then go ahead and open it if he's dying or what." Jackson demonstrated the lock to the main door and a lock on a cell door in the middle of the row; inside were two cots with clean, stained sheets and a toilet between them. "Your bunk, if you want it," he said. "Usually I hang out somewhere in the office and check him every fifteen or so."

Suppertime, I microwaved Tod a frozen dinner from the department's freezer and slid it under his cell door. He looked up at me from his seat on the bunk as if to say something, but I beat it down the hall.

Around midnight, after a dozen trips down the hall to unlock the main door and check on Tod, who was either sleeping or pretending to, the open cell two doors down began to appeal to me. I stretched out on a bunk in there. The cell lights were out, but the hall lights stayed on all night; it was bright enough that I thought I would stay sharp. Still, I fell asleep and jerked awake what felt like thirty seconds later. It was after three.

I took off my boots and walked silently down to Tod's cell. A fluorescent glow reflected from his eyes in the dark. He reclined on his cot, one leg crossed over the other.

After a moment I said, "You good?"

He raised his eyebrows and said, "Pull up a chair." I did so. He hitched himself up in the cot to where he was almost sitting. "Do you think," he said, "when the time comes, you're going to believe it? How are you going to handle it?"

"Why are you asking me that?"

"Why am I asking you that, or why am I asking *you* that?"

"Pick one."

Tod exhaled a sigh that reached me in stale sweet breath. "I want to picture how you take it when it comes," he said. "When, not if. That's why."

"What did I ever do to you?" I said, smiling in his face.

"Oh, you didn't do nothing to me. I'm just passing through," he said. "But I hate leaving work undone. And now that I'm in here, I don't know who's out there to pick up the slack."

"Well, whoever they are," I said, "I hope they leave a good-looking corpse."

SUMMER WAS drawing to a close. Most cottagers would be spending a final week or two out in Wild Thyme before they shut their places up and drifted away for the year. I had been promising to spend some time with Julie and her people on Walker Lake, and with the weekend, that time had come.

I left my truck squeezed between the tree line and the side of the dirt road, took my bag and my fiddle. Far below on a dock, a half dozen or so people lounged in the late summer sun, and I picked out Julie among them. A pontoon boat was tied to the dock.

Off to my right, Willard Meagher sat in an Adirondack chair smoking a small cigar. He tapped ash into a standing brass ashtray beside him, held up the cigar, and said, "You know how it is."

I followed the stone wall over to him and stuck out my hand, which he shook. He wore a magenta tennis shirt, cutoff jeans, and no shoes. A battered plastic cooler stood beside him on the ground. He reached into it, found a can of pale ale, and placed it on the arm of an empty chair beside him. I sat and snapped it open. We sat and listened to the people teeming below at Walker Lake.

"You from here?" he said suddenly. "Originally?"

"Yessir. Then the service, then back here, then Wyoming for

a while." For some reason I needed this family to know that I'd been other places.

"I've been to Wyoming. I like it better here."

"If you say so," I said.

"I've been a lot of places and here's better," he said, flapping a hand as if I didn't know my own mind. "You served where?"

"Somalia, tail end of it, just out of high school."

"I was Coast Guard. In the seventies, drug enforcement off Florida? Chasing smugglers in yachts and fishing boats. Waste of time. Waste of money."

"Yeah?"

"Well, you of all people can see it didn't do a bit of good. Fun, though." He twisted his cigar in the ashtray. "For a while I thought: Florida, why not? That's where I met Tina, she was on her spring break with her parents. Here's better. Come on, I'll show you around."

We left my bag on a creaky old bed in a second-floor room with nobody else's things in it. He told me to put on my bathing suit and I did while he waited in the hall. It felt strange to be staying over at a house not twenty minutes from mine, but I guess that was the point. I had forgotten flip-flops, so I just slipped my bare feet back into the work boots I wore every day. Willard showed me the cottage. His paintings were sprinkled throughout: glacial shards of blue, green, and white competing for space. Hints of other, sharper colors, tailings from a strange mine. Many of the pieces featured scraps of burlap or threads sewn onto the canvas. He didn't explain and I didn't ask. The living room had a wall of novels whose spines had been bleached from the sun.

He and I each took the handle of a large cooler full of beer, ice, and a bottle or two of white wine and walked straight to the shore. There, four women lolled reading by the dock, wearing swimsuits and wraps on this last hot day of a turning season. Julie had two sisters, one younger, Dierdre, who went by Dee, an unmarried asset manager in New York City. The elder sister was Georgia, a schoolmarm at a private academy up the Hudson River. She was married, with two boys ages five and seven. Her husband had not come, claiming too much work as a consultant or lobbyist up to Albany. And with the sisters was Julie's mother Tina, a slow-talking, eyebrow-arching, silver-haired lady in an elaborate beach wrap.

With predatory patience, Tina roused herself from her lounge chair, stepped into the family's pontoon boat, and rearranged herself on a bench seat exactly as she'd been on the dock, except with a life preserver around her neck as a kind of pillow. I understood through the course of the day that Mom's drawling fanciness was a kind of running family joke, that she had never quite adjusted to the rough-and-tumble of her husband, and knew it only too well. She handled herself like a lady from olden times, fallen and making the best. And her daughters were happy to play along, the more ridiculous the better, waiting on her, offering a beach blanket every time there was a breeze, and regularly inquiring after her condition as we cruised the lake. Mom answered only in murmurs and almost never cracked.

But the pontoon came under fire from neighboring boaters armed with water balloons. As the rainbow of blobs pelted our boat, it was down to me, Julie, and Georgia's boys to defend us. I went so far as to dive down under the attacking boat and make a grab for their bucket of balloons as I surfaced on the other side. I took a hit to the face for it. But when Tina got blasted, Will had the good sense to surrender and flee. I heard her say, "Ugh. It isn't funny."

Afternoon blurred into evening and we returned to shore, baffled on too much sun and beer and ready to put our feet up. I washed under a showerhead the size of a Frisbee. When cocktail hour arrived I headed to the living room. Just keep smiling, I told myself, and think twice before you open your damn mouth.

Dee sat cross-legged in a wing-backed chair in ripped jeans, scrolling through her BlackBerry. She looked up, smiled, and looked down again. "I hate this thing," she said. "It's a desert island and still there's email."

"I know what you mean," I said, thinking of my radio.

Willard swept in, went to the bar, and placed a lowball glass in my hand: scotch. Tina followed, carrying what looked like a vodka tonic.

"I snooped," she told me, "in your room. To make sure you had everything you needed. Lo and behold, you brought your violin. I hear you're good. You'll play for us. A private show!"

"Leave him alone, Mother," said Dee.

"Oh, please, you're no fun, Dee."

"Let him be, Tina," said Will. "Come on out to the smoking lounge," he said.

Outside, the boys were playing manhunt. Their bird voices carried all the way up the slope. From my Adirondack chair, through a mare's tail of Willard's cigar smoke, I caught a glimpse of Julie down the hill, sneaking from under some pine trees and across the lawn to the lee of a moss-covered boathouse.

"You got any young ones in your world?" Willard asked me.

"My sister's got three kids. But they're in North Carolina. One of them I've never even met yet. I'd like to. She's one year old."

"I know Julie'd like to have kids. Not with you! Necessarily. I mean . . ." He shifted in his chair. "What I mean is, she left it a little late, but it's not as if she's got a career in the way."

"You don't think?"

"I don't know what I think." Will abandoned his empty lowball for a cold beer. He tossed me one, too. "What do you think?"

"I couldn't say."

"Thinking is dangerous," he said. "I'm going to retire from it. You don't retire from working, you retire from thinking, did you know that? Maybe I should retire from talking too." He put an ankle across his knee. "You'll get used to us."

After supper, Julie fetched up beside me where I sat on a stone wall. The scent of her sweat pulled at me, quickened my heart, cut into the buzz and flower scent of ironweed and aster left to grow against the deck, almost wild. I wondered would she sneak into the guest room and see me later. The lake reclined below us, and above us was a field that had yet to be mowed, with a trail leading up to the work site. She caught me eyeing at the escape route and said, "Come on."

Up to the field we went with my fiddle, a blanket, and what remained of a bottle of rosé wine. The lightning bugs were out again, looking for love in the tall grass. The night deepened and our little branch of the galaxy locked into place above me.

A series of high-pitched screams sat us bolt-upright. Close by. I caught two sets of green eyes low to the grass. They dropped out of view. The creatures screamed again, sounding like women in anguish except for the tone that threatened, that marked territory.

"Fishers," I said. Black little foxlike animals, long like weasels, and fearless. They move like water pouring from glass to glass.

"Tell them to go away," Julie said.

"Greedy little things. They just kill and kill, stash what they've got and move on, leave food on the table. They'd bury us in a second if they could."

'VE BEEN wandering seventeen years," Tod said to me, and to the world.

It was high noon. He and I were standing side by side in a ravine that ran under 37, through rocks and a six-foot culvert, and continued east. He'd claimed there was a deer trail on the uphill side. If we took it through the red pine, we'd find a girl buried by a car-sized boulder with coins hammered into its layers. Sleight stayed with us while the ID Services team searched the forest.

"Seventeen years beyond the pale," Tod said. He shrugged as far as his shackles would allow. "Who in life can say they did that?"

I moved up the hill, as far away from him as I dared get. I heard a few steps and I thought at first he was following me, and I turned. I felt the shot pass before I heard it: a high-caliber rifle from a distance. Tod's head burst into a red cloud, and pieces of his skull scattered into the creek. I slid down the way I came. For an instant Tod remained standing, and then fell over dead. Sleight removed his glasses, and wiped the killer's blood and brain from his face. He pointed back up the hill and I ran.

On 37, Hanluain was leaning into his patrol car's window to get to the radio. I sprinted along the shoulder, around a bend in the road, to catch a glimpse of any vehicle taking the shooter away. There was nothing, nothing, and then Hanluain raced past me at about a hundred in his car. I gave up and turned up the hillside on foot. Past the high-water mark of road dust and litter I moved into a world of deep green. I kept part of my focus on the position of the body as a point of reference, and the rest clung to what entered my senses from the woods: no birds singing, no footsteps moving away, the huffing of two or three cops approaching the hilltop. I met Mason and Riva in an open space, lightly trampled, with a view into the ravine where the world had caught up with Coleman Tod.

I paced farther north into the forest, away from 37. Eventually I came to an electric fence strung around a paddock of several dozen cows. Skirting it, I came to a farm with its farmhouse long gone, in its place a double-wide dwarfed by the barn next to it. A long dirt driveway led to what I eventually recognized as Tanner's Hill Road. A sagging farmer of about fifty emerged from the barn to stare at me as I placed my hands on my knees and sucked air.

NOBODY IN Wild Thyme claimed to have seen or known Coleman Tod. We had been followed or someone had leaked our location; that was plain. But who would have risked the kill and why— that was less clear. Of course Bobbie Stiobhard swore she hadn't yet reached her boys, and I'd never given her any idea of our position out by 37. Still, when the hill had been combed over and nothing turned up but my tracks, and given the length of the shot, I had to take the absence of evidence as a meaning all its own.

Once again I called Louis Resnik out in Beaver to see if he'd turned up Sage Buckles, and to keep a watch out for Kevin O'Keeffe, both of whom were of interest in Tod's death until I could rule them out. Resnik had nothing on Buckles, but he gave me some news: Hope Martinek had died a lonely death that early fall. Before a landlord had unlocked the cinder-block cottage she rented month to month, she had decomposed considerably. The universities didn't want her and she was given a simple burial in the county graveyard out in Beaver. I pressed Resnik on the investigation, but he was steadfast: it was an overdose, nothing more.

It took two weeks to wind up Tod's death with an inquest and an investigation taken over by PSP that is open to this day. I had some long conversations with a state detective. Whatever suspicions I may have had about the Stiobhards, I kept them to myself, and turned the exchange toward Binghamton and the operation that Tod threatened to bring down every day he took breath and dredged up another body. Meanwhile, Alan did me the favor of staying out of Holebrook County, or at least out of sight. All good things in all good time.

I threw myself into timber framing once again. Working on the building, as the song goes. Willard's studio took form, piece by piece, day by day, and the crew was drawn to the hilltop above Walker Lake. Ed was a month or three past the deadline, but Willard had been drawn into the process more so than end result, and had stopped looking at the calendar.

Bright blue sky, maples gone red and orange among the yellow and green hills surrounding the work site. A white puff of breath, cold morning water seeping into my boots from the tall grass. The air smelled like the timbers we'd worked, numbered, assembled, disassembled, loaded onto flatbeds, and secured with ratchet straps. Soon we'd raise the barn, throw a party, and shake our fists at the autumn already elbowing summer aside with a morning frost, a little chuckle at our earthly pursuits.

Some personal prayers were said as Ed's aged Ford L8000 turned up the dirt track to the meadow above Walker Lake. It made the climb, and the crew unloaded and stacked timber, siding, and sheets of steel roofing around the site.

My cell phone rang: I recognized Andy Swales's number. I didn't answer it, and it rang again.

"Yeah?"

"He's back."

"Who?"

"O'Keeffe. He's got somebody with him."

"Don't leave the house," I said. "I'll take care of it."

I had warned Kevin about going up there anymore, and he had not listened, and now I was being pulled away from my own life to deal with it. Damned if I wasn't going to take him in for trespass and we were going to talk—Penny's death, Coleman Tod, what he knew and wasn't telling me, his future here in Wild Thyme. I got to my truck, reconsidered, pulled Willard aside, and asked for the use of his over-under. It would only be a prop, but better to have it and not need it.

As I neared the Swales place, I could see Sage Buckles's sedan parked in the driveway with the trunk open. I saw Kevin O'Keeffe standing beside Buckles in the space where the trailer had been. One of Buckles's legs was loose at the knee and could hold no weight, and his wrists were fastened behind him with wire. His hands were purple. I stopped my truck in the middle of the road and got out with the shotgun in my hand. Kevin knocked Buckles to his good knee and raised a machete over the back of his neck. In his other hand was an automatic pistol, which he pointed dead at me.

"Kevin," I said.

"Do you want to live?"

"Yes," murmured Buckles. His face was white, his nose was flattened completely to one side, and black blood dripped from his chin.

"Not you." Kevin never took his eyes off me. I laid the shotgun down. "'Ahead of you are butchers and killers to drag you along,'" he told Buckles, tapping the back of his head with the blade. "You a butcher? That's how she'd see it. You're a demon. But you know what? So are we, all of us. And we're going to become something else now. We're all going to become something else."

"No," said Buckles. Tears streamed down his face.

"This is important," Kevin said. He gestured for me to move forward, and I did, away from my weapon. I kept my hands on the back of my head. He smiled at me, a lucid, happy smile. "You feel her here?"

"Sometimes," I said.

"We need to help her leave."

"Kev. I know who killed her," I said.

"That makes two of us."

"You don't know everything."

"I saw a name in your file. I saw this name, Hope Martinek. She was this guy's wife, so-called? But I didn't know any Hope. I never seen her before. So when I got out and tried to put my shit together, put that night together, she was a missing piece. Maybe she saw something I didn't." Kevin took a casual step on Buckles's bad leg. Buckles let out a scream that circled back into tears. I took a step forward.

"Stop crying," Kevin said, "just fuckin stop it." He turned back to me. "Hope Martinek. I checked her addresses, I checked the rehab. But I couldn't find her any of those places. Why is that, Sage?"

Buckles didn't reply.

"What did Hope know?"

"I didn't kill her," Sage managed, his voice thick, his eyes unfocused. "She got drunk and shot up. It was too much; she died."

I took another step.

"Henry, I'll kill you right now," Kevin said. I stopped and held my hands up. "It didn't take five minutes to check her record. Hope was on three months' house arrest and outpatient with a fuckin bracelet. Until June last year. She completed. So how'd she get up here in May? I didn't see her then. Nobody fuckin saw her. So why did Sage say she was with him all that time? He killed Penny. Hope knew. So he killed her too."

"Okay, man," I said. "It doesn't have to be that way." But I was not so sure.

"Here's what we say: Om mani padme hum. Om mani padme hum. Repeat it."

I repeated it. Buckles tried and didn't quite get there. "Oh, no, oh, no," he said.

"Here's why it's important to say the words," said Kevin. "You killed my girl. She wasn't ready to die. And she didn't die easy, did she?"

"I didn't kill her," Sage choked out. "You going to shoot this cop, too?"

"You put Coleman Tod right next to her while you dragged me through that fuckin lake house job. Nobody would've got through me otherwise."

"You think you could protect her? She was going to die for one thing or another. She was already gone."

"No."

"She ran her mouth," the big man said. "She ran her mouth and got a talking-to. You want to say I killed her. She was already laid out dead in my fuckin house when I got back. By that fuckin devil. He left me to deal with her."

"You thought you'd get to have your way first." Kevin stepped on the leg once more. "Right now, where Penny is?

She's not where you put her. She's with the terrors in between. Do you know what she sees? Charred stumps, black spots, dark ravines, and shadows. And you're with her too. We all are. Om mani padme hum. Do you know what the words do, Sage? The words dissolve that place—the earth where Penny is—into water, the water into fire, the fire into fireflies, into wind. The candle's flame into wind."

"All right," said Buckles.

"The wind into consciousness, consciousness to luminance, luminance into radiance, radiance to imminence, and imminence into what?"

"I don't know."

"Clear light," Kevin said. "Let's try again."

We tried again. My mind raced. I said the words but did not mean them. Buckles couldn't get them right and gave voice only to his pain.

"It's all right," said Kevin, not unkindly, and pressed the pistol to Buckles's head. I started for my weapon but an unseen hand stopped me. The hand was the sound of a shot. Its echo went on and on. Kevin watched me sink to my knees, then to my side on the ground. Then he shot Buckles clean through the head. I tried to move and a fire ripped through my shoulder to the shredded flesh above my heart.

I didn't want to die. But if I was going to, I might as well get into the spirit of it. Penny came to me. Wherever she was, she was still beautiful. I thought of her as the same as myself, and as Kevin, and Shelly, and Julie, and dead faceless Coleman Tod, and Dopey Hopey, and even dead Buckles right there with his mind spread out over the unmowed grass like vomit, and as the bobolinks in the field, and the field itself and everything in it, and the forest at the edge of the field that grew on and on, and as every great old tree in the commonwealth. And, though it took some effort, I saw her as my own Polly.

With my lips not quite touching Penelope Pellings's ear, I began to chant. Kevin listened, smiled, and spoke words out of a dream. Strange and familiar, his words, though I can't remember them now.

PART THREE

I SAT ON a kitchen chair under a maple tree with leaves the color of cherry bubble gum. Where I pressed the fiddle to my shoulder, the place felt foreign, still raw: muscle healing around a through-and-through gunshot. A gang of antibiotics for the wound, a valve for a collapsed lung, and bracing for a collarbone fracture. Two weeks of PT and it was still going on. But the fiddle came alive as I drew a bow across the strings. While I watched from the shade of my tree, folks swarmed the Meaghers' hilltop to see the barn-raising and maybe swing a hammer or haul on a rope. Ed had told me that my job was to set a steady pace. I let the bow take over and it veered into "Ways of the World."

Since early morning, they'd knocked the sill beams together, put up corner posts and plates, and with the aid of two real draft horses and a pulley system had gotten a start on the second-story bents. The building's ribs called to mind a cathedral when you look up inside it and imagine climbing to the ceiling, or at least a church of some grandness.

Holding the fiddle's neck with my left hand, something as natural as walking to me, had changed. Without the sling, my torn muscles worked, and after a few numbers an ache drew my attention, every now and then a twitch.

With the second-story plates joined to the bents, it'd be time to send up the rafters on either side to meet the frame and be attached with pins of yellow locust.

They tell me Andy Swales called for help and watched Kevin as he sat beside me cross-legged and silent. Kev tossed the 9mm in the driveway where all could see, but still they tackled him when he wouldn't lie flat. I guess he's in the lotus position still, somewhere in the belly of SCI Waynesburg, waiting for his date. Whatever he needed to do out here, he did it, and pled to it. Even to Charles Michael Heffernan, once they matched the gun up.

In the days that followed, Sleight's and Dally's people combed Sage Buckles's property and unearthed a blue plastic barrel. Inside, dirt and an entire skeleton, Penny Pellings's. With my testimony and evidence from Cy Stokes and the truck, DA Ross was able to conclude that Coleman Tod had killed her and planted blood evidence in Kevin's truck as insurance; the matter ended with a brief inquiry. The family took her remains and I don't know what they did after that.

Wild Thymers drifted in and out of our work site, in and out of the life of a long-gone era we could only wonder at now. Willard Meagher bounced from one task to another, never quite in time to be helpful, always just in time to get in the way. Julie walked the upper tier of the frame, hauling timbers up as they were passed to her. I yawned, a great world-eating yawn, and I played.

I'D SPENT THE NIGHT before with Lieutenant Sleight. He had borrowed his wife's car and, from Columbus Park up to Prospect Street, he drove us through downtown and its walking wounded. At a gas station on Clinton and Glenwood we stopped for beer. In the parking lot a tiny hatchback with tinted windows idled, pulsing with music. I walked into the store, chose a sixer of Flower Power, and waited to pay behind a young woman buying flavored cigars. She slipped into the hatchback, which stayed put as Sleight drove away.

We ended up in a lot kitty-corner to Stingy Jack's, drinking beer from a six-pack turning warm. Above us, travelers sped to and fro on the overpass. When you watch a bar's entrance long enough, the people seem to move in and out like air. Around eleven some angry lumps stepped out yelling, and we perked up in hopes of entertainment, but their shoving went nowhere. We called it a draw.

"I hear from Special Investigations that they're looking at a new crew now," Sleight told me. "You can't keep up with it, not anymore."

"A new crew."

"Yeah," he said. "A new old crew, maybe. Bunch of kids all grew up together on the same block downtown. Whatever stream Blaine was running has dried up." At this I was downcast, but I hadn't expected the world. "Too much mess up north and down your way. A dead cop and so on, that crew is scurrying for their holes. And Blaine, I'm sure he knows what's good for him. Nobody's seen him since fall last year."

We'd sat long enough across from Stingy Jack's in the car's forced air, listening to right-wing talk radio, that we were out of beer and dry. We decided why not go in. It was a Friday, a loud, busy night, and my shoulder sling attracted no attention under my jacket. Sleight ordered a bourbon and I stuck to IPAs, and we stood and watched the girls behind the bar filling drinks in constant motion. When Sleight leaned over the bar to ask one a question, I couldn't hear what either of them said, but the lieutenant nodded and we left soon after.

"She thinks Ohio," he said as we got back in his wife's car. "He can run, but who owns the place, owns the place."

"And who's that?"

"Same folks that bought the apartments where Heffernan got shot," he said. "They're registered in Pennsylvania; I looked it up." He scribbled something on a Post-it and handed it to me. I was not surprised: on the paper was written, *Ton L, LLC*, with a Scranton address. "You know who the managing director is. The members aren't on the certificate, don't have to be. You could try to get to them with a subpoena if you could work it up. Blaine isn't connected that I can tell, not on paper, except for the bar and the house in Airy. The group also owns that, or used to. They'd paid some property taxes on it, sold it to a bigger investment group that looks legitimate. I wouldn't be surprised if the next we heard, Blaine was dead or back in prison. Henry, even if they knew, they won't have touched any of Blaine's business directly," he said. "Not Swales, not nobody. That's what they had Blaine for."

"And Blaine had who he had." All down the line to Penny Pellings. Who's been here since I've been gone, pretty little girl with the red dress on.

"Anyway," Sleight said. "I've got my mess. You've got yours."

RALPH LILLY arrived with the first chill in the afternoon air and joined me under the tree to swat at his wooden box. Liz brought out the banjo, and we competed with noise from the raising. After a couple tunes I let them two hold it down, slipped into the tree line to toughen up, and then circled the structure and stretched my legs. Next week would be next week. Was it a shame what happened to people, of course it was. You can mourn it without end or deal with it the best you can. The setting sun broke up among the trees and timbers and shot wild pink beams across the field. The crew hammered decking across the rafters. Miss Julie appeared beside me, catching her breath and sweating out her troubles, almost as if she had always been there.

WORKING ON A BUILDING

Emily Bouman, Barbara Jean Bouman, Pete and Kate Bouman, Joyce Wilbur and Ed John, and my whole family. Neil Olson at Donadio & Olson. Tom Mayer, Sarah Bolling, Elisabeth Kerr, Mary Kate Skehan, Sam Mitchell, Meredith McGinniss, Steve Colca, Don Rifkin, Julia Druskin, Bill Rusin, Brendan Curry, Golda Rademacher, Deirdre Dolan, Dan Christiaens, Karen Rice, and W. W. Norton & Company. Angus Cargill, Sophie Portas, and Faber & Faber UK. Adrienne Brodeur, Isa Catto, Daniel Shaw, and Aspen Words for the space and time in Woody Creek. Judi Farkas at Judi Farkas Management. Dave Cole for his sensitive copyediting. Jennifer Widman at the South Dakota Festival of Books. Chad Buckley and Tim Burgh provided background on law enforcement; any errors are mine alone. Carolyn Finch, Sue Millard, Peg Miller, and the Silver Lake Volunteer Fire Company and Rescue Squad. Professors Butler, Gildin, Pearson, and Skladany of the Dickinson School of Law at Penn State, and the staff of the H. Laddie Montague, Jr., Law Library. Bill Cokely, for the OJT, in memory. Dante Di Stefano, Peter Fallon, Bill Luce, John McNamara, and Nick Mullen.

SELECTED WORKS CONSULTED

A History of Bluegrass in New York and Northeastern Pennsylvania by Ken Oakley and Carol Ripic; *Celtic Folklore: Welsh and Manx, Volume One* by John Rhys; *Timber Frame Construction* by Jack A. Sobon and Roger Schroeder; *Historic American Timber Joinery* by Jack A. Sobon; *The Tibetan Book of the Dead* translated by Robert A. F. Thurman; *The Celtic Twilight* by W. B. Yeats.

Dry Bones in the Valley

WINNER of the *LA Times* Book Award – Thriller/Mystery
WINNER of the Edgar Best First Novel
NOMINATED for the CWA John Creasey New Blood Dagger

When an elderly recluse discovers a corpse on his land, in Wild Thyme, Pennsylvania, Officer Henry Farrell follows the investigation to strange places in the countryside, and into the depths of his own frayed soul.

As a second body turns up, Henry's search for the killer opens old wounds and dredges up ancient crimes which some people desperately want to keep hidden.

In these derelict woods, full of whitetail deer and history, the hunt is on . . .

'An elegiac debut that brings pastoral America to life as surely as if it were written by William Faulkner . . . It is a tour de force.' *Daily Mail*

'I loved every word of it.' DONALD RAY POLLOCK, author of *Knockemstiff*

'Tremendous, Officer Henry Farrell is a character I hope to read about for years to come.' WILLY VLAUTIN, author of *The Motel Life* and *Lean on Pete*

'An exciting and disturbing debut . . . mesmerizing and often terrifying.' *Washington Post*